NG

"Iles squeezes every drop of suspense out of the prolonged standoff."

—*Publishers Weekly*

"Might be Iles's best . . . a novel that demands—and rewards—more than one reading."

—*Booklist*

### TRUE EVIL

"Engrossing. . . . A lush, full-tilt thriller."

—*The Washington Post*

"Fasten your seat belt. For 500-plus pages, this mystery thriller will keep you zigging, zagging, speeding, and cornering hard."

—*St. Louis Post-Dispatch*

"A pulse-pounder."

—*Publishers Weekly* (starred review)

"One hell of a ride."

—*Booklist*

### TURNING ANGEL

"*Turning Angel* will have you wondering where Greg Iles has been all your life."

—*USA Today*

"The job of great fiction is to entertain, elucidate, and educate while keeping readers nailed to their chairs; this does all of that brilliantly. . . . Gripping."

—*Publishers Weekly* (starred review)

"Iles has a flair for drama. . . . Enveloping."

—Janet Maslin, *The New York Times*

"Explosive . . . a powerful piece of popular fiction."
—*Chicago Sun-Times*

"An insider's heartfelt picture of a Southern town. . . ."
—*The Washington Post*

## *BLOOD MEMORY*

"Greg Iles mixes action and suspense like a master."
—Stephen Coonts, *New York Times*
bestselling author of *The Traitor*

"Surprising and exciting. . . . The stakes—and the rewards for readers—are especially high."
—*Chicago Tribune*

"Fascinating. . . . Genuinely moving . . . with some unsuspected twists."
—*The Denver Post*

## *THE FOOTPRINTS OF GOD*

"Alarming, believable, and utterly consuming."
—Dan Brown, #1 *New York Times*
bestselling author of *The Da Vinci Code*

"A riveting page-turner in the tradition of Robert Ludlum."
—Vince Flynn, *New York Times*
bestselling author of *Protect and Defend*

"Amazing and multi-layered . . . breathtaking."
—Nelson DeMille, *New York Times*
bestselling author of *Wild Fire*

"Mix[es] hot-off-the-press science with off-the-wall theology."
—*The Denver Post*

# GREG ILES

# THIRD DEGREE

POCKET BOOKS

NEW YORK  LONDON  TORONTO  SYDNEY

Pocket Books
A Division of Simon & Schuster, Inc.
1230 Avenue of the Americas
New York, NY 10020

First Pocket Books paperback edition October 2008

POCKET and colophon are registered trademarks of Simon & Schuster, Inc.

For information about special discounts for bulk purchases, please contact Simon & Schuster Special Sales at 1-800-456-6798 or business@simonandschuster.com.

Cover art by Jae Song

Manufactured in the United States of America

10  9  8  7  6  5  4  3  2  1

ISBN-13: 978-1-4165-2454-0
ISBN-10:      1-4165-2454-1

*Bone of my bones, and flesh of my flesh.*
Genesis 2:23

# THIRD
## DEGREE

# CHAPTER

# 1

Floating in the half-world between sleep and wakefulness, Laurel reached down and slipped her hand into the crack between the mahogany bed rail and the box springs, searching . . . searching for her connection to life. The cool metal of the Razr pricked her nervous system enough to make her freeze; a millisecond later she was fully awake and turning her head slowly on the pillow—

Her husband's side of the bed was empty. In fact, it looked as though Warren had not come to bed at all. Resisting the compulsion to check the Razr for a text message, she slipped the cell phone back into its hiding place, then rolled out of bed and padded quickly to the bedroom door.

The hall was empty, but she heard sounds from the direction of the den. Not kid sounds . . . something else, a strange thumping. Laurel whisked down the hall and peered into the great room. Across the vast open space she saw Warren standing before a wall of bookshelves in his study. Half a dozen medical textbooks lay at his feet, more on the red leather sofa beside him. As she watched, Warren stepped forward and with an angry motion began pulling more books off the shelves, six or eight at a time, then piling them haphazardly on the couch. His sandy blond hair spiked upward like bushy antennae, and unless she was mistaken, he was wearing the same clothes he'd worn to work yesterday, which meant that he really *hadn't* come to bed last night. On any other day this would have worried Laurel, but today she closed her eyes in gratitude and hurried back to the master suite.

When she entered the bathroom, her throat clenched tight. She had put this decision off for days, praying in vain for deliverance, but now she had no choice. Only now that she was set up to go through with it, something in her rebelled. The mind would do anything to deny certain realities, she thought, or at least to postpone them.

Kneeling before her washbasin, she reached into the cabinet, removed a Walgreens bag, and carried it into the private cubicle that surrounded the commode. Then she latched the slatted door, opened the bag, and took out a large tampon box. From this box she removed the small carton she'd concealed inside it yesterday afternoon. The side of this carton read *e.p.t.* With shaking fingers she removed a plastic bag, ripped it open, and took out a testing stick not much different from the one that had struck terror into her heart as a nineteen-year-old. Remarkably, she felt more fear in this moment than she had as an unmarried teenager.

Holding the stick between her legs, she tried to pee, but her urine wouldn't come. Had someone walked into the bathroom? One of the kids? Hearing no breath or footfall, she forced her mind away from the present, to the parent/teacher conferences she had scheduled today. As she thought of the anxious mothers she would have to deal with later on, a warm rush of fluid splashed her hand. She withdrew the stick from the stream, wiped her hand with tissue, then closed her eyes and counted while she finished.

She wished she'd brought the Razr in with her. It was crazy to leave that phone in the bedroom with Warren home, crazy to have it in the house at all, really. The cell phone Laurel called her "clone" phone was a second Razr identical to the one on their family account, but registered in someone else's name, so that Warren could never see the bills. It was a perfect system for private communication—unless Warren saw both phones together. Yet despite the danger, Laurel could no longer stand to be apart from her clone phone, even though it hadn't brought her a single message in the past five weeks.

Realizing that she'd counted past thirty, she opened her eyes. The testing stick was fancier than the ones she remembered from college, with a tiny screen like the ones on cheap pocket calculators. No more trying to judge shades of blue to see if you were knocked up. Before her eyes, written in crisp blue letters on the gray background, were the letters *PREGNANT*.

Laurel stared, waiting for a *NOT* to appear before the other word. It was an infantile wish, for part of her had known the truth without even taking the test (her too tender breasts, and the seasick feeling she'd had with her second child); yet still she waited, with the testing company's new slogan—*We call it the Error Proof Test*—playing in her mind. She must have heard that slogan twenty times during the past week, chirped

confidently from the television during inane children's sitcoms and Warren's overheated cop melodramas, while she waited in agony for her period to begin. When the letters on the stick did not change, she shook it the way her mother had shaken the thermometers of her youth.

*PREGNANT!* the letters screamed. *PREGNANT! PREGNANT! PREGNANT!*

Laurel wasn't breathing. She hadn't exhaled since the letters first appeared. Had she not been sitting on the toilet, she might have fainted, but as it was, she sagged against the nearby wall, her face cold. The sob that broke from her chest sounded alien, as though a stranger were wailing on the other side of the door.

"Mom?" said Grant, her nine-year-old son. "Was that you?"

Laurel tried to answer, but no words came. As she covered her mouth with shaking fingers, tears streamed down her face.

"Mom?" asked the voice behind the door. "Are you okay?"

She could see Grant's thin silhouette through the slats. *No, I'm not, sweetheart. I'm going insane sitting right here on the toilet.*

"Dad!" called Grant, staying put. "I think Mom's sick."

*I'm not sick, baby, I'm watching the goddamn world end. . . .* "I'm fine, sweetie," Laurel choked out. "Perfectly fine. Did you brush your teeth already?"

Silence now, a listening silence. "You sound funny."

Laurel felt herself gearing down into survival mode. The shock of the positive pregnancy test had caused a violent emotional dislocation; from there it was only a small step to full-blown dissociation. Suddenly her pregnancy became a matter of academic interest, one small factor to be weighed in the day's long list of deceptions. Eleven months of adultery had schooled her well in the shameful arts. But the irony was shattering: they had ended the affair five weeks ago, without a single moral lapse since; and now she was pregnant.

She shoved the stick back into the e.p.t carton, carefully fitted the carton back into the tampon box, and stuffed it into the Walgreens bag. After stashing the bag on the floor behind the toilet, she flushed the commode and stood.

Grant was waiting beyond the door. His face would be alert for any sign of anxiety in his mother. Laurel had seen that watchful face many times in the past few months, and every time she did, a blade of guilt sliced through her. Grant knew his mother was in emotional turmoil; he knew it better than his father did, being far more perceptive when it came to such things.

Laurel carefully wiped away her tears with tissue, then gripped the doorknob, willing her hands to stop shaking. *Routine,* she thought. *Routine will save you. Play your usual role, and no one will notice a thing. It's June Cleaver time again—*

She opened the door and smiled broadly. Wearing nothing but a Tony Hawk skateboard T-shirt, Grant stood looking up at her like a nine-year-old interrogation specialist, which he was. He had Laurel's eyes in his father's face, but the resemblance grew less marked every day. Lately, Grant seemed to change at the rate of a fast-growing puppy.

"Is Beth awake?" she asked. "You know we need to go over your spelling before we leave."

Grant nodded irritably, his eyes never leaving her face. "Your cheeks are red," he noted, his usually musical voice almost flat with suspicion.

"I did some sit-ups when I woke up."

He pursed his lips, working through this explanation. "Crunches or the real thing?"

"Crunches." Laurel used his preoccupation to slide past him and head for her closet. She slipped a silk housecoat over her cotton nightie and walked down the hall toward the kitchen. "Can you make sure Beth is up?" she called over her shoulder. "I'm going to start breakfast."

"Dad's acting weird," Grant said in a jarring voice.

Sensing something very like fear, Laurel stopped and turned, focusing on the slim figure framed in the bedroom door. "What do you mean?" she asked, walking back toward her son.

"He's tearing his study up."

She remembered Warren pulling books from the shelves. "I think it's just the tax thing we told you about. That's very stressful, honey."

"What's an audit, anyway?"

"That's when the government makes sure you've paid them all the money you're supposed to."

"Why do you have to pay the government money?"

Laurel forced a smile. "To pay for roads and bridges and . . . and the army, and things like that. We talked about that, honey."

Grant looked skeptical. "Dad says they take your money so lazy people won't have to work. And so they get free doctor visits, while working people have to pay."

Laurel hated it when Warren vented his professional frustrations to the children. He didn't understand how literally they took everything. Or maybe he did.

"Dad told me he's looking for something," said Grant.

"Did he say what?"

"A piece of paper."

Laurel was trying to stay tuned in, but her plight would not let her.

"I told him I'd help," Grant went on in a hurt voice, "but he yelled at me."

She squinted in confusion. That didn't sound like Warren. But neither did staying up all night in yesterday's clothes. Maybe the audit situation was worse than he'd led her to believe. However bad it was, it was nothing compared to her situation. This was *disaster*. Unless . . .

*No*, she thought with desolation, *even that would be a disaster*. She knelt and kissed Grant on the forehead. "Did you feed Christy?"

"Yep," he replied with obvious pride. Christy was the children's increasingly overweight Welsh corgi.

"Then please go make sure your sister is awake, sweetie. I'm going to start breakfast."

Grant nodded, and Laurel rose. "Egg with a hat on it?"

He gave her a grudging smile. "Two?"

"Two it is."

Laurel didn't want to look Warren in the eye this morning. On any given day, she had about a 70 percent chance of not having to do it. Half the time, he left early to put in between five and fifty miles on his bicycle, an obsessive hobby that consumed huge chunks of his time. To be fair, it was more than a hobby. During his early twenties, Warren had been classed as a Category One rider, and he'd turned down slots on two prestigious racing teams to enter medical school. He still completed Category Two races, often against men fifteen years his junior. On mornings when he wasn't training, he sometimes left early to make morning rounds at the hospital while she was getting the kids ready for school. But today, since he obviously hadn't showered, he was likely to be here until after she left.

Her mind jumped to the Walgreens bag sitting under the commode. The odds were one in a million that Warren would even notice it, much less look inside. And yet . . . their commode sometimes spontaneously began to run water and wouldn't stop unless you jiggled the handle. Warren was compulsive about things like that. What if he rolled up his sleeves and got down on the floor to fix it? He might move the bag out of his way, or even knock it out of his way in frustration—

*It's the little things that kill you,* Danny had told her, enough times for it to stick. And he was speaking from experience, not only of extramarital affairs, but also as a former combat pilot. After a moment of doubt, Laurel went quickly back to the bathroom, opened one of the windows, then took the bag from beneath the toilet and dropped it out the window. She leaned out far enough to watch it fall behind some shrubbery; she'd retrieve it before she left for school, then toss it in a Dumpster at a gas station somewhere.

As she closed the window, she looked across her lawn, a vast dewy expanse of Saint Augustine grass dotted with pecan trees greening up for spring. There was almost no chance of her little disposal mission being seen; their house stood on a ten-acre lot, with their nearest house on this side—the Elfmans'—almost two hundred yards away, with much foliage between. Now and then Laurel saw the husband cutting grass where the property line ran near her house, but it was early for that.

Before the full psychic weight of the pregnancy could crash back into her thoughts, Laurel pulled on some black cropped pants and a white silk top, then applied her makeup in record time. She was putting on eyeliner when she realized she was avoiding her own gaze as much as she might her husband's. As she stepped back from the mirror for a final appraising glance, a wave of guilt hit her. She'd put on too much makeup in a vain attempt to hide that she'd been crying. The face looking back at her belonged to what more than a few women privately accused her of being—a trophy wife. Because of her looks, they discounted her education, her work, her energy, her devotion to causes . . . all of it. Most days she didn't give a damn what people thought, especially the women who gossiped nonstop about her. But today . . . the pregnancy test had confirmed every savage insult those witches had voiced about her. Or it almost certainly had, anyway.

"How the hell did I get here?" she whispered to her reflection.

The reproof in the large green eyes staring back at her was enough. She pulled down a curtain of denial in her mind, then turned and hurried down the hall to face her family.

• • •

The kids had almost finished breakfast before Warren looked out of the study. Laurel had just washed the skillet and was turning back to the granite counter where the kids were eating the last of the biscuits when she caught Warren's deep-set eyes watching her from the study door. He hadn't shaved, and the shadow on his chin and jaw gave him a look of unusual intensity. His eyes looked hollow, and his expression gave away nothing, except perhaps a sense of malice, but she wrote that off as hatred of the IRS. She raised her eyebrows, silently asking if he needed her to walk over for some private words, but he shook his head.

"If the earth keeps getting hotter," asked Beth, her six-year-old, "will the oceans boil like when you boil eggs for tuna fish?"

"No, punkin," Laurel assured her. "Although it doesn't take much of a temperature change to melt a lot of ice at the north and south poles. And that can have very serious consequences for people living at the beach."

"Actually," Warren said from the study door, his deep voice carrying easily across the great room, "the oceans *will* eventually boil."

Beth knit her brow and turned on her barstool.

Warren said, "The sun will eventually heat up and grow into a massive ball of fire, and the oceans will bubble away just like water in a pot on the stove."

"*Seriously?*" asked Beth, her voice filled with concern.

"Yes. And then—"

"Daddy's talking about millions of years from now, punkin," Laurel cut in, wondering what the hell had got into Warren to be telling Beth that kind of thing. She would worry about it for days. "Your great-great-great-great-great-great-granddaughters won't even have been born by then, so it's nothing to worry about."

"Supernova!" cried Grant. "That's what they call that, right? When a star explodes?"

"Right," said Warren with obvious satisfaction.

"That's *so* cool," Grant said.

"It's a boy thing," Laurel explained to Beth. "The end of the world sounds really cool to boys."

Despite her predicament, Laurel was tempted to give Warren a chiding glance—it's what she would have done had things been normal—but when she looked up again, he had gone back into the study, and she could no longer see him. More thumping sounds announced that he was still searching for something. On any other day, she would have gone in and asked what he was looking for and probably even helped him. But not today.

Grant slid off his stool and opened his backpack. Now Laurel felt some satisfaction. Without a word from her, he had begun reviewing his spelling words for the day. Beth went to a chair at the kitchen table and started putting on her shoes, which always had to be tied with equal tightness, a ritual that occasionally caused paroxysms of obsessive-compulsive panic, but on most days went fine.

Laurel sometimes felt guilty when other mothers complained what a nightmare it was to get their kids off to school in the mornings. Her kids pretty much did their preparations on autopilot, running in the groove of a routine so well established that Laurel wondered if she and Warren had some sublimated fascist tenden-

cies. But the truth was, for someone who spent her days
teaching special-needs students, handling two normal
children was a no-brainer.

*Should I go into the study?* she wondered again.
*Isn't that what a good wife would do? Express con-*
*cern? Offer to help?* But Warren didn't want help with
things like this. His medical practice was his business,
and his business was his own. He was obviously preoccupied with the audit. And yet that prolonged stare
from the door had disturbed her on a deep level. It
seemed months since Warren had given her even a long
look. It was as though he were intentionally giving her
the space she had silently requested. He never looked
too deeply, because she didn't want to be seen, and
he didn't want to see. It was a conspiracy of silence, a
mutual denial of reality, and they had become expert
at it.

"We're going to be late," Grant said.

"You're right," Laurel agreed without looking at
the clock. "Let's move."

She helped Beth get her backpack on, then picked
up her own computer case and purse and walked toward the door to the garage. With her hand on the
knob—almost out!—she glanced back over her shoulder, half expecting to find Warren gazing at her, but all
she saw was his lower legs. He had climbed a small lad-
der to search the top shelves of his custom bookcases,
ten feet up the wall. She breathed a sigh of relief and
led the kids out to her Acura. Grant called shotgun—
Beth never thought of it in time—but Laurel motioned
for him to get in back, which earned a smile from her
daughter and an angry grunt from her son.

After they were belted in, Laurel mock-slapped the

side of her head and said, "I think I forgot to turn off the sprinkler last night."

"I'll check it!" cried Grant, unbuckling his seat belt.

"No, I'll get it," Laurel said firmly, and quickly got out of the car.

She hit the button on the wall and ducked under the rising garage door as soon as it was four feet off the concrete, then trotted around to the back of the house. She would retrieve the Walgreens bag, crush it into a ball, then slip it into her trunk and dispose of it sometime during the school day, at a gas station or convenience store. (She'd done the same with a valentine card and roses and a few actual letters during the past year.) She was making for a gap in the shrubbery when a woman's voice called out, "Laurel? Over here!"

Laurel froze and looked toward the sound. Just twenty-five yards away, almost obscured by some boxwoods, knelt a woman wearing a straw hat and bright yellow gloves. Bonnie Elfman was about seventy, but she moved like a woman of forty, and for some reason she had chosen this morning to beautify the western boundary of her considerable property.

"I'm just adding some nasturtiums to this bed!" Bonnie called. "What're you up to?"

*Retrieving a positive pregnancy test so my husband won't find it.* "I thought I left the sprinkler on," she called back.

"That'll sure kill your water bill," Bonnie said, standing and walking toward Laurel.

Laurel felt a flutter of panic. To compound her troubles, Christy came tearing around the corner of the house, desperate for someone to play with her. If

Laurel picked up the bag from behind the shrubs, the corgi might just leap up and rip it out of her hands. She gazed along her own line of shrubs with exaggerated concern, then waved broadly to Mrs. Elfman. "I guess I got it after all! I've got to run, Bonnie. The kids are waiting in the car."

"I'll find your sprinkler and make sure," Bonnie promised.

Laurel's heart thumped like a bass drum. "Don't trouble yourself! Really. I thought I'd left it out here, but I took it back to the storeroom. I remember now. Don't you get too hot, either. It's been really warm for April."

"Don't worry about that, it's going to rain," Bonnie said with the confidence of an oracle. "It's going to cool off, too. By the time you get back from school, you'll need a jacket."

Laurel looked up at the sun, clear and bright in the sky. "If you say so. See you later."

Bonnie looked miffed over Laurel's escape. She would have much preferred to stand around gossiping for a half hour. Laurel knew from past experience that like most gossips, Bonnie Elfman was as quick to repeat stories about her as she was to confide in Laurel about others.

"Shit, shit, shit," Laurel cursed, as she hurried back around to the garage. The Walgreens bag would have to wait until after school. Christy was trotting at her heels, so the dog was no problem. But Mrs. Elfman wasn't going anywhere soon. Laurel prayed that the old busybody would stay on her own property until school was out.

# CHAPTER

# 2

Laurel pulled her Acura up to the elementary-school door, leaned over, and kissed Beth on the cheek. Mrs. Lacey had door duty today, and she helped Beth out while Grant sprang out of the backseat like a monkey escaping from a zoo cage and darted into the school building to find his buddies.

After Mrs. Lacey escorted Beth through the door, Laurel drove around the elementary school and parked in her reserved space beside the Special Students building. It was a small brick box, two classrooms with a unisex bathroom and an office, but it was better than nothing, which was what Athens Country Day had had for the past fifty years. A generous endowment by a local geologist had made the building possible. He had a niece in New Orleans who was mildly retarded and so understood the need.

Laurel looked down at her computer and purse, which had lain under Beth's feet during the drive over, but she didn't reach for them. The engine was still running; she made no move to switch it off. She wasn't sure she could face what lay ahead. Her students could be trying enough, but today she had parent conferences, and her first was with the wife of her former lover.

The prospect of facing Starlette McDavitt while pregnant by the woman's husband was almost unendurable. If Starlette weren't the first appointment, Laurel would have tried to cancel the meeting. But it was too late for that.

She didn't know she was crying until she tasted tears in her mouth. It wasn't the impending appointment, she realized. It was that she didn't know for sure whose baby she was carrying. The odds were, it was Danny's. They had ended their affair five weeks ago, but in the three weeks prior to that—the three weeks after her last period—they had made love at least a dozen times. She'd only had intercourse with Warren twice since her last period, both times after she and Danny had ended it. She hadn't even wanted sex with Warren, but how else could she make an honest try? And what alternative did she have but to try, given Danny's decision? Walk out on Warren to live alone in some lonely apartment, surrounded by other divorcées and waiting for a man who couldn't come to her for another fourteen years, if ever? Not an attractive option even before she was pregnant. Now . . .

Laurel wasn't even sure whether a fetus conceived while you were on the pill was viable or not. She would have to look it up on the Internet. She should already have done it, but that kind of practical act didn't square with her strategy of intense denial. She still couldn't believe she was pregnant. She was on the pill, for God's sake! Ninety-eight percent effective! How could she be in the unlucky 2 percent? She'd had some bad luck in her life, but never the *worst* luck. It was the rotavirus, she knew. Last month, she had somehow contracted the same gastrointestinal virus that had required the quarantining of major cruise ships. CNN had said the virus was sweeping the country: people were simultaneously puking and pooping from coast to coast. Three to five days of that, Laurel had learned, could eject from the system the progestin contained in a woman's birth control pills. Since she'd had sex almost every other day last month, pregnancy must have been a near certainty.

She laid her forehead against the steering wheel and allowed herself a single sob. She'd always believed she was a strong woman, but now fate had colluded with chance—and stupidity—to make the prospect of raising an illegitimate child in her husband's house a reality.

And that she could not face.

*There are probably women doing it,* said a rebellious voice in her head. *Right here in this town.* Desperate to avoid thinking of her impending meeting with Starlette, Laurel spun through the possibilities. If you were going to be stuck in a loveless marriage for the rest of your life, that "love child" might be your only link to sanity, or at least to the life that might have been. But could she live a lie for the rest of her life? She had found it difficult enough to lie about even small things over the past year, to bring off the thousand tiny deceptions that an extramarital affair required. The thrill of the forbidden had lasted about three weeks for her, and after that, the lies had begun to produce a sort of psychic nausea. Every lie generated the need for a dozen others—lies and sub-lies, Danny called them— sprouting like heads on an endlessly replicating Hydra. Yet she had worked hard to maintain the charade of normalcy. She'd even become good at it—so good that lying had become automatic. She felt the dishonesty corroding her soul, yet still she lied, so desperately did she need the love that Danny McDavitt gave her.

Yet what she was contemplating now was no simple deception. She wouldn't be the only one lying. She would be forcing her unborn child into a lie from the moment of its birth. Its very life would be a lie. And what about Warren? He would try to love this baby, but would he actually *feel* love? Or would he sense something alien in the little interloper in his house? Something inexplicably but profoundly wrong? A disturbing scent? A genetically dissonant sound? A shiver at the touch of skin or hair? And of course, the baby wouldn't *look* like Warren—it couldn't—except by the merest chance.

Laurel actually knew one woman who had done it. Kelly Rowland, a sorority sister at Ole Miss who had become pregnant by a one-night stand while engaged to the boy she had been dating for three years. Kelly's fiancé had been a good, stable, somewhat bland boy of medium attractiveness and excellent financial prospects; in short, the ideal husband for a sorority girl at Ole Miss. Kelly had always insisted that her fiancé wear condoms religiously during sex, so it struck Laurel as odd when Kelly allowed one of the houseboys—a devastatingly hot soccer player—to screw her brains out sans protection one night after a candlelight ceremony for one of the other sisters. But when Kelly learned she was pregnant, she had simply moved up her wedding date, scheduled her own candlelight ceremony, and never looked back. That was thirteen years ago, and the couple were still married and living in Houston.

Laurel drew no inspiration from this memory. But what was the alternative? Abortion? How could she abort the child of the man she truly loved? And even if she convinced herself she could bear that, how could she tell her husband she wanted an abortion? *You get the abortion without telling him you're pregnant,* said a cold, Darwinian voice. With dread she pictured herself running a gauntlet of antiabortion protesters to sit alone in the waiting room of some distant women's clinic. She'd have to go at least three states away to avoid any possibility of being recognized, and even then the physician might—

A fist rapped on the window beside Laurel's head.

She jerked away from the noise like a woman being carjacked, then looked back to see Diane Rivers, the third-grade homeroom teacher, mouthing her name with obvious concern. Diane was a big-haired Southern belle with a heart of gold, almost a throwback to Laurel's mother's generation, though she was only forty-three. Laurel had seen pictures of Diane in a glittering sequin unitard as she twirled two batons at a national college competition. Diane made a cranking motion with her hand, meaning that Laurel should roll down her window, though almost no cars had window cranks anymore, at least not in the parking lot of Athens Country Day.

Laurel wiped her tears on the shoulder of her blouse, smearing mascara on the white silk, then pressed the window button. The glass sank into the door with a low whir.

"What's the matter, honey?" Diane asked. "Are you all right?"

*Do I look all right?* Laurel silently responded. But

what else was someone supposed to ask when they found you crying in a parking lot? Some teachers would have derived savage ecstasy from finding her in this state, but Diane wasn't one of them. She really meant well.

"I think I'm getting a migraine," Laurel said. "I'm getting that aura, you know?"

"Christ on a crutch," Diane said with empathy. "Seems like a long time since you had one."

"Over a year." *Since before Danny and I got together,* Laurel realized.

"Do you think you can handle your conferences? If it was just classes, I'd sit with your kids, but I wouldn't know what to tell special-ed parents."

"I'll be all right," Laurel asserted, leaning down to lift her purse and computer off the floor. "Sometimes I just get the aura but not the headache. They call that a silent migraine. I'm hoping this is one of those."

Diane shook her head. "Oh, honey, I don't know. You don't have one of those shots with you? The stuff that heads it off?"

"Imitrex? It's been so long since I had a migraine that I stopped carrying the kit."

Diane gave her a look of maternal reproach.

"I know," Laurel said, getting out of her car. "Stupid."

"You should run to Warren's office," Diane suggested. "Get that shot, you know? What's the use of having a doctor for a husband if you don't take advantage now and then? I could cover for you till you get back. My homeroom knows I'll skin them alive if they misbehave."

Laurel almost laughed. Diane had a glare that could

paralyze a mischievous boy from a hundred paces. After locking the Acura, Laurel started toward the Special Students building. "I'll be all right, Di, seriously. I saw some spots, that's all."

"You were sobbing in pain, girl."

"No . . . I was just overwhelmed. I really believed I might be over them. That's why I was crying. Facing reality."

"Reality's a bitch, all right," Diane said under her breath. Then she giggled like a 1950s wife who'd accidentally said *shit*.

She squeezed Laurel's wrist as she left the door of the Special Students building. Her touch was oddly comforting. Laurel felt an irrational urge to pour out her heart to the older woman, but she didn't say a word. Diane couldn't possibly help with her predicament, even were she so inclined. And Diane was unlikely to feel sympathy for the deranged slut who was cheating on her husband—Diane's personal physician—and was stupid enough to get pregnant while doing it. Laurel nodded once more that she was okay, then walked down the short hall to her classroom, easily found by the raucous chatter of special-needs kids in the grip of their morning energy.

After an aide escorted her students to the playground, Laurel sat at the round table she used for parental meetings. Sitting across a desk made parents feel they were being lectured to; the round table made them feel like partners in educating their children. Laurel had eleven special-needs children in her program, almost too many, given that she had only limited help from an aide. But Athens Point was a small town, and parents had few options. She hated to turn anyone away. Her kids' problems ran the gamut from ADD and oppositional/defiant disorder to mental retardation and autism. Handling such a broad spectrum was hard work, but Laurel relished the challenge.

To insure that parental meetings went as smoothly as possible, she kept meticulously organized records during the year, and none was more detailed or better organized than the file on Michael McDavitt. *The way to get through this,* she thought, *is to focus on my second meeting. That way I can keep Starlette at arms' length—psychologically speaking—until I'm actually facing her across this table.*

It was a nice idea, only Laurel couldn't manage it.

Even when she closed her eyes, she saw the former Tennessee beauty queen sweeping into her classroom wearing her latest catalog purchases, her bleached hair perfectly coiffed, her nails flawlessly painted, her waist pathologically thin, her fancy cowboy boots (which must surely be passé by now) shimmering. Laurel's negative feelings toward Starlette McDavitt had not begun during the affair. That happened during their first meeting, when it became clear that Mrs. McDavitt saw her autistic son as a burden dumped on her by an unjust God. Starlette had run on for half an hour about how some parents claimed that autism was caused by mercury in government-mandated vaccinations, but deep down she knew it was a divine punishment. Something so deeply destructive simply had to be God's will, she believed. And it wasn't necessarily anything *you'd* done. It could be retribution for some sin committed far back down the ancestral line, rape or incest or something you didn't even know about.

In less than an hour, it had become clear that Michael McDavitt's primary caregiver was his father, Daniel, who was fifteen years his wife's senior.

Danny McDavitt was a soft-spoken man a year shy of fifty. He looked younger, but his eyes held a quiet wisdom that bespoke considerable experience. It wasn't long before Laurel learned that McDavitt was a war hero, an Athens Point native who had left town at eighteen and returned as a prodigal, thirty years down the road. All he'd told her during the first weeks of Michael's assessment was that he'd flown helicopters in a couple of wars, that he was now retired due to wounds received, and that he was giving "fixed-wing" flying lessons out at the county airport. Laurel soon decided that either flying or combat experience must be good training for men dealing with special kids, because in nine years of teaching, she had never seen a father work harder to connect with a developmentally challenged son than did Danny McDavitt.

The problem was his wife.

The only mystery about Starlette McDavitt was why Danny had married her. This single act betrayed a serious lapse of judgment, which seemed uncharacteristic in him. Of course Laurel had noticed that even brilliant men could be out-and-out fools when it came to picking women. They were like little boys at a Baskin-Robbins. *I'll have some of THAT. Hmm, that tastes good, I want some more.* Pretty soon, they bought the whole bucket of ice cream, to keep a steady supply. But once they had access to that bucket all day every day, they didn't like the taste so much. That ice cream didn't even look the same as it had behind the frosted glass with the big silver scoop stuck in it.

Starlette looked tasty enough, and her looks matched her name. She was a former Miss Knoxville or something, not quite a Miss Tennessee, but something higher up than a Soybean Queen. Yet her TV spokesmodel beauty was offset by bitter eyes that told you she'd already learned the lesson that pageant victories only take girls a short way down the road of life. The real irony was that in Starlette's view, Laurel had won the marital lottery. She'd married a doctor— count your blessings and keep your mouth shut, honey (and your legs open, if you know what's good for you). Starlette had never verbalized any of this per se, but it had seeped out between her little digs at other doctors' wives (none present to defend themselves) and in her limited observations on her own lot in life.

Danny had married Starlette seven years ago, a year before he'd planned to retire from the air force. First marriage for both of them. He'd waited a long time to make that mistake, he told her, but the waiting hadn't made him any wiser. After nineteen years in the service, he'd flown to Nashville to buy a house in anticipation of working as a songwriter in his retirement, something he'd always done during downtime in the air force. To protect his savings, he'd lined up a job with a local flying service. The owner was a big admirer of Danny's war record, and one job perk was flying country music stars around the state. Starlette had been working for a real estate agency, and she'd showed Danny a couple of houses in Franklin. His songwriting aspirations hadn't impressed her; in fact she'd questioned his ability to buy in that neighborhood. But his upcoming gig flying country music stars had the glamour she'd come to the city to find. Danny still had a year left at Eglin

Air Force Base in Florida to round out his twenty, but he was soon commuting to Nashville on every leave, to shop his songs and to spend time with Starlette. When she turned up pregnant, they decided to marry, and six months later, their daughter, Jenny, was born—beautiful and healthy.

Danny was only two weeks from retirement when the World Trade Center was attacked. After that, he'd refused to consider quitting, despite Starlette's protestations. She didn't have to wait long for his return. He deployed to Afghanistan but was shot down three months later, in an incident he was lucky to survive. He took this as a hint from fate and returned to Nashville with his discharge papers in hand. Soon he was dividing his time between flying singers, selling songs, sleeping with his new wife, and raising his daughter. The only problem in paradise was that he quickly tired of being a flying chauffeur. Jet-set hillbillies were getting on his nerves. Some were truly wonderful people, but others were real jerks. With the fans they were warm and sincere, but as soon as they hit the chopper, they were bitching about the hassles of dealing with the public. After six months without selling a song, Danny was ready to bail out. He hadn't returned to Mississippi except for funerals and one high school reunion he'd enjoyed, but ever since he hit forty-five, he'd had an inexplicable itch to head back South. The next time a singing cowboy millionaire said the wrong thing, Danny told him off, and that was that. It took some talking, but he finally convinced Starlette to give his hometown a try, promising that if it didn't work out, they could move back to Tennessee.

Laurel set aside Michael McDavitt's file and forced

herself to stop thinking about his father. Her strategy had been to focus on the conference *after* Starlette, and all she had done was rewind to the beginning of her relationship with Danny. God, was she messed up.

She pulled out her file on Carl Mayer, her most serious ADD case, and tried to focus on the words and numbers on the page. *Mean, median, stanine . . .* no matter how hard she stared, the data wouldn't coalesce into anything coherent. And why should it? In less than five minutes, she would be face-to-face with a woman she had willfully betrayed for almost a year. A woman who had never liked her, probably out of anxiety about being judged a bad parent. There was no way to avoid making those kinds of judgments, but Laurel always tried to keep them out of her eyes. The problem was, she didn't respect Starlette McDavitt. Most of the mothers Laurel worked with bordered on sainthood when it came to dealing with their children; Starlette was on the opposite end of the spectrum. Laurel didn't think she could have betrayed a woman she respected, although that might just be wishful thinking. As Danny had often said, you never knew what you would do until life tested you.

A soft knock sounded at the door, which should have given her a moment's warning, but she was so busy putting up her defenses that she forgot Starlette always made grand entrances. So Laurel was totally unprepared when Danny McDavitt stepped into her classroom looking like a man hovering in some netherworld between life and death.

# CHAPTER

# 3

"I'm sorry," Danny said, closing the door behind him. "Starlette wouldn't come."

"Why not?" Laurel almost whispered.

Danny shrugged and shook his head. *You know what she's like,* said his eyes.

"She found an excuse not to come."

He nodded. "I had to cancel a flying lesson to get here."

Laurel studied him without speaking. She hadn't laid eyes on Danny for a week, and then she'd only caught a glimpse of him in his beat-up pickup truck, dropping Michael at the front door. The pain of not seeing Danny was unlike anything she had ever known, a hollow, wasting ache in her stomach and chest. She felt purposeless without him, as though she'd contracted an insidious virus that sapped all her energy—Epstein-Barr, or one of those. She was glad she'd been sitting down when he opened the door.

"Should I come in or what?" he asked diffidently.

Laurel shrugged, then nodded, not knowing what else to do.

She watched him walk toward the rows of miniature chairs near the back wall. *He's avoiding the table,*
she realized, *giving me time to adjust.* Danny moved
with an easy rhythm, even when he looked as if he
hadn't slept or eaten for days. He stood an inch under
six feet, with wiry muscles and a flat stomach despite
his age. With his weathered face and year-round tan,
he looked like what he was: a workingman, not a guy
who had grown up privileged, moving from private
school to college fraternity to whatever professional
school he could get into. The son of a crop duster,
Danny had gone to college on a baseball scholarship
but quit after his second season to join the air force.
There he'd aced some aptitude tests and somehow
gotten into flight school. He was no pretty boy, but
most women Laurel knew were attracted to him.
His curly hair was gray at the temples but dark elsewhere, and he didn't have it colored. It was his eyes
that pulled you in, though. They were deep-set and
gray with a hint of blue, like the sea in northern lati-
tudes, and they could be soft or hard as the situation
demanded. Laurel had mostly seen them soft, or twinkling with laughter, but they sometimes went opaque
when he spoke of his wife, or when he answered questions about the battles he'd survived. Danny was in
every respect a man, whereas most of the males Laurel
knew, even those well over forty, seemed like aging
college boys trying to find their way in a confusing
world.

He turned one of the little chairs around and sat
astride it, placing the back between them, as if to emphasize their new state of separation. His gray-blue
eyes watched her cautiously. "I hope you're not angry,"

he said. "I wouldn't have come, but it wouldn't have looked right if one of us hadn't."

"I don't know what I am."

He nodded as though he understood.

Now that she was over the shock of seeing him here, need and anger rose up within Laurel like serpents wrestling each other. Her need made her furious, for she could not have him, and because her desire had been thwarted by his choice, however noble that choice might have been. The only thing worse than not seeing Danny was seeing him, and the worst thing was seeing him and being ignored, as she had been for the past month. No covert glances, no accidental brushes of hands, no misdirected smiles . . . nothing but the distant regard of casual acquaintances. In those crazed moments the hollowness within her seemed suddenly carnivorous, as though it could swallow her up and leave nothing behind. To be ignored by Danny was not to exist, and she could never convince herself that he was suffering the same way. But looking at him now, she knew that he was. "How could you come here?" she asked softly.

He turned up his palms. "I wasn't strong enough to stay away."

Honesty had always been his policy, and it was a devastating one.

"Can I hold you?" he asked.

"*No.*"

"Because there are people around? Or because you don't want me to?"

She regarded him silently.

"I'm sorry for how it's been," he said haltingly. "It's just . . . impossible." His eyes narrowed. "You look really thin. Good, though."

She shook her head. "Don't do this. I'm not good. I'm thin because I can't hold down any food. I have to pretend to eat. I'm barely making it, if you want to know. So let's just stick to Michael and get this over with. There'll be another parent outside my door in fifteen minutes."

Danny was clearly struggling with self-restraint. "We really do need to talk about Michael. He knows something's wrong. He senses that I'm upset."

Laurel tried to look skeptical.

"Do you think he could?" Danny asked.

"It's possible."

"All I'm saying is, when I'm not okay, he's not okay. And I think you come into it, as well."

"You mean—"

"I mean when you're hurting, he knows it. And he cares. A lot more than he does about his mother."

Laurel wanted to deny this, but she'd already observed it herself. "I don't want you to talk like that anymore. There's no point."

Danny looked at the wall to his right, where clumsy finger paintings of animals hung from a long board he had attached to the wall last year. While he drilled the holes, he'd confided to her what he thought the first time he saw the pictures: that the kids who'd drawn them were never going to design computers, perform surgery, or fly airplanes. It was a shattering realization for him, but he had dealt with it and moved on. And though Laurel's students were unlikely ever to fly a helicopter, every one of them had ridden in one. With their parents' joyful permission, Danny had taken each and every child on spectacular flights over the Mississippi River. He'd even held a contest for them, and the winner got to fly with him on balloon-race weekend, when dozens of hot-air balloons filled the skies over Natchez, thirty-five miles to the north. This memory softened Laurel a little, and she let her guard down slightly.

"You've lost weight, too," she said. "Too much."

He nodded. "Sixteen pounds."

"In five weeks?"

"I can't hold nothing down."

Improper grammar usually annoyed Laurel—she had worked hard to shed the Southern accent of her birthplace—but Danny's slow-talking baritone somehow didn't convey stupidity. Danny had that lazy but cool-as-a-cucumber voice of competence, like Sam Shepard playing Chuck Yeager in *The Right Stuff*. It was the pilot's voice, the one that told you everything was under control, and made you believe it, too. And when that voice warmed up—in private—it could do things to her that no other voice ever had. She started to ask if Danny had seen a doctor about losing so much weight, but that was crazy. Danny's doctor was her husband. Besides, it didn't take a doctor to diagnose heartbreak.

"I wish you'd let me hug you," Danny said. "Don't you need it?"

She closed her eyes. *You have no idea . . .* "Please stick to Michael, okay? What specific changes have you noticed in his behavior?"

While Danny answered, slowly and in great detail, Laurel doodled on the Post-it pad on her table. Danny couldn't see the pad from where he sat; it was blocked by a stack of books. After covering the first yellow square with spirals, she tore it off and started on the next one. This time she didn't draw anything. This time she wrote one word in boldface print: *PREGNANT.* Then, without knowing why, she added *I'M* above it. As soon as she wrote the second word, she realized she meant to give the note to Danny on his way out. She wasn't going to tell him out loud—not here. There would be no way to avoid a tense discussion, or maybe something far less controlled.

The note would work. He could dispose of it on the way home, the same way she had disposed of the scrawled missives hurriedly passed to her at her classroom door. Like the e.p.t box she would ditch later today. All the detritus of an extramarital affair. *Like that baby you're carrying,* said a vicious voice in her head.

The thing was, she couldn't be sure the baby was Danny's. She certainly wanted it to be, as absurd as that was, given their situation. But she didn't *know.* And regardless of what Kelly Rowland had done in college, Laurel needed to find out who the father was. Only a DNA test could determine that. She was pretty sure you could analyze the DNA of an unborn child, but it would require an amniocentesis, another thing she'd have to go out of town to have done, if she was going to keep it from Warren. She would have to get some of Warren's DNA without him knowing about it. Probably a strand of hair from his hairbrush would be enough—

"So, what do you think?" Danny concluded. "You're the expert."

For the first time in her life, Laurel had not been listening to what Danny was saying about his son. For more than a year, Michael McDavitt had been her highest priority in this classroom. It wasn't fair, but it was true. She loved Danny, and because Michael meant everything to him, she had let the boy far inside her professional boundaries. Not that he was more important than the other kids; but until last month, she had believed she would one day become his stepmother, and that made him different.

"Danny, you've got to go," she said with sudden firmness.

His face fell. "But we haven't talked. Not really."

"I can't help it. I can't deal with us right now. *I can't.*"

"I'm sorry."

"That doesn't help."

He stood, and it was clear that only force of will was keeping him from crossing the classroom and pulling her close. "I can't live without you," he said. "I thought I could, but it's killing me."

"Have you told your wife that?"

"Pretty much."

A wave of anxiety mingled with hope swept through Laurel. "You told her my name?"

Danny licked his lips, then shook his head sheepishly.

"I see. Has she changed her mind about keeping Michael if you divorce her?"

"No."

"Then we don't have—"

"You don't have to say it."

She could see that he hated his own weakness, which had brought him here despite having no good news. Nothing had changed, and therefore nothing could change for her. He put his hands in his jeans pockets and walked toward the door. Laurel quietly tore the I'M PREGNANT Post-it off the pad and folded it into quarters. When Danny was almost to the door, she stood.

"Are you sleeping with Starlette?" she asked in a voice like cracking ice.

Danny stopped, then turned to face Laurel. "*No,*" he said, obviously surprised. "Did you think I would?"

She shrugged, her shoulders so tight with fear and anger that she could hardly move them. The thought of Danny having sex with Starlette could nauseate her instantly. Though he'd sworn he wouldn't do it, her mind had spun out endless reels of pornographic footage in the lonely darkness before sleep: Danny so desperate from going without Laurel that he screwed his ex-beauty-queen wife just for relief—and found that it wasn't so bad after all. Laurel was sure that Starlette would be trying extra hard to make Danny remember why he'd married her in the first place. Midnight blow jobs were her specialty. Laurel had dragged this out of Danny one night when he'd drunk more whiskey than he should have. Apparently, Starlette would wait until he was sound asleep, then start sucking him while he slept. Sometimes he wouldn't wake until the instant before orgasm, and his expression when he'd told Laurel about this said all she needed to know about how much he enjoyed this little ritual. Once or twice she had thought of trying it herself, but in the end she decided it was better not to compete with Starlette at her game; better to stick to her own bedroom tricks or invent some new ones—and she had.

"We're broken up," Laurel said. "She's your wife. I just assumed . . ."

Danny shook his head. "No. What about you?"

"No," Laurel lied, hating herself for it, but too afraid

of giving him an excuse to make love with Starlette to tell him the truth. Besides . . . if she admitted to sleeping with Warren—even just twice, which was the truth—the pregnancy would become a nightmare of doubt for Danny.

Danny was watching her closely. Then, as he so often did (and Warren almost never), he read her mind and did exactly what she wanted him to do. He marched up to her and smothered her in his arms. His scent enfolded her, and the strength in his arms surprised her, as it always did. When he lifted her off her feet, she felt herself melting from the outside in. The note stayed clenched in her hand, for until he let go, there was no way to slip it into his pocket. When he finally let her down, she would squeeze his behind, then slide the folded square into his back pocket. She could text him later and tell him to look in his pocket.

He was murmuring in her ear, *"I miss you . . . Jesus, I miss you,"* but she felt only the moist rush of air, which sent bright arcs of arousal through her body. As he lowered her to the floor, he slid her crotch along his hard thigh, and a shiver went through her. She would be wet in the time it took him to slide his hand past her waistband. She was thinking of helping him do just that when she saw a dark flash at the window in the door, as though someone had looked in and then jerked suddenly out of sight. She clutched Danny's arm with her right hand and dragged it away from her stomach.

"Keep hugging me," she told him. "You're an upset parent."

"What?" he groaned.

"There's someone at the door. I think they saw us."

Danny's body went limp, and Laurel patted his back

as though comforting him. Then she pulled away and assured him that everything was going to work out eventually, that Michael might make surprising progress before the school year ended. Danny stared back like a lovesick teenager, deaf to her words, his eyes trying to drink in every atom of her being.

"I love you," he said under his breath. "I think about you every minute. I fly over your house every day, just hoping to get a glimpse of you."

"I know." She had seen the Cessna he taught lessons in buzzing over Avalon several times in the past five weeks. The sight had lifted her heart every time, in spite of her vows to forget him. "Please shut up."

"It's better that you know than not. I don't want you thinking there's anything between me and Starlette other than the kids."

She felt a surge of brutal honesty. "But what's the *point*? Either you talk some sense into your wife, or you may as well start sleeping with her again. This is the last hug we'll ever have. I mean it."

He nodded soberly.

"Danny?" she said, realizing that she had not yet given him the note.

"What?"

She moved forward, but now there was a face at the door, and this time it did not retreat. It belonged to Ann Mayer, mother of Carl, the severe ADD case. Ann was staring at Danny with undisguised curiosity.

"To hell with her," Danny whispered, stepping between Laurel and the door. "What were you going to say?"

"Nothing. Don't worry about it."

"It was important. I could tell."

Laurel waved Mrs. Mayer in, and the door opened immediately. "Michael's going to be fine, Major McDavitt," Laurel said, using Danny's retired rank to put some distance between them.

"I appreciate you saying so, Mrs. Shields," Danny replied, a note of surrender in his voice. "I'm sorry I got upset like that."

"Don't give it another thought. It's tough raising a special boy. Especially for fathers."

Mrs. Mayer nodded encouragingly to Danny; at last she thought she understood what she'd witnessed.

"Good-bye," Laurel said, and then she turned and led Mrs. Mayer over to the round table, not even looking up when Danny closed the door.

"Is he all right?" Mrs. Mayer asked, her eyes hungry for details.

"He will be."

"Lord, he really lost it, didn't he? Looked like he flat broke down to me."

Laurel frowned. "I'm sure he wouldn't want anyone to know."

"Oh, of course not. You don't have to worry about me. I'm just surprised, that's all."

"Why?"

"Well, my husband told me Major McDavitt killed dozens of Al Qaeda terrorists over there in Afghanistan. He flew with some kind of commando unit. That's what the newspaper said, anyway."

This local legend was partly true, Laurel knew, but in some ways a gross exaggeration. "I think he saved more people than he killed, Mrs. Mayer."

Her eyes flickered. "Oh, really? Did he tell you that?"

Laurel pulled Carl Mayer's file from her stack. "No, Major McDavitt taught my husband to fly last year. He doesn't like to talk about his war experiences, but Warren dragged a few things out of him."

"Oh, I see," said Mrs. Mayer, relieved—or bored—to hear the word *husband* brought into the equation. Laurel could plainly see that in Mrs. Mayer's eyes, she and Danny made far too natural a couple to spend any innocent time alone.

Laurel felt precisely the same.

# CHAPTER

# 4

Laurel was in the middle of her seventh conference when her vision started to go. The rapt face of the mother across the table wavered as though fifty yards of broiling asphalt separated them; then the center of Laurel's visual field blanked out, leaving a void like a tunnel through the world.

"Oh, God," she said, in utter disbelief. "Oh, no."

She had lied to Diane Rivers about having a migraine; now the lie was coming true. Already the blood vessels were dilating, pressing on the cranial nerves, interfering with her vision. Soon those nerves would release compounds that would drop her to her knees in unremitting agony.

"What is it?" asked Rebecca Linton, a woman of fifty with a mildly retarded daughter. "Are you all right?"

*Could the pregnancy be causing it?* Laurel wondered. She'd read that some women's migraines worsened during their first trimester, but in other women they improved. *It's probably the shock of finding out I'm pregnant, on top of all the other stress.* Ultimately, the cause didn't matter. But coming on the heels of the positive pregnancy test, the incipient migraine made her feel she was being pursued by furies intent upon delivering retribution for her moral transgressions. A wave of nausea rolled through her, which might be part of the prodrome or merely fear of the crippling agony that would soon lay her low. A shower of bright sparkles burst like fireworks beside Mrs. Linton's right ear. *"Jesus,"* Laurel breathed, pressing her fist into her eye socket.

"You're covered in sweat!" cried Mrs. Linton. "Are you having a hot flash? I mean, you're too young for it, but that's what happens to me when I get them."

Laurel gripped the edge of the table, trying to get her mind around the situation. Best case, she had forty-five minutes before the headache hit. Worst case, fifteen. Just enough time to make arrangements for the kids and get home to her dark and silent bedroom. "I'm afraid I need to cut our meeting short."

"Of course. Is there anything I can do?"

"Could you wait here and tell my last appointment I had to leave? I'm about to have a migraine headache."

"Of course I'll wait, darling. Who's coming next?"

Laurel looked at her schedule sheet. A blank spot like a bull's-eye hovered in the middle of it. "Mrs. Bremer."

"You go on, sweetheart. I'll call Mary Lou. All us moms are like family now."

"Thank you so much," Laurel said, grateful for the graciousness of Southern women. "I don't get these much, but when I do, they're severe."

"Say no more. Go, go, go."

She picked up her purse and computer case and hurried across the driveway to the elementary building's office. She told the secretary that she had to leave, then walked down to Diane Rivers's classroom and poked her head through the open door. Twenty-nine third-graders looked up as one. Diane looked over from her desk and saw instantly that Laurel was in distress. She got up and walked out into the hall, her face lined with concern.

"Migraine worse?"

"Deadly. I have to go home. Do you think you could drop my kids off after school?"

"You know I will. It's right on the way."

Laurel squeezed Diane's hand, then walked to the door at the end of the hall. She was crossing the drive to her car when her aide called out from the playground behind the school, where the children of the parents Laurel had been meeting were playing. Erin Sutherland was a local girl in her early twenties, an education major from USM. Laurel didn't want to stop—if her students saw her, some would come running—but Erin waved both hands as she jogged to the fence, so Laurel walked over and forced a smile.

"Hello, Erin. Is something wrong?"

"I wanted to tell you one thing. Early this morning, Major McDavitt came out and sat with his son for a while. I figured it was okay since you and he are friends, and I know how much he does for all the kids."

Laurel nodded warily, then cringed as another wave of nausea hit her.

"The thing is," Erin went on, "he looked really upset. I think maybe he was crying. Michael definitely was."

Laurel had known Danny was upset, but crying was totally out of character for him. She looked past Erin, scanning the playground until she found Michael. He was sitting alone on a motionless swing, a small, dark-haired boy with his hands floating before him as he rocked forward, then back, again and again. "Did Major McDavitt say anything to you?"

"No. I went up and asked if everything was all right, but he just kind of waved me away. You know, like, mind your own business."

"And then he left?"

Erin nodded as though worried Laurel would scold her. Laurel was about to reassure the girl when her cell phone vibrated against her left thigh. It had been so long since Danny had texted her that she ignored it at first. Then she remembered that her clone phone was in her left pocket, and her legit one in her right. The clone was registered to a friend of Danny's, and Danny paid the bill in cash. Danny also carried a duplicate phone, so that he could speak to Laurel without Starlette finding out about it. This message could only be from Danny.

Laurel patted Erin's arm, then turned and walked briskly to her Acura, flipping open the Razr as she went. Danny's text read, *Sorry about today. Please call. Star gone to Baton Rouge for the day.*

Laurel shut the phone without typing an answer, then climbed into her car and drove quickly out to Highway 24. In her mind Michael still sat on the motionless swing, endlessly rocking. With a stab of maternal guilt, she forced the image from her mind. She needed to drive to Warren's office and get a shot of Imitrex. But Warren was the last person she wanted to see right now. He rarely noticed when she was angry or upset, but he would have to be brain-dead not to see that she was on the ragged edge of a breakdown today. Besides, she was pretty sure that her old Imitrex injection kit was still at the house, in the back of Warren's medicine cabinet.

Only . . . there was Danny's message to consider. Her pride told her to ignore it, but she had been praying for just such a message for more than a month. And now she'd gotten it. Danny was waiting to hear from her *right now*. Waiting in his lovely old cypress house on fifty acres at the end of Deerfield Road—less than five miles from where she stood. That was where they'd spent most of their extended time together, except for a couple of overnight trips they'd managed to take last summer. Starlette frequently left town, usually driving to Baton Rouge to shop in the upscale stores there, or to have her hair and nails done in a "real" salon. Her expensive habits had given Danny and Laurel hundreds of hours to get to know each other over the past year, so that instead of a frenetic affair that consisted of hurried sex in cramped and inconvenient places, they'd enjoyed long afternoons taking walks, swimming, riding horses, and even flying together.

The temptation to turn north on Highway 24 was strong. All Laurel had to do was send a reply, and Danny would be waiting in the clearing he had cut out of the forest just for her. Ostensibly a "feed plot" designed to attract deer, the clearing was a circular opening in the trees about fifty feet across, covered with clover a foot deep. Laurel had often lain in that fragrant green lake with Danny inside her, watching the clouds drift from one edge of the sky to the other. To get to the clearing, she used a small gate in the barbed-wire fence that lined Deerfield Road. Danny had given her a key, which she kept in the inside zip pocket of her purse, but whenever he knew she was coming, he unlocked the gate, so that she could nose her Acura through it without even getting out. Thirty seconds later, she would be in the clearing, where Danny sat on his four-wheeler, waiting to chauffeur her up to his house.

Sometimes, sitting behind him, she would open his belt and squeeze him as he drove along the trail. On rainy days, he'd let her drive and cup her breasts to protect them as the four-wheeler bounced along the deep ruts like a tractor crossing rows in a cotton field. If he sensed that she was in the mood, he would rub gentle circles around her nipples as she drove, so that by the time they reached the house, she was well and truly ready.

Laurel shifted on the seat as she stopped for a traffic signal. Five weeks without Danny had given her a constant low-grade ache down low, and sex with Warren had done nothing to alleviate it. The stoplight was a Robert Frost moment: a left turn would take her home; a right would carry her toward Danny's property. Even with blank spots floating before her eyes, she felt compelled to turn right. Two or three shattering orgasms might just nip her migraine in the bud. But then where would she be? Back in an affair with a man who wouldn't leave his wife—or his son, rather. Whichever, the result was the same: the second-class citizenship of Other Womanhood.

Laurel turned left and angrily gunned the motor, her mind on the Imitrex waiting at home. As she neared the stately new homes of Avalon, the seemingly idyllic sameness of the place began to close in on her: perfectly manicured lawns, oceans of pink azaleas, well-placed magnolias, brick border walls, wrought-iron gates, and cookie-cutter Colonials that held every antique armoire, top-end deer rifle, and flat-screen television that the upper crust of Athens Point could buy on credit. Much of it had been purchased to distract the owners from marriages in various states of decomposition, or so it seemed to Laurel, who heard the inside story on every couple in the teachers' lounge at school.

As she turned onto her street, Lyonesse Drive, instinct suddenly got the better of her pride. She took out her clone phone and texted Danny without taking her eyes off the road. She had sent so many text messages in the past year that she could work the keypad as effortlessly as any high school girl at Athens Country Day.

*Give me 30 mins,* she typed.

Driving as swiftly as she dared between the mountainous speed humps, she slid the Razr back into her pocket. She needed Imitrex in her system as fast as she could get it, but she needed Danny just as bad. Images of past lovemaking fragmented into another shower of sparkles, and she clenched her shoulders against what could be the first hammer blow to the side of her head.

*Why am I going to Danny's place?* she wondered. *To pour out my heart to him?*

So what if she was pregnant? Would Danny abandon his autistic son to take care of a child that only *might* be his? What if he suggested that she get an abortion? She'd probably kick him in the balls—something to hint at the pain she would have to endure on an abortionist's table. There was no equivalent analog of the emotional loss she would endure in that case, not for a man.

With that thought, Laurel's father popped into her mind. This was strange, because she hadn't seen him for more than three years. God, would he rant if he knew about her situation. At least she didn't have to worry about that. The "Reverend" Tom Ballard was off on a "missionary trip" in Eastern Europe, an endless one, apparently. He'd tried to explain his goals before he left, but the more he'd told Laurel, the more it had sounded like recruitment for some sort of Christian cult, so she'd tuned out. Her father was a lay minister who'd spent more time and money on other people's children than he ever had on his own. Nominally Baptist, but really more of a roving tent show built around his own unconventional beliefs, Tom's ministry was based in Ferriday, Louisiana, forty miles up the river from Athens Point. This one-horse town had also produced Jimmy Swaggart and Jerry Lee Lewis, and Tom carried the spirits of both men within him. Itinerant by nature, he traveled ceaselessly to spread his version of the Good News, which always included music and sometimes involved an intimate laying on of hands.

Laurel's clearest and most embarrassing childhood memories were of squatting on the shoulders of highways in half the states in the union, while her father tried to repair whatever broken-down junker he happened to be driving at the time. Laurel would wait in mute rage, sweating or freezing as the case might be, while her mother implored her father to let her flag down a passing motorist (translation: a man with more practical sense than the one she'd entrusted her future to). Tom wasn't a bad man, but he was a poor father. About the only two benefits Laurel had derived from his peripatetic lifestyle were world travel and books. Their rickety old house in Ferriday contained more books than many of the big houses by the country club in Athens Point. She had spent her preteen years reading a moth-eaten *Cambridge History of the Ancient World*—all fifteen volumes—and vowing to marry a man opposite from her father in almost every way.

In Warren Shields, she had found that man. Warren was so organized that at twenty, he'd kept meticulous records of his mileage and car maintenance. In hindsight, that should have signaled a seriously anal-retentive personality, but to Laurel Ballard, those records were flags marking a safe harbor. Warren hadn't come from a rich family, but during his first year of medical school he was already buying bargain stocks and calculating which specialties would allow him to retire soonest. (Only later did she begin to see the dark side of these traits, such as being kept on a strict household allowance, one that barely allowed her enough money to buy decent clothes.) Warren also attended a real church with hardwood pews and stained glass, not a one-room saltbox with an aluminum steeple clapped on top with baling wire. In Warren's church, the congregation spoke softly and needed hymnals to follow the hymns. The minister always acted with great rectitude, and no one ever— ever—danced or fainted in the aisles.

By marrying Warren, Laurel got exactly what she'd thought she wanted. And then she'd begun the long, slow realization that financial security could be expensive to the soul. Warren, too, discovered that life didn't unfold according to even the best-laid plans. During the second year of his surgical residency—in Boulder, Colorado, which Laurel had *loved*—Warren's mother had been diagnosed with a progressive nerve disease. Warren's father, a school principal who'd preached "toughness" his whole life, had proved unequal to the task of caring for his wife as she moved toward death. And because Warren's mother refused to move to Colorado for palliative care (she claimed she had to take care of her husband while she could), Warren decided to "take a sabbatical" from his residency to return home and care for his mother. Laurel understood his motives, but she had taught special ed for years to put Warren through medical school, and she finally had a year of architecture school under her belt. She didn't think either of them should stop their educations, even for one year. But when Warren pressed her, she gave in, and they returned to Athens Point.

When Mrs. Shields lived longer than her doctors expected, the "temporary" sabbatical slowly became permanent, like a mining encampment becoming a town. Warren took a position in a local family practice, and real money began flowing in. Then Mrs. Shields let it be known that the one thing that might bring some joy to her last days was to see a grandchild born. This time Laurel dug in her heels, her eyes on the receding horizon of their former future. But how could she deny Warren's mother's last request? After some terrible arguments, she relented, and nine months later Grant was born. Mrs. Shields lived ten months after that, and Grant certainly brought her joy. But less than a month after her funeral, as Laurel was prodding Warren to get everything in order for their return to Colorado, Warren's father had a crippling heart attack. Thirty seconds after they got the call, Laurel realized that they would never go back to Colorado.

She'd tried to make the best of her life in Athens Point. Since there was no four-year college in town— much less a school of architecture—she'd joined the clubs that medical wives were expected to join to further their husbands' careers: the Junior Auxiliary, the Medical Auxiliary, the Garden Club, the Lusahatcha Country Club. She went to church every Sunday, and even taught Sunday school, an immense personal sacrifice, given her background. But all this frenetic social networking did nothing to replace the dream she had given up; rather it created an emotional tension that fairly screamed to be released. For years Laurel had tried the traditionally accepted outlets: step aerobics; Tae Bo; reading groups (invariably chick lit, which made her want to slash her wrists in frustration at the heroines' actions, or lack of them); she'd even circulated through various walking groups, in the hope of finding a friend who shared her frustrations with Martha Stewart Land. But in none of those clubs and groups had she discovered a single kindred spirit.

Her ultimate solution had been to go back to work. Teaching solved several problems at once. It gave her life a single focus, one that excused her from the wearisome club duties she was accustomed to taking on. She really cared about her students and felt she was giving them help that might otherwise be denied them in a small town. Teaching also brought her money that she could spend on whatever she wanted, without the auditing glance Warren always gave her when she made a purchase of even minor extravagance. Finally, teaching had given her Danny McDavitt, the kindred spirit she had been searching for all along. Moreover (an unexpected lagniappe), this kindred spirit came with an anatomically correct, fully functioning penis. And *that*, she thought bitterly, is what got me where I am now.

*At least I hope it was his,* she thought, passing the Elfmans' flower-lined driveway. Her own house appeared on a gentle rise farther on, but the sight gave her no pleasure. It was a contemporary version of a Colonial, at six thousand square feet, twice the size of the homes that had inspired it. Laurel had wanted to design their home herself, in conjunction with a professional architect—her year of architecture school had made her proficient with the top CAD programs—but Warren had been against it. He'd marshaled a half dozen excuses for his opposition: teaching wouldn't allow enough time for her to adequately supervise the project; time spent dealing with contractors would steal hours from the children; but the real reason was simpler: Warren knew that if she designed their home, it would look nothing like the rest of the houses in Avalon. His instinct toward conformity was so strong that he could not bear what the neighbors might say about something that broke the carefully established pattern of the development. And so Laurel lived in a house much like those of her neighbors, one her mother thought perfect, but which she herself saw as one more cell in the suburban hive called Avalon. She swung into her driveway and hit the brakes.

Warren's Volvo was still parked in the garage.

She sat with her foot heavy on the brake, unsure what to do. Something told her to back out and leave;

but there was no rational reason to do that. Besides, Warren might have seen her pull up. The kitchen had a direct line of sight to the driveway.

*Why is he still home?* she wondered. *Did he come home early for lunch? No. He was running late when I left for school this morning. If he skipped hospital rounds and went straight to the office, he would have had to make rounds at lunch. He wouldn't be here. Has he been here all morning? No . . . that's impossible.* Warren didn't take off from work unless he was seriously ill; it took the full-blown flu to hold him down. A paralyzing thought surfaced in the swirling sea of speculation: *What if he found the e.p.t carton? The used test strip from the pregnancy test?*

"No," Laurel said aloud. "No way." *Not unless he went behind the shrubs under the bathroom window . . . and why in God's name would he do that? There's no garden hose or anything else back there. There's only—*

"Mrs. Elfman."

Could the old busybody have seen her drop the box from the bathroom window? Doubtful. Even if she had, why would she give it to Warren? Not even Bonnie Elfman was idiotic enough to congratulate her doctor on something he might not yet know himself. *But she might be malicious enough to do it. . . .*

Laurel and Mrs. Elfman had once quarreled over the boundary line of their lots (a dispute resolved when a second survey proved Laurel correct). Was the woman still bitter enough to take her revenge in such an extreme way?

*No,* Laurel decided. *Warren's still here because of the IRS audit.*

The situation was probably worse than he'd admitted. Warren never burdened her with business worries, and he also knew that Laurel had never trusted Kyle Auster, his senior partner, not even during the honeymoon years of the partnership. Auster's smile was too broad, his patter too slick for a physician with his priorities in line, and he spent far too much money. For the first few years, Warren had defended his older partner—only ten years older, but that was sufficient to engender a little blind hero worship—but in the last couple of years, some of the shine had rubbed off of the statue in Warren's mind. He had seen Auster's human side too many times, and he'd revised his opinion accordingly. She recalled the wild look in Warren's eyes as he'd searched the bookshelves this morning. It took a great deal of stress to make her husband betray any emotion at all. Given his mental state this morning, she wondered whether Auster might have gotten them into serious legal trouble. *That must be it,* she decided, worried for Warren, but also relieved for a distraction to keep him occupied during her present crisis.

She eased her foot off the brake and idled toward the garage, wondering what she could do to soothe his nerves. She was putting the car in park when she remembered the note in her pocket, the one she'd meant to give Danny this morning. A note saying *I'M PREGNANT* might give Warren a stroke today, even if he thought the child was his. Laurel considered stashing the note in her car, but something told her not to take any chances. Depressing the cigarette lighter with her thumb, she rolled down her window and switched the AC control to MAX. Then she fished the yellow Post-it from her pocket and touched the red-hot lighter to its corner. The glue-coated back of the note caught first, then the draft from the air conditioner stoked the flame. Soon the note was burning in the ashtray. Laurel leaned out of her window to keep the smoke out of her hair. When nothing remained but ash, she grabbed her purse and computer and walked up to the house just as she would have on any other day.

Squeezing past Warren's Volvo, she remembered that she still had both Razrs in her slacks. Habit was a strong force. It would probably be better to leave the clone in the car, but Danny was liable to text her with more information about their meeting, and she needed to stay abreast of the situation, so that she could tell Warren whatever would get her the most free time. She took out the clone Razr, switched it to SILENT, then slid it into her back pocket on the opposite side from the legit phone in front. At least Warren wouldn't see the flat bulges of two phones from any angle.

As soon as Laurel entered the pantry, she knew something was wrong. Moving into the kitchen, she sensed that things were out of place, as though they had been moved and then put back by someone who didn't know exactly where they went. She heard nothing, but there seemed to be a residue of anger in the air, as though the house itself were disturbed. She thought she smelled alcohol, a faint trace coming from deeper in the house . . . and maybe burnt food. *Yes*—there was a microwave carton in the sink, with something black leaking out of it. Warren had never been much of a cook. He didn't care about food.

She left the kitchen and stepped down into the great room with its two-story windows and oversize fireplace. Several seconds passed before she realized that she was not alone. Warren was sitting so still that he didn't seem to be alive. But his eyes were open, and they were watching her. Warren was hunkered down on the ottoman of Laurel's Eames lounger, which he had dragged up to their thick glass coffee table. He was still wearing yesterday's clothes.

"Warren?" she said. "Are you all right?"

The eyes blinked slowly, but he said nothing.

She took a step closer, then stopped, still five yards from him.

"Come sit down," he said. "I need to talk to you."

He motioned toward the sectional sofa that half surrounded the coffee table. Laurel started forward, then checked herself. Something in his voice had set off an alarm in her head. Or maybe something *lacking* from it. That was it. All the life had gone out of his voice.

"Warren, what's the matter?" she asked gently. "Is it something to do with the tax audit?"

He pointed at something on the coffee table. A piece of paper. "I want to know about that."

Laurel leaned forward and looked down, and an explosion of panic detonated at the base of her brain. Now she understood everything. The frantic searching she'd witnessed this morning had nothing to do with the IRS. Warren had somehow discovered the sole handwritten letter Laurel had kept from her relationship with Danny. She'd recognized it instantly, because Danny had written it in green ink. The block-printed letters shrieked up at her like an accusation of adultery. *When did Warren find that?* she thought frantically. Since he hadn't come to bed last night, it was possible that he'd found the letter many hours ago. Found it, read it, and then begun tearing the house apart looking for more evidence. Probably the only reason he hadn't snatched her out of bed and confronted her last night was because the letter wasn't signed (except for the word "Me," which on the day Laurel had received the letter made it sound like a note from a junior high school boy, but which she now thanked God that Danny had done).

"I'm surprised you kept that," Warren said. "You're usually such a detail person. I guess that letter means a great deal to you."

Laurel stood frozen, her eyes on the letter. Other than outright panic—squashed by survival instinct—her mind was blank. She gazed at the green letters, trying to keep the muscles of her face motionless. She felt Warren staring relentlessly at her, not blinking, and blood rushed into her cheeks. Nothing could stop that. She could blame it on Warren's confrontational posture, but that would only postpone the inevitable. From the moment Warren found that letter, the truth was bound to come out.

"Well?" he prompted, his voice exquisitely controlled. "Are you going to stand there and lie to me?"

Laurel knew what his exaggerated control signaled: rage. Danny had always warned her to be prepared for this moment. For getting caught. Anyone might have seen them on any day, without their even knowing it. Danny had told her that people who had affairs behaved as though they were invisible, as though passion created some sort of force field through which common people couldn't see. But this was a chemical illusion, and it took only a single unexpected glance to destroy it. Danny's letter was much more than that. It was as deadly as a shot fired through the heart, and it had probably destroyed Warren to read it. Worse, that shot had triggered an avalanche from the frozen heights above their marriage. Even now, mountains of denial and repression were hurtling down upon them at two hundred miles an hour. The silence in the room was the prelude to the roar of being buried alive.

"You're not going to say anything?" Warren demanded.

Her mind grasped at the nearest concrete detail. "I'm getting a migraine. That's why I came home early."

"You poor thing."

"Whatever," she said, turning away. "I'm going to try to find the Imitrex."

"Don't try to walk away from this."

As she looked back at him, Danny's voice spoke softly in her mind: *Never admit anything. No matter what he confronts you with, deny it. Deny, deny, deny. It may seem ridiculous, but he'll be desperate for any excuse to believe you. If you admit cheating on him, you'll regret it later. Think before you act.* She knew Danny was right, but looking at Warren now, and knowing what was in the letter, she saw how impossible that advice was. She had no option but to tell the truth, even if it meant living alone forever. But first she needed the Imitrex. She couldn't complete the destruction of her marriage while having a migraine.

"I'm going to find the Imitrex," she repeated firmly, and walked away before Warren could respond. "Will you give me the injection?"

"Come back here!" he shouted. "Don't walk away from me! Laurel!"

She waved acknowledgment but kept walking, her eyes brimming with tears.

*"I said turn around, goddamn it!"*

It was his tone that turned her, not the "goddamn." There was something in it she had never heard before, a fury that bordered on madness, and she could imagine nothing more alien to Warren Shields than madness.

Facing him again, she saw that he'd gone pale. His right hand gripped the edge of the coffee table like that of a drowning man clinging to the gunwale of a lifeboat. The sight triggered something deep within her, something far deeper than thought, an impulse concerned with her survival alone. And then she saw why: Warren's other hand was holding a gun. A black revolver, pressed against the outside of his thigh. Only part of the gun was visible, but there was no mistaking what it was.

"My head is about to *explode,*" she said, her eyes locked on to his by force of will alone. "Whatever that piece of paper is, I've never seen it before in my life."

# CHAPTER

# 5

"You're lying," Warren said, still clutching the gun beside his leg. "I have to say, that's the last thing I expected from you."

Laurel refused to acknowledge the gun's existence, yet it filled her mind with terrifying power. Where had Warren gotten a pistol? He owned a rifle and a shotgun, but so far as she knew, there wasn't a single handgun in the house. Yet he was holding one now. Should she acknowledge it? Was it riskier to pretend the gun wasn't there? Would that reinforce the idea that she was lying? Warren was almost hiding it from her, though. For now, she decided, she would pretend she hadn't seen it.

"I don't know what you're talking about," she said in a level voice. She pointed at the letter on the coffee table. "What is that?"

He slid the letter toward her. "Why don't you read it?"

She picked up the note and scanned the words she knew by heart, her eyes swimming.

"Aloud, please," Warren said.

"What?"

"Read the letter aloud."

She looked up. "You're kidding, right?"

"Do I look like I'm kidding? It'll be so much more powerful that way."

"Warren—"

*"Read it!"*

"Will you give me the injection when I'm done?"

He nodded.

She'd read Danny's last letter so many times that she could recite it from memory. She reminded herself not to glance away from the paper as she read, a mistake she might pay for with her life. She began reading in a lifeless monotone: "'I know the first rule of this kind of relationship is Never Write Anything Down. But in this case I feel I have to. A—'"

"You skipped the salutation," Warren said coldly.

She sighed, then backed up and gave him what he wanted. "'*Laurel,*'" she said. "Blah, blah, blah. 'A transient wisp of electrons won't do it. There's no need to go over the facts. We've both done that until we're almost insane. But before I say what I want to say, let me remind you that I love you. I feel things for you that I've never felt before—'"

She looked up and spoke sharply, "Warren, this is bullshit. Where did you get this?"

He looked back at her without speaking.

"Did someone give you this?"

An odd smile touched his lips. "I actually found it in your copy of *Pride and Prejudice*. But then you know that already, don't you?"

"I told you, I've never seen this before in my life."

He shook his head. "Deny till you die, huh? I *really*

expected more from you than this. Where's the woman
of principle who's always criticizing people? Why can't
you tell me the truth? Because this guy dumped you?
Are you scared to leave me without another man to
run to?"

The words rolled right over her. She couldn't get past
the gun. It seemed unreal in Warren's hand, a mockery
of everything he stood for. He had never liked guns.
He knew how to shoot, of course, like any man raised
in a small Southern town. But he wasn't like a lot of
the men she knew, who had fetishes about guns. Many
homes in Athens Point held half a dozen firearms, and
some forty or fifty. A couple of doctors actually carried guns on their person and had built pistol ranges
on their property. She'd heard Warren make disparag-
ing comments about those men, something to the effect that they used the idea of self-defense to justify the
macho feeling that guns gave them. Laurel agreed, but
Warren's take on things had surprised her, because unlike most people, he had actually used a gun to defend
his family.

When he was fifteen years old, a prowler had broken into his parents' house, looking for anything he
could steal to buy drugs. Warren had awakened, crept
down the hall, and found a hopped-up teenager pointing a gun at his father's chest and demanding money.
Without thinking, Warren rushed to his parents' room
and grabbed his father's loaded .45 from the top shelf
of the closet. Then he ran back to the front room and
shot the yelling prowler in the back. He didn't yell out
a warning or call 911. He saw his parents in mortal
danger, and he responded with deadly force. The police
saw things the same way, and within hours, Warren

Shields was a local hero. A week later, the NRA sent a reporter to town to get the story, to run it in their "The Armed Citizen" column in *American Rifleman*. Warren and his parents declined this celebrity. As it turned out, the boy Warren had shot was only three years older than Warren himself. Warren had played baseball against him when he was still in high school. As far as Laurel knew, Warren had never fired another pistol since that day.

Yet now he was holding one in his hand.

*Don't look at the gun,* she told herself. "Somebody's screwing with your head, Warren. That's the only explanation for this."

Another faint smile, as though he could appreciate her efforts to deny the obvious, the way Grant tried to deny peeing on the toilet seat. "Then it shouldn't bother you to keep reading," he said. "Maybe together we can figure out who wrote this."

"Warren—"

"*Read!*"

She closed her eyes for a few moments, then continued. "'I think of you in everything I do. You're as much a part of my being as I am. This emotion feels unselfish, but it's not, because you are my salvation. And not only mine, as you know. No lesser thing could keep me from coming to you. I know you know that, and that's not why I'm writing you. I'm writing to tell you something else you already know, hopefully to give you the last push you need.

"'You deserve more than I can give you, and that's why we're not together. But you also deserve more than Warren can give you. Much more. You have to leave him, Laurel. He can never make you happy, and you know it. He doesn't even know you. If he did, he would never have let you give up so much to come here.'"

Over the top of the letter, she saw Warren's mouth tighten into a grimace of hatred. She stopped, but he motioned for her to go on.

"'You and Warren are complete opposites. He is cold, logical, held-in, almost sterile. You're warm, vibrant, creative, sensual, all the things you've shown me this past year. I'm not trying to denigrate him. I know he has good qualities. He's an honest man, a good provider. I don't care much for his parenting style, but I'm not sure we have much choice in that. We're all victims of our fathers that way. But your needs are so deep. Emotionally, sexually, intellectually . . . while his seem so limited and concrete. You've told me that yourself. He doesn't really want a wife, but a beautiful servant. That role will never be enough for you, and the sooner you admit that, the better off you'll be. Warren will be, too. The only way you could stay with him is by becoming a lifelong martyr to your children. I've known women who did that. Zoloft for the daytime, sedatives at night, a vibrator in the drawer, and too many glasses of wine at parties. They all regret it later.'"

Laurel paused for breath. Too afraid to look up, she pushed forward on autopilot.

"'Please don't choose that life. Don't sell yourself short. The simple truth is that you married too young. Should you pay for that mistake for the rest of your life? I know, I know . . . Do as I say, not as I do. But we're in very different situations. Grant and Beth will be all right. No matter what you choose, I'm going to abide by our agreement. I never thought of myself as weak until I was inside you. Now I know how weak I truly am. I'll never get myself out of you, and I'll never get you out of me. I'm sorrier than you'll ever know.'" She paused, trying to blot Danny from her mind, as though not thinking of him might somehow protect him. "It's signed, 'Me.'"

"How convenient," Warren said acidly. "Don't you think? And the writer seems to have his finger on the pulse of our marriage, doesn't he? Or he thinks he does, anyway. Who do you think might know us that well?"

She kept staring at the paper, wishing harder than she had as a child forced to sing in front of her father's congregation that she could magically be transported elsewhere. As she stared, the periphery of her vision shrunk and went dark, until she was staring at the letter through a round window. Her dread of pain returned with enough force to take her out of the moment—almost.

"Just tell me the truth," Warren said softly. "Please. I won't be angry."

Glancing up at his slitted eyes, she felt she had just heard a rattlesnake hiss, *Just step right here on my tail, I promise I won't bite you.*

"I have told you the truth. You don't want to hear it." She dropped the letter on the floor. "I got a migraine aura thirty minutes ago. If I don't get that injection, I'll be flat on my back all afternoon, unable to speak. You won't be able to continue this ridiculous interrogation."

He regarded her coolly. Withstanding his scrutiny as best she could, she tried to make a plan of action. Given the as-yet-unmentioned gun, she should probably get out of the house as fast as possible. But that wasn't as simple as it sounded. She couldn't outrun Warren, and no one could outrun a bullet. It seemed inconceivable that he would actually shoot her, but if someone had asked her whether Warren would threaten her with a gun, she would have declared that impossible, too. No . . . she was going to have to talk her way out of this. Talk and bluff.

"Is that a gun in your hand?" she asked in a neutral voice.

He lifted the pistol into plain sight. "This?"

"Yes, that."

"It is."

"Is it loaded?"

"Of course. An unloaded gun is useless."

*Oh, boy.* "Where did you get it?"

"I bought it a couple of months ago. Some punks hassled me one night when I was riding my bike on the south end of town. I carry this in my seat bag now. I've got a permit for it."

Warren was still an obsessive cyclist; he'd won dozens of regional races, and even a couple of nationals a few years ago. He rode countless miles in training, but she'd heard nothing about any gun, or any incident where he'd needed one.

"You keep that in the house, with our children?"

She'd tried to sound suitably shocked, but Warren ignored her apparent concern. "I have a lockbox for it in the storeroom. Top shelf. It's kidproof, don't worry."

*It's not the kids I'm worried about right now.* "That doesn't mean it's Grant-proof."

A smile crossed Warren's face as he thought of his mischievous son.

"Why are you holding it now?" she asked.

"Because I'm very angry. And this makes me feel better."

*Oh, God—*

"Apparently," he went on, "you don't want to tell me the truth. But you should know this: you're not leaving this house until I know who wrote that letter."

"I don't want to leave the house, Warren. I want a shot of Imitrex."

He frowned as though he were being greatly inconvenienced. "Give me your cell phone."

A shiver of panic went through her, until she remembered she was carrying both phones. There had been days when she'd only had her clone phone in her pocket.

"Hand it over! Your car keys, too."

She slid her hand into her right front pocket and drew out her legitimate Razr. Warren reached out and took it, then laid it on the coffee table.

"I've already gone over your cellular records online. I've got a couple of questions for you."

She shrugged. There was no danger there. She had always used her clone phone to call Danny.

"The keys, come on."

She drew her car keys from her left front pocket and passed them to Warren, who shoved them into his own pocket. She hated to give them up, but she couldn't risk him searching her and finding the clone phone in her back pocket. Danny was probably trying to call her right now. He would be sitting in the clearing on his four-wheeler, expecting to see her Acura come rolling between the big oak trees. He'd wait awhile, thinking she was only running late. Then he would start to worry. She had to contact him. A sickening wave of nausea hit her, and she tensed against it. As it passed, she got an idea about how to text Danny.

"I want your computer, too," Warren said. "Where is it? In the kitchen?"

The blood drained from her face. There were things in her computer that could destroy her. Danny, too. "I'm going to throw up," she groaned.

She ran for the master bathroom.

"Goddamn it!" Warren cursed, jumping up and rushing after her.

She ran all the way to the toilet cubicle, hoping that Warren would stop in the bedroom, but he didn't. He stood over her as she fell to her knees and put her face in the toilet bowl. She had no choice now. Retching loudly, she stuck her finger down her throat and brought up what remained of her breakfast.

Warren didn't flinch. He'd seen things in his medical career that made a little vomit look like a picnic. She was terrified that he would notice the flat, rectangular bulge of the second Razr in her back pocket, but he suddenly walked out of the cubicle. She heard him rummaging in the medicine cabinet on his side of the marble-floored bathroom. Could she risk texting Danny now?

"Is the Imitrex in there?" She coughed. "Did you find it?"

"I've got it. Come lie on the bed, and I'll give you the shot. Stay away from the bathroom windows. I noticed Mrs. Elfman nosing around out there this morning."

Laurel's throat constricted in terror. She prayed that

the e.p.t box still lay behind the hedge beneath the bathroom window.

"Hurry up!" Warren said irritably, suddenly standing above her again. "You're done, aren't you?"

"I'm still nauseated."

"The sooner the better, then."

He grabbed her pants right above the pocket that held the Razr. As she screamed and tried to protect the phone, he yanked down her waistband and jabbed a needle into her hip. After what seemed a savage twist, he yanked it out again.

"*Ow!*" she cried. "What's wrong with you?"

"Me? I'm 'cold, logical, held-in, almost sterile.'" He slapped the spot where he'd injected her, something nurses did to distract patients from the pain of injections—usually *before* the needle went in—but his slap was hard enough to bruise. "Tell me who wrote that shit. Tell me who else has been looking at that ass."

His voice had a proprietary edge. "No one! I told you."

"When was the last time you fucked him?"

Laurel tried to stand, but Warren seized her neck and pressed her back down. In twelve years of marriage he had never laid a hand on her in anger. Fresh fear twisted her insides. "Warren, that hurts! Please think about what you're doing."

"You want to talk about pain? That's funny. I don't need to think about this."

"Yes, you do. I haven't cheated on you. I'd never do that to you!"

"You're a liar." He shoved her against the toilet, then walked away again.

She scrambled to her feet and ran to her side of the

bed. There was no point in trying to flee the house unless she could slow him down first. Pulling back the
comforter and sheets, she crawled under them and
pulled them up to her neck.

"Get up," Warren said from the foot of the bed. "I
want to check your computer."

"Go get it, then. I'm going to lie here until the aura
goes away."

"If I leave you here, you'll climb out the window."

*Damn right I will.* "Ten minutes in the dark, Warren.
Please. If the aura stops, I'll do whatever you want."
She closed her eyes. "You can lie here with me, if you
want to."

"I don't," he said, but he flicked off the light switch.
"The windows are locked, by the way. All of them."

She shifted under the covers, then slid her hand into
her back pocket and eased out the clone Razr. In one
continuous motion, she opened the phone and slipped
it into her front pocket. Warren was a black silhouette
in the dark, leaning on his bureau.

"When I read that letter," he said hoarsely, "I felt
like someone had stabbed me in the heart."

She slid her thumb lightly over the Razr's keypad.
Keying in a message was child's play, but blindly pressing the proper sequence of buttons to put the phone
into text mode wasn't. She turned her head and looked
at Warren as she worked her thumb over the faintly
tactile buttons, trying to keep his eyes focused on her
face.

"I'm not having an affair," she said softly. "I haven't
had one in the past, either. I would never do that to
Grant and Beth."

Warren flipped out the cylinder of his revolver and

spun it. "I wouldn't have thought you could." The cylinder snicked home. "But the letter says different."

"That letter is bullshit." Laurel had the Razr in text mode. She began keying her message to Danny, her eyes never leaving her husband's face. "Someone faked it to mess with your head."

To her surprise, Warren seemed to be considering her suggestion. "Who would fake something like that?" he asked, as though talking to himself.

"Somebody who wants to drive you crazy. And it's obviously working. Warren, if you lift a hand to me again, I'm calling the police and hiring a divorce lawyer."

This was pure bravado. Even in near darkness, she could see his neck and jaw muscles tightly flexed. Danny's letter had utterly transformed him. With an infinitesimal movement of her right thumb, she pressed SEND and slid her hand out of her pocket.

"I still have the aura," she said with genuine anxiety. "My arms are tingling, and I'm craving ice cream."

"Imitrex only shortens the headache, you know that."

She closed her eyes again.

"You've got to get up," Warren said. "I want to see your computer. You can lie on the sofa in the great room."

Laurel prayed that Danny was already reading her message. She'd risked a lot to send it, and she hadn't sent the message Danny would have wanted her to. But she still had the phone, and in her heart she still believed she could talk Warren down from this flight of rage—so long as her computer concealed its secrets. At bottom, the idea that Warren Shields, M.D., might shoot the mother of his children was preposterous. But what he might do to a man who had fornicated with and impregnated her was another matter.

"Get up, goddamn it!" Warren snapped, kicking the side of the mattress.

The violence of his anger was what worried her, for it was wholly new. Laurel stood slowly, gathered the comforter around her shoulders, and padded into the hall that led to the kitchen. *Run, Danny,* she thought. *For Michael's sake, run.*

# CHAPTER

# 6

Danny McDavitt was lying on his back in a sea of clover when his cell phone chirped, signaling the arrival of a text message. He hadn't heard that sound since the day he'd told Laurel that he couldn't leave his wife and watched her crumble before him.

Danny didn't reach straight for his phone. He knew the true worth of lying in sun-drenched clover, waiting for the touch of a woman who loved him. There had been more than a few moments in his life when he'd been certain that he wouldn't survive into the next minute, much less live to lie in a fragrant bower like this one, waiting for a beauty like Laurel Shields. In the air force, Danny had been known as an even-tempered guy, even among pilots. But falling in love with a woman he could not possess had rewired part of his brain. An emotional volatility was loose in him, and it frightened him sometimes. The chirping phone, for example. Laurel's reply to the text message he'd sent after their "parent-teacher conference" had lifted him from depression to blissful anticipation in the span of four seconds. But this time the chirp had sent a tremor of fear through him. Laurel was already late, and a new text message was likely to tell him she'd decided not to meet him after all.

He couldn't blame her. It had been unfair of him even to ask. Nothing had changed in his marital situation. He'd simply reached a point of such desperate longing that he'd been unable to keep from begging. He hated himself for the weakness he'd shown this morning. It was true that Starlette had bailed on the teacher conference; that was par for the course. But the second she'd started making excuses, Danny's heart had soared. Her avoidance would give him an excuse to see Laurel—in private—and even though he'd known she would be upset, he'd gone to her classroom anyway.

Danny dug his hand into the deep clover and found his phone, but still he didn't read the text message. He didn't want to shatter his dream yet. Twenty-one years of military service had taught him to let good things linger while he could, even if they were illusory. Danny had seen the world from the cockpit of an MH-53 Pave Low helicopter, starting with the original bird in anti-drug operations out of the Bahamas in 1982 (not the dream duty it sounded like), and winding up in the futuristic Pave Low IV in Afghanistan, where in late 2001 he was shot down and finally retired. In between, he had served on almost every continent, with Bosnia and Sierra Leone proving particularly memorable. Pave Lows from Danny's group, the elite Twentieth Special Operations Wing, had opened Gulf War One by crossing the desert in pitch blackness and taking out Iraq's air defenses, opening the skies for the army's better-known AH-64 Apaches. Danny still remembered the unparalleled rush of flying a massed formation of birds into what everyone knew was going to be the first real war since Vietnam (his own personal *Apocalypse Now* moment). His sound track, rather disappointingly in hindsight, had been Willie Nelson's "On the Road Again," rather than Wagner's "Ride of the Valkyries." Though Desert Storm had ended faster than anyone expected, there'd been no shortage of adrenaline-charged missions to follow. But they paled in comparison to what he'd endured in the hellish mountains of Afghanistan, a land that bred warriors the way America now bred lawyers.

"Give me some good news," he murmured, raising the cell phone at last. He held the device far enough from his aging eyes to read the tiny letters on the screen and pressed READ. Laurel's message materialized almost instantly.

WARREN KNOWS GETMICHAEL
LEAVETOWNASAP NO HEROICS

Danny stopped breathing. This was the last thing he'd expected. After all the times they might have been caught—and there had been some close calls—he'd thought the danger had finally dropped to zero. He re-read the message as he got to his feet, trying to work out what might have happened.

Some sort of confrontation, obviously. But why was she telling him to run? Did she think he was in danger? That was difficult to imagine. Danny had given Warren Shields flying lessons for four months, and he'd come to know the doctor as a quiet, restrained, methodical man, just what you wanted in a physician, and indeed in a pilot. The idea of Warren Shields harming his wife seemed silly, and the possibility of him coming after Danny even more far-fetched. And yet . . . Danny had seen enough men under severe stress to know they were capable of wildly unpredictable behavior. He'd seen soldiers do things in battle zones that no one back home would have believed—some good things, but more of them bad.

There was no question of taking Laurel's advice. If she was in danger, he wasn't about to cut and run. The question was, what could he do to help her? If he shed his anonymity as her lover, he would bring about the very thing he was trying to avoid by remaining with Starlette: he would lose custody of Michael. But if Laurel was truly in danger . . .

He started to text her back and tell her that she wasn't alone, that he would solve whatever problem had come up. But she *was* alone, at least in the sense that he wasn't with her. And fighting with Warren, almost certainly. One call or text message from Danny might give away everything or hurt her in some way that he couldn't guess at.

He trotted to his four-wheeler, cranked the engine, and wrestled the Honda onto the track that led up to the house. His chest thrummed with nervous energy. The shock of her message had been profound. He'd been dreaming of the moment that Laurel would rush into his arms. After five weeks apart, she would melt under his hands. Hell, she'd started melting in her classroom. To be ripped from that fantasy into this reality had disconcerted him. But Danny knew how to shift neural gears in a hurry. Countless times he'd been roused from dreams by a klaxon calling him to battle, or to rescue men barely clinging to life, their limbs shredded, guts puddled in their laps like bowls of pasta. His ability to adapt quickly was one reason he was still alive.

He jiggered the Honda into his garage, hit the kill switch, and jumped off. First he needed to know where Laurel was. The school? Home? Warren's office? He started to get his car keys from the kitchen, but stopped at the door. Danny drove a 1969 Dodge Charger he'd restored himself. Warren knew the car well, so it was useless in this context. Climbing back onto the Honda, Danny drove down to the shed where he kept his lawn equipment. He'd bought an ancient Ford pickup to make runs to the hardware store and to the nursery. He and Michael used it to tool around the property together. Michael had steered it from Danny's lap several times, an experience akin to flying over Baghdad on a bad night. Danny parked the four-wheeler, jumped into the cab of the truck, backed out of the shed, and drove across his lawn toward Deerfield Road. As he passed his house, he considered stopping to get his nine-millimeter from the bedroom. But that would be plain crazy, he decided. Serious overkill.

"Hold on, babe," he said, pushing the old truck toward the paved road. "I'm coming."

Laurel lay silently on the great room sofa, her comforter pulled up to her neck. Warren was sitting on the ottoman he'd dragged over to the coffee table and staring at Laurel's Sony Vaio, which hummed in front of him like a willing informer. His forefinger slid steadily over the computer's trackpad; he was working methodically through her file tree in Windows Explorer.

Laurel's computer posed several risks, some minor, others grave. She kept some files on it that, while they would not implicate Danny directly, would certainly make Warren suspicious. There were stored AOL messages that could cause her trouble, but he was unlikely to see them as significant unless he cross-referenced everything he found against a calendar. But there was one thing she absolutely could not afford for him to discover—the digital equivalent of an atomic bomb.

Laurel maintained a secret e-mail account that Warren knew nothing about. Ostensibly, they both used AOL as their mail server, and Laurel did use AOL for her "official" e-mail life: notes to friends, school announcements, and the like. But her correspondence with Danny was run through a free Hotmail account protected by a password. Laurel's Hotmail username was misselizabeth2006@hotmail.com. Corny, perhaps, cribbing a digital alias from Jane Austen, but what else was she going to choose? Agent 99? Hester Prynne? The Sony was programmed to "forget" her username and password every time she logged off, but she knew that these keys to her secret life must reside somewhere on the hard drive, as did her past e-mail messages. A forensic computer expert would doubtless be able to call up that data like a boy rubbing a genie's lamp. What Warren could accomplish on his own was open to question. He knew how to operate most mainstream Windows programs, but he was no wizard. He was patient, though. And if he was willing to hack at the Sony for hours, who knew what he might uncover? If he stumbled onto that Hotmail account or, God forbid, somehow guessed her password, her secret life would be served up on a platter—a poisonous platter that would kill Warren even as he devoured it.

His eyes glowed with feral hunger as his fingers flew over the keys, and his orbits, almost black from lack of sleep, gave him a desperate mien. Danny had said

Warren would want to believe that she'd been faithful despite evidence to the contrary, but she saw no such desire in his face now. Warren wanted only one thing: the identity of the man with whom she had betrayed him. As he punched at the keys, she noticed how unhealthy he looked. Competitive cycling had sculpted Warren into a figure of toned muscle, prominent veins, and limber tendons, but in the past couple of months, she'd noticed an unusual puffiness in his face, his neck, and even on his body. He still had heroically defined leg muscles, but he was looking soft around the edges, with a womanly sort of fat accruing around his hips and upper back. She'd assumed this was due to age, or maybe even depression, but the truth was, she'd been too self-absorbed to ask about it. Besides, Warren had always been touchy about his body, and a question like that might offend him. Looking at him now, she saw a depth of fatigue that could not be explained by a single night of sleep deprivation.

*It's got to be work,* she decided. *Kyle Auster must have finally gotten the practice in bad trouble.* Kyle was capable of anything, in Laurel's estimation. He'd made it clear from the outset of the partnership that he would dearly love to sample her physical charms. And Warren stayed so busy with his patients that he might easily be duped into anything. But what exactly? Warren wouldn't get this bent out of shape over some tax penalties. What was the next step? Prison? Surely that was impossible. You had to commit outright fraud to go to jail, and Warren would never have let Kyle go that far. She wondered, though, if the senior partner could have committed fraud without Warren's knowledge. If so, then today's manic persecution made at least some sense. Warren might be displacing the anger he felt at his former mentor and venting it on her. *What was Warren looking for when he found Danny's letter?* she wondered. *Should I ask him? Or is it safer to lie here with my mouth shut and pray that my digital secrets remain inviolate?*

With a giddy rush Laurel realized that the blank spots in her visual field were gone. The Imitrex was working. She still had the dislocated feeling of a migraine aura, but the aura wasn't metastasizing into a headache. That could still happen, of course, and at any moment. She wondered if the imminent danger, rather than the Imitrex, had shut down her headache. *Get back on point,* said a voice in her head. *You're drifting. The kids will be home before you know it, and then you're looking at a real nightmare.* Even the thought made her breath go shallow.

It was well after noon already. She couldn't know exactly how late it was without checking her cell phone, which was what she used for a watch these days, and that was buried in her pocket. She considered asking Warren the time, but asking questions would only emphasize that she wasn't free to get up and walk into the kitchen. Trying to gauge elapsed time was tricky under stress (she remembered that from her labor with Grant), but she figured that in two hours, more or less, Diane Rivers would drop Grant and Beth off at the end of the sidewalk. The children would race up to the front door, unaware that their father was waiting inside with a loaded gun.

*I can't wait for that,* she decided. *I can't bank on talking Warren around to reason before the kids get home. Because I might not be able to talk him down.*

She stole another look at his eyes, which tracked across her computer screen with laserlike precision, sucking up every character on the screen. *He's not going to stop until he finds out what he wants to know. And he's not going to accept innocence until he's turned over every goddamned rock he can find. Even then, will he believe me? Once somebody begins to doubt your honesty, wiping away suspicion is almost impossible. That's why people never survive public investigations. Some of the mud always sticks, justified or not. And in my case, it is. I'm guilty, and on some level Warren knows that. If he gets deep enough into my Sony, he'll have the proof he's starving for. Or what if he doesn't? What if he finds my Hotmail account but not my password? Would he use the kids as leverage over me?* Searching for a crack in the mask of jealousy that was Warren's face, she began to wish she'd sent Danny a very different message. *I should have dialed 911 the second I saw the gun. I'm like one of those stupid babysitters in a slasher movie. TSTL. Too stupid to live.*

She still had her clone phone, of course. She could dial 911 right now, if she wanted. But Warren had once explained to her that there was no autolocation system in place for cell phones yet—not in Mississippi, anyway. If you didn't tell the 911 dispatcher where you were, it could take a long time for help to reach you, if ever. What if she called 911 and simply left the line open? The dispatcher might eventually hear enough of Warren's threats to realize a dangerous situation was in progress, but again—how would they find her? If she dialed 911, it would have to be from the house phone. They knew where you were the second you dialed in from a landline. Laurel had already taught Grant and

Beth this. If she could get close enough to one of the home extensions, she could definitely bring the police to the house, even if she simply opened the line and said nothing. And yet . . .

Calling the police might be the most dangerous action she could take. Athens Point was a small town: sixteen thousand people. Avalon was outside the city limits, in Lusahatcha County, home to another ten thousand souls. That meant it was policed by the Sheriff's Department. Laurel didn't know how much training local deputies had, but she was pretty sure there was no state-of-the-art crisis management team or hostage negotiator. An image of the local sheriff standing outside her house yelling into a bullhorn came into her mind. What were the odds that this situation could peacefully be resolved by a man like Billy Ray Ellis? He'd been a petroleum land man before winning the post of sheriff, and he was a patient of Warren's. How long would he wait before ordering an all-out assault on the house? His deputies would probably be ex-high-school jocks with an excess of testosterone. Warren could easily wind up dead or locked in Parchman Farm for the rest of his life. And even if he chose not to punish her for calling 911, she might be killed by a stray bullet or tear gas canister. She'd seen that kind of thing enough times on CNN. Such thoughts might be extreme, but he had threatened her with a gun. No . . . she needed to resolve this situation herself, and soon.

Before the kids got home.

*I can text Diane!* she thought with dizzying relief. *Tell her to take the kids home with her rather than drop them here.* Laurel was about to slip her hand into her pocket when she realized the risks that such a move would entail. She'd be texting from her clone Razr, which was registered to Danny's helpful friend. The unfamiliar number might confuse Diane enough to make her call the house. Or what if Diane had something else to do after school? What if she tried to call back? Laurel's Razr was set to SILENT, but if Diane got no answer, she might call the house phone. Warren would answer, and in less than a minute he'd learn that Laurel had just texted Diane from a cell phone. Game over. Laurel slid her hand away from her pocket. She couldn't risk losing the clone phone yet.

*I've got to get out of here*, she thought. Could she hit Warren hard enough to disable him? If so, she could take back her car keys, which would seriously shorten the distance she had to run. She looked around the great room for a heavy object. A thick blown-glass vase on the console table against the far wall might do. But she'd have to choose her moment perfectly. If she tried to hit Warren and missed, there was no telling how he might react. At the very least he would tie her up, and then she'd be truly helpless when the kids walked into this horror show. With that thought came the first ripples of true panic, fluttery jerks in the heart muscle that made her swallow hard even as the saliva evaporated from her mouth.

*Don't give in to panic,* she told herself. The phrase made her recall her days as a counselor at a girls' summer camp, where she'd taught lifesaving to young teens. *Panic will kill you. So do everybody a favor, remain calm, and focus on safety, even if you're partying—* "Safety," she said softly.

"What?" asked Warren, looking over at her with red-rimmed eyes.

"Nothing. I'm out of it. My head's starting to hurt bad."

"The Imitrex will kick in. It's working on those vessels now."

Warren was talking on medical autopilot. She'd heard that robotic voice thousands of times, when nurses called the house at night for instructions. But Laurel wasn't listening now. She was thinking about a room that she'd insisted be added to the house before they moved in. Some people called it a panic room, but the architect they'd worked with had simply called it the safe room. Located under the staircase, it was a windowless, eight-by-ten-foot cubicle with steel walls, a reinforced door, and an electronic lock that operated from the inside. The safe room also had a dedicated phone line that ran underground to a box at the street. Warren had stocked the safe room with canned food and water for use during hurricanes, and also with blankets and pillows for comfort. Grant and Beth had "camped out" in the safe room a couple of times; they called it their "fort," the place they'd run to if "bad guys" broke into the house. Laurel had never imagined a day when the "bad guy" she would need to escape would be her husband. But that day had come.

She knew she could reach the safe room before Warren stopped her. He was so deep into her computer files that she could be halfway there before he got up off the ottoman—

*Wait,* she thought, already flexing her calf muscles beneath the comforter. *Think it through. So I get to the safe room. Then what? Call 911? No. Call Diane and tell her to take the kids to her house without telling anyone else about it. If I say "family crisis," Diane will handle it, no questions asked.*

Once the kids were safe, Laurel could call the police. Or better yet, a lawyer she knew who was friendly with the sheriff. He would get a more serious hearing. And when the law arrived at the house, Warren would have no hostage to threaten. He would effectively be alone with his gun and his wife's computer.

The most likely risk at that point, Laurel realized, would be suicide.

She closed her eyes, wondering if Warren could really be that far gone. He seemed more angry than depressed, but more was going on inside him than she knew. There had to be. But now wasn't the time to question him about it.

*Leave that to the TSTL girls . . .*

She flexed her fists beneath the covers, then her forearms. When she felt the blood flowing, she tensed her biceps, shoulders, and abdomen. Then her thighs. *Flex, release, flex, release.* It was like warming up for one of those classes at Curves, only her life might depend on this little exercise. She wasn't about to spring up off her sofa like a lioness and then collapse in a heap because her feet were asleep.

*Should I grab the computer?* she wondered. *That would be a tacit confession of guilt.* Plus, Warren might tackle her before she could get clear with it. She could wait until he walked farther away to make her move, but that might not happen for hours. Warren could go for most of a day without urinating, and he might well be expecting her to try to damage the machine.

While she debated when to run, Warren stood without a word and walked away from the Sony. Laurel didn't follow him with her eyes. She flexed her calves but maintained the illusion of a woman at rest. His footfalls stopped, then started again. She risked cutting her eyes to the left. Warren had walked most of the way to the door that led to the master bedroom, but now he'd stopped again. He was watching her with obvious suspicion.

*What the hell is he doing?* she thought.

As if in answer, he muttered something, then took the blown-glass vase off the sideboard, unzipped his pants, and began to urinate into the vase. He looked straight at Laurel as he did this, a cloud of self-disgust over his features. *See what you've brought me to?* he seemed to be saying. Laurel didn't give a damn. She used his primitive act as an excuse to sit up. Then she gave him a withering glare.

"That's gross," she said, listening to the steady splash of piss in her expensive vase. "Can't you use the toilet?"

"I didn't think you'd want to get up."

She shook her head as though this were beneath contempt. Warren often peed for more than a minute, but she wasn't counting on that. As though battling nausea, she hung her head between her knees. Then she exploded off the couch, snatched the Sony off the coffee table, and raced for the front stairs.

The AC cord nearly jerked the computer out of her hands, but it popped free as Warren screamed. The urine-filled vase rang against the maple floor as she reached the first door and cut left. Warren roared with anger, and heavy footsteps pounded after her.

"*Go, go, go!*" she cried, darting through the foyer and snatching open the wooden closet door that concealed the steel entrance to the safe room. Joy flooded through her as she grabbed the handle and pulled—

And almost ripped her shoulder out of its socket.

At first she thought Warren had yanked her arm back, but the truth was simpler: the safe room was locked. A racking sob burst from her throat as she wrenched the handle once more, but it was no use. Then she realized what was wrong. There was a child-protection mechanism to keep children from inadvertently getting locked inside the safe room: a three-digit code that could seal the safe room from outside but not override the master lock, which was controlled from the inside. Laurel frantically punched 777, then jerked the handle again. It didn't budge.

Horrified, she whirled to try for the front door, but Warren was already standing outside the little closet, staring at her with a malevolence she had never suspected in him.

"I changed the code," he said.

She felt tears on her cheeks.

"You're like a five-year-old caught in a lie," he went on. "Totally predictable."

Nothing he could have said would have enraged her more.

"Give me the computer," he demanded, holding out one hand.

She lifted the lightweight Vaio and hurled it at the floor with all her strength.

Warren's foot shot out to deflect the computer, and the machine hit the carpet with no more force than her cell phone did when she dropped it at the market. Laurel balled her hands into fists and screamed at the top of her lungs. She didn't know what she was saying, but whatever it was, it was the wrong thing. Warren raised the gun, aimed at her face, and pulled the trigger.

Fire spurted from the muzzle, and something stung her face. She reeled back in shock, her ears ringing from the blast in the confined space. Her left cheek hurt badly, but she didn't think she'd been hit by a bullet. The pain was in her skin. Warren must have aimed just to the right of her ear. She wanted to slap him, but she didn't dare risk it.

"That shut you up," he said, his eyes like blue ice. "And don't think the police will come running because of that shot. Not even the Elfmans heard it, and they're the closest to us. Now, pick up that computer and hand it to me."

She blinked away tears of impotent rage. "No."

He stepped forward and laid the hot barrel flush against her forehead. She jerked away from the scalding steel and stared back at the man she had slept with for more than a decade and saw no one she recognized. She bent at the waist, picked up the Sony, and handed it to him.

"What now?"

Warren smiled like a wolf at cornered prey. "Let's see what you're hiding."

Danny McDavitt turned his pickup truck east off of Highway 24 and rolled into Avalon. He drove as fast as he could without drawing attention to himself. In this neighborhood, in this truck, everyone would assume he was coming to cut someone's grass or to fix a faucet.

Danny had been to a few parties in these palatial

houses. Some moneyed folk in Athens Point didn't mind mixing with the common people, and he had actually been making some pretty good money himself for the past year. He'd sold two songs before March, but that was chicken feed compared to what he was making on his oil deals with John Dixon. The geologist had invited Danny to buy into a couple of wildcats he felt good about, and one had come in with twelve feet of pay. At $60-a-barrel oil, even Danny's one-eighth interest was worth real money. But the timing was bad, maritally speaking. That oil well—plus the four others they were working over now—was the main reason Starlette wanted to stay married to him.

Danny turned left onto Lyonesse Drive and slowed down. The Shields house was a big Colonial set well back from the road on a wooded lot. If the garage door was shut, he wouldn't be able to tell a thing. But three seconds later, Danny saw Laurel's midnight blue Acura parked behind her husband's gray Volvo, which stood halfway out of the open garage.

*They're both at home,* he thought. *In the middle of the day.*

He knew from experience that this almost never happened. For one thing, Laurel should still be at the school. For another, Dr. Shields didn't usually get home until after his evening rounds, unless his kids had an athletic event scheduled. Danny could hardly believe that he'd coached soccer with Warren Shields only last year, but he had. Their daughters were the same age, and since Danny had been teaching Shields to fly, the doctor had suggested that they coach a team together. All in all, the experience had been good, but Danny had discovered that Warren Shields approached everything with deadly seriousness, even soccer for five- and six-year-old girls.

Danny drove to the end of Lyonesse, then executed a three-point turn and rode back by the house. Nothing had changed, of course. He felt like a high school boy cruising past the home of a girl he had a crush on. As a teenager he'd swing past a girl's house five or six times a night, just on the off chance of catching a glimpse of her. Stupid, and yet as primal as the mating rituals of Cro-Magnon man.

"Jesus," he muttered, pulling to the curb. "What the hell am I supposed to do now?"

Laurel's message had been too vague. *Warren knows.* How about a little detail with that, lady? Warren knows *what,* exactly? Did he know that his wife had recently had an affair? Or did he know she'd had an affair with Danny McDavitt? Danny had to assume the latter; otherwise, why would she warn him to get out of town? And to take his son with him? That was the worrisome part. Why the hell would Laurel think Michael was at risk? Maybe she knew Danny wouldn't leave town without his son, so she'd named Michael in the message. But then again . . . maybe things were worse than Danny was letting himself believe.

He craned his neck over his shoulder and looked at the house. Worst case, what could be happening in there? Shields could be beating the hell out of his wife. He might even be threatening her with a weapon. *Truth be told,* Danny thought, *he could have killed her already.* But that was nuts. Warren Shields was no killer. Danny hated to make assumptions, but Shields wasn't going to shoot the mother of his children—not for screwing somebody on the side. Maybe if he'd

walked in on Danny doing her doggy-style in the conjugal bed . . . *maybe*. But certainly not based on hear-
say evidence, which was all he could possibly have,
barring a confession. Someone must have seen Danny
and Laurel together somewhere. It could have been the
hug they'd risked this morning. And that was easily
deniable. Danny had coached Laurel on what to say in
this type of situation; she knew to deny everything, no
matter what.

He didn't envy her having to bluff it out with her husband. Warren Shields was smart, and not just regular-
doctor smart. Danny had known doctors who couldn't
pour piss out of a boot with the instructions printed
on the heel. But Shields wasn't one of them. He was
obsessive about everything he did. He had only been
flying for a year, but he probably knew more aerody-
namics than Danny did after thirty years in the cockpit.
If Warren really suspected that Laurel was cheating on
him, he'd tear at it like a bulldog until he was satisfied.
On the other hand, he was like any other man. Deep
down, he didn't want to believe that his wife would
open her legs for anyone but him. It just went against
the grain of the masculine mind. If Laurel stuck to the
plan and denied everything, she would be fine.

Danny wondered if he should risk sending a reassuring text message. If Warren had possession of Laurel's
secret cell phone, it was all over anyway. He would
already have seen Danny's message about "Star" going
to Baton Rouge for the day. From that alone he could
figure out everything. Even if Laurel had deleted that
message as soon as she read it, Warren could trace the
phone to Danny's obliging friend. So where was the
additional risk in texting her? Another possibility was

that Laurel's clone phone was stashed safely in her car, as it should be. But Danny knew from experience that she sometimes risked taking it into the house with her. At least on those occasions she always set it to SILENT. His only other option—the only one that didn't involve losing Michael—was reporting a Peeping Tom at the Shields house. Or better yet, a bomb threat. The Sheriff's Department would have to go inside, then. But if Laurel had things under control, that kind of intrusion would only make things worse. Best to leave it at sending a reassuring text message.

"Hey there!" called a scratchy male voice in the upper register. "You lost or something?"

Danny looked across the passenger seat at the sunburned face of a bald man in his late seventies. "No, sir. Just sitting for a minute."

"You making a delivery out here?"

"Nope."

"I thought you might be bringing me my crossties."

"Pardon?"

The man spread his arms as far as they would go. "Railroad ties! To border my garden, shore up the bank."

Danny smiled. "No, sir. But I've used some of those myself, now and again."

The man stared at him as though awaiting an explanation of what Danny was doing on this street.

"Well," Danny said, grinding the truck into gear. "I guess—"

"Do I know you?"

"I don't think so."

"Sure! I saw you in the newspaper. Something about

the war. Iraq or somewhere. You won some medals over there, right?"

Military fame is a funny thing. You can leave a town as a pimply faced teenager and not come back for anything but funerals, but as long as you have a living relative there, or somebody still remembers you, your picture will pop up in the Sunday paper above an announcement of your latest promotion or, rarely, an item trumpeting the receipt of a medal for bravery under fire.

"No, sir," Danny lied. "I'm over from McComb, checking out sites for cellular towers."

The man's face scrunched into a near parody of suspicion. "*Cell towers?* Here in Avalon? Now listen, we got restrictive covenants against that kind of thing."

"Is that right?"

"Damn straight we do! That's why these lots are so expensive. You need to just drive on down to Lake Forest or Belle Rive, mister. Ain't gonna be no cell towers round here."

"I reckon not," Danny said, smiling. "My mistake. Thanks again."

"Don't thank me. You get on out of here."

Danny drove off, wanting to make a last pass by Laurel's house, but knowing he was already late for a flying lesson with a lady lawyer. He wondered if the old man had noticed that his truck had Lusahatcha County plates.

Warren held the barrel of his revolver against Laurel's right ear as he searched a pantry drawer with his free hand. His motions were jerky, his breath bad. *He hasn't brushed his teeth since yesterday,* Laurel realized. Her left cheek stung as though someone had poured acid over it, and when she ran her fingers over the skin, she felt hard particles embedded in her flesh. Gunpowder. The idea was too surreal to fully accept. Then Warren lifted a heavy roll of duct tape from the pantry drawer.

*He's gone over the edge,* she thought. *I'm in serious fucking trouble here.*

"Get back into the great room," Warren said, shoving her ahead of him, driving her through the kitchen and back down to the sectional by the coffee table. When Laurel reached the sofa, he forced her down onto it.

"Lie on your back," he ordered.

"Warren—"

"Shut up!" He ripped a long strip of tape off the silver-gray roll and wrapped it tight around her ankles.

"Why are you doing this? I don't understand."

"You understand, all right. It's because I can't trust you. You've proved that." Another long strip of tape tightened around her ankles. "All that remains is to find out how deeply you've betrayed this family."

"Warren, you don't have to do this. Can't we just talk?"

"Sure we can." A false smile split his lips. "Tell me why you're so afraid of me looking into your computer, and I'll send you on your way right now."

*Send me on my way? What the hell does that mean? Freedom? Or death?*

"More love letters?" Warren asked. "Pictures? What? Just tell me where the files are, and you can sit with me and have a glass of pinot noir while we look at them together."

She couldn't think of a thing to say.

He nodded slowly, as though settling something in his mind. "Every word that comes out of your mouth is a lie." He wrapped two more lengths of tape around her calves. "I ought to tape your goddamn mouth shut. Hold out your arms."

Laurel began to cry. She didn't want to, but the realization that she was now helpless was overwhelming. Not in her deepest troughs of guilt had she imagined something like this. Warren bound her wrists with the thick tape, then pulled her into a sitting position.

"Don't move unless I tell you to."

He dropped the tape roll onto the coffee table and retrieved her Vaio from the kitchen, where he'd left it. He set it up on the coffee table again, carefully plugging in the AC cable, which looked as though it had suffered minor damage when Laurel ripped the computer loose. "Let's see if this baby survived your little escape attempt." He pressed the power button, avidly watching the screen.

Laurel prayed that the Sony's hard drive had been smashed, but a moment later she heard the halting mechanical sounds of the computer booting up. Then the clicking stopped. Prematurely, she thought. Warren's face was taut. He unplugged the Sony, removed its battery, shook the computer, then reinserted the battery and plugged the AC cord back in. This time the Vaio booted normally.

"You just dazed it," he said with a smile.

Laurel smelled adhesive as her skin warmed the duct tape. When she moved her wrists farther apart, the tape tugged painfully at the hair on her arms.

"You may as well come clean now. I know there's

something on this computer, or you wouldn't have tried to stop me from looking at it."

"You're wrong," she said in a shaky voice. "That's my computer. Mine. Those are *my things* on it. My personal things. I have a right to my own things, you know. My own thoughts. You don't own me. I'm your wife, not your property."

He shook his head. "I've treated you like a queen for twelve years. And this is how you repay me."

She closed her eyes, trying to find some way to break through to him. "Warren, what were you looking for when you found that letter? Will you please tell me that? You were awake all night. You must have been looking for something related to the IRS audit, right?"

The skin around his eyes tightened. "What do you know about that?"

"I know what you've told me, which is almost nothing. As usual."

His stare intensified.

"Why won't you tell me what's really going on?" she asked.

"You're the only one in this room who knows what's really going on."

Laurel shook her head in frustration. "I know *nothing*. Please tell me what you were looking for last night."

He was studying the computer screen again. "The letter. That's what I was looking for."

"Why would you be looking for a love letter?"

His gaze came back to her, and his eyes smoldered with fury. "Because someone in this world actually cares about me. A lot more than you do, obviously."

This floored her. "Are you saying someone told you to look specifically for a letter in this house?"

Warren snorted. "You don't get it, do you? I already know who wrote the letter. And I already know who you're fucking behind my back."

Cold sweat popped out on her neck. Had someone spotted her and Danny together after all? Maybe. Because no one—not even Danny—knew she had kept that letter. Laurel paid a cleaning lady to come in once a week, but it seemed unlikely that her maid would flip through her collection of Jane Austen. Cheryl Tilley had got married in the eleventh grade and, by her own admission, had read nothing since her graduation two decades earlier but *Star* magazine, which she bought religiously after her weekly grocery shopping at Wal-Mart. Even if Cheryl had accidentally found Danny's letter, would she have told Warren about it? The two had hardly spoken to each other since she began working at the house, nor was Cheryl a patient of Warren's.

"I see goose bumps," Warren said, his eyes glinting. "Piloerection."

"Who told you I was having an affair?" Laurel asked. "Whoever it is, they're lying to you."

"Does it matter? It's someone who's offended by adultery, unlike you and your lover. And half this goddamn town, I think sometimes."

"Warren, I didn't—"

"*Did you think I wouldn't find out?*" he shouted, his eyes blazing. "Did you *really* think that?"

She drew back from the force of his fury.

"Right in my fucking face, both of you! You've lied every single day. Him, too! Every day! Smiling and acting like a friend . . . goddamn him. Both of you!"

Laurel sat stunned, trying to puzzle out Warren's words. *Him, too? Acting like a friend?* Warren didn't see Danny every day. Not even when Danny had taught him to fly. Could Warren be referring to the time they'd spent coaching together?

"Who are you talking about?" she asked softly.

"Don't insult my intelligence!" Warren screamed.

She squinted against the roar of his voice. "Please, Warren. Tell me."

He leaned over her and spat the words like a priest naming a demon. *"Kyle Auster."*

Her mouth fell open. Did Warren really believe she was sleeping with his partner? *"Kyle?"* she asked, still in shock.

Warren raised his hand as though to strike her, but then he turned away and muttered, "All those times you told me he came on to you when he was drunk . . . Christmas parties, weekends at the lake. You told me he repulsed you. Lies, every damn bit of it."

He turned to face her again, disgust etched into his tired face. "Do you know how many nurses that bastard has slept with? It'll be a miracle if you don't have every STD in the book. Me, too, by now. *Jesus.*"

Laurel felt hysterical laughter rising in her throat, but she didn't dare release it. "Why in God's name would you think I'm involved with Kyle Auster?"

Warren picked up his revolver and pointed it at her face. "I don't think it," he said with certainty. "I *know.*"

# CHAPTER

# 7

Nell Roberts hibernated the insurance computer and looked over at her sister, Vida, who was talking to an angry patient at the reception window. This morning had been hell, mainly because Dr. Shields hadn't shown up for work. Nell couldn't remember Dr. Shields missing a single day because of sickness, and he always called ahead if he got hung up at the hospital. Dr. Auster had instructed the sisters to call every number they had for Dr. Shields, but Warren remained unreachable. Even his wife's cell phone went unanswered. Vida was so surprised by this that she'd called the ER to find out if Dr. Shields had been in a car accident. Unlike Vida and Dr. Auster, Nell was not surprised by Warren Shields's uncharacteristic absence. She had a pretty good idea why he hadn't shown up for work this morning.

Two days ago, Nell had overheard Dr. Auster and her sister talking about their recent business problems, in the coffee room after work. They thought she'd left the office already, but Nell was in the storeroom, culling some old files. *Problems* was actually a mild word for what had been going on around the clinic for the past ten days. First had come the letter from the IRS. The agency was doing an audit of the Auster/Shields medical partnership. This had sent both physicians into a barely controlled frenzy, Dr. Shields because he deeply resented the government's intrusion into every sphere of medicine, and Dr. Auster for darker reasons. For the past three years, Kyle Auster had been defrauding the government in various ways, some of which Nell knew about, while others were known only to her elder sister.

Nell kept her emotions under tight rein, but she was easily the most frightened person in the office. Dr. Auster's scams were only possible because she and Vida made them so, and Nell was deathly afraid of prison. Twenty-seven years old was too young to live behind bars, especially if you were white and pretty and basically innocent. Looking back now, she couldn't quite believe she'd done the things she had, but it was like Pastor Richardson used to say: a slippery slope. You started small, looking the other way while your sister did this or that, fudging a couple of small things because she asked you to, and pretty soon you were outright lying to help steal from the Medicaid program. It was easy to justify if you tried, like cheating on your taxes. The government did so much to screw doctors out of fees, and Vida made it sound as if they were only getting Dr. Auster his due. But if that was the case, why were she and Vida getting a big cut of the money?

And the IRS letter was only the beginning. Next had come a phone call, informing Dr. Auster that an IRS investigation was under way. That ratcheted things a little tighter and pushed the doctors closer to panic. *Then* came the call from a friend of Dr. Auster's in Jackson, a school friend who worked in the state government. This friend had apparently tipped Dr. Auster that the Medicaid Fraud Unit was investigating his practice. No announcement, no courteous letter filled with legalese to give them plenty of time to cover their tracks. Just a late-night warning that someone had made Kyle Auster a target. And why? Because somebody—probably a pissed-off patient—had called the Medicaid office and told them that Dr. Auster was lying to the government. Presto, an investigation began. A *secret* investigation. That was all Nell knew, and more than she wanted to know.

The scariest thing was that Vida had started it all. Nell had been working in New Orleans when her sister called and told her there was a job waiting for her in Dr. Auster's clinic, no experience required. To someone making decent money as an assistant manager at an uptown hotel, working as an insurance clerk in Athens Point sounded like a step backward. But Vida had cryptically promised that she was likely to earn double what she'd been making in New Orleans—and Vida hadn't exaggerated. She *had* omitted to say exactly what Nell would be doing for the money.

According to Vida, the scams started this way: she'd been skimming a little money from Auster's till—on cash payments only—and fudging the books to cover it up. Just enough to cover essentials while her husband missed some work at the paper mill, certainly no more than she deserved. But there was a blue-haired lady working as Auster's insurance clerk, an old battle-ax named Bedner who should have retired years before, and she hated Vida. After catching on to Vida's scheme, she had gone straight to Dr.

Auster. At this time, Dr. Shields was only an associate; he hadn't yet bought into the practice and so had no involvement in the business side of things.

Dr. Auster confronted Vida after work one day, armed with evidence supplied by Mrs. Bedner. He told Vida he was letting her go but wouldn't press charges if she left immediately and without a fuss. True to her nature, Vida denied all wrongdoing and claimed she was being framed. Dr. Auster said that if Vida believed she was being framed, she could explain her side of the story to the police. Vida sat quietly for a few moments, then asked Dr. Auster whether, in exchange for a first-class blow job, she could explain her side of things to him instead. Vida had always been pragmatic about sex; she'd been shocking people with her frankness for years. She knew that Kyle Auster had screwed a couple of hospital nurses, and she'd caught him looking down her top whenever he thought he could get away with it. After he heard her offer, Auster told her he'd decide what to do about the embezzlement after evaluating how good a job she did.

Apparently, she'd done pretty well, because Dr. Auster gave her plenty of time to talk afterward, and Vida used her time well. She'd spent her adult life working in medical offices, and she'd learned some sweet accounting tricks. Though Vida only had a year of junior college, she'd always been quick with numbers. When Auster heard how easy it was to hide cash, he decided to listen to the rest of Vida's ideas on increasing his income. She sold him in half an hour. The key to it all, she told him, was having control of the front of-fice. You couldn't have church ladies like Mrs. Bedner looking over your shoulder while you were up-coding

Medicaid claims. Two weeks later, Dr. Auster called a puzzled Mrs. Bedner into his office and told her she'd been mistaken about Vida, and that she couldn't continue working for him after making that kind of accusation.

Nell replaced Mrs. Bedner the next day.

That was the beginning. The crest of the slippery slope. Once the money started rolling in, Dr. Auster only wanted more. He was that kind of doctor. Cars, motorcycles, gambling trips to Vegas, wild investments, big charity donations, expensive medical equipment . . . he wanted everything bigger than life, and his wife wanted the same. Of course, he and Vida went full-time after the scams started. She stayed late almost every day, working on the second set of books, the one the government would see if it ever came to an audit (which it finally had). Dr. Auster stayed late about half the days and on most others stopped by for a quickie before going home after evening rounds. Nell liked to leave right at five thirty, so as to witness as little illegality as possible (and none of the illicit intimacy between Auster and her sister). That had bothered her from the beginning, and nowadays she couldn't stand the thought of it. It was too pathetic.

Because as pragmatic as Vida could be about life, she actually believed that Dr. Auster was going to leave his wife and marry her. Nell figured the chance of this happening was about the same as the chance of Toyota building an automotive plant in Athens Point. But her sister believed, and without that faith, Nell knew, Vida would have nothing in her life but two high-school-dropout sons and an ex-husband on the dole.

The strange thing was, Nell now believed she'd been

wrong about Auster. He *was* willing to leave his wife—
only not for Vida. Two days ago, Nell had overheard
him talking on his cell phone to someone whose name
she hadn't picked up. She'd only heard a few seconds
of the call, but Auster's tone had definitely been intimate, and he'd been talking about getting married.
Nell didn't know how a married man could remarry
without getting divorced first, but then she realized
that Auster was talking about down the road. She was
pretty sure he'd said, "I just have to keep you-know-
who on my side until Warren takes the fall. After that,
I can leave and we can be together." There'd been a
pause while the woman replied (a tinny sound with a
cadence Nell was strangely certain she'd heard before),
and then Auster said in a bitter tone, "I'm so tired of
servicing that little redneck, I could kill myself. She
scares me. But she'll have too much at risk to retaliate." He'd ended the conversation with a whispered "I
love you, too," then crossed the hall and walked back
into his private office. Nell stood shaking in her tracks
for almost a minute, then put on a fake smile and went
back to the front desk, where her sister sat working
diligently to protect the man she loved from the law.

*I'm so tired of servicing that little redneck. . . . She
scares me.*

One overheard conversation had split open Nell's
world. She and Vida had been living in a dream. Auster
was cheating on his wife *and* his mistress. And just
as disturbing to Nell, he was planning to blame Dr.
Shields for everything that had been going on in the
office. Auster was obviously counting on Vida to back
this story up in court, if necessary. Nell couldn't believe her sister would be willing to do that, but when

she thought about all that was at stake, she realized that Vida would probably see the situation as a case of straight survival. *Him or us.* If somebody had to go to jail, better it be Warren Shields than the man she loved. Vida would solemnly swear that every illegal act she had committed was at the express order of Dr. Shields, and that Kyle Auster had known nothing about it.

Nell couldn't live with that.

The truth was *so* different. Warren Shields was not only innocent of fraud, he was also a good and con-scientious physician. Moreover, he'd always treated Nell with respect. He'd never even remotely crossed the line into inappropriate behavior with her, which made him different from almost every other man she'd ever worked with. Dr. Shields had a beautiful wife at home, but in Nell's experience that wasn't enough to keep a man faithful, especially after twelve years of marriage. She figured Dr. Shields really loved his wife, and that made Nell sad for reasons she couldn't quite understand. She was only three years shy of thirty, and though most men found her attractive, her faith that she would find a husband like Warren Shields—a good provider and father who would truly love her for her-self—was almost gone. She had held out a long time for her Prince Charming, turning down two proposals of marriage from decent men. She felt intensely jealous of Laurel Shields, and yet also protective of her. Nell had enough generosity of spirit to wish another woman well, if that woman had indeed found happiness.

With all this in mind, Nell had called Vida at home last night, after Leno's monologue. She'd been on the verge of telling Vida about Auster's shady phone call when Vida warned her that there were likely to be some "big doings" at the office over the next couple of days. When Nell asked why, Vida told her that the less she knew, the better off she'd be. Vida also said that if she or Nell was arrested, they shouldn't say a world until they met with a lawyer. "Kyle" would arrange for that. When Nell heard the word *arrested,* she'd almost peed in her pants. After getting up the nerve, she asked why they would be arrested. Vida took some time, then said softly, "There's something in Dr. Shields's house, honey. And if someone searches, they're going to find it. I hate that it's come to this, but things are worse than you know. A lot worse. We have to think about ourselves now. Do you understand?" Nell had mumbled that she did, then told Vida she'd see her at work the next morning.

After hanging up, she'd sat hunched over the phone for several minutes, regretting every dollar she'd ever taken from Dr. Auster and wishing she'd never left the quiet old hotel on Tchoupitoulas Street. She cried for a while, then petted her cat and cried some more. Then she'd put on her coat and gone out for a walk. She did a lot of thinking during that walk, and when she got back, she sat down at her computer and typed a brief e-mail to Dr. Shields. She'd never sent him anything before, but she knew his AOL address from work. She used her Hotmail address, which not even Vida knew, and which had no obvious connection to her real name. After she was sure the message had gone through, she took two lorazepam copped from the samples room, washed them down with a glass of white zinfandel, and crashed so hard that she was an hour late getting to work this morning.

When Dr. Shields failed to show up, Nell had felt

a quiet, somewhat nervous satisfaction. She assumed that he'd found whatever had been planted in his house, and that he would know what to do with it. Smart guys like Dr. Shields always knew what to do. For most of the morning, Nell had been expecting the FBI to come crashing through the door with Dr. Shields behind them, ripping computers off the desks and confiscating files. It would almost be a relief at this point.

"Nell, honey?" said Vida.

Nell looked up at her sister, who, as usual, was wearing too much blue eye shadow. Vida was watching her intently from the front desk.

"Are you all right?"

"I'm fine," Nell assured her.

"You've been staring at the same insurance claim for ten minutes. You're real pale, too, honey. You look like you're in a daze."

Nell summoned her cheerleader smile, the best fake smile in her repertoire, and said, "I drank too much wine last night, that's all. I'm fine."

"Wine?" Vida's eyes twinkled. "Did you hook up with somebody? That drug rep didn't come back to town, did he?"

Nell quickly shook her head. "God, no. That's *so* over."

"Are you sure you're all right? This could be a rough day."

*You have no idea, Vi.* "I'm fine, I swear."

Several seconds passed before Vida looked away, and Nell sighed inwardly with relief. It would only be a matter of time before Dr. Shields straightened everything out. And when he found out it was Nell who had warned him in the nick of time, well . . . it was only natural that he would be grateful. It wasn't hard to imagine the office running just fine without Dr. Auster in it. *Or Vida either,* she thought with a pang of guilt. It would definitely be a nicer place to work, and Nell was sure she could find a hundred ways to make Dr. Shields's days less stressful.

All she wanted was a chance to show what she could do.


Laurel's hands were almost numb. She'd lost the sensation in her feet fifteen minutes ago. When she complained to Warren, he'd assured her that there was no real danger unless her skin turned black. She asked about blood clots in her legs, but he waved away her fears and went back to searching the hard drive in her laptop.

Two improbable facts kept pinging around in Laurel's brain. First, that someone had told Warren she was having an affair with Kyle Auster. And second, that Warren had believed it. Kyle's interest in Laurel had been obvious years ago, when Warren entered practice with him. Auster was a well-known ladies' man who got out of hand when he was drinking. She'd warned Warren about Kyle's advances, and Warren had told her to be firm with him but not to make a big deal of it, so long as the incidents remained rare. This hadn't been the answer Laurel was looking for, but they had a lot riding on the success of the partnership, not least the matter of paying back Warren's school loans. Auster's interest in her never faded, but he did stop making overt passes, which allowed everyone to settle down to a tolerable undercurrent of anxiety about the issue, if not to put it behind them altogether.

Clearly, someone had resurrected the issue by lying to Warren about an affair. But why would he be willing to view her as Auster's paramour, rather than a put-upon wife? It must have to do with the identity of the informer. That person must be someone in a position to know about such an affair, if it were really happening. But what reason could someone have for telling such a lie? The longer Laurel thought about it, the more confused she became. According to popular rumor, Auster (who was currently married to his second wife) was involved with a nurse at St. Raphael's Hospital (blond and busty, naturally) and possibly someone in the office as well. Why anyone would believe that Laurel would waste time on him was beyond her.

Then suddenly she saw the logic. If she was miserable at home, and she blamed Warren for her misery, might not she get involved with Auster simply to hurt Warren? To publicly embarrass him as profoundly as she could? Some wives she knew had played that game. But Danny's "anonymous" letter hadn't exactly bolstered this scenario. It had painted a picture of soul mates finding each other after years of searching. But considering Warren's mental state when he'd discovered the letter, she could understand his glossing over the details.

She thought back over what he'd said about the informer. Supposedly, it was someone who cared about his welfare more than Laurel did. Someone "offended by adultery." But had that person told Warren to look specifically for a letter? The informer couldn't have betrayed the existence of Danny's letter, because no one—not even Danny—knew that she'd kept it. Warren claimed to be certain she was having an affair with Auster, yet how could he be certain without hard evidence? A photograph. Or a tape recording. But if he had seen such evidence, why would he care so much about the unsigned letter he had found in *Pride and Prejudice*? Instead of searching her computer, he'd be waving the evidence in her face.

The facts didn't add up. Not as she knew them, anyway. But if Warren had been told to search their house (and he had *claimed* to be looking for the letter, not anything to do with the IRS audit), then the informer's warning must have been more general—

Unless there was another letter waiting to be found. A *planted* letter, whose purpose she could not know. Or maybe it wasn't a letter. Maybe some other incriminating piece of evidence had been planted in the house, one that Warren had been prompted to find. If so, he had stopped searching for it, because he had stumbled onto Danny's letter instead.

Laurel thought of voicing her reasoning to Warren, but there was no point. He'd only think she was trying to stop him from searching her computer. Rather than ponder what the planted evidence might be, she focused on who might have planted it. Who could possibly profit from Warren thinking his wife was screwing his partner? A woman who wanted Warren for herself? Laurel couldn't believe that Warren had given any woman enough encouragement to take such drastic steps.

As she watched him probing her computer, a flash of insight struck her. What if the source of the lie about Laurel and Kyle was *Auster himself*? If Kyle had committed crimes at work—crimes that had come to the attention of the authorities—he would desperately need to distract Warren while he tried to save his own skin. It would take a lot to distract Warren from an IRS investigation, but a bombshell like marital infidelity would do it. (Witness today's freak-out.) And once Warren began to hate Kyle for something so personal as cuckolding him, he would be unlikely to see him straight in business matters. Moreover, any subsequent accusations of mismanagement that Warren might make about Auster would be viewed through a distorted lens.

Laurel could admire the logic of the scheme, if she removed herself sufficiently from the reality. As she thought it through from various angles, excitement began to build inside her. If she was right, her salvation might still be waiting in the house for Warren to discover it.

*What might Kyle have planted?* she wondered. *An article of clothing? Underwear? A cuff link? (Auster actually wore French cuffs whenever he went out.) A nude photo of himself? What about a love letter in his own handwriting? A crudely sexy letter, knowing Kyle.* Laurel thought back over the past couple of weeks, trying to remember if Auster had visited their house. She didn't think so, but the house usually stood empty for most of the day, and she wouldn't be surprised to learn that Kyle had a key of his own. If they had ever lent him a key—and she was pretty sure they had, early on, during a Disney World vacation—then he still had a copy in his possession. Kyle was that kind of guy. Laurel counted herself lucky that he hadn't simply let himself in one day when Warren was off at a bike race and climbed into the shower with her.

Regardless of how it had happened, the odds were

that someone—possibly Kyle Auster—had planted something far more damaging than Danny's letter in the house, and it was still waiting to be found. Whatever that something was, there was a good chance that it might not jibe with Danny's letter, since the person who planted it had known nothing of that letter. A strange pair of underwear or a used condom wouldn't help her case, but a different letter written in a different hand—and outlining a different scenario—might sell Warren on her frame-up theory. Going in that direction was certainly less risky than letting him continue to dig through her computer.

"Warren?" she said evenly. "We need to talk."

He glanced up, then returned his attention to the screen.

"I think I have an idea what's really going on here."

No response.

"I think I know who's sent you on this wild-goose chase."

Warren seemed to have frozen in his chair.

"What is it?" she asked, panic fluttering in her chest.

"Well, well!" he crowed. "Isn't this special. A hidden folder, under the Windows System folder. It's labeled ROPN. Any idea what this could be?"

Her belly knotted. She wished she could twitch her nose like Samantha Stephens and delete the folder in question. "Look and see," she said, trying not to sound defensive.

Warren stared at her for several seconds, then clicked on the folder. She didn't know what he'd expected to find, but his eyes quickly widened as he scrolled through the images and video clips she kept in that folder.

"Where did you get this stuff?" he asked without looking up.

"The Internet."

"Did you pay for it?"

"No. I downloaded it off LimeWire. And it's not really hidden, you know. I made the folder invisible so Grant or Beth wouldn't stumble onto it if they booted up my computer. By next year, Grant will know how to find that kind of folder."

Warren's eyes jerked right and left; he was probably scanning thumbnail images of her explicit video clips. He bit his upper lip, looking angry and disturbed. "Why haven't you ever told me you look at this stuff?"

"I don't know. I didn't think you'd be interested."

He snorted. "You know that's not true."

"Look . . . I know you, okay? I didn't think you'd like me looking at that kind of thing by myself."

His eyes remained riveted to the screen. "Why do you look at it by yourself?"

"Why do you look at porn by yourself?"

He shrugged as though the answer were self-evident. "That's different."

"How?"

"I'm a guy."

She couldn't believe it. "So?"

"So I just use it to masturbate."

"I see." She waited a few moments. "What do you think I do with it?"

His eyes opened wider. "Are you serious?"

"What else would I do with it?"

Warren wrestled silently with this for a while. "How long have you been doing this?"

"Since it got easy to get video clips like those on-line."

"So you've been unsatisfied for that long."

*Of course I have, for God's sake,* she replied in the silence of her head. *And you should have known that long before you found my porn cache. You would have known, if you'd paid any attention at all.* But what she said aloud, considering the gun and Warren's fragile mental state, was "Haven't you always masturbated?"

He nodded rigidly.

"Have you been unsatisfied with me all that time?"

"No. But I'm a guy."

"Jesus."

"I mean, of course I'd like to do it more often. I just . . . you don't seem like you want to, so I don't push it."

She wasn't sure how to respond. For the past three or four months, Warren had hardly touched her, yet he seemed to be speaking as though this sexual dry spell had not occurred. She decided to take a chance. It was a risk, but if she played doormat and acquiesced to everything he said, he wouldn't believe she was telling the truth about anything. "That's not very perceptive. Haven't you ever noticed that after you finish, I still want more?"

"Not really. You never come out and say that."

"That's because I don't want to hurt your feelings, in case you can't perform again right away. But I've tried to show you."

"Well, no guy can do it again right away."

She nodded, though she knew this assertion to be untrue. "I'm sure you're right."

Warren's eyes hardened with suspicion. "Are you?"

"I don't have much to compare you to, as you know."

"So you told me. To tell you the truth, I never really believed the number you gave me. Not deep down. How many people did you really sleep with before me?"

*Here we go.* "Warren . . . do you see why I don't talk to you about these things? I'm trying to be honest with you, and the first thing you do is accuse me of lying even before we got married."

He stared at her a long time before replying, "This isn't spontaneous honesty. You're caught in a lie already. And you're trying to sell me a bill of goods."

"Two men before you," she said flatly. "Two boys, actually." *God, don't strike me dead,* she thought, as Warren looked down and clicked the mouse again. Cries and groans came from the laptop's tiny speakers, as though miniature humans were copulating inside the carbon-fiber case.

Warren would have freaked out at any number higher than two, and even that made him nervous. It bothered him no end that he hadn't taken her virginity, but at least he understood that. Everyone had to lose it to somebody, and that wasn't usually the best sexual experience anyway. But the "second guy" had always worried him. Warren wanted to know exactly how many times she'd had sex with him, and every act she'd ever tried with him. Laurel had strained her imagination to invent a bland physical relationship with a college boyfriend of six months, someone from

a Northern state whom they would never run into in
the future. After seeing Warren's reaction to even this
small "revelation," it hadn't taken a brain surgeon to
figure out that it was best to banish her other partners to the female Bermuda Triangle of "never happened." After all, it wasn't as if she'd slutted around or
anything. She'd held on to her virginity until eighteen,
which was a record in her high school class. But during
college she'd had a couple of inebriated hookups that
went further than she'd initially planned. Handsome
boys she had screwed on the first date, for no reason
other than she was lonely and they'd made her feel
good and she just by God wanted sex.

Then there was the architecture professor she'd slept
with for eight months, all on the DL because he was
married. Warren would have lost it over that. The affair had been Laurel's real initiation into sex, and if she
had left any corner of her body or psyche unexplored,
it wasn't for lack of trying. She'd actually tried a few
things she learned in that relationship on Warren, and
sometimes they'd worked, after a fashion. But anything really edgy always brought probing postcoital
questions, so she'd stopped experimenting. She had
mistakenly thought he'd be glad for the variety, but
Warren was different from most men. Or maybe most
men were more like Warren than she knew. Twelve
years of faithful marriage had effectively removed her
from the research pool.

She'd had no trouble telling Danny about her sexual
past. He wouldn't have minded if she'd slept with a
half dozen or more men before him, so long as she
ended up with him. In that relationship, *she* was the
insecure one. Danny had made love with women all

over the world, and no matter how much he said to boost her confidence, Laurel felt that she could never outdo the exotic courtesans who now populated her mind. But then trying to was half the fun.

"God," Warren exclaimed, breaking her reverie, "some of this stuff is *sick*."

Laurel felt herself blush. "I'm human, okay?"

"This stuff turns you on?"

"Some of it wasn't what I thought, based on the file names. But most of it does, yes."

Warren looked at his wife as though seeing her for the first time. "Do it right now, then."

"What?"

"Masturbate."

She searched his face for sarcasm but found none. "You're joking, right?"

"Not at all."

"Don't be ridiculous."

"I'm dead serious, Laurel. We've been married twelve years, and I've never seen you do that. Not for real. Today seems as good a day as any."

"I'm not going to do that, Warren. I couldn't anyway."

"Why not?"

She closed her eyes, then screamed her answer at nearly full volume: *"Because I'm duct-taped like a fucking Al Qaeda terrorist and you're holding a gun on me! How about that for starters?"*

Warren remained unmoved. "From what I see in these videos, you ought to like the idea."

"Sorry, wrong girl."

"Maybe so," he said softly. "I don't know you at all, do I? You've never really been honest with me."

She looked hard into his eyes. "You never wanted me to be honest. Not really."

He drew back, then looked away. "How often do you do it? Play with yourself, I mean."

In Laurel's experience, if she wasn't having much sex, she felt little need to masturbate. She would have thought the opposite would be true, that during dry spells she would need to do it more, but she'd found that the reverse applied to her. It was when she was being well looked after that she needed constant release, whether she had access to her lover or not. After she became involved with Danny, masturbation had become as important a part of her sex life as intercourse. On days they couldn't meet, it was essential, and when they could meet, she sometimes did it just to warm up for the rendezvous, so that he wouldn't be ahead of her on the arousal curve. Then they could share everything equally from the beginning.

"Laurel?"

She looked up. For the first time today, Warren looked as vulnerable and confused as Grant sometimes did.

"So, I guess this guy you're seeing is some kind of sex god or something, huh?"

"Warren. I'm not having an affair."

He grunted in stubborn disbelief.

"Besides," she said, "what do you mean 'this guy'? I thought you said you know it's Kyle."

He laid his hand on the letter beside the computer. "This doesn't really sound like Kyle. I know he'd fuck you without a second's hesitation. And I don't know what you might do to hurt me. But this letter . . ." Warren shook his head. "This really hurt."

Even sitting duct-taped like a prisoner awaiting execution, Laurel felt guilt surge within her. Had getting involved with Danny been the only answer to her marital problems? Of course not. She simply hadn't been brave enough to confront them directly, or to face what leaving Warren might mean. She'd waited for an emotional parachute, and only by chance had she found real love.

"Tell me what it's like," Warren said dully. "With the guy who wrote this, I mean. Tell me what you feel when he does it to you."

*You mean* with *me,* she thought. *Not* to *me.*

Warren's transition from fury to depression had been almost instantaneous. Laurel felt as if someone had slammed on the brakes of a speeding car, and she hadn't yet recovered. All she knew was that she wasn't about to tell her husband one detail about how being with Danny compared to her conjugal sex. Warren was like the boys she had known in high school; he had a powerful biological urge that needed release, and her body was the vehicle for that release. His sexual routine hadn't varied significantly in years. The tension would build in him for a few days, or even a couple of weeks, and then he would come to her and spend himself. She occasionally managed a vaginal orgasm by sitting astride him. But the only reliable orgasms she got were from his licking her, and as the years passed, he had become less and less willing to devote the time required to bring her off this way. She was always left wanting more, and the few times he'd been able to go back inside her, she'd been unable to reach the peak she sensed just beyond the horizon.

Danny, on the other hand, instinctively understood

the dynamics of female arousal and release. Some days Laurel wanted hours of foreplay punctuated by staggered moments of release, and other days she wanted to be stormed like a city under siege, plundered until nothing remained but a faint pulse of life and dreamless sleep. Danny knew within moments of seeing her which kind of day it was, and he could often tell by the timbre of her telephone voice as they arranged their rendezvous. Laurel had once arrived at a hotel room only to have a gloved hand clapped over her mouth from behind, her skirt hiked up, and her body ravished from behind without ever seeing the man's face. Only after he had ejaculated and let her fall to the bed had she been positive it was Danny. She didn't want that kind of adventure regularly, but to know that it might happen at any time . . . that was the thing. Warren could pound violently at her in a fit of drunken passion and still leave her unsatisfied, while Danny might force her to lie absolutely still while he moved at a glacial pace within her, yet by the time he finished, her body felt like a desiccated husk of fruit, sucked dry of all moisture.

Laurel watched her husband from a bottomless well of sadness. The truth might set people free—in theory—but it was difficult to see any upside to sharing her most intimate secrets with Warren. His jealousy had always followed his insecurities. He'd never worried about buff pool boys or bohemian types, however sexy they might be. Warren worried about other doctors, or businessmen who earned more money than he did, anyone who might be ahead of him in the eternal competition that was life. If he were to learn that his whole worldview was wrong, that the greatest threat to his

marriage had come from a man who wasn't compet-
ing with him in any way—who in fact cared nothing
about competition, but was only and profoundly glad
to be alive (and who touched a part of Laurel so deep
that her husband had never even glimpsed it)—Warren might not survive that. Watching him now, Laurel
suddenly understood the essential nature of what was
unfolding before her. Warren was a control freak who
sensed control slipping inexorably away. First at work,
and now at home. The fear growing inside him probably had no limit.

"Hey," Warren said softly. "If I untaped you now,
would you go in the bedroom and make love with
me?"

She closed her eyes involuntarily. "If you really
want it, I suppose I would. But what we need to do
right now is talk. I think someone is trying to hurt you,
Warren. Maybe to destroy you."

His chin began to quiver like Grant's when the boy
tried not to cry. "Yeah," Warren said, his voice completely different from the one he'd spoken in a moment
ago. "*You*. I don't know what I was thinking, asking
you for sloppy seconds. I just wish I knew how long
I've been getting them."

The words stung her more deeply than she would
have imagined. "Warren, please listen to me—"

"I'm going to find out," he vowed, slapping the side
of the Sony's screen. "This porn is just the beginning,
I'm sure. I'm going to dig out every last secret in this
pile of garbage before I'm through."

Laurel felt tears coming again.

A savage light had entered his eyes. "Maybe we
should show some of these pictures to the kids when

they get home. Show them what Mom does in her spare time."

Her heart seized at the mention of the kids. So Warren was well aware that they would soon be home. But how did he think they would get here, with her trussed up like a turkey? Did he plan to lock her in the trunk of his Volvo and pick them up himself? The idea didn't seem as impossible as it would have an hour ago.

"Screw you," she said. "You want them to stay up and watch you jerk off to soft-core on Cinemax after we're asleep? Dictating medical charts, my ass."

He stared at her with visceral hatred.

"God, we're pathetic," she said, meaning it.

She had no idea what to do or say next. Warren wasn't going to listen to anything from her. His obsession with her infidelity had nothing to do with love. It was about possession. *Ownership*. Someone had appropriated his personal property, and he wanted revenge. She was like all his other possessions, something to be jealously guarded, not because of her intrinsic worth, but because she was *his*. That concept was laughable now. The issue of ownership had been decided within two weeks after she first kissed Danny McDavitt. No matter whose ring Laurel wore, no matter who mounted her in the dark of the night, Danny owned her, body and soul. That was the reality, and nothing but death could change it.

# CHAPTER

# 8

Kyle Auster sat on the stool in examining room five and silently regarded his nineteenth patient of the day. Arthur M. Johnston. White male, fifty-three years of age, forty pounds overweight, high cholesterol, hypertension, enlarged prostate, erectile dysfunction, history of persistent alcohol abuse, osteoarthritis—the chart went on and on. An intern might look at Johnston's record and think, *This guy is sick,* but Auster knew he was looking at a classic malingerer. After working seven years at the now defunct chemical plant, Johnston had somehow talked his way into a full Social Security disability (for back pain, of course). That was a couple of decades back. Now he spent his days cushioned on a carpet of pain medication, watching daytime TV, working in his garden, and taking his grandkids fishing in a boat purchased with government money.

As he droned on about his need for constant pain relief (which only opiates could provide), Auster wondered how he'd gotten to this little chamber of hell. He'd been a goddamn ace in medical school. The only reason he hadn't specialized in surgery was that he'd had to get out into the real world and start making money. It wasn't as if he'd had a choice. He had an expensive lifestyle, even then. People had no idea how much money changed hands in a frat house during football season. You could dig a deep hole without ever rolling out of bed.

"What do you think, Doc?"

The patient's question penetrated Auster's reverie. "I think you're doing about as well as you're going to do, Mr. Johnston. You're not going to play ball for the Yankees, but you're not going to drop dead anytime soon either. You'll probably still be fishing when·they bury me."

Johnston gave a little laugh. "I hope so, no offense. But I was thinking, Doc, you know. . . . I might need some tests."

Auster looked back in puzzlement. Johnston had the tone of a patient who'd read some article on preventive medicine in *Reader's Digest*. He probably wanted a goddamn sixty-four-slice CAT scan of his heart. "What kind of tests?"

Johnston's face looked blank as a baby's. "Well, you're the doctor. I thought maybe you could tell me."

Auster's financial antennae went on alert. He glanced at the upper-right corner of Mr. Johnston's file, searching for a faint check mark in pencil. There was none, as he had suspected. If there had been, it would indicate that Mr. Johnston was a "special" patient, meaning that he'd undergone some tests that might have been unnecessary in a strictly medical sense, but which had proved lucrative for both doctor and patient. But there was no pencil mark. So what the hell was Johnston hinting at?

"What are your symptoms, Mr. Johnston?"

A sly grin now, minus three front teeth. "Well, Doc, I thought maybe you could tell me that, too."

A few months ago, Auster would have been happy to oblige Mr. Johnston. Thorough lab work was good, sound medicine, and a chest X-ray never hurt anybody. But given the present state of affairs, Mr. Johnston's not-so-subtle hints were like the blare of a fire alarm. Auster put on his soberest countenance, the face he used when telling people they had a disabling or deadly illness.

"Mr. Johnston, in the past, I've worked with patients to solve their health problems as creatively as I could, given the state of government regulations. But recently the government has taken a dim view of that kind of alternative medicine. It's become very risky to do anything unconventional these days. Anyone who does could be subject to severe penalties. Abusing the Social Security disability program would be a good example."

Mr. Johnston blanched.

"Am I being clear enough, sir?"

Johnston was already getting up. "You know, I think I'm doing fine, Doc, except for this back of mine. If you could just renew that prescription, I'll be on my way."

Auster stood and patted him on the shoulder. "Happy to do it."

He wrote out another prescription for Vicodin, then, cursing under his breath, marched out of the exam room and down the hall to his private office. Things were spinning out of control. Vida was doing everything she could to erase all trace of questionable activity, but people kept crawling out of the woodwork with their hands out.

The patients weren't even the main problem. The real threat was the state's Medicaid Fraud Unit. Five attorneys, eleven investigators, and four specially trained auditors bird-dogging every medical practice in the state that accepted Medicaid patients. The injustice chapped Auster's ass no end. Many doctors refused even to treat Medicaid patients, so pathetic was the level of reimbursement. It was the humanitarians who found it in their hearts to treat the poor and indigent who got raped by the government. It made you want to leave the damn country.

Auster knew the Fraud Unit was on his tail. Patrick Evans, his doubles partner on the high school tennis team, was an executive assistant to the governor. Pat was wired into every agency in the state, and a week ago he'd quietly informed Auster that Paul Biegler, the pit bull of the Fraud Unit, had begun investigating him, based on a tip called in to the attorney general's office. The whistle-blower could have been anybody, but it was probably a disgruntled patient, someone who'd made a little extra money off Auster, then wanted more and got angry after being turned down. Or maybe it was a woman. Auster didn't get many attractive female patients, but when he did, he wasn't above a little horse-trading. An ER doc had taught him this racket during his residency. Five Mepergan could get you a hell of a blow job from a strung-out woman, and that beat seventy taxable dollars for an office visit any day of the week.

Medicaid investigations typically lasted months before an indictment, but Auster sensed imminent danger. He felt like a rebel village waiting to be hit by government troops. The blow could fall at any hour of the day or night. The IRS was already auditing the partnership's Schedule Cs for the past five years, and probably his personal returns, too. God knows what they'd found already. His gambling income was the problem there, although lately all he'd had to report were losses. Auster was a good gambler; he just didn't always know when to stop. That was why he'd spent a lot of weekends working seventy-two-hour shifts in emergency rooms. Doctors were so reluctant to move to Mississippi that rural hospitals would pay large sums for ER coverage. But Auster was too old to be scrounging extra money that way. His colleagues thought it unseemly, and worse, the work itself was becoming a lot more technical. The standard of ER care was higher. Auster didn't have time for the continuing-education classes he needed to stay competent in that arena, so that extra income had faded away.

It was Vida who'd helped him replace it. They'd started small, sliding a little cash off the books, for example. What smart businessman didn't do that? But they'd quickly moved on from there, and soon Auster had found himself making serious misrepresentations of fact. Up-coding Medicaid claims—charging for a Level 4 exam when you'd only spent five minutes with the patient, that kind of thing. But it was the collusion with patients that had really kicked up the cash flow. Vida got the idea from an Internet story about some Korean doctors in New York City. They'd persuaded members of the Korean immigrant community to pretend to have various ailments, then had done loads of tests and procedures on those patients and paid them a fee for their trouble. Vida figured the poorer African-American patients would jump on a chance like that, if Auster put it to them right. But she'd been wrong. *Everybody* jumped on it in a big way. Not one patient Auster had ever pitched had turned him down. It was a no-brainer. Everyone felt dehumanized by the health-care system and thus eminently justified in screwing it back—just as Auster did. When he thought about how many hours he'd spent with indigent patients for no pay, he had no qualms about finding another way to get compensated for his time.

The Medicaid Fraud Unit wouldn't see it quite the same way, of course. Guys like Paul Biegler were congenitally blind to the color gray. *If I hadn't pushed it so far so fast,* Auster thought uselessly. But he knew enough psychiatry to diagnose his own problem: poor impulse control. Nature had combined with nurture to make him the kind of man who, confronted with a hundred grand in blackjack losses, would double down rather than walk away from the table. He had the same habit with women. Two were better than one, and three better still. Ideally, you had several available at various hours of the day, every day of the week, including Sundays. That way, you moved so fast from woman to woman that you never had to focus on the complications with any particular one. Nevertheless, Auster had somehow acquired two wives along the way, probably because he tended to tell people what they wanted to hear, regardless of his true feelings.

Just now he was managing three women full-time: wife number two, Vida, and a drug rep from Hoche. He had a backup stable of part-timers, but lately he'd been unable to do much there. His problem was Vida. She was the classic double-edged sword: an asset and a liability rolled into one. For an ex-waitress with a year of junior college, she was a whiz at accounting. And she gave great head, no question. But she had some very unrealistic expectations about the future. She'd cling to him like a terrier biting his leg, or in her case, his prick. Vida definitely didn't fit into any of the scenarios he saw in his future. She probably wouldn't cause much of a stir in Vegas, but they'd laugh her out of the clubs he liked to frequent in L.A., or even Atlanta.

Auster was thinking of taking out the bottle of Diaka vodka he kept in his bottom drawer when his phone buzzed. He put his hand on the drawer handle, dreaming of the transparent fluid that dedicated Poles filtered through diamonds before bottling it in crystal. One sip could erase an hour's worth of stress—

"I have a phone call for you, Doctor," Nell said through the phone's staticky speaker. "An Agent Paul Biegler, from the Medicaid office in Jackson?"

Auster let his hand fall from the handle. He had the sensation of a sailor who has stared for days over threatening seas finally seeing an enemy periscope rise in front of him. At least it wasn't a complete surprise. For the hundredth time he congratulated himself on making the right political donations over the years. That was how you stayed wired in this state—in any state, for that matter—and staying wired was how you protected yourself. "Ah, is Vida up there, Nell?"

"No, sir. I think she went out for a smoke break. You want me to try to find her?"

He thought about it. The last thing he wanted was Vida standing at his shoulder trying to coach him through a phone call. This couldn't be too bad. If it were, Biegler would have shown up at the clinic door with a search warrant, not called him on the telephone from Jackson.

"Did the guy say he was in Jackson, Nell?"

"No, but the caller ID shows a state-of-Mississippi number."

Auster suddenly had visions of a government surveillance van parked outside his office, a convoy of black cars filled with agents ready to tear his office apart. "Could it be a cell phone?"

"Looks like a landline prefix to me. But I can't be sure. You want me to take a message?"

Auster didn't want Biegler thinking he could be intimidated by a phone call. He'd been expecting a surprise search for the past few days. That was the government's style. They'd show up with a search warrant, a stack of subpoenas, and a team of agents. They'd confiscate your files, your computers, every damn thing you needed to run your practice. They'd act friendly and have "informal" chats with you and your staff, every word of which would be recorded and used against you later. Then they'd stop all Medicaid payments to your business, before you'd had a chance to say one word in your defense. In short, they would ruin you, months before you ever saw a courtroom. Sometimes they even denied you a jury trial. Auster's lawyer had given him careful instructions on how to respond in the event of a surprise search, but no advice on how to deal with an informal phone call. He would just have to wing it.

"That's all right, Nell," he said expansively. "I'll take the call." He pressed the button that transferred the caller. "This is Dr. Auster. What can I do for you, Agent Biegler?"

"Hello, Doctor. Nothing today, actually. This is an informal call, for your benefit more than mine."

*Right . . .*

"I'm calling as a courtesy, to let you know that you've been the subject of a Medicaid fraud investigation for some weeks now. Were you aware of that?"

"How could I be aware of that?"

A pregnant silence. "Are you one of those people who answers every question with a question, Doctor?"

*This might actually be fun,* Auster thought. "That depends on the question."

"Well, up to this point, we've mostly been conducting interviews. I wanted to let you know that we're about to move to the more proactive phase of the investigation, and that's likely to disrupt your normal business affairs for a short time."

*Jesus Christ. How would an innocent person react?* "I'm not sure I understand. Who have you been interviewing? And why?"

"Patients of yours, sir."

*Sir* always sounded bad in the mouth of a cop. "Patients? Why have you been talking to my patients?"

The answering silence felt smug somehow. "Do I really need to explain that to you, Doctor?"

Fear and anger rippled through Auster's gut. "I'm afraid you do."

He heard paper shuffling. Notebook pages? "Do the names Esther Whitlow, George Green, Rafael Gutierrez, Quinesha Washington, or Sanford Williams mean anything to you?"

Auster swallowed hard against a geyser of gastric acid rushing up his esophagus. Pulling open his top drawer, he took out a half-empty bottle of Maalox and chugged it. "They're all patients of mine," he coughed.

"I'm glad we can agree on that, at least. That's probably all I should say at this time. I just wanted you to know that we're moving to the next phase of our investigation. We've sometimes been criticized in the past for conducting surprise searches. I've even heard the phrase 'storm trooper tactics' used. In your case, I want to make sure that you have every opportunity to prepare your staff for the disruption. I don't want you to feel we've made our investigation unduly burdensome in any way."

*What the hell is this guy up to?*

"In my experience, you need to take certain steps if you want to be able to continue practicing medicine during the investigative process. You'll probably want to make copies of your business software. I would also suggest purchasing some new computers, since we almost always remove the on-site computers from the practice."

Auster's head was spinning. He opened his bottom drawer and unscrewed the cap from the Diaka bottle. A hundred dollars' worth of vodka slid down his throat as Biegler continued.

"You should photocopy any and all documents necessary for the running of your business, since we'll probably be taking those away as well. It could be months before you see them again."

"And when are you moving to this next phase?"

"Eight a.m. tomorrow."

*Tomorrow!* "Agent Beagle, I—"

"Biegler," the agent cut in, his irritation plain.

"Right, listen, I couldn't do the things you just suggested by tomorrow if I kept the staff working overnight."

"You're getting eighteen hours more notice than most people do, Dr. Auster."

*Stay calm, be courteous and professional at all times*—his lawyer's voice in his ear. "Be that as it may, sir, tomorrow presents real problems. My partner, Dr. Warren Shields, is out due to illness, and consequently I have an especially heavy patient load tomorrow. It would be a huge help if you could delay your search until after the weekend."

Biegler cleared his throat. "Dr. Auster, perhaps this might be a good time to inform you that destroying medical records that are under subpoena constitutes obstruction of justice. In your case, those would be felony charges."

Anger began to override the fear in Auster's pounding heart. "Are you saying my records have already been subpoenaed?"

"That's correct, sir. And I should inform you that digital files are no less a legal record than hard copies. If anyone attempts to erase any digital files, we will know it, and we will recover them. The penalties are quite severe."

"I see." Auster took a quick slug of vodka, then wiped his chin with the sleeve of his lab coat. "You know what I think, Agent Biegler? I don't think you called me out of courtesy. I think you called to kick my blood pressure up. You called me to *gloat*. This is how you get your rocks off, isn't it? You've got a bug up your ass about doctors, and you spend every day trying to bankrupt them or put them in jail. Well, I've got news for you. You've picked on the wrong doctor. First of all, I'm not guilty of anything. Second, I've got lawyers out the wazoo, and I can afford to pay them for a long, long time. And third . . ." Auster tried to remind himself that this conversation was almost certainly being recorded. It wouldn't be good to threaten bodily harm or death by the intervention of third parties he might know in a questionable line of work. "Never mind about third," he ended lamely. "You get the idea."

"Yes, I do," said Biegler. "You paint a vivid picture, Doctor. Now let me paint you one. You're going to be indicted under a number of federal statutes, many of which have been newly created to deal with predatory physicians like you. You have violated the False Claims Act, the False Statements Act, several sections of the Social Security Act, and most importantly, the Kennedy-Kassebaum Health Insurance Portability Act. Also, by mailing fraudulent bills to patients in Louisiana, you've violated the Federal Mail and Wire Fraud Act, each instance punishable as a separate offense. Furthermore, there are civil penalties for all the above crimes. You have violated the Civil False Claims Act and the Civil Monetary Penalties Law . . ."

Auster was having difficulty breathing. The Diaka wasn't going to do it this time. He opened a prescription bottle in his drawer and swallowed twenty milligrams of propranolol to slow his heart.

"Are you still there, Doctor?"

"Of course."

"To sum up, under the new sentencing laws, you are

facing the possibility of one hundred and seventy-five years in prison, and sixty-five million dollars in penalties. That doesn't include punitive damages, which the government is entitled to pursue, up to three times the cost of actual damages. In each instance, of course."

Auster felt a sharp pain radiating down his left arm. Even the hint of a heart event sent his pulse into the stratosphere.

"Dr. Auster?"

Auster shut his eyes and forced himself under control. All these sensations were simply a stress reaction. Paul Biegler had ambushed him, and the panic now redlining his vital signs was exactly the result Biegler had sought to produce. But he would not give the agent that victory. This was like tournament poker in Vegas. It was all about balls. Cojones. Nerves of steel. You might have bet heavy on the come and drawn a shit hand, but you couldn't let anybody know that. Especially the guy sitting across the table from you, daring you to call. You knew he had the cards—you could read them in his eyes as surely as if his corneas were mirrors reflecting what was in his hand. But you had to call the bastard and play it out. Anybody could win with a royal flush. It was how you played the shit hands that proved your mettle.

"Did you hear what I said, Doctor?" Biegler repeated. "Sixty-five million dollars."

Somehow, Auster found it within himself to chuckle. "That figure is a fantasy, Agent Biegler. None of that will ever happen. You know why? You're rattling off all those numbers to scare me into settling out of court. You want me to pay Uncle Sam a big chunk of extortion money. Well, guess what? I have committed no crimes. None. And I already pay the government my fair share of extortion money. It's called *taxes,* and I shell out close to a million dollars every year. So *kiss my sanctified ass, you pencil-pushing cocksucker.*"

For a few glorious moments, Kyle Auster felt the euphoria of having done what every hardworking American wanted to do in his heart of hearts, tell the government to go to hell—and it felt good.

Then Agent Biegler started laughing. "You're something, aren't you?" he said, his voice betraying something like admiration. "I heard that about you. High-stakes gambler, they tell me. Boy, this one's gonna be fun. By noon tomorrow, you're going to think you're dealing with a proctologist, not a Medicaid investigator."

"What exactly are you, Agent Biegler? Are you really an investigator? Because I smell a lawyer. I can respect a cop, you know? But a lawyer's something else again."

"I have a law degree."

"Couldn't pass organic chemistry, huh?"

Biegler's laughter stopped. "I should also inform you that as of nine a.m. tomorrow, all Medicaid payments to the partnership of Auster-Shields Medical Services will cease. You are being excluded from the Medicaid program pending the outcome of your criminal trial. Have a nice day, Doctor."

Auster slammed down the phone before Biegler could hang up. "Vida!" he yelled at his door. *"Vida!"*

Nothing.

He buzzed the front. "Nell, tell Vida to come back here!"

"Yes, Doctor."

Auster put away the Diaka bottle and took three deep breaths to try to calm down. A moment later, Vida stepped into his office, her face lined with worry.

"Nell told me who it was," she said. "You shouldn't have taken that call, Kyle."

"Yeah, well, you should have been here to tell me not to take it."

"Let me guess. You got into a pissing contest."

Auster shrugged helplessly. "Do you know what he said I'm facing?"

"Jail, I guess."

Auster leaned forward and looked hard into Vida's heavily made-up eyes. "Not just jail. A hundred and seventy-five years in prison."

She didn't flinch. "No way. Never happen."

"Then there's the little matter of sixty-five million dollars in penalties."

At last her face lost some color. "Sixty-five *million*? Can that be true?"

"Oh, yes. And that's not counting punitive damages. You need to start researching the Kennedy-Kassebaum law. If you want to know what the rest of your life looks like, that is."

Vida walked halfway around the desk and looked down at him. "Don't let that asshole get to you. He's just talking tough, like all cops do."

"He's pretty good at it."

"It doesn't matter. I've been sterilizing records for the past ten days. We never did anything stupid. I've been working in medical offices for eighteen years. Everything we billed for can be defended on medical grounds."

"But the special patients . . . they can blow us out

of the water. The stuff we did on them was based on total fiction."

"Wrong. They said the words to you, Kyle. They made the complaints. You did what any conscientious physician would do, even if you thought the complaints might be psychosomatic."

"Jesus, Vi."

She reached out and brushed some hair from his eyes. "You've got to hold your nerve, baby."

"We paid them to say that stuff!"

Vida shook her head. "Never happened. Untraceable cash, and long gone now, I promise you."

"But if they testify—"

"They won't. Where's the upside for them? From us they get cash and free medical care. From the government they get jack shit. Anybody makes trouble, we'll buy them off."

"What if somebody has an attack of conscience?"

"They won't. I didn't pick a bunch of Holy Rollers to do this, I picked good, compromised Christians. The only thing we have to worry about is somebody you pissed off. Somebody testifying out of revenge. Like a woman, say."

Auster's mind flew back to a couple of attractive female patients, one of whom Biegler had called by name. In the natural course of things, they had offered him certain sexual favors in exchange for certain prescriptions, and he had not resisted as he should have. When their requests got out of hand, he'd had to cut them off, no matter what they offered. One or both of those women might present problems, particularly if the government had leverage over them based on drug-related charges.

"I see we've got a problem," Vida said harshly. "Who is she?"

"Nobody. I was just going over it all in my mind."

"Bullshit. Spill it, Kyle."

Paul Biegler needed Vida working for him. She was relentless. Auster sighed heavily. "Quinesha Washington."

Vida went pale. "That crackhead? You went with that skank?"

"Just a blow job—I never touched her otherwise."

Vida shuddered in disgust. "Well, I hope it was a good one. She's going to cost us plenty."

*A good one? More like a dozen good ones.* "Sorry."

"You go tell JaNel to draw blood for an HIV test."

"Come on, Vi—"

"*Now,* damn it! You don't have the sense God gave a tomcat."

Auster held up his hands in surrender. "I'll do it when we're done."

"We're done until you get that test back. I'm going back up front to try to save you from yourself." She turned on her heel and stormed out.

Auster leaned back in his chair and waited for his heart to slow. A few blistering images of Quinesha Washington on her knees before him arced through his brain, but they vanished as Paul Biegler's threats came rushing back. The funny thing was, the patients and the records weren't what really worried Auster. What worried him was his partner.

Taking on Warren Shields had been a mistake. Auster had assumed that Shields, like all the young docs, was hungry for money. And Warren certainly had nothing against making money. But he was constantly checking himself against a code of ethics that belonged to an older generation of doctors—hell, the generation behind Auster, even. It was maddening. On the other hand, the affluent patients in town loved the guy, so he was still good for business.

Then, like a gift from heaven, Shields had suddenly come around on the money issue. About a year ago, he'd walked into Auster's private office after work and said point-blank that he needed to make more money. Auster told him it was no problem, that the money had always been there for the taking, had Warren been ready to earn it. Warren had just nodded and said he was, and that was that. Auster didn't know what had precipitated Warren's sudden venality—a mistress, a drug habit, an expensive hobby—nor did he care. In short order he'd put Vida in charge of Shields on a day-to-day basis. Before Warren checked the billing code after seeing a patient, Vida would ask him a few questions, then check the appropriate box herself. A busy physician like Shields didn't have time to be bothered with trying to figure out the finer shades of what constituted a Level 5 exam.

Within a month, Shields's income almost doubled.

That abrupt uptick in billing might have been what attracted the attention of the Medicaid Fraud Unit. But Auster knew why he'd pushed it. Warren Shields's reputation was spotless; he was the last doctor anyone would suspect of padding his charges. And Shields truly resented government intervention in medicine. Auster had no doubt that, confronted by an accusing government lawyer, Warren would experience a primal burst of outrage. If that pencil pusher Biegler went after Shields, he would get a blast of righteous anger that would set him back on his heels. Then Shields would use his considerable medical knowledge to defend every bill for every patient he'd ever examined. Auster would do the same. And if Vida could really keep the special patients quiet . . . then everything would be all right.

# CHAPTER

## 9

Laurel lay bound on the sofa, trying to keep her mind from going as numb as her extremities. She felt the minutes draining away like blood from a wound. All thoughts of marriage, adultery, and even pregnancy had fled. She lived only to discover the time. Only when she knew how long she had before the children got home could she plan her next move, which might be something she would have thought abhorrent an hour ago. Escape had been her first priority, but given Warren's crazed emotional state, she could not limit her goal to breaking out of the house. The heavy glass vase he had urinated into—and then dropped during her race for the safe room—had come to rest against the wall that separated the great room from the kitchen. The hand-blown vessel, heavy and round at the bottom with a long, tapered neck, had the makings of an ideal club. A blow from that might crush Warren's skull, but anything was preferable to letting her children walk into this nightmare.

"I told you, I'm about to pee on myself!" Laurel cried for the fifth time.

Warren didn't even look up from her computer.

"Why don't you take a break from that thing and search the house some more? I told you, there's something else waiting for you to find it."

He chuckled softly. "What I want to find is buried in the circuits of this machine."

"What you need to find is what Kyle Auster planted in here, so you can start taking out your anger on the person who's your real problem."

Warren ignored her.

She tried another tack. "Do you really want our children to see me taped up like a hostage? With urine-soaked pants? How are you going to explain that?"

"You don't have to use the bathroom. You just want to get loose."

"I'm about to burst! Can't you see the sweat on my face?"

He gave her a brief glance. "If you have to go that bad, go in your pants. I'll throw them in the washer before the kids get here."

New anxiety awakened within her. "How are they supposed to get here if I don't pick them up? Are you going to get them?"

"Maybe I e-mailed one of the girls at the office to get them."

She hadn't considered the idea that Warren might be e-mailing people while he was carrying out his exercise in paranoia. "Who?"

"Nell Roberts."

Laurel pictured a pretty, dark-haired Louisiana girl, the younger sister of the bleached-blond receptionist people said Auster was sleeping with. What would Diane Rivers do when Nell Roberts showed up at school to pick up the children Diane had been asked to drop off? She'd call Laurel's cell phone, which was now tucked into Warren's back pocket, and he'd give some smooth explanation to allay any suspicion. End of story.

"How long till they get out of school?" Laurel asked casually.

Warren shrugged. "They'll get here when they get here. But Nell's not bringing them. I didn't e-mail her. You're such a perfect mother that I realized you would already have arranged to get them here. Right?"

His sarcasm angered Laurel, but at least she had learned that the possibility to intervene with Diane remained.

"Warren, I'm begging you to let me go to the bathroom. Don't you have enough simple human decency left to allow that?"

At last he looked over at her. "Tell me the password to your Hotmail account. Then you can go. "

*Okay,* Laurel thought angrily. *You asked for it.* She closed her eyes and relaxed her urinary sphincter. Within seconds her crotch was soaked, then her inner thighs and bottom. The smell would hit Warren in a minute, and he was unlikely to maintain a stoic front. The sofa beneath Laurel's behind was a leather Roche-Bobois imported from France, $17,000 and change through a boutique store in West Palm Beach. She was still peeing when Warren sat up straight on the ottoman.

"Fuck!" he cried. "You didn't pee on that couch?"

"I told you I had to go."

*"Get off the damn sofa!"*

"Screw you. Cut this tape off me and I'll get up."

He glared as though he wanted to hit her, but Laurel sat as calmly as a Buddha, almost blissful in the relief of her empty bladder.

"You're disgusting," Warren said.

"You asked for it, you got it."

He went into the kitchen and came back with a razor-sharp steak knife. Then he knelt and began cutting the duct tape away from her lower legs. They burned as blood began flowing back into her skin. She held out her hands for him to cut the tape from her wrists, but he shook his head.

"Forget it. Take off your pants and throw them in the wash. Then we'll get you some new ones."

Stripping off her pants presented a problem, since her pants were the only thing concealing her clone phone. Carefully, she slid them down her legs and bunched them around the pocket that held the Razr, then headed for the laundry room. The pungent odor of urine reminded her of the days when Grant and Beth still wore diapers, a memory that broke loose a calcified layer of fierce maternal instinct. As she passed through the kitchen, she glanced at the wall clock: 2:11 p.m. Fifty minutes, max, until the kids burst through the front door. Fifty minutes to break out of the house or to hurt Warren so badly that she could do anything she liked without fear of retribution.

He seemed to sense her hardening resolve. He followed no closer than ten feet behind her as she walked to the laundry room, and his gun stayed in his hand. That distance allowed her to palm the Razr as she tossed the dirty slacks into the washer. But this presented another problem. If she tried to sneak the phone to the bedroom while naked from the waist down,

Warren was bound to see it. She considered trying to slip it up under her arm, but she could feel him watching her from the bifold doors.

"Get moving," he said. "Come on."

"Just a sec." She wanted to check the phone for text messages, but she didn't dare. As she reached for the big jug of Purex on the shelf above the machine, she slid the Razr onto the shelf and left it there. Just before the phone slid out of sight, she saw 2 NEW MESSAGES on its tiny exterior LCD screen. Her heart leaped, for the messages could only be from Danny, but she didn't even consider trying to open the phone and read them. That would have to wait. After she got the wash going, she left the Purex on top of the dryer and walked half-naked back to the master suite, trusting that Warren would prefer to watch her receding derriere rather than double-check the laundry room.

She got into the shower and cleaned herself as well as she could, considering the duct tape on her wrists. Rather than loosening under the spray, the tape became even stickier, a gooey gray mess. To her surprise, Warren hung a towel on the shower door while she scrubbed. She dried herself with it, pulled a fresh pair of panties from her drawer, and selected a pair of stretchy, black yoga pants from the closet—just the thing for sprinting, if she got the chance.

As she sat on the bed to pull them on, she caught Warren staring at her pubic triangle. He'd always liked her to keep it shaved, and she usually obliged him. But Danny had liked her natural, and she'd been more than happy to please him. Warren hadn't complained about the difference, though he had mentioned it a few months back. But now he was staring at her mons like a detective who'd stumbled onto a clue that could solve the case of his life.

"What?" she asked. "Comments from the gallery?"

"Kyle likes them shaved," Warren said almost to himself. "I've heard him say it a hundred times."

"He would."

Warren's eyes narrowed. "What does that mean?"

Laurel sighed, debating whether to be honest. "I just think it's juvenile the way men want women shaved down there. I mean, what's the deal? Do you really want a prepubescent girl, and a shaved woman is the closest thing you can get?"

Warren had gone red. "Your new friend is above all that, right? More mature than the rest of us?"

*You'd better believe it.* "I'm not going to dignify that." She pulled on her panties and then the yoga pants. "What now, General Pinochet?"

"Don't act like this is my fault. You put yourself in this position."

"Ah. So torture is the new legal remedy for infidelity?"

"It ought to be. Even if it were, the betrayed person would still suffer more."

She dismissed his words with a flick of her hand and walked back toward the kitchen.

"Back to the couch," he told her. "If there's room beside your wet spot."

"No more duct tape. My children will *not* see me like that. And you're going to cut this tape off my wrists before they come in."

Warren wasn't looking at her anymore. He was staring at the computer on the coffee table as though seeing it for the first time. She felt a sudden compulsion to distract him but saw no way to do so. She knew that look. Warren could be maddeningly stupid when it came to human relations, but when it came to quantitative matters, he could be as smart as a treeful of owls, as her grandfather used to say. She could almost smell the rush of his neurotransmitters kicking into overdrive.

He started to laugh, sending a chill through her.

"What is it? What's funny?"

He perched on the Eames ottoman and reached for the trackpad. "All this time I've been searching for *data*. I've ignored the actual programs."

A worm of fear squirmed in Laurel's belly. Warren was already clicking away, this time with his sights set squarely on her true vulnerability. It took him less than five minutes to nail her. She knew the exact moment, because he smiled like the Cheshire cat, then looked up and spoke with almost obscene satisfaction.

"Hello, misselizabeth2006. How are we today?"

Adrenaline blasted through Laurel's system like a hit of pure cocaine, but she looked back at him like a deaf woman who couldn't read lips.

"Don't even try," Warren said. "You're not Meryl Streep, okay? You're not even Tori Spelling. I want your password."

"I don't have the password for that account."

"Jesus! Would you stop it already? What's the point of denying anything now?"

"I got that account when I first got my computer. It was free. I used it once or twice, then never again."

"Uh-huh. So it's just a coincidence that I found that love letter in your copy of *Pride and Prejudice*, and that your Hotmail alias is Miss Elizabeth, as in Elizabeth *Bennet*?"

That Warren would know even a single character from an Austen novel stunned Laurel.

"You can thank Keira Knightley for that one," he said.

When Laurel didn't respond, he squeezed his fists into his eye sockets in some sort of brutal massage, then began stabbing the Sony's keyboard again. "Let's just check out your little story, shall we?"

An almost irresistible compulsion to flee gripped Laurel. Only the memory of Warren firing the pistol at her head kept her on the sofa. The revolver now lay inches from her laptop—and from Warren's right hand.

"O-kay," he said, like a desk clerk locating a hotel reservation. "Here's the Microsoft file where old e-mail is stored for Hotmail accounts. Your file totals exactly 226 megabytes of data." He looked up again, his eyes glowing with triumph. "That sounds like about five hundred e-mails to me. With a few candid snapshots thrown in, maybe. Are we going to see some of your *personal* porn this time?"

*Not without my password,* Laurel thought, but her confidence was wavering. Warren was driving her ever deeper into a corner—

"This file was last accessed two days ago," Warren said. "At eleven forty a.m. So, you read your love notes while in your classroom at Country Day? Is that why I donated money to get Wi-Fi out there? What were your poor students doing then, *Miss Elizabeth*? That sounds like negligence to me."

Laurel stared determinedly at the floor. The entire

dynamic between them had changed, but she could not acknowledge this.

"I guess I'll have to figure out your password on my own," Warren said cheerily.

The keyboard started clicking again.

Laurel hugged herself and tried to think of a way to stop him, but nothing came to her. With the screen facing away from her, she couldn't be sure what he was doing. But he would almost certainly begin with her birthday, then the kids' birthdays, then her Social Security number. Then he'd move on to various inversions of those numerals. Warren had always excelled at puzzles, so this kind of thing was very much to his taste. Yet after several abortive attempts to log into her account, he got up, hurried over to his study, and quickly returned holding her copy of *Pride and Prejudice*.

"I should have started with this," he said. "I guess we'll try *Darcy* first? Any thoughts?"

Retrieving this book had been a brilliant intuitive leap, but it didn't worry Laurel as much as Warren probably thought it did. Even with a copy of *Pride and Prejudice* to work from, it would take hundreds of hours to ever hit on *FitzztiF*, the password to her account. She'd created it by playing with the first half of Mr. Darcy's Christian name: Fitzwilliam. It was an almost childish choice, but the odds against Warren trying that particular sequence of letters were astronomical.

"I wish I had a PET scanner that could read the folds of your traitorous little brain," he said with sudden bitterness.

She pretended to ignore him, but she was rejoicing inside. Trying to guess someone's password was about as much fun—and as difficult—as trying to open a safe by random turns of the dial.

"I know why you're doing this," he said over the screen. "Stonewalling, I mean. It's because he doesn't want you. The letter was definite about that. He used you and then he dumped you."

She gave Warren nothing.

"If he'd wanted to run away with you, you'd be gone, wouldn't you? You're just afraid to jump ship without a lifeboat waiting to catch you. You're gutless. That's the ugly bottom of all this. I don't know what the hell I ever saw in you."

She knew she shouldn't take the bait, but she couldn't let this pass. "If that's how you feel, why would you care if I'm seeing someone?"

"Because I'm stuck with you," he said, still not looking up from the screen. "I take my marriage vows seriously. And I take our children's well-being seriously. I happen to have the fortitude to stick it out and try, even with a slut who hasn't got the nerve to bail out without a golden parachute."

"Me?" she whispered. "*I'm* a coward? I'm gutless? What about *you*?"

The righteous indignation in her voice got his attention. He peered over the top of the screen. "What are you talking about?"

"You know. That night on Highway 24. On the way home from the Criterium race in McComb."

Warren had gone still. His face was pale but for the dark circles around his eyes. He remembered, all right. They stared at each other over her computer, each recalling the night that had opened a chasm between them, one that had not been bridged since. Almost a year ago now, after one of the few bike races Laurel had traveled to watch. Warren had taken third place, which most riders would have been happy to win, but because it was only a regional race, he had dumped the diminutive trophy in a garbage can and demanded that they leave for home immediately.

They'd covered about half of the sixty-mile drive when it happened. Flames exploded out of the darkness far ahead, as though from an impacting meteor. As they drew closer, Laurel made out the silhouette of a burning pickup truck on the right shoulder, its nose wedged tight against a massive oak tree. More chilling, she saw a prone form on the asphalt, and it seemed to be moving. She kept waiting for Warren to hit the brakes, but he never did, and before she knew it, they were hurtling past the flaming wreck, the acrid stench of burning gasoline flooding through the AC vents like a ghostly accusation.

"Stop!" she'd cried, grabbing his arm, but he'd continued on, his jaw set tight. The argument that followed had altered her view of her husband forever. While she pleaded for him to turn back and use his medical skills to save the victim she had seen on the road (much less those who might be trapped inside the truck), Warren had calmly described the risks of such an act for him. Wasn't there a Good Samaritan law on the books in Mississippi? Laurel shouted. Wouldn't make a bit of difference, Warren told her, not once the personal-injury lawyers got into it. She'd been sobbing by then.

"Someone could be dying back there!" she screamed. "Right now, while we drive away. I saw someone moving on the road!"

But Warren remained unmoved. She still remembered his quiet soliloquy as they fled the scene: "Listen to me. That's probably some drunk black guy wrapped around that tree. Or white trash, take your pick. He probably never paid a dime for car insurance in his life. I, on the other hand, studied for twenty grueling years to become a doctor. I'm not risking everything I've built for you and the kids to try to help somebody who'll repay me for my efforts by suing me."

While Laurel gaped in disbelief, Warren went on, and his words were still engraved in her soul. "I've gone so far out of my way to help those people . . . and I don't mean all of them, you know that. But I drove a blood sample to Jackson late one Friday so a family could find out as soon as possible whether their kid had leukemia or not—he didn't—and did I get one word of thanks? No, ma'am. Just a blank stare, and they're gone. No 'Thank you,' no payment, no nothing. So tonight, we drive on."

Laurel had settled back in her seat and closed her eyes, but the flaming truck still burned behind her eyelids, and the broken body still crawled along the lightless road. The next morning, she read in the newspaper that two people had died in a one-car accident on Highway 24—no witnesses, according to the highway patrol. The couple had been traveling home from the funeral of their grandson. Laurel could tell by their names that they were black. She never looked at Warren the same way again after that night, and two weeks later, she'd begun her affair with Danny McDavitt. Danny, she knew, would never abandon someone in trouble on the side of a road. He had the medals to prove it.

"You don't know half what you think you know," Warren said with eerie certainty. "You think I'm a coward because of that night?"

"I don't want to think about that night ever again."

He nodded slowly. "That's a luxury you have, I guess. You think I don't have reasons to check out of this marriage?"

She shrugged. "If you do, then you should."

He shook his head like a man amazed. "Is it really that easy for you? You can look at Grant and Beth, smile, and say, 'Sayonara, kids? It was fun while it lasted'?"

"You know it's not that simple."

Warren clenched his jaw muscles, then got up and stood over her with the pistol in his hand. She watched it hanging beside her head, an efficient little machine of death, dangling like a child's toy in his tanned hand.

He pressed the barrel against the crown of her skull. "This is how simple it is. I know you had an affair. I know because you won't give me that password. You think you're sparing me pain by keeping the truth from me, but you're not. You're making it worse. For me *and* for you. Be sure you understand that. You're not leaving this house until I know who's been fucking you. Do you understand that?"

Laurel wanted to be brave, but she felt herself trembling.

"DO—YOU—UN—DER—*STAND*?!"

She waited until she knew she could speak without sounding terrified. "I want you to listen to me, Warren. I want you to think about all the things that have frightened us through the years. Everything that could take us away from our children. Cancer. Car accidents. Child molesters. An intruder in the house. We've taken steps to prevent all those things. But right now"—the gun barrel scraped her scalp as she lifted her face to look at him—"right now *you* are the greatest threat to this family. What if I did have an affair? I understand you would feel hurt. But does *anything* justify this? Would you murder the mother of your children? Think about Grant and Beth for just ten seconds. Picture them in your mind. How innocent they are."

The smell of gun oil entered her nose. After a few moments, Warren lowered the gun, bent his knees, and squatted before her. Seeing a change in his eyes, she was sure she had broken through the anger and pain to reach him. He still looked shell-shocked, but the tenderness in his gaze had not been there before, however wounded it might be.

"Do you know what a family is?" he whispered. "What makes a family?"

She nodded, but Warren shook his head.

"*Trust,*" he said. "That's what separates a family from the rest of the world. Blood isn't enough. They say blood is thicker than water, but brothers betray each other all the time. Trust is the glue that protects a family from the chaos outside."

She wanted to respond, but it was coming to her that Warren saw the world in a way that she did not, and never could.

"*You,*" he said with quiet force, "have destroyed that. Irrevocably. The damage is done, and I can never take you at your word again. Grant and Beth can never trust you again."

"Warren—"

"Don't speak!" he commanded, standing suddenly. He looked down at her like some kind of Old Testament judge. "You chose to place your selfish desires over the welfare of your children. And you must pay the price for that. All of us will have to, I'm afraid."

"Warren, you're not yourself," she said, starting to rise.

He slapped her with his left hand, driving her down to the floor. His palm had struck her right ear, which was now ringing like the three-o'clock bell at school. It hurt, but the shock of being hit far outweighed the pain. She held up her hands to prevent another blow.

*"Do you think I haven't been tempted?"* Warren shouted. "Do you think I haven't had nurses offer me any damn thing I wanted, no strings attached?"

"I'm sure you have."

"Not only nurses. Wives of friends, teachers at the school, *friends of yours!* The signs are always up: 'Pussy for rent'! Nobody has any honor anymore. Nobody keeps their promises."

Laurel stayed on the floor, trying to recall a dark religious strain in Warren's childhood, but she didn't remember one. But the way he was talking . . . it was like he'd been possessed by some wild-eyed minister from another age. Or by her father on his worst day. But not even her father would have resorted to violence. He would have gotten her down on the floor to pray until God sent some sign that forgiveness was at hand. But Warren wasn't waiting for a sign. He saw himself as the instrument of God's punishment.

"I'm sorry you're hurting," she said. "But there's no reason for it. I wish you'd believe me. I would never do anything to hurt our children. Never."

*"Get up!"* he yelled, almost jerking her arm out of joint.

She scrambled to her feet. Warren seemed about to drag her somewhere, but then he shoved her back down on the sofa.

"I'm so *stupid,*" he said. "How could it take me so long to see it? My blood sugar must be in the basement." He sat on the ottoman and started pecking at the computer again. "You can buy just about anything on the Web these days. I read an article in *USA Today* about identity theft and computers. Apparently, hackers have these programs called password crackers that will crank away for fifty hours in a row, if necessary, trying every possible combination of numbers and letters until they break into your e-mail account, or whatever. I'll bet for the right price, I can download one of those cracker programs right into your little Sony."

Laurel had mistakenly invested in the idea that the gun was the greatest danger in the room. This new digital wrinkle destroyed that illusion. Her computer was the real weapon, or rather the detonator that could trigger the use of the gun in earnest. If Warren actually got into her Hotmail account, he would have Danny's name almost instantly. Soon after, he would read every piece of e-mail that had passed between her and Danny during the eleven months they had been together. There were even *photos* embedded in some of those messages! Some were intimate, others not, but every one had the power to shatter what remained of her husband's sanity.

"Here we go," said Warren, a note of triumph in his voice. "Merlin's Magic. Sounds like just the ticket. Two hundred eighty-nine bucks, and they won't even let you download a trial version. That means they know their program works, and they know the kind of situation someone's likely to be in when they need it. A one-shot deal, with a lot riding on the outcome."

Just as she began to hope that Warren would have to get up to retrieve a credit card, he said, "I'm going to use your PayPal account to buy this. Isn't that sweet? One click, and we're in business."

Laurel closed her eyes while his fingertips clicked the keys. How many minutes until the kids got home? If she jumped up and raced for one of the house phones to call 911, would Warren shoot her? Even if he didn't, had things deteriorated to the point that an armed siege was the best solution? *They have,* she said silently. *As long as the kids aren't in the house*—

"All done!" Warren said brightly. He cut his eyes at her. "You might want to rethink your denial. It's only a matter of time until I read those e-mails. And remember, confession is good for the soul."

*My soul is my own business, thank you,* she thought, looking past him to the heavy vase lying against the wall. *But if you turn your back on me before the kids get home, adultery might end up being one of the lesser sins marked against my name.*

# CHAPTER

# 10

"I have to tell you something, Vi," Nell whispered. "I don't want to, but I think you need to know. You deserve to know."

She and Vida were sitting in the reception area of the office, and Nell had rolled her chair over next to her sister's, away from the big patient window. JaNel, the lab tech, had passed by in the hall a couple of times, so Nell kept her voice low.

"Well, don't take all day," Vida said. "There's work to do. I'm listening."

Nell felt her lower lip quivering.

"Go on, baby girl. Whatever it is, I can take it."

*I hope so,* Nell thought. *I dearly hope so.* "I think Kyle is cheating on you, Vi."

Vida stared back in silence. "With who?"

"I don't know."

"What did you see? Or hear?"

"I heard him talking on his cell phone."

Vida glanced over her shoulder at the hall door, then leaned closer. "When was this?"

"Day before yesterday. Back in the surgery room."

"Go on."

"Well, the conversation was pretty intimate. He had that tone, you know?"

"Lovey-dovey?"

"Mm-hm. It seemed obvious that he's involved with whoever it was. And I—"

"Listen, honey," Vida cut in. "I don't doubt you. I'm sure Kyle's poking God knows who all, and I wish he wasn't. But let me tell you something you're gonna learn one way or the other someday. *They all do it.* Every damn one of 'em. That's the way men are. They live for tail, and they're gonna chase it whether they're married or single or whatever. It's a natural law, like freakin' gravity. Like the sun rising in the east. Soon as they get their ashes hauled, they're trying to figure out how to get away from whoever did the haulin'. Unless they need you for something else. And *that's* why I'm not worried."

Nell sat quietly, working through her sister's logic. She'd known Vida was hard, but she hadn't thought her sister would be willing to put up with infidelity to keep a man at her side. Most of all, she hoped Vida was wrong about men—at least a few of them. She considered keeping back the rest of what she'd heard, but if she did, she'd regret it later. She could see Vida standing outside her apartment one night waiting for Dr. Auster's Jaguar to swing by and pick her up, like a black carriage come to sweep her off to a castle. But that Jaguar would never arrive. It would be long gone, to pick up some princess who fit more smoothly into the castles of the rich and conscienceless.

"Let me finish, Vi," she said, louder than she'd intended. "Please."

Vida laid a comforting hand on her knee. "Go on, baby."

"It wasn't just sex talk, okay? He apologized to the person, and then he said he had to keep putting up with—with *somebody*—for a while longer, before he could leave and be with whoever was on the phone."

Something changed in Vida's face. She had the look of someone walking along a path as night fell, one moment sure she knew the way home, the next knowing she was lost. "Keep going," she said in a flat voice that told Nell her walls had gone up.

"Dr. Auster said, 'I hate servicing that little . . .'"

"That little what?" asked Vida, her eyes as dead as marbles. "You can say it."

"'That little *redneck*,'" Nell whispered, and Vida flinched. "Then he said, 'But she scares me.' Next was something else I couldn't hear, but then he said, "'But by then it'll be too late for her to retaliate.' Or something like that."

Vida's face had lost its color. "And you think he was talking about me?"

Nell couldn't bring herself to drive the last nail home. She shrugged. "I can't say for sure."

"I will *castrate* his sorry ass," Vida hissed. "That no-count son of a bitch. After all I've—oh, never mind. Serves me right for believing a man about anything."

"Was I wrong to tell you?" Nell asked anxiously.

"You had to tell me, baby. Blood's thicker'n water. Thicker than anything. It's sure thicker than what comes out of a man. Christ almighty."

Nell watched her sister adjusting to this new reality. Vida usually projected an air of coarse vitality, but at this moment she looked like a road-weary woman from a Depression-era photograph. Nell had tried—subtly—to suggest a few things to soften her older sister's appearance. Skin lotion, for one thing, which Nell applied religiously every night before bed, and all during the day on her face. Decades of smoking had turned Vida's face into a hard carapace with a yellowish tint, and her hair, once a lustrous brown, had become dry and frizzy and always stank of cigarettes. When she went out at night, she dressed one notch up from white trash: halter tops and blue eye shadow worn like some sort of mask—not to mention the line of mascara under her lower eyelid, circa 1985. Vida's great claim to fame was winning a televised wet T-shirt contest in Destin—she'd beaten 150 other competitors—but two children and ten thousand cheeseburgers had deflated her prized assets and hidden her waist in a roll of hard fat. It was testament to her black sense of humor and lively personality that Dr. Auster—who had his pick of twenty-something nurses—had looked past her obvious flaws.

"What are you going to do?" Nell asked softly.

A hard glint appeared in Vida's eyes. "Don't you worry about that. I can take care of myself. Always could, you know that."

Nell was afraid to be honest about her other fears, but she knew she had to speak up if she was to help in any way. "I'm worried about Dr. Shields, Vi."

Vida looked long and hard at her. "He's a lot better man than Kyle, isn't he?"

Nell nodded soberly.

"You've got a thing for him, don't you?"

She closed her eyes and nodded again.

"Jesus, girl. Have you done the dirty with him?"

Nell shook her head vehemently.

"You swear?"

"I swear. He's never touched me."

"Do you talk to him? Secretly, I mean? On the phone? E-mail, like that?"

"Nothing, Vi, I swear to God. He's not like that."

Vida chuckled softly. "They're all like that, once the right woman comes along. But I know what you mean."

"I'm just afraid he'll go to jail."

Vida buried her face in her hands and rubbed it harder than Nell would have dared. Then she looked up and said, "I'll be honest with you, sweetie. Until five minutes ago, that was the plan. Him or us, you know?"

Nell waited without breathing.

"But now . . . maybe it's him or Kyle, you know?"

A glimmer of hope. "What do you mean?"

"I'm not sure yet, baby. I need to think."

Nell was shivering. Vida took her hand and said, "How about this? Whatever happens today, I'll make Kyle go over to Warren's house and take out the stuff he put there."

"You promise?"

"I promise."

"Today?"

Vida patted Nell's knee. "Today."

"But what if Dr. Shields is home? Or his wife?"

"Oh, Kyle's slick enough to get it out even if they're there. Some things he is good at, I'll give him that. He's a born con man."

"But where *is* the stuff? *What* is it? I don't even know that."

The hardness returned to Vida's face. "You don't

need to know. But I'll tell you where it is. It's in that room they have under the stairs. Did you know about that?"

Nell shook her head.

"It's like in that Jodie Foster movie, only not so fancy. Where you go if there's a tornado, or somebody breaks in. It's a rich people's thing."

Nell said, "I remember Mama used to throw us in the closet when a tornado came."

"That was me. Mama was too drunk to worry about any tornado."

Shame and love reddened Nell's face.

"Don't think about it," Vida said. "Anyway, Kyle went over to Dr. Shields's house last Saturday night when they were all gone to the movies. He put the stuff behind some canned goods or something. But you just stop worrying. I'm going to take care of Kyle and make sure your boyfriend is safe, too. As safe as he can be in the middle of this mess, anyway. Safe as you and me."

Nell forced herself to smile. This was the best she could hope for.

Vida leaned forward and hugged her tight, the smell of Marlboro Ultralights wafting from her hair. "You're such a pretty girl," Vida cooed with maternal pride. "Everything's gonna turn out perfect for you. It has to." She pulled back far enough to wink at Nell. "One of us deserves a happy ending."

Nell felt like crying, but she held it in.

Vida stood and walked to the patient window, her hands accepting a form from a patient, but her mind already plotting her next move. Nell didn't envy Dr. Auster's next meeting with her sister. Vida was hell on wheels when she was angry—scarier than most men.

Nell rolled her chair back to her computer, but the longer she stared at the screen, the less relieved she felt. Things were moving too fast, and yet not fast enough. What if the cops did something today? What if they searched Dr. Shields's house before Dr. Auster went over and removed the planted evidence? Could she afford to wait for that? Could she even trust Dr. Auster to do what he was supposed to do, even if he promised Vida that he would? The answer to that question was an unequivocal no. Nell couldn't leave Warren Shields's future in the hands of his sleazy partner. She would have to take responsibility herself. After a quick glance at Vida, she opened her Hotmail account and began to type.

Two thousand feet above the city, Danny told his flying student to bank the Cessna northward and head away from the Mississippi River. They'd been in the air forty minutes, mostly on the south side of town, but Danny wanted to know if both cars were still parked at the Shields house. Laurel had not replied to his last text message, and he was worried that he'd made a mistake by sending it.

A bad mistake.

"You want me to go all the way to Fort Adams?" asked Marilyn Stone, a local attorney who'd dreamed for years of learning to fly.

"No, let's do our usual run out here. When you get to Avalon, execute an S-turn over Belle Chêne Plantation, then head back to the barn."

Marilyn nodded, her eyes on the GPS unit mounted on the instrument panel. "Why Avalon all the time? You buying a lot there or something?"

"You never know," Danny said with a forced laugh.

He looked down at the loess hills below and tried to settle his nerves. Athens Point was a beautiful place, and the verdant forests below reminded him why he'd chosen to return after his military career. Unlike so many places that he had lived, this city had a long and colorful history. Athens Point had been founded in 1753 by a classically educated Frenchman venturing downriver through the Natchez Territory. The land was inhabited by the Choctaw Indians, but they lasted only seventy years before vanishing into Oklahoma or worse places. Removal was accomplished the way Hemingway's Bill Gorton went bankrupt, slowly and then all at once. After the Treaty of Dancing Rabbit Creek, all that remained of the Choctaw in that corner of Mississippi was a few names, like the one taken by the county, Lusahatcha ("Black Water"), which today seemed a misnomer since the great river stretching away behind the Cessna looked reddish brown under the sun. But the Mississippi River had many faces, and Danny had seen them all while growing up beside it.

Unlike Natchez, thirty miles to the north, Athens Point had resisted the Yankee invasion during the Civil War. The town sent three companies to fight under Lee in Virginia, and those who remained behind held out until July 11, 1863, being forced to surrender after the fall of Vicksburg. While the Father of Waters thereafter flowed "unvexed to the sea," as President Lincoln put it, the inland areas of southwest Mississippi remained vexed indeed. Gangs of Confederate deserters roamed the land, and marauding Union cavalry units under

Colonel Embury Osband pillaged what remained of the state's resources.

For a hundred years afterward, the town's hero was Jean Larrieu, a diminutive but feisty planter who shot six cavalrymen from the windows of Belle Chêne plantation before being cut down on his porch by a saber during a parley. A Union private had struck his wife, and Larrieu refused to let the insult pass. His statue still stood atop a column in the town square. Even today, antebellum city buildings bore the scars of the shelling that resulted from the town's firing on Admiral Porter's passing ironclads in 1863. A historical marker commemorated the seventeen citizens who perished in the fires that day, while beside it a second marker memorialized six African Americans who died in Lusahatcha County during the struggle for civil rights.

The prejudice so prevalent in Danny's childhood had diminished to a mild undercurrent between the races, but even today black and white remained largely divided in the physical sense. Black families tended to congregate in the city proper or to the south, while affluent whites and a few wealthy blacks built shining new subdivisions in the forests along Highway 24 to the north. Avalon was the newest and most exclusive of these, patterned after subdivisions of the same name in Gulfport and Natchez. Apparently the developer intended to replicate his utopian concept across the state. Danny could just make out the serpentine bends of Larrieu's Creek, which marked one boundary of Avalon.

*There,* he said silently.

Avalon had been tastefully carved out of forestland that had been locked up in the trust of an old Athens

Point family for a hundred years. A massive wrought-iron gate greeted prospective buyers as they turned off Highway 24 onto Cornwall, a broad street that wound its way eastward through the upscale development. Only fifteen houses had been built so far, with a handful of others under construction. The smallest lots available were 6.5 acres. The Shields house was easy to spot from the air, because its acreage was bordered by a bend of Larrieu's Creek.

"I've been thinking," Marilyn said, "I might want to try for an instrument rating after I get my VFR license."

Danny chuckled. "You're always pushing, aren't you?"

She grinned. "I'm a trial lawyer. I guess it's in my blood."

He knew she expected him to keep up the banter, but his mind was on the land below. He could see the Shields house coming up on his left. "Drop down to five hundred feet. I think I see a herd of deer."

Marilyn responded smoothly, and the Cessna quickly descended.

"Good. Stay well clear of those houses." Danny would have liked to let Laurel hear the plane, but if there was any chance that Warren suspected Danny was her lover, then drawing attention to the Cessna would be insane. Warren had flown this plane so often that he would recognize it at a glance. And since Laurel—or Warren, for that matter—had not responded to the two text messages he had sent her, he had to play things very cool. "Somebody complained to me at the hardware store the other day," Danny added. "Asked if we're planning to bomb the neighborhood."

Marilyn laughed and slid the plane a quarter mile to the east.

Danny got a perfect view of Laurel's Acura parked behind her husband's Volvo. The sight tied a knot in his stomach. What the hell was going on down there? *Maybe they're getting it on,* he thought, surprised that he almost wanted this to be true. Because any alternative was bound to be worse.

"See any bucks?" Marilyn asked.

"What?"

"The deer. See any bucks?"

"Nah. Nothing but does, and they skipped into the trees."

"Should I start my turn?"

"Yeah. Go ahead." Danny closed his eyes and tried to think logically, but his nerves kept getting in the way. Or was it his emotions?

"An S-turn over Belle Chêne?" Marilyn asked.

"Let's skip that," said Danny, glancing at his watch. "Let's take her back to the airport. I've got something I can't be late for."

"Suits me," Marilyn said, watching him from the corner of her eye. "I've got a deposition this afternoon. Big case coming up."

"I pity the lawyer you're up against."

She laughed. "You don't know whether I'm a good lawyer or not."

He clicked his tongue against the roof of his mouth. "Oh, yes, I do."

"How?"

He tapped the bridge of his nose. "I'm a good judge of character."

Marilyn elbowed him in the side, and he saw some

color come into her cheeks. "I'll bet you are," she said, looking as if she wanted to say more.

Danny resisted the urge to look back toward Avalon as she made a controlled 180-degree turn.

"Are you all right?" she asked in a concerned voice.

"Sure, I'm fine."

"You look worried to me. I don't think I've ever seen you worry before."

*This is why you're a good lawyer,* Danny thought. "Little bit of a headache, that's all."

"If you say so. But if you need any help . . . don't hesitate to call me."

He tried to laugh this off, but the more he thought about the situation, the more worried he became. The Cessna headed southwest toward the Mississippi River, where it curved between Angola Prison and DeSalle Island. "Marilyn, do you know anything about family law?"

She sighed. "I thought it was something like that. Yes, I know a lot. I used to handle nothing but divorces, until I got enough oil-business work to keep me going."

Danny rubbed his forehead for a while. He'd talked to a couple of lawyers already, but neither had seemed to grasp the special nature of Michael's educational problems. Praying that Marilyn was different, he said, "I need to ask you about a custody issue."

She looked him in the eye and nodded, more serious than he'd ever seen her.

"It's complicated," he said.

She smiled encouragingly. "That's why you need a professional. Fire away, Major."

. . .

Laurel was nearly mad with fright. The Merlin's Magic
program had been hammering steadily at her Hotmail
account for the best part of an hour, and sooner or
later, the mindless digital battering ram would break
through. It was fast and efficient, a brute-force strategy
that guaranteed success, given sufficient time. Laurel
didn't know enough about probability theory to guess
how long it might take for the program to hit on her
password—surely longer than the fifteen or twenty
minutes until Grant and Beth got home—but what was
to stop Warren from keeping her and the children prisoner all night? He could run Merlin's Magic until the
contents of her secret files finally poured into his lap,
even if it took until morning.

Shortly after Warren installed the program, Laurel
had heard what she thought was the faint sound of an
airplane engine far to the east. She was unable to get
up and look, however, because Warren had retaped her
ankles and calves, probably so he could focus on the
password program without worrying about her. She
was almost afraid to hope that the sound had come
from Danny's plane. And yet she did. Who else could
help her? The fact that she had not answered his last
two text messages might have worried him enough to
overfly the house. But what more could he do?

*You have to help yourself,* said a voice in her head.
*Don't wait to be saved.* So she hadn't. After a few minutes' thought, she had hit on one possible method of
escaping the duct tape. When Warren wasn't looking,
she had reversed her engagement ring—a radiant-cut
two-carat diamond that he had bought three years
ago to replace the sliver of a stone that had graced the

ring when he proposed—and tested its ability to saw
through duct tape. Where the tape was stretched tight,
the raised edges of the diamond worked reasonably
well. The problem was Warren, who had a clear line
of sight to her. After complaining that the wet duct
tape was itching badly, which was true, she began
scratching often. Whenever Warren seemed entranced
by the computer screen, she would saw at the vertical
rip she'd made in the tape binding her lower legs. She
worried that the diamond might pop out of its setting
if she sawed too hard—white gold was a soft metal—
but she was bracing the stone with her thumb as she
cut, and besides, she saw no alternative.

A few minutes ago Warren had typed on the Sony's
keyboard for nearly a minute. At first this frightened
her, but when she realized he had not broken into her
account, she decided he must be writing or answering
an e-mail. She'd used this time to work harder at the
duct tape. Yet even if she managed to free her legs,
her wrists would remain bound. It would be difficult,
if not impossible, to retrieve the vase and hit Warren
over the head with it if her hands were bound together.
And even if she succeeded at that, there remained the
problems of trying to get her keys, reach her car, and
drive away. Warren wasn't going to lie peacefully on
the floor while she did all that.

She was pretending to scratch her ankles when he
got up from the ottoman and stared at her like a man
trying to hypnotize someone.

"Why did you run to the safe room?" he asked.

"Because I thought I would be *safe* there. Duh."

"Is that the only reason?"

"What other reason could there be?"

He pointed his right forefinger at her, then wagged it right and left like some cranky middle-school teacher. "Let's find out." He shoved the gun into his waistband, then walked out of the great room and into the kitchen.

Laurel bent nearly double on the couch and sawed frantically at the tape. A few seconds later Warren walked out of the kitchen with a knife and came straight to the sofa. Kneeling beside her, he cut through the tape around her calves, then the strips binding her ankles. She was terrified that he would notice her saw marks, but he was in too much of a hurry. He pulled her to her feet and marched her toward the foyer.

"Who are you talking to online?" she asked.

"Why do you think I'm talking to someone?"

"You've been typing and reading something. I figured it was e-mail. Or IMs. And you said before that someone told you to search for the letter. They just told you to look in the safe room, didn't they?"

"Aren't you the little detective."

"I told you there was something else in the house. Somebody's screwing with your head, Warren. Big-time."

"We'll see when we find out what it is, won't we?"

*I was right!* Laurel thought anxiously. *What the hell are we about to find? Just don't let it be something I can't explain—*

He opened the closet that concealed the steel door of the safe room and told Laurel to turn her back to the door. After she did, he punched his new code into the child-protection key pad, which opened the steel door unless the master lock had been set from the inside. As Warren stepped into the metal room, a spark

of excitement flashed through her. If she could get inside the safe room and somehow shove him out, then
she could slam the door and lock it. With him outside, the kids would still be in danger, but there was a
secure phone in the safe room, and she could use it to
call Diane Rivers and stop her from bringing the kids
home.

Laurel took a furtive step backward, instinctively
realizing that this was the way to get into the safe
room. Warren would be nervous that she was trying to
break for the front door. As if on cue, he said, "That's
far enough. You come stand here, in the doorway."

She shuffled forward like a reluctant prisoner. The
air in the safe room was musty and stank of mildew.
Warren began removing the canned goods stored on
the shelves, grabbing shrink-wrapped packs of Bush's
baked beans and stacking them on the floor. Next
came the bottled water. Laurel was ready to risk her
life to get Warren out of there, but he outweighed her
by sixty pounds, minimum. And that sixty pounds was
almost all muscle. To complicate matters, her wrists
were still taped together, and Warren was almost flush
against the shelves on the back wall. How could she
get behind him and shove him out the door?

She found her chance less than a foot away.

Where the reinforced wall met the steel door, a
sharp piece of sheet metal protruded a half inch into
the open doorway at shoulder level. It looked a lot like
an old-fashioned razor blade, and she wasted no time
testing it. As Warren cursed and dropped a six-pack of
Dasani onto the pile behind him, she raised her arms
and dragged the duct tape along the protruding metal.
Warren paused at the ripping sound—which sounded

like Velcro being unhooked—but by the time he turned, Laurel was holding her wrists together again.

He knelt before the deep shelves, then grunted in surprise.

Laurel picked up a heavy can of beans and drew it back as if to hurl it at his head. It seemed safer than moving close enough to hit him, but if she missed, he might shoot her out of simple reflex. Warren groaned in frustration. He was trying to pull something off the back of the bottom shelf. A white cardboard box. A banker's box.

She sprang forward and drove the can down toward the base of his skull, aiming for the brain stem. With her children in danger, there was no point in half measures. Warren must have heard her approach, because he turned his head back and upward just as the can reached the end of its arc. Instead of knocking him into a vegetative coma, the flat of the can crashed into his neck and jaw.

He fell against the shelves, his eyes blank.

Laurel raised the can to deliver another blow, but Warren toppled sideways, out of reach. She darted forward, meaning to grab the gun from his waistband, but the light of awareness flashed in his eyes. She froze, aware that she had moved within his grasp, then whirled and lunged for the door.

The gun thundered like a cannon in the tiny room.

*"DON'T TAKE ANOTHER STEP!"* Warren screamed.

Laurel was too close to freedom to obey. She kept moving, and the pistol exploded again. A hole appeared in the foyer wall ahead of her. This image somehow penetrated the rush of panic driving her forward.

She turned and saw Warren crawling through the door of the safe room with the pistol in his hand. She darted to her right, which carried her out of his line of sight and to the front door.

The door was bolted shut, but the key was in the lock. She was turning the key when a car horn sounded outside. Two quick blasts that told her Diane Rivers had just pulled to the end of the sidewalk with the kids. As the bolt clicked open, a shadow fell across the door. Laurel put her hand on the knob.

"Open that door, and I'll kill you," Warren said. "I'll kill you with Grant and Beth watching."

She gripped the brass knob with all her strength, willing herself to open the door. *No way will he shoot me in front of them,* she told herself. *He'd spend the rest of his life in prison, and not one person would ever visit him. Not even his mother—*

"And then I'll shoot myself," Warren said quietly.

Laurel froze, a thousand images from news stories she'd seen over the years playing in her mind. *Murder-suicide! Distraught Dad barricades home and executes family! Stabs wife, strangles kids in their beds! Father crashes plane into mother-in-law's house with children aboard!* She let her hand fall from the knob.

Warren seized her by the neck and dragged her away from the door.

# CHAPTER

# 11

Kyle Auster gripped his office telephone with an almost bloodless hand. The man on the other end of it was Patrick Evans, executive assistant to the governor and Auster's line into the Medicaid Fraud Office. Evans had opened the conversation with the warning "No names," then explained that he was calling Auster from a pay phone. At Evans's next words, Auster's face went slack with fear.

"I don't know what you said to Paul Biegler today, but he's on his way down there with two other agents to chain your goddamn office shut. You are out of business, Kyle. For a while, anyway. It's time to hire a good criminal lawyer."

"But . . . but" was all Auster could sputter. "Today? Biegler said he was coming in the morning."

Evans didn't bother to respond to this evidence of idiocy. Auster heard traffic zooming by whatever pay phone Evans was using. He could see his old schoolmate standing by some shady downtown pay phone, watching every vagrant like a potential mugger.

"Patrick," Auster said in a halting voice. "Isn't there any way I can head this off?"

"I'm sorry, man. The ship has sailed. And . . . I've got to say this. Our relationship has to end at this point. I know we go back a long way, but I'm in a high-profile job. You're a liability now. I can't risk everything because we played ball together in high school."

A big truck ground its gears in Auster's ear. He felt as if Evans had just walked away from the roulette table, leaving him half a million down. "I've got to go," Evans said. "Are we clear on that last? No calls to the governor's office, not even from home, much less jail."

Fear and indignation rose as one in Auster. "What about all the contributions I've given you guys? Hell, this year alone—"

"Wake up, Kyle. This is survival. Get a good lawyer. I'm out of here."

The phone clicked in Auster's hand. No more traffic sounds. Nothing but the hum of his air conditioner and the sound of a patient's voice in the corridor outside. He felt the world collapsing around him, crushing him with its density. His allotted time as Kyle Auster, noted Athens Point physician, had shrunk to the time it would take Paul Biegler to cover the one hundred and twenty-six miles of road between Jackson and Athens Point. With traffic, that was about two and a quarter hours, but if Biegler really pushed it, he could do it in ninety minutes.

*Christ, when did he leave?* Auster fought the urge to race out to his car, visit the bank, empty his cash accounts, and skip town. *I should have kept my damn mouth shut.* He pressed the intercom button on his phone and waited for Nell to answer.

"Yes, Dr. Auster?" she said in a strangely cold voice.

"Would you ask Vida to come to my office?"

"Um . . . she's not here, Doctor."

"What? Where is she?"

"She went to the store."

"The *store*? What store?"

"I'm sure I don't know, Dr. Auster."

Auster was flabbergasted. Vida never left the office during the day. Maybe she'd run out of cigarettes.

"Should I send her to you when she gets back, Doctor?"

"Ah . . . yes, Nell. Thank you."

Auster's heart was galloping. He scrabbled in his top drawer for another beta-blocker, which he swallowed with the remains of a flat Coke from his morning snack. Then for good measure he stuck an Ativan under his tongue. What the hell could he do to save himself in ninety minutes? Call Biegler and send him to Warren's house to find the planted evidence? Claim that everything he'd done had been to protect his younger partner? Would Biegler buy that? Probably not. There was still too much evidence to be found at the office. Too many patients to buy off. Ten days simply hadn't been enough warning. He needed Vida. *Now.*

He speed-dialed her cell phone, but it kicked him straight to voice mail. Either Vida was on the phone with someone else, or she was purposefully not answering his call. At a loss, Auster started to get up and see one of the patients waiting in his exam rooms. Then he sat back down, took the crystal Diaka bottle from his bottom drawer, and gulped a heroic slug right from the mouth.

"She'll be back soon," he gasped, thankful for the burn of alcohol in his gullet. "She'll know what to do."

Warren dragged Laurel down the hall to the guest room and threw her onto the bed. The horn sounded again outside, and then the doorbell rang.

"Let me answer it!" she begged. "I won't try anything! I swear to God."

Warren wasn't listening. He shoved a chair under the doorknob, then began rummaging in the guest room closet, which they used to store junk that had no other place.

"What are you doing?" she cried, praying that since the front door was still locked, Diane would take the kids home to her house. But of course she would see both cars in the driveway. "Please don't tape me up again, Warren. I don't want the kids to see that!"

"No tape," he said, walking out of the closet with a three-foot length of plastic-coated cable. A bicycle lock.

"No!" she yelled, but it didn't matter.

He sat astride her chest and looped the cable twice around her neck, then cinched it tight and passed it through two slots in the wooden headboard. By the time he clicked the lock shut, she could hardly move without cutting off her air supply.

"I'll be back in a minute," he said. "Don't do anything stupid."

He vanished into the hall. Laurel heard the front door open, then a squeal of joy from Beth at unexpectedly finding her father home early. The voices dropped to a muffled hum, and a moment later Laurel heard feet going up the front stairs.

*Why?*

Struggling to breathe with the bike lock choking her, she agonized over her decision at the front door. She'd read that experts advised women to try everything for freedom in a kidnap situation, even to risk being shot rather than be taken captive. But this was different. When Warren said he would kill himself, she had known by the timbre of his voice that he would do it. He would kill her and himself, too. For an instant, she'd wondered if even that would be better than letting the children fall under his power, but in the end she'd decided that they represented her last hope of bringing him to his senses. Warren had come unmoored from reality, but perhaps Grant and Beth could coax him back.

She heard soft footsteps in the playroom upstairs. The kids' couch groaned under Warren's unaccustomed weight. In that moment Laurel hated Danny McDavitt. Five weeks ago her life had been a beautiful dream. They had each decided to tell their spouse that they wanted a divorce on the same night, a Thursday. That way, no matter what happened, Warren would have to go to work the next day, and Danny would have flying lessons scheduled. They could almost surely find a way to see each other, even if Warren or Starlette had freaked out. They parted that Thursday afternoon with a feeling of elation that masked the deep anxiety Laurel felt at broaching the subject of divorce with Warren. After eleven months of soul-withering secrecy, they were finally stepping into the light.

Danny stuck by his side of the agreement. After he put his kids to bed, he sat Starlette down in the kitchen and told her he didn't love her anymore. When she asked if he'd met someone, Danny admitted that he had and told her that he was truly in love for the first time in his life. Starlette went ballistic. Not only did she make clear that she had no intention of granting Danny a divorce (in Mississippi you had to have grounds), but she also stated that if Danny somehow forced her into one, his ideas on custody—him keeping Michael, for example—would never become reality. She would keep Michael, first to make Danny suffer as she would be suffering, and second because she wouldn't let any of her friends think she was capable of relinquishing her autistic son with only minor regret (which was the truth). Danny spent that night in their kitchen, trying to find a way out of the cage he had constructed for himself.

In the Shields house, things unfolded differently. When Warren got home from his hospital rounds, he was more taciturn than usual, and he actually ignored the children for several minutes, though they tried desperately to get his attention. Worried, Laurel sent them into the backyard and asked him what was wrong. Warren told her that Jimmy Woods had died that afternoon. Jimmy had gone to school with Warren from nursery school through the twelfth grade, and they'd lived on the same street as boys. He'd developed diabetes some years ago and had a hard time keeping it under control. An hour before Warren got home from work that Thursday, Jimmy had gone into a diabetic coma while driving on Highway 24 to pick up his son from baseball practice. He ramped off a low shoulder, went airborne, and slammed into a pecan tree. Warren had been in the hospital when Jimmy was carried into the ER, and the attending had called him to help try to stabilize Woods, whose neck had largely been crushed. Jimmy died under Warren's hands, as blue as a bruise and paralyzed from the neck down.

Warren had never before showed emotion when he lost patients, but as he recounted Jimmy's death, he wiped tears from his eyes. He had personally broken the news to Jimmy's wife, who'd shown up at the ER with their son in tow. Strangely moved, Laurel walked to Warren and hugged him tight, but he stiffened and tried to change the subject. She held him by force for a moment, then went back to the kitchen to finish cooking supper.

After she put the kids to bed, she came downstairs and found Warren on the sofa, blankly staring at MSNBC. Despite her desire to be with Danny, she could not find it in her heart to tell Warren then that she was leaving him. The packed suitcase hidden in her car trunk would have to stay there one more night. Danny would be upset, but they could certainly wait one day. She had decided to go take a shower when Warren turned to her and said, "What would you do if I died like that? If I was here one day and gone the next? Out of the blue?"

"Don't talk like that," she replied, not wanting him to go any deeper with his morbid musings.

"I think you'd be all right financially. I've been working on my estate this year."

"Thank you for telling me," Laurel said awkwardly. "But it would be such a blow to the children, I just don't want to think about it."

Warren nodded distantly. "Death is part of life, though. I see it every day. Men younger than Jimmy die every month in this town. Children, too. But it's you I'm thinking about. Would *you* be all right? Would you be able to move on and find a new life?"

*Dear God.* Laurel closed her eyes, almost unable to deceive him a moment longer. But that was definitely not the moment to tell him she was leaving. Warren believed that adultery was a profound betrayal not only of one's spouse, but of the entire family. The very concept of family. And she had never seen him as emotional as he was that night. No, the breakup conversation would definitely have to wait.

"I'm going to take a shower," she said helplessly, wondering why Warren had decided to unburden himself on this night of all others. He never had before, and that was one of the roots of their marital problems—maybe even the taproot. Flustered and angry, she checked her clone phone in the bathroom and found a text message from Danny: DON'T TELL HIM! I'LL EXPLAIN TOMORROW.

They met the next day in the woods near Danny's house. She arrived to find Danny pacing back and forth in the little glade, looking as though he hadn't slept at all. She asked if he'd told Starlette last night, then immediately launched into her own explanation of why she hadn't told Warren. She'd expected Danny to get angry, but instead he looked relieved. In a subdued voice, he told her he'd decided he couldn't divorce Starlette after all. The reason was as simple as his son. He'd already talked to a lawyer, and the lawyer had confirmed the bleak visitation picture painted by Starlette. Laurel knew that Starlette was capable of following through on her threats. The irony was that Danny's best chance of convincing a judge that he was Michael's primary caregiver was Laurel herself; but her testimony would be useless if she was exposed as his paramour, a fact that even a semiprofessional investigation would probably uncover.

Eleven months of dreams had vanished in a span of seconds. She had given Danny everything, or almost everything, and she'd promised him the rest. Yet he was rejecting her. He had a valid reason, yes. But it still seemed unfair. How could all his promises evaporate in the face of his wife's selfishness? Laurel had waited thirty-five years for true love, and having found it, was she doomed to watch it float away like smoke? She felt as though fate were mocking her, showing her what was possible and then snatching it away at the last moment. And what about the previous night? What if she had told Warren she was leaving him, only to learn that Danny had chickened out? Talk about jumping out of a plane without a parachute. When Danny tried to hug her, she shoved him away. If she couldn't have everything, she'd decided, she wanted nothing.

A creak in the hallway made her tense, and the bike lock constricted around her throat. Then the guest room door opened as slowly as a door in a horror movie.

Warren looked down at her with eyes every bit as wild as those of an ax murderer. He had a stack of boxes in his arms, and these he dumped right on top of Laurel. When she flinched to avoid injury, the cable lock cut off her airflow.

"I can't breathe!"

"Sounds like a personal problem," Warren said, sitting on the edge of the bed with apparent disgust. "Let me know how it comes out."

Laurel twisted her neck enough to get some air, but

the terror generated by her need for oxygen overrode almost everything else. She dug her fingers under the cable and held it out just enough to take a long, sweet breath.

"I knew I was right," Warren said. "For a while you had me doubting. The letter, too. It didn't sound like Kyle. But you never know what somebody's really like. You're a perfect example of that. My pussyhound partner turns out to be a closet romantic, and my wife a lying whore." He clucked his tongue. "You learn something every day, right?"

Laurel had no idea why Warren was back on the Auster kick. It must have something to do with the boxes. "How are the kids?" she asked. "What did you tell them?"

"Mommy's having a migraine."

Laurel tried to guess every possible effect of this explanation.

"They're very worried about you," Warren said with false concern. "They've promised not to make one little peep, or to come downstairs. If they need something, they'll call me from the upstairs extension."

She nodded thankfully. At least they wouldn't see her in this condition or be anywhere near Warren's gun.

He opened one of the boxes and pulled out what looked like an accounting ledger, bound in red faux leather. "At first I figured you were storing these for Kyle. But that's not it, is it?"

Laurel shrugged warily. "I don't even know what that is."

"You never give up, do you? I can understand why. You know what's likely to happen, don't you?" He held out the ledger. "This is some kind of duplicate set of books for the office. Only it shows all sorts of payments that never made it onto our tax returns. Cash payments, I guess. And there are codes beside certain patients' names, codes I've never seen before. God only knows what they mean. God and Kyle, anyway." He gave her a pointed look. "And you, right?"

Laurel risked cutting off her air to shake her head.

"You're not just storing this stuff as a favor. The reason I know that is because I found *these*." He held up a stack of what looked like stock certificates, bound with a tight paper band. "Bearer bonds. Two hundred thousand dollars' worth, if I'm doing my conversion correctly."

Laurel blinked in confusion.

"These are just like cash," Warren said. "Totally liquid. You have them, you own them. They're illegal in the U.S. now. But these, conveniently, were issued by a Guatemalan company."

"I've never seen those before, Warren. I don't even know what they are."

He laughed. "That's odd, don't you think? They're hidden in our house, and I've never seen them before. If you didn't hide them, how did they get here? The bond fairy? Santa Claus?"

"Kyle must have hidden them here. He's setting you up for something."

"You're right about that. And you're helping him."

Laurel knew there was no point, but she shook her head anyway.

Warren reached out and closed his hand around her windpipe. "Stop denying it, Laurel. Stop *lying*. And maybe—just maybe—you'll live through this."

"Tell me what you want. What do you want me to do?"

He pursed his lips. "I want to know how you feel when you suck Kyle's cock. Do you like knowing fifty women have done it before you? Or that he just pulled it out of Vida an hour before he saw you?"

Laurel shut her eyes and began to cry. This was what happened when you decided to break the rules. She hadn't wanted any of this, but her acts had made it all happen. By reaching for Danny's love, she had drawn this nightmare around herself. She had put her children's lives at risk.

*God forgive me,* she thought.

"You like degrading yourself, don't you?" Warren said. "This life we have, this perfect life . . . you hate that. You need drama, don't you? You need to feel low. It gets you off. Like that porn in your computer. The nasty stuff gets you off. It must have something to do with your father, the preacher. Did old Tom give you a little private Communion after Mom went to sleep at night? A little wine and romance?"

"Baptists drink grape juice at Communion."

Warren barked a laugh. "That's in public. In private they do it all, don't they?"

Crying was making her throat swell, and that made it still harder to breathe. "Please take this off my neck," she gasped. "I really can't breathe."

"I will take it off," he said, smiling strangely. "You know why? Because you're about to make a phone call."

"Who am I going to call?"

"Kyle, of course."

"Kyle? What do you want me to say?"

Warren thought about it for a moment. "You want an afternoon quickie. You're horny. You can't go another minute without it."

Laurel couldn't believe his words.

"You were watching your porn, but it's not enough. Use your imagination. I'm sure he's fucked you right in our bed and loved every second of it. As much because of me as you, probably."

Warren left the guest room, then quickly returned with two cordless handsets. *He must have the phones hidden somewhere,* she thought. Laurel lay still as he unlocked the cable, loosened it a little, and then, to her horror, shut the lock again. He had no intention of releasing her from this torture device.

She watched him dial a number on one of the handsets, then hold the phone up to her face. He put his head against hers, crushing the phone between, so that he wouldn't miss a word Kyle said.

With his other hand he stuck his pistol against her ribs.

When Auster's cell phone rang, he assumed it was Vida returning his call to her cell, but the LCD said WARREN SHIELDS. Auster breathed a heavy sigh of relief, though he wasn't sure why talking to Shields should calm him down. Maybe because they were both in the same boat, even if Shields didn't understand how leaky the boat was.

"Warren?" he answered. "Where are you, man?"

"Kyle?" said a female voice that Auster thought might belong to his girlfriend, but then he decided against it. This woman sounded more mature.

"This is Kyle. Who's this?"

"Laurel."

*Laurel Shields? What the hell?* "Laurel? What's going on?"

"Nothing. I've been thinking about you, that's all."

Auster sputtered in confusion. "You have?"

"Mm-hm."

"What about me?"

"You know. What we've been doing together."

"What we've been doing?"

"Yes. You know."

"Ah, I'm a little confused, Laurel. I like your tone, but why don't you help me out here?"

"I want you to come over and fuck me. Now. The kids have a birthday party, and they're not here now."

Auster was stunned speechless.

"I want you to do me the way you did the last time. Can you handle that?"

*The last time?* "Laurel . . . this is some kind of joke, right? Like *Candid Camera* or something. *Punk'd* or whatever?"

"No joke, Kyle. You know me better than that."

"What I know is that I've dropped hints for years, and you've kept me at arm's length the whole time. What's changed?"

There was a long pause, during which Auster sensed a hand pressed over the mouthpiece on Laurel's end. He'd downed several shots of Diaka, but through the vodka-generated fog it struck him that since Warren had not come in to work today, he might be home now. He might even be on the phone with Laurel, though Auster couldn't imagine what they might be playing at.

"Kyle?" Laurel said plaintively.

"I'm here."

"What do you think? Don't you want me to suck you off?"

Auster was about to hang up when a new scenario struck him. What if Warren had been cheating on his wife? God knew he'd been acting screwy for the past couple of months. Longer, really. If he was cheating on Laurel, and she'd found out about it, maybe she was out for a little revenge. This wasn't the best time for it— with Biegler on the way, it would be insanity—but he'd had his eye on her for a long time. Laurel Shields was a thoroughbred. She made his latest girlfriend look like a plow horse (despite Shannon's being ten years younger than Laurel) and Vida Roberts like something destined for the glue factory. Laurel had *class,* and there was nothing better than a woman with class looking in the gutter for revenge.

"Ah . . . I can't say I would turn that down. What do you have in mind?"

"Just drive over here. Pull into the garage, and I'll be waiting for you. Bring some Viagra with you. I need a serious workout."

The mention of Viagra pushed back the fog a little. Then he thought he heard another voice, heavily muffled. "What about Warren, babe? Where is he?"

"Warren's not at work?"

"He never came in today."

"Huh. I don't know, then. And I don't care. I know what I want."

Auster felt his sluggish blood pumping faster.

"Don't worry about Warren," Laurel said. "He never comes home during the day. Maybe he's playing golf."

Auster closed his eyes and forced himself to think beyond the moment. Biegler was driving hell for leather from Jackson to shut down the office. Vida would be getting back any second. Yes, nailing Laurel seemed like the ideal escape from all that, but what it really amounted to was professional suicide. He would have to walk away this time. For once in his life, he would leave money sitting on the table.

"I sure appreciate the offer," he said. "But I have to pass, Laurel. There's just too much going on, and I keep thinking of something my daddy taught me early on."

"What's that?"

"Don't shit where you eat."

She gave a feminine snort of contempt. "You've broken that rule too many times to count."

"Yeah, I know. But Warren's my partner. Maybe I've finally learned something. Be careful, honey. You're too sweet to waste it, you know?"

He hung up before his darker instincts could betray him.

Warren slammed the phone against the guest room wall. Laurel cringed, but hope was surging through her. She had been sexually explicit, as Warren had instructed, but that strategy had backfired, as she had known it would. The more forward she was, the more confused Kyle was bound to be. Her only worry had been that he would ignore the absurdity of her offer and accept it on the outside chance of getting sex from a delusional woman. He had certainly lusted after her long enough. At one drunken Christmas party Kyle had confessed that he often thought about Laurel while having sex with other women. She'd shoved him away, but what more could she do? How could she prove he'd said something like that? The only upside of this unsavory history was that Kyle knew her well enough to know she'd never be the pursuer, even if she decided she wanted him.

"I told you someone was messing with your head," she said softly. "Kyle had no idea what I was talking about. Do you believe me now?"

"You've got some kind of code!" Warren shouted. "Something you say if I'm around. Or something you *don't* say. That's it, isn't it?"

A Kafkaesque dread descended in her soul. "Warren . . . the kids. Please keep your voice down." She took a deep breath, then spoke with utter sincerity. "If you don't believe what you heard with your own ears, I don't know what I can do. The only place I've ever cheated on you is inside your head."

"Are these in my head?" he cried, snatching up a bundle of bearer bonds.

"I can't explain those," she said with conviction. "But I'm not involved with Kyle Auster in any way. I'll take a lie detector test, if you want."

Warren was staring at the bonds, not at her.

"*Think,*" she said. "Use that big brain of yours. Who could have told you where to find this stuff except the person who put it there?"

"Maybe that's how it is," he said slowly. "Maybe when Kyle dumped you, you kept his money for revenge. Maybe he's trying to get back at you like this."

"That's crazy!" she cried, causing the lock to jerk taut against her throat. "Think of the risks. And he'd never get his money back."

"Maybe it's his wife, then. E-mailing me, I mean. *She'd* damn sure have a reason to get back at him."

"You think Kyle would tell his wife about hidden money? Come on."

"I don't know. But I guess you do."

"I'm just guessing, for God's sake. Just like you. All I care about are those two children upstairs. They're going to know something's wrong pretty soon, if they don't already."

Warren gave her the same odd smile as before. "You don't have enough faith in them. They're fine. Whatever I tell them, they'll believe. They trust me, Laurel. They know who protects them."

*They know who takes care of them,* she thought. "You're right about one thing today. There's something bad going on around you. But you're wrong about me being part of it. Look how Kyle reacted just then. I offered the man a blow job, and he said no. Does that sound like Kyle Auster to you?"

Warren picked up the red ledger. He seemed to be trying to stare a hole through it.

Laurel said, "You need to forget about who's screwing who and ask Kyle about this financial stuff. Before something really bad happens."

She heard a bump upstairs. Then another. The kids were still up there.

"Maybe I will," Warren said, staring at the other phone. "Maybe I will."

Auster was swigging from the Diaka bottle again when his office door opened and Vida swept in the way his mother used to when he'd misbehaved as a boy. She shut the door behind her, then stood before his desk with a look so harsh that all his glib opening lines fled his brain.

"Are you drunk?" she asked.

"Vida . . . we're in trouble. Bad trouble."

Her expression didn't change. "You just figured that out, Sherlock?"

Auster studied the bleach-blond harpy standing with her arms crossed over her chest and wondered why he'd ever gotten involved with her. He could hardly bear to look at her anymore, much less give her what she wanted after hours. Worse, he sensed that she didn't even want the sex herself; it was simply a tool in her campaign to protect herself from a world that had always been less than kind to her.

"What's happened now?" she asked.

"I got a phone call while you were gone."

"From who? Biegler again?"

"No. Evans, up at the capital."

"And?"

Auster blew out a lungful of air. "He said Paul Biegler's driving down from Jackson to padlock the office. Now. As we speak."

This shook Vida from her pose. Shock pinned her painted eyelids back for several seconds, but then her features went hard again. "Let me guess. When you had Biegler on the phone, you got up on your hind legs and roared like a drunk frat boy. You can't keep that ego reined in, can you? I bet he's ready to put you under the jail."

Auster nodded in despair. "And I don't see what we can do besides sic him on Warren and hope he's content with that."

Vida gaped as though Auster had suggested driving

into a brick wall at sixty miles per hour. "Listen to me, *Doctor*. You're as crooked as a barrel of fishhooks, but when it comes to actually committing a crime, you're about as smart as a barrel of hair. The mystery is how you made it through medical school. They must have had a lot of lady professors up there, that's all I can figure—"

"Vida—"

"Damn it, Kyle. Blaming Shields depended on a low-key investigation and things falling just right. On sanitizing this office of anything and everything that could contradict our version of things. Losing a lot of records. And most of all, on our special patients keeping their goddamn mouths shut. But we're not near ready yet." She dug a cigarette out of her back pocket, lit it, and began puffing furiously.

"I wish you wouldn't do that."

"Shut the fuck up, Kyle. I'm thinking. The only way we could dump this thing in Shields's lap now is if he shot himself in the head with the evidence in his house. Then we'd be the only ones left to tell what happened, other than the patients. They'd be expensive, but—"

"What about the records?"

"Shut *up*! I'm trying to keep your ass out of jail."

He reached into his bottom drawer for the vodka.

Vida watched him take a slug with obvious contempt. Then she blew out a long stream of smoke and said, "I know what you're up to, mister. You've got some high-toned slut on the side, stashed and waiting for you to bug out with her. I don't know who she is, but I will in about twenty seconds, because you're going to tell me."

Auster reached for the bottle again, but Vida lashed

out with her hand and knocked it off his desk. The precious fluid gurgled onto the carpet.

"Don't sit there gasping like a landed fish. Tell me who she is."

"Vida, I wouldn't cheat on you."

"Jesus wept. Whoever she is, the slut is out of your life as of this moment. In exchange, I'm going to save you the indignity of nightly anal sex in Parchman Farm, where you most definitely would *not* be the top."

"Shannon Jensen," Auster whispered with the sound of a deflating balloon.

Vida's eyes flashed with fury and disbelief. "The drug rep from Jackson?"

He nodded.

"She's only twenty-three!"

Before Auster could reply, Vida said, "Of *course* she's only twenty-three. Young enough to buy into your bullshit and throw her life away before it's begun. God, you're a prick. That smug little sorority princess prancing up these halls with a corncob up her butt . . . *Jesus.*"

Vida was turning pale; primal anger was threatening to take over her higher brain functions. Before she could wind up again, Auster said, "I'm sorry, I'm an idiot. She's history. Just tell me what to do."

Vida flattened both hands on his desk and leaned over the charts lying there. "I've got half a mind to let Biegler clean your clock for you. I could turn state's evidence, send you to Parchman for twenty years, and walk away rich. They give rewards for that kind of evidence now. Monetary rewards. I'd be getting a massage in Cabo, while you'd be doing research on whether size really does matter or not."

Auster felt dizzy. "Vida, don't lose sight of what's—"

"I could do that," she went on, as though he hadn't spoken. "But I'm not. I don't want Nell getting in any kind of trouble."

"How can you prevent that?"

"By getting us all out clean." Her eyes drilled into him like twin X-ray beams. "I just need to know two things, bub."

"What?"

"One, that you're done with that sorority slut."

Auster nodded eagerly. "And?"

"Make the call, Kyle."

"What call? To Shannon?"

"Who else?"

"But Biegler's on the way!"

"I can't think of a better time. Make it short and not so sweet."

Auster took out his cell phone and speed-dialed Shannon Jensen. She answered with a husky tone, "Mmm, I wasn't expecting this. I'm on the road between Oxford and Tupelo, and it's *lonely*."

Auster banished phone sex from his mind. "Shannon, I need to tell you something."

"What?" Her alert business voice had come online.

"I have some bad news, honey. It's . . . it's not going to work out like we thought. It's just too complicated here. My marriage, I mean. I have to end it. You and me, I mean." Shannon gasped, but he pushed on before she could gather herself. "You deserve a lot better than me, you know that. I know you'll bounce back like nothing ever happened." The girl was screaming now, and sobbing, but the only word he could make out was

"Why?" He started to embellish his excuse, but Vida leaned closer and gave him his cue line.

"You're in love with someone else," she whispered.

Auster closed his eyes.

"Say it," Vida commanded.

"I'm in love with someone else, Shannon."

"Oh my God," Shannon cried. "Someone besides your wife?"

"That's right."

"I don't believe you!"

"Tell her who," Vida ordered.

"It's Vida," he said in desolation. "From up front. She's always been the one."

"Even when we were together," Vida whispered.

Auster grimaced, but he had no alternative. "Even when we were together, I was with her."

The line was dead. He prayed Shannon had hung up before she heard the last of it.

"There," Vida said with supreme satisfaction. "Doesn't that feel better?"

He forced himself to nod. "I was telling the truth. You have always been the one. I just . . . you know me. She made it so easy, and—"

"You're embarrassing yourself." Vida leaned back and put her hands on her hips like a drill sergeant. "Are you ready to do what you have to do to save us?"

He nodded.

"Can you grow a freaking backbone for five minutes?"

"Absolutely."

"Okay. I want you to drive over to Dr. Shields's house and get the stuff you planted there."

This stunned him. "What do you mean, get it?"

"Retrieve it. Take it out of the safe room and drive it to where I tell you."

"But why?"

"We need it to disappear. Forget blaming Warren. We need everything in that house to disappear. The second set of books, the coded records, everything. Most of all, the bonds. Biegler may have frozen your business accounts by now. Maybe even the personals."

"Jesus!"

"Do you understand?"

"Yes, but what if Warren's at home? He didn't come in today, which is pretty strange, and . . . oh, God."

"What?" Vida asked, her eyes narrowed.

"What if Warren is working *with* Biegler?"

Vida thought about this for a few seconds, then dismissed the idea with a shake of her head. "No. He'd never admit to the things he's done, not even for a big reward. His reputation means everything to him."

"He might do it to stay out of jail."

"I don't think he's at risk of going to jail. Not really. Even if they threw the book at him, he could plead out. We're the ones who could go to jail. But I'll tell you, there's something weird going on with our Warren. For five years, he's a Boy Scout. Then he walks in and says he needs money. Big money. And he starts breaking rules left and right. It doesn't add up. There's something fishy about that life insurance he got last year, too. I don't know what, but I know Warren's not about to start cooperating with the Feds. He hates the government. And in his eyes, he's got more to lose than any of us."

"Okay," Auster said, calming a little. "But if he's at home, I can't just waltz into his safe room and start carting stuff out. He'll freak out."

"Screw him, okay? This is life or death, Kyle. If you have to, go in with your key, grab the stuff, and get out. You know the code. Whatever he says or does, humor him, but get that shit out of there. Tell him the FBI planted it there. Or just ignore him. Shields won't hit you or anything. He's not the type. Not unless you were fucking his wife or something." Vida froze, her eyes boring into Auster's. "You're not, are you?"

"Hell, no!"

She returned his gaze without the slightest bit of faith. "If you're not, it's only because she wouldn't touch you with three sets of gloves on."

*That's what you think.* "You know Laurel, all right."

Vida chuckled. "Yes, I do. Way too much class for you."

He was surprised by how deeply this assertion stung. "What will you be doing while I'm at Warren's?"

Vida sat on the edge of his desk and looked at him with a strange light in her eyes. "Burning this office to the ground."

A bolt of terror went through him. "What? Burning . . . ?"

"You heard me. It's the only way, Kyle. And we've only got a few minutes to do it. Biegler and his guys are probably driving ninety miles an hour from Jackson, which makes it about an eighty-five-minute trip."

Auster felt sick. "But—"

"They've probably got somebody watching the office, too, to make sure we don't try to cart the files and computers out of here."

"They'll follow me when I leave," he thought aloud.

She nodded. "They will, if they recognize you."

"How could they not?"

She smiled. "Wait here."

Sixty seconds later, Vida walked in with some threadbare pants, a polyester work shirt, and a green John Deere cap.

"Where'd you get those?" he asked.

"Mr. Chaney. He's lying on the X-ray table in a paper gown. I think he's getting a good trade myself, and so will he. Your pants and button-down together probably cost three hundred bucks." She tossed the clothes into Auster's lap. "I doubt they'd take these rags at the Goodwill."

A reek of BO rose from his lap. "They stink!"

"Life's rough. Get changed, Doc."

"Do I take my own car?"

"Sure you do, chunkhead." Vida dug into her jeans and brought out a jingling key ring. "Mr. Chaney drives a black Chevy pickup. It'll be in the front lot. If we're lucky, Biegler's spy will be watching your Jag in the employees' lot. Change clothes, damn it!"

Auster removed his butter-soft Charles Tyrwhitt pinpoint and folded it carefully on his desk. Then he raised the stained work shirt and slid an arm into it. "*Ugh,*" he grunted, wrinkling his nose. "Is this the only way?"

Vida gave him a blue steel stare. "You'd better believe it."

"Don't you dare give Chaney the keys to my Jag."

"Forget the Jag, and forget your cell phone. Don't use it for anything, unless I tell you to. That's why I didn't answer your call before."

Auster's mind filled with images of his office burning, a black column of smoke bringing all the doctors and nurses out of the hospital three blocks away.

"I'll tell you one thing, buster," Vida said. "You're gonna owe me after this. For a very long time."

Auster nodded in surrender, but he knew Vida wouldn't buy it. Her father had been a pathological liar, and she saw all men as reflections of him. Sometimes he wondered if she was far wrong.

# CHAPTER

# 12

Nell sat at the reception desk and tried to look like a normal person, but inside she was a wreck. In the last few minutes the office had gone crazy. Vida was acting like some sort of secret agent, and a few minutes ago a strange man had shambled past in the hall, coming from the direction of Dr. Auster's office. Then an old man in X-ray had started yelling that someone had stolen his clothes. JaNel was looking for Dr. Auster and couldn't find him, and Vida had told Nell to hold down the front while she took care of some necessities. When Nell asked what was going on, Vida had leaned close and whispered, "Give me five minutes, hon. Then I'll tell you what to do." That was five minutes longer than Nell could stand, but she'd gritted her teeth and tried to look calm.

Then Dr. Shields called, and her legs turned to jelly. "I need to speak with Kyle," he said in a stiff voice.

"I don't think he's here, Dr. Shields," Nell said nervously.

"What kind of answer is that? Either he is or he isn't."

"Um . . . that's all I know at this point."

"Listen, if that son of a bitch is trying to avoid me, you tell him I said to get his ass on the phone."

Nell sat blinking in the wake of Dr. Shields's profanity. From Warren Shields, a curse word in the office was like an explosion. "Dr. Shields?" she ventured tentatively.

"Yes?"

"Can I tell you something?"

"What?"

She lowered her voice to a whisper. "I'm the one who's been e-mailing you."

Silence.

Nell was suddenly sure she'd made a mistake, but then Dr. Shields said, "You e-mailed me to look in my safe room?"

"That's right."

"But . . . how did you know what was in there?"

"I didn't. I still don't. But I knew it was dangerous. My sister told me about it. I was trying to help you. I mean, I *am* trying to."

"You did help me, Nell. Look, do you know anything about a letter? A love letter written in green ink?"

She thought back over all the papers she had seen in the past few days. "No, sir. Nothing like that."

There was a long pause. "What's going on up there today?"

Nell blinked away tears. Being able to talk to Dr. Shields directly was more relief than she could stand. "Things are out of control. I think some kind of agents from Jackson may be on their way here. Because of all the stuff Dr. Auster and my sister have been doing. You know what I'm talking about?"

"I'm afraid so."

"I haven't been a hundred percent perfect in my life," Nell said, "but I never meant to hurt anybody. And I know *you* didn't. And . . . I just don't want anything to happen to you. You don't deserve that, Dr. Shields."

"I'm going to be fine. Don't worry about me."

"I don't know. You're too trusting, and you sure can't trust Dr. Auster. Not a lick. Listen, if I hang up all of a sudden, it's because Vida's come in. I'll do whatever I can to help you, but you'd better not call back here. Not with those agents coming. You just do whatever you think is right. You can count on me to back you up."

Dr. Shields didn't speak for several seconds. Then he said, "Nell, I need to ask you something."

"Hurry."

"Is Kyle having an affair?"

"Well . . . yes, sir. With my sister."

"I know that. I'm talking about with someone else."

Nell wasn't sure she should say more, but she didn't want to hold anything back from Dr. Shields. It might hurt him in some way. "I did hear Dr. Auster on the phone with somebody two days ago. I think he's planning to run off with somebody new."

"Who?"

She sensed a sudden urgency in Dr. Shields's voice. "I don't know."

"Are you sure? Don't hold back to spare my feelings."

This comment confused her. Why should Dr. Auster's affair hurt his feelings? "I really don't. But you'd better—" Vida's cheap heels were clacking down the corridor. "Sorry, I have to go." Nell set the phone in its cradle and began typing entries on a Blue Cross insurance claim.

"Patients still calling?" Vida asked, walking in with two stuffed Walgreens bags.

"What do you think? It's like a tidal wave without Dr. Shields here."

"You just keep blowing them off, honey. And it doesn't matter what you tell them. Say we're gone to the NASCAR races. This shop is closing for good."

Nell stared openmouthed at her sister.

Vida gave back her "I meant what I said" look, then began opening the file cabinets against the back wall.


Laurel watched Warren's face as he hung up the phone. He had looked puzzled while he was talking, but now he wore an expression she couldn't begin to read.

"That was Nell Roberts?" she asked.

He didn't answer.

"Nell is the one who's been sending you e-mails?"

"Apparently. She's worried about me."

Laurel had met Nell a few times, but only in passing. A pretty girl in her late twenties, she looked as if she'd come from a different family than her putative older sister. "How could Nell possibly know anything about me?"

Warren seemed to be working something out in his head. "Through Vida, I guess. Vida's got a vested interest in protecting her relationship with Kyle."

Laurel saw where this was going. "Warren, don't try to bend things around to fit your preconceptions. Look at the facts. You obviously didn't even know who was telling you this stuff. What if Nell has an ulterior motive herself?"

"Like what?"

"Maybe she's in love with you."

"That's ridiculous."

"Why? She's young and single, and you're a handsome doctor, her boss—"

"I'm not going to listen to that crap. Nell is the only good person in that whole snake pit. She doesn't even belong there."

"She can be a good person and still do not-so-good things. And anybody can be mistaken about things they see or hear."

Warren raised his eyebrows. "Well, she's apparently heard that Kyle is planning to run away with someone. A new girlfriend, she said. And that seems to square with the two hundred grand in bonds hidden in our safe room. Guatemalan bonds, huh? Were you planning to take our children with you?"

Laurel suddenly realized that reason would never get her out of this. No matter what facts surfaced, Warren would find a way to fit them into his betrayal scenario. "Listen to me. I'm not going to discuss Kyle anymore. I haven't had sex with him, I don't even like him, and I can't answer any of your questions. I don't know what those bonds are doing here, or the ledgers, or anything else. I know *nothing,* okay? Kyle is your partner and your problem. End of story."

Warren looked at his watch for a long time, as though calculating the number of hours he'd been awake. Laurel guessed thirty-four. How rational could anyone be after that kind of sleep deprivation? He yawned as if trying to swallow his head with his own mouth, stretching his arms back until his shoulders popped.

"Do you want to see the kids?" he asked.

She looked at him in disbelief. "You're going to untie me?"

"If you promise to behave."

"Can I clean up before they see me?"

"You worry too much about your looks. We go upstairs as is, or forget it."

Laurel wasn't sure she should let the kids see her in her present state. But somewhere in the back of her brain simmered a fear that she might not survive this encounter. "Okay."

With a quick turn of the dials, Warren opened the bike lock. One moment she was a chained prisoner, the next she was free. Free to move, at least. She was still a prisoner.

She'd expected to be led straight upstairs, but he took her arm and walked her back to the great room, where her laptop sat clicking on the coffee table. Interposing himself between Laurel and the machine, he looked down at the screen to check the progress of the password-cracking program. Around his back, Laurel saw the Hotmail log-in page superimposed in miniature over a background page, which showed a gray-bearded wizard staring wisely up from the screen. Lightning flashed from the staff in his hand, but what held Laurel's attention was the numerical ticker below the wizard. It was seven digits long, and the last three digits were increasing almost too fast to see, like the digital readout of a gas pump filling a bottomless tank. Above this, a line of asterisks filled the PASSWORD field of the Hotmail log-in page, and a red error message

read SIGN IN FAILED. The asterisks and letters appeared
to be permanent, but as Laurel stared, she realized that
they were blinking so rapidly that she almost could not
detect it. Somehow, the cracker program had disabled
the feature that kicked people off after ten failed attempts. She felt as though a ghostly robot were sitting
at her computer, trying to break into her e-mail account at the speed of light.

"Any minute now," Warren said, glancing around
at her. "Nervous?"

She turned away. "Let's go see the kids."

"Yes. Let's do that."

He led her up the front stairs, only letting go of her
arm when they reached the top. Laurel heard the TV
blaring through the closed door of the kids' playroom.
She tried to steel herself, but she knew she would cry
when she saw them. She had once burst into tears
upon seeing them after a five-day education seminar in
Dallas. She expected Warren to warn her in some way,
but he simply pocketed his gun, opened the door, and
cried, "Hey, hey! Look who's here!"

Laurel heard a scuttling sound to her left, but saw
nothing there. Her eyes were drawn to the couch,
where Grant lay sprawled on his back watching the
big-screen TV. He'd changed his royal blue school
uniform shirt for a ripped GIRL skateboard T-shirt,
and his New Balances for Adios with stripped black
laces. On the screen before him, Tony Hawk leaped
and spun over the lip of a massive half-pipe, which
Grant never tired of begging Warren to build in the
backyard.

"Hey, Mom," Grant said, moving his eyes but nothing else. "How's your headache?"

"A little better," Warren said quickly. "She's not over it yet. Where's your sister?"

"Over *here*," said a small voice. "Ta-da!"

Beth jumped out from behind the closet door. Laurel had to cover her mouth to hide the pain that pierced her at the sight. Beth was wearing the Snow White costume Laurel had bought her during their last trip to Disney World. Not the cheap one-piece costume, but the full-blown ensemble of yellow satin and dark blue velvet, with bright red ribbons like the ones in the Disney classic. Beth's proud smile and flashing eyes made her look impossibly alive and happy, like a character who had leaped out of a movie herself.

"How do I *look*?" she asked.

Laurel bit her lip and knelt before her daughter. "Did you put this on all by yourself, Snow White?"

Beth curtsied with elaborate ceremony.

"I helped," Grant said from the couch.

"No, you didn't!" Beth cried.

Grant shrugged.

"He just tied my bow," Beth explained. "Nothing else."

"*Riiiight,*" Grant drawled.

"Shut up, Butt Face."

Grant broke up at this.

"Stop provoking her," Warren snapped. Then he looked down at Beth. "And you stop saying 'Butt Face,' young lady."

"Well, he is."

As Grant stifled more laughter, Laurel hugged her daughter as tightly as she dared. "Mama?" Beth's small voice in her ear. "Are you okay?"

"I'm fine now, baby. I just had to see you."

"I don't want your head to hurt."

Hot tears slid down Laurel's cheeks. She bent her neck and wiped her cheeks on Beth's cape. Then she pulled away.

"Mama, your hands are all sticky. And your mascara's running!"

Laurel stuck out her bottom lip and blew air over her face, hoping to dry the tears. "It's just my headache, darling. Are you guys all right for food and stuff?"

"I'm hungry," Grant said. "Can we come down and mikeywave something?"

"Not yet," said Warren. "I'll bring something up to you in a minute. But first we need to talk."

A frisson of fear went through Laurel's chest. She turned to Warren, but he wasn't looking at her. He took Beth's hand and led her over to the sofa, where Grant lay.

"Sit up, Son," he said. "Come on, get your behind in gear. This is a family conference."

Grant groaned loudly. "But I'm *starving*."

Laurel wanted to bolt from the room. She saw now that Warren had brought her up here not to ease her mind, but to torture her more painfully than he ever could downstairs. Grant and Beth sat side by side on the sofa, their upturned faces curious but unworried. Snow White and a skateboard prince. A more innocent pair of angels she could not imagine. Warren pulled two chairs over in front of the couch and sat facing the kids, then motioned for her to join him.

She couldn't move.

"Come here, Laurel," he said. "This won't take long."

"What is it, Daddy?" Beth asked. "Did Christy poop inside the house again?"

"No, sweetheart. This is more serious than that."

When Laurel refused to move, Warren shrugged as if to say, *All right*. Then he turned to the children and said, "Your mother has something to tell you, guys. So pay close attention." He turned to Laurel expectantly.

"Warren," she said evenly, "I need to speak to you outside."

He smiled in apparent sympathy. "Mom's having a hard time finding the right words, kids. So I'll help. While you kids have been going to school, and while I've been working hard at the hospital, Mom has been making a new friend."

Grant's eyes narrowed. "Really? Who is it, Mom?"

Laurel stared at her husband, silently begging him not to go on. But the hatred in his eyes was unveiled now, and it was absolute. Nothing was going to stop him. She thought of grabbing the kids and trying to get out of the room, but that would only result in a fight with Warren, which might scar them even more.

"It's a man," Warren said. "I don't know who it is yet, because Mom won't tell me. But she's been going to a secret place every day and hugging and kissing this man."

Beth's eyes were wide. They moved from Warren to Laurel, filled with questions. Laurel wanted to say, *That's not true, sweetheart*. But it *was* true. She had been doing exactly what Warren was accusing her of doing.

"I know it seems hard to understand," Warren went on, "but Mama's getting tired of us. Our family is starting to bore her, so she's looking for another one. One that might make her happier."

Her children's faces were moving in ways Laurel had never seen before. She was witnessing the implosion of innocence. And she, not Warren, was responsible. Though Warren was the one talking, she felt as if she were holding down her children and hitting them in the face again and again, and they could not fight back.

"Mama?" Beth said, her voice scarcely a whisper. "Is that right? Are you tired of us?"

Laurel realized that her hands were shaking. And not just her hands. Her chin was quivering, and her legs were turning to water.

"Why are you crying, Mom?" Grant asked worriedly. He no longer looked like a smart-aleck teenager, but the terrified nine-year-old he really was. "Dad, what's wrong? I don't like this game."

"I don't either, Son. But Mom hasn't given us any choice. She's already made her decision." He waved Laurel over to the chair beside him. "Come on, honey. I want you to explain things to Grant and Beth as best you can. They deserve to know the truth."

*There's no way I'm staying married after this,* Laurel thought. *And if Danny had left his wife five weeks ago, like he said he would, I would have faced a scene a lot like this one. Warren wants me to tell them I had an affair? All right, I'll tell them what I would have told them five weeks ago. Not that I'm in love with someone else, but that I don't love Daddy anymore. That* should *be easy enough. I don't love Daddy anymore. But I love them more than I ever have. They'll know I'm telling the truth about that, because that* is *the truth—*

"Get over here!" Warren snapped. "Have the courage of your convictions, damn it."

"I'm scared," Beth whimpered through glistening tears. She held out her arms for Laurel to pick her up, but when Laurel moved, Warren stood and blocked her path.

"Dad, you're scaring us," Grant said with surprising force. "You're scaring Mom, too!"

"That can't be helped, Son. Mama's done a very bad thing."

"No!" Beth cried. "She *couldn't* do something bad. Mama's good!"

Warren looked as though he might be crying himself. "I know you believe that, Elizabeth, but I'm afraid it's not true. That's one of the hard things about growing up—facing the fact that adults aren't all good. And your mother is capable of doing some very bad things. You two get punished when you do bad things, don't you?"

Grant nodded reluctantly.

"Then Mom should, too. We all have to follow the same rules. That's—"

"You sorry son of a bitch," Laurel said under her breath. "You should be ashamed."

Warren turned to her, his eyes red. "*I* should be ashamed? The shame is all yours today, my love. Did you ever think about these children when you were betraying them? Did you think about them for five seconds while you—"

"*STOP IT!*" Beth screamed. "*STOPITSTOPIT-STOPITSTOPIT!*"

"Be quiet, Elizabeth!" Warren snapped.

"*AAAAAAAAHHHHHHHHHHHHHHHHH!*"

Beth's earsplitting scream made all other communication impossible. Warren stood over her as if to make her stop, but he was faced with the fact that nothing short of violence could do it, and that was likely to provoke even more screams—or worse, total silence. If Laurel could have snatched the gun from his pocket at that moment, she might have shot him through the heart. She had betrayed her duty to her children, yes. But nothing justified the psychological torture he was putting them through now. And for what? For revenge, the most useless thing in the world.

"Warren, you have to stop," she said, while Beth recharged her lungs between screams. "You've made your point."

"Have I?" he asked, scowling over his shoulder.

Beth cut loose with another shriek, and this time Laurel rushed forward and snatched her up off the sofa. "I've got you, darling, I've got you," she murmured in Beth's ear. "Everything's all right now. Daddy was just telling a story."

"Were you?" asked Grant, hope in his eyes.

"No, Son. I'm afraid not. And soon we're all going to know who Mom's new friend is."

Something in Laurel snapped then. She turned far to the left, winding up, then flung out her right arm and backhanded Warren with all the force she could summon. The slap resounded through the room, leaving total shock in its wake. While Warren rubbed blood from the end of his nose, Grant gaped in shock.

"Mom just hit you, Dad," he said, as though trying to get his mind around what his eyes had just seen. "She knocked the *crap* out of you!"

"It's just a game," Laurel said, gently rocking Beth

in her arms while Warren watched her with madness in his eyes.

"What game is that?" Grant asked.

"Austin Powers," Laurel replied, grabbing the first suitable image she could find amid the clutter of her pop-culture memory. "I think Beth needs a nap, gentlemen."

She started to carry Beth to her bedroom, but Warren's right hand slid into the pocket that held his pistol. "Think," she said softly. "Think about what you're doing."

"You didn't think."

"You're right. I should have—" Laurel stood with her mouth open, but no sound emerged. The doorbell had just rung. The echo of its musical ping was still fading.

"Someone's at the door," Grant piped up. "Maybe it's UPS with my new trucks!"

The bell rang again, three times in quick succession.

"Nobody move," Warren said in the voice of a TV cop. He went to the dormer window and looked down toward the front entrance of the house.

"Who is it?" asked Grant.

"Probably some guy wanting to pressure-wash the house," Warren muttered. "There's a beat-up pickup parked at the end of the sidewalk."

Wild hope flashed through her at the thought of Danny's old Ford pickup.

"Jesus Christ," Warren said, his whole body tensing at the window.

"What?" Laurel asked, her heart beating against her sternum.

Warren turned from the window, his face pale with
fury. "It's Kyle Auster."

Ever since talking to Dr. Shields, Nell had been terrified that he would call back and speak to her sister. If he repeated some of the things Nell had told
him, Vida would flip out. And Vida angry was not
something anybody wanted to deal with. At sixteen,
she'd become too much for even their father. But Dr.
Shields hadn't called back, nor had Dr. Auster reappeared. Vida kept leaving the reception desk and
then coming back. The lights in the office had blinked
a couple times, and once they'd gone off completely
for a full minute, which kicked the computers into
emergency-power mode. When Nell asked what was
going on, Vida had just put her finger to her lips and
smiled.

Now Vida returned from one of her little excursions
and slid her chair right up to Nell's. She smelled of
rubbing alcohol.

"What's going on?" Nell asked. "I'm nervous as a
cat."

Vida smiled and ran her hand through Nell's hair
the way their mother used to do. "So pretty. So dark
and fine."

"Vi—"

"Shhh. I want you to get your purse and go home,
sweetie. Right now."

Nell drew back in surprise. "Go home? Now?"

Vida nodded. "Things are getting out of hand. I
don't want you around here for the last act."

Nell felt a surge of concern for her sister. "What's
going to happen?"

"Nothing too bad. I told you there were revenue agents watching the office. There's more coming to close us down this evening."

Nell blinked in disbelief. "Close us down?"

"Yep. Padlock the building."

Nell shook her head like a child hearing that her parents' home was about to be repossessed. "But . . . are you saying it's over? Everything?"

Vida smiled again. "I wouldn't say that. You know I always keep a card or two up my sleeve. But the easy part's over with. You need to get home, throw some clothes in an overnight bag—nothing too big—then go down to the bank and take out your money."

Nell's anxiety escalated into outright fear. "All of it?"

"You've got most of the liquid part in your brokerage accounts, right? With UBS?"

"Yes, just like you told me."

"The government may have frozen those accounts, but I doubt it. They wouldn't want to tip their hand. They'd freeze Kyle and Warren's money first, not ours. Your real money's in the house in Texas anyway, and they can't take that from you. That's where you should go. Withdraw about eight thousand in cash and light out in your car. Tell the girls at the bank you're buying a used car and the seller wants cash. If things get dicey here, I'll call your cell phone. If that happens, stop in Baton Rouge and get on a plane to Cancún. I don't care what it costs, just haul tail. South of the border, you hear me?"

Nell nodded, but she was close to crying. "What about Dr. Shields?"

"He's going to be fine, baby. Don't you worry about

Warren. Kyle's on his way over there now to take out the stuff he planted."

"You promise?"

"Honey, I scared the bejesus out of Kyle. That stuff is probably already in a Dumpster somewhere."

Nell wiped away her tears, but more followed.

"I tell you, though," Vida said thoughtfully, "there may be trouble in paradise."

"What do you mean?"

"Kyle thinks Laurel and Warren are having marital problems. You think maybe you could be part of the reason for that?"

"Oh my God, no," Nell protested, wishing it were true. "No way."


Warren stood rigid in the foyer, his left hand clutching Laurel's wrist, his right hand holding his gun. The doorbell rang again, for the sixth time. Kyle had obviously seen the cars in the driveway and did not intend to go away. Laurel wondered why Warren didn't simply answer the door.

Then she saw why.

There was a scratching sound in the lock, and the bolt turned with a decisive snick. He backed her against the wall, so that they would be behind the door if it opened. The lock in the doorknob turned next. Then the door opened about twelve inches. Kyle stuck his head through the crack and looked toward the stairs.

The barrel of Warren's gun touched his temple. "Come on in, partner," Warren said softly. "Nice and easy."

Auster stepped inside with his hands up and his eyes wide. If he hadn't stuck his head in first, Laurel might not have recognized him. The noted clotheshorse was wearing garments that looked as if they'd been bought at the Salvation Army store downtown. And he *stank*.

"What the hell are you wearing?" Warren asked.

"This is my new look," Kyle said, but the fear in his voice killed his attempt at levity.

Warren studied him for a few seconds, then said, "It's a disguise, isn't it?"

Auster nodded, his face downcast.

"You decided you wanted that quickie after all?"

"Hell no," Auster replied, slowly lowering his hands. "That's not why I'm here. I knew that was a joke."

"You've got a key to our house, though, huh?"

"You gave it to me. Don't you remember? I fed your dog when y'all went to the Bahamas that time."

Warren thought about this. "You gave that key back."

"Well, I had a copy made. In case I lost the original. You know I'm always losing my keys. I didn't want your kids' dog to starve because I can't keep up with anything."

Warren looked at Laurel. "He's a compulsive liar. Did you know that? I've seen him lie to patients, drug reps, other doctors, anybody—even when he doesn't have to. It's like an addiction or something."

Kyle wasn't listening. His full attention was on the pistol. "Warren, man . . . what's with the gun?"

"I want truthful answers. This helps."

*It hasn't helped so far,* Laurel thought.

Auster looked at him long and hard. "No offense, buddy, but have you lost your mind? There's no need for this kind of theatrics. We're all friends here, right?"

"I lost my mind the day I went to work for you," Warren said in a somber voice. "Only I didn't know it."

"Come on, partner. What kind of talk is that?"

"Straight talk."

Auster held up his hands as though he knew where Warren was headed. "Look, I don't need a Boy Scout lecture, okay? I'm a lost cause. Anyway, I thought you gave up all that Dudley Do-Right stuff last year. Huh?"

Laurel had no idea what Kyle was talking about, but Warren certainly seemed to. He looked as though Auster's words had wounded him deeply. She glanced up the staircase to make sure the children hadn't come to the rail to listen. Warren had warned them to stay in the media room, but they were so rattled, there was no telling what they might do. "Could we move this to another room?" she asked. "I don't want the kids hearing this stuff."

Warren grabbed Kyle's wrist and dragged him down to the great room. Kyle was three inches taller than Warren, but Warren was in peak physical condition. Auster had spent the last twenty years going soft. They stood between the fireplace and the Roche-Bobois sectional like two boxers who might close at any moment. Laurel leaned against the sofa back and glanced over it at her computer, terrified that the Merlin's Magic program might have cracked her password while they were upstairs. The Sony was still clicking away, but Warren seemed to have forgotten it.

"First you push me to bend the rules," Warren said. "Then to break them. Then—"

"Whoa there, Dr. Welby," said Kyle. "Sure I tried

to get you more focused on the bottom line. But when you told me to back off, I did. It was you who came to me that last time, remember? Out of the blue. 'I need to make more money, Kyle.' That's what you said. And do you remember what you said after that?"

Warren had turned to stare out the tall windows. There were two rows of them, one atop the other, and through them Laurel saw the pale, virginal green of early spring in the budding leaves. A hundred yards from the house, Christy trotted toward the line of trees that marked the creek's ravine, her orange coat giving her the appearance of a well-fed fox. Only the darkening sky kept the picture from being perfect. It seemed that Mrs. Elfman's augury of rain might be proved accurate after all.

"You said, 'I don't care how you do it,'" Kyle continued. "'Just don't tell me about it.'"

Warren scowled at him. "I didn't mean for you to—"

"I know what you meant, brother. So I doubled your income, and you took the money. And here we are. That's the way it works."

Laurel stared at Warren in amazement. She couldn't imagine the words Kyle had quoted ever coming from her husband's mouth. But apparently they had, because Warren wasn't arguing the point.

"We'll have to agree to disagree about that," Warren said. "But you going behind my back to screw my wife was definitely not what I asked for."

Auster was clearly stunned, but he was a quick study when it came to matters sexual, and Laurel could see him working out the particulars of the current situation. Her strange telephone come-on, the gun, all of it.

"You really hate me, don't you?" Warren said.

"Hate you? Warren, I love you, brother. You're my hero, which is weird since I'm ten years older than you. But you've got to be the most dedicated doctor in this town. Like a young Doc Adams on *Gunsmoke* or something. You think I *hate* you?"

Warren was studying the maple floor. Kyle took this moment to risk full eye contact with Laurel, and the words she read in his face were *What the hell is wrong with him?*

"It doesn't matter," Warren said to the floor. "Just tell me what you're doing here."

"What do you think?" Auster's eyes kept darting to the gun. "You didn't show up for work, and that was a first. We were overrun with patients, but I thought I'd take the first chance to come see how you're doing. I'm sure Laurel's been taking good care of you. I figured she'd be at school, though."

Warren looked up. "You figured she was at school when she called and asked you here for a quick fuck?"

"I figured she'd gone back, I mean."

"It's after three, Kyle."

Auster couldn't hide the blood rushing to his cheeks. "Look, bro, I don't know what's going on over here, and I don't want to know. You guys are having some marital discord? That's cool. I've been there. Everybody has. But I've got nothing to do with you guys' problems, I'm happy to say."

Warren moved closer to him, aiming the gun from his waist. "I'm not so sure of that, buddy. Not sure at all."

"Why not?"

"What's happening at the office, Kyle? Nell said there are Medicaid agents coming down."

Auster's face twisted with exasperation. "You know the government. Always interfering. They want six sets of paperwork on every patient, and they go batshit when you don't give it to them."

"Stop lying, Kyle. I know why they're coming. But I have a feeling things are even worse than you've told me. What have you been doing besides up-coding?"

"Nothing, man. Nothing illegal, anyway. They just . . . they don't agree with me about the necessity of certain tests on certain patients. Maybe some procedures, too, but you know how that is. They're pencil pushers. They don't have any sympathy for defensive medicine, because nobody's gonna sue their ass if a patient croaks unexpectedly."

Laurel wasn't sure why they were talking about work when Warren's primary obsession had been whom she might be sleeping with, but it was clear that they were in serious trouble.

"Tell me about your girlfriend," Warren said.

Auster looked perplexed. "My girlfriend?"

"Aren't you planning to run away with somebody? Isn't that what you were going to use the bearer bonds for?"

At the mention of bonds, Kyle's mouth hung slack. Then he gulped and started talking fast. "So you found that stuff? Thank God it's safe. Are the ledgers in there, too?"

Warren nodded slowly.

"Good, good. Because that stuff's dangerous, man."

"Back to your girlfriend."

Auster seemed to have trouble following the change of subject. "You mean Vida?"

"No. Your *other* girlfriend."

Auster's eyes flicked back and forth between Warren and the gun. "You mean Shannon?"

"Shannon?"

"Yeah, the drug rep for Hoche. The one with the tits and the eyes?"

Now Warren looked confused. "You've been seeing Shannon Jensen?"

"Uh-huh."

"How old is she?"

"Twenty-three. Jesus, what's the big deal? She's legal. Everybody asks that."

"That's not who I'm asking about, Kyle."

"Who, then? Come on, man, we don't have all day here."

Warren tilted his head toward Laurel. Auster held out his hands like a rustler about to be hanged by angry ranchers. "Brother, I don't know where you got this idea, but you are wrong. *Way* wrong."

"What exactly have I got wrong?"

"This whole idea is ridiculous! Laurel wouldn't touch me with a ten-foot pole." Kyle looked at her with complete confidence. "Would you?"

"No, I wouldn't. I think I've always made that clear."

Auster turned to Warren and held up his palms in apology. "I won't say I never squeezed her ass at the hospital Christmas party, okay? But that's just vodka talking. I do that because she's hot and because I know it gets to her and because nothing's going to come of it. Man, you don't really think I'd try to snake your wife?

That's nothing but trouble for me. I'm gonna lose a productive partner over some tail? No way. Not in my DNA."

Warren's eyes flickered with a glow Laurel couldn't read. "That kind of challenge is the cornerstone of your DNA, Kyle. But Laurel is more than the usual compulsive conquest. You've always been jealous of me. The way patients talk about me, the fact that so many of them request me specifically. Even the scores I made on my boards. You know you'll never beat me at those things, so what do you do? You go after Laurel. Maybe she's my weakness, right? If you can screw my wife and make her come, all will be right with the world. That's how your mind works."

Auster's face fairly shone with disbelief. "Jesus, pal, you need to get a life. Or a psychiatrist. I don't even try to compete with guys like you, except in income. That's where I show my stuff. Medic for hire, that's me. I leave the Doctors Without Borders shtick to you guys."

"What are those bonds doing in my house?" Warren asked doggedly.

Something changed in Kyle then. The boyish facade fell away, and a weary man appeared from behind it. "We needed a storage room. That's all. A safe one."

"We?"

"Vida and me. It was her idea. Who was going to search *your* house, you know?"

"The Medicaid Fraud Unit, I imagine," Warren said.

"That's why I'm here. Today is the day of reckoning, partner. I came here to remove the threat, to get you and your family out of harm's way. So why don't you let me do what I came to do? Then you two can continue your little tête-à-tête."

Laurel surprised herself by speaking. "What exactly is going on here? What have you two been doing at work?"

"Ask him," said Warren. "But you don't have to, do you? You already know. You're playacting just like he is."

"*Damn* it," Laurel said, "would you get over it already? I don't know anything, and I'm sick of being in the dark. What kind of trouble have you geniuses gotten us into?"

Warren turned back to Auster. "She has a secret Hotmail account, and she refuses to give me the password. I have a special program working to crack it. If your name doesn't pop up as her secret pen pal, then you can go."

Rather than calming Auster down, these words sent him into apoplexy. "Are you *shitting* me? That could take all night! The cops could be here in five minutes! With *handcuffs*!"

Despite Kyle's panic, Warren remained unmoved. "Then you're out of luck, unless the program finishes before then."

Kyle turned on Laurel. "Give him the fucking password."

Warren's eyes flashed with interest.

"Give it to him, goddamn it!" Auster screamed. "This is my life here!"

*And mine, you bastard. And the life of someone I actually love.* "I don't even know the password," she said. "Warren's gone paranoid."

Warren was watching Auster, trying to judge whether

he was sincere or not. Without a word, Warren walked around to the coffee table, picked up Danny's letter, then came back and held it out to Auster. "If you're bored, here's some reading material to pass the time."

Kyle took the letter like someone forced to accept literature from a Hare Krishna. He scanned it quickly, then looked from Laurel to Warren. "You *know* I didn't write this crap, partner."

"Do I?"

"All that hokey can't-live-without-you stuff? Are you kidding? You of all people should know I couldn't even make that up. My love letters read like something out of the *Penthouse* Forum."

"Maybe they did until you fell for my wife."

Auster was turning purple. He had the face of an innocent man being dragged bodily into prison.

"Besides," Warren went on, "I've recently discovered that my blushing bride might be a fan of the *Penthouse* Forum. She's a closet porn addict."

"This is insane," Laurel muttered.

With sudden defiance, Kyle shook Danny's letter under Warren's nose. "This isn't my handwriting, kemo sabe. It's not even close."

"Do you know whose it is?"

"How could I? It's block print. It could be anybody's. Or nobody's. I don't know any grown men who write this way. I think somebody's messing with you. And you don't have *time* for that right now. Look around you, man. You're married to one of the greatest women ever. You've got two fine kids. Get past this high school bullshit and think about what really matters. Being free to raise your children, not stuck in a cell somewhere."

Laurel found herself nodding. Amazingly, when the shit hit the fan, it was Auster who had his priorities in line, whereas Warren seemed lost.

Kyle dropped the letter on the floor and stared hard into Warren's eyes. "You want the truth, buddy? Listen up. We were going to let you take the fall. Vida and me. That's why the bonds and the ledgers are here. But it's all happening too fast. The only way out for any of us now is to get rid of *all* the evidence. Everything, ASAP. Those ledgers have to go, and the bonds have to disappear."

His pragmatic tone broke through Warren's sarcastic front. "And how do you suggest we manage that?" Warren asked.

"We go down to the creek behind your house and have a little bonfire. Then I'll take the bonds somewhere safe."

Warren laughed. "As a favor to me, right? You'll take that two hundred thousand off my hands?"

"Do you want the bonds for yourself? Is that what this is about?"

"I want to know what they're really doing here!"

Kyle spoke as he might to a child. "I just told you. I planted them here last week—with the ledgers—so that you'd take the fall for what's been going on at the office. That's it. End of story."

When Warren didn't respond, Kyle turned to Laurel. "What the fuck is wrong with this guy?"

"He won't take yes for an answer."

Kyle tapped Warren on the shoulder. "You want my secrets? I was screwing Shannon Jensen, okay? Midlife crisis maximus. But Vida caught me, so I ditched her. But *your wife* was nowhere in my plans." Kyle glanced at Laurel, then pushed on, his voice ragged with fear. "We're standing on the edge of a cliff, partner. You wouldn't believe the penalties they have now. I'm talking fifty years in prison and millions of dollars in fines. Tens of millions. That's buried so deep you'll never get another chance at life. We've got to take care of each other now."

Contempt chilled Warren's eyes. "Like you've taken care of me all along?"

Kyle groaned in frustration. "Buddy . . . most of the time, life is every man for himself. But *sometimes,* we all have to pull together. We have to hang together, or we'll all hang separately, right? Ben Franklin said that."

"The circumstances were rather different."

"Yeah, well, the sentiment's the same. Come on, bro. Don't be a sucker."

"But I am. That's what I've always been." Warren pursed his lips, his gaze far away. Laurel tried to read his face, but her old systems of spousal interpretation were no longer reliable. She had no idea how this new version of Warren reasoned. He looked from Kyle to her like a man trying to judge the lesser of two evils.

"The computer will decide," he said finally. "That's the only thing I can trust. If you're not Laurel's e-mail buddy, you can go."

Auster stared at his junior partner for several seconds. "You're crazy if you think I'm staying here. I'm not spending my last good years in prison because your wife is poking somebody else. You'll just have to shoot me." He turned and started walking toward the foyer, which probably meant the safe room.

Warren raised his pistol and cocked it with a loud click. "It's your choice."

Auster took two more steps. Then he stopped and looked back, his face sagging under the strain. Laurel saw a wet glint in his eyes.

"You're committing suicide," Kyle said. "Okay, fine. But why make me do it with you?"

"Because we're partners," Warren replied, smiling with irony. "We share everything, right?"

# CHAPTER

# 13

Nell was standing in line for a teller at the Planter's Bank when a blast of precognition so strong it made her dizzy hit her. She didn't know what to call it: foreboding, ESP, the heebie-jeebies, whatever. She just knew in her heart that something was dreadfully wrong at the office. Something about Vida's manner had rattled her to the bone, but without her quite realizing it. It was a delayed reaction, like somebody dying in the night from a blow to the head during the day.

Vida was too calm.

The situation was unraveling, yet she was walking around and joking like a jaded undertaker at a funeral. Nell hurried out to her car, drove down the frontage road, and crossed Highway 24 onto Audubon Boulevard. Then she turned into the employee parking lot, which was practically deserted, except for Dr. Auster's Jaguar and Vida's old Pontiac. She ran to the back door of the office, which was locked and bolted. She let herself in with her key, then moved quietly into the hall.

The door to exam room six was partly open. She

saw stockinged feet sticking off the examining table. So there were still patients here. But she saw no staff whatever. As she passed X-ray, she looked in, but Sherry wasn't at her counter. Same in the lab. No sign of JaNel, and the lights were off. The blood-chemistry machines were still running, though.

A cold chill raced the length of her body, and her shoulders jerked as though a static charge had suddenly left her. The building seemed alien to her, as though she had entered an office that *looked* like the one where she worked, but was not. Some of the office buildings near the hospital were almost identical. But not this one. Dr. Auster's building had a hipped roof and dormers, unlike the "modern" boxes with flat tar roofs standing in front of the hospital.

Suddenly Nell understood the reason for her anxiety. The computers were silent. She had never been inside the office when the computers were shut off. It seemed a different place without their steady, reassuring hum. The machines gave the building a sense of being alive, whereas now the whole place seemed dead.

The clinic had always smelled of rubbing alcohol, but as Nell neared the reception area, its biting odor became overpowering. And there was something else in the air, too. Something even more volatile . . .

*Gasoline.*

She rounded the arch that led to reception and saw Vida leaning over an open file drawer. Vida was pouring something into the drawer, right onto the papers. It was alcohol, Nell realized. Rubbing alcohol from one of the brown push bottles they used in the exam rooms. Twenty other file drawers stood open to various lengths.

"Vi?" she said softly.

Vida jerked erect and whirled, but relaxed when she saw it was only her sister.

"What are you doing?" Nell asked.

"TCB, honey. In a flash. Like Elvis always said."

"What?"

Vida laughed. "Taking care of business in a flash. I forget how much younger you are sometimes."

"Not that much," Nell said, very afraid and not quite sure why.

"A lifetime, baby girl. I thought I told you to clear out."

"I had a bad feeling. Like I get sometimes, you know?"

Vida looked down at the file drawer and sighed.

Nell scanned the room, and what she saw sent her to the edge of panic. Empty alcohol bottles were all over the room. Most stood in a row on the floor by her computer, but some lay atop the file drawers. A red metal gas can stood right beneath Vida's desktop. If someone lit a match in here, they would all die in a giant fireball.

"Why are you doing this?" Nell asked.

"No other way." Vida opened another bottle of alcohol and dumped its contents into a drawer full of patient records. "We're having a fire sale. Everything must go! No exceptions!"

Her laughter had a hysterical edge that scared Nell. "Is this why you went to the store today?"

"Mm-hm. We didn't have enough alcohol. But they had loads of it at Walgreens. I had to sneak it in, inside an old Dell computer box. The Medicaid people have somebody watching the back door. They're waiting for their pit bull to get here."

"Pit bull?"

Vida's humor evaporated. "You need to go, baby. Now."

"But . . . how can you light this stuff without killing yourself?"

Vida's smile was cagey. "I go down to the switch box and shut off the main breaker. Then I come back here and plug the computers and copiers back in. One more trip down the hall, flip the breaker on, and *boom!* Gone with the wind."

"How do you know about this kind of stuff?"

"I had a boyfriend who did insurance jobs. Torch jobs, you know? Remember Randy?"

Nell vaguely remembered a scrawny, unshaven Cajun of indeterminate age.

"But we don't have time for nothing fancy," Vida said with regret. "You do the best you can with what you got."

Nell stepped farther into the room. "There are still patients in the back, Vida. I saw somebody on the way in."

"Just a couple. I'll take them out with me." Vida tossed the empty bottle on the floor. "A heroic rescue will make it look more like an accident. As if anything could. But we try."

"Where's everybody else?"

"I sent them home. Told them we'd had a computer crash and couldn't keep up with billing or insurance. They were out of here like a shot."

"And Dr. Auster?"

"He's getting that stuff out of Warren's house, like I promised he would."

Nell felt a warm rush of gratitude. "Vi . . . why don't

we just get out of here? You've got money squirreled away, I know you do. Let's *both* go down to Cancún. We could rent a condo by the month and just figure out what to do next."

Vida smiled dreamily at this fantasy. "I'd love to, sweetie, but I can't. I've put in with Kyle, and I'm going to stick by him all the way. If we get through clean, he'll have to stick by me."

Nell closed her eyes, nearly overcome with sadness. "But he *won't*, Vi. You know he won't. As soon as he's sure you've saved him, he'll find some other girl. Somebody younger, who doesn't know what a jerk he is."

Vida's smile stretched so tight that Nell thought it would crack at the corners. Then it changed to a grimace. Nell heard a man's voice behind her. She turned.

A black-haired man wearing a gray suit stood in the hall door. He looked like a lawyer or maybe an FBI man—what they looked like on TV anyway.

"Afternoon, ladies," he said in a deep, Yankee-sounding voice. "Where's Dr. Auster?"

"Gone," said Vida. "We've been having some trouble with our computers. I think he might've gone to RadioShack for some parts."

The newcomer's eyes roamed over the computers and open file drawers. He must have seen the alcohol bottles, but he didn't mention them.

"Ladies, I'd like you to walk slowly toward me and step out of the room. I want to talk to you for a few minutes. Nothing serious. Please don't make any sudden movements on your way out. We're all in grave danger at this moment."

Vida looked back at him with an almost playful smile. "You think?"

"Just step away from the wall, Ms. Roberts. And please join me in the hall."

Vida almost preened like a cat being petted. In some perverse way, Nell knew, it gratified her sister that they knew her by name.

"Are you Biegler?" Vida asked.

"That's right."

"The pit bull with a tick up his ass?"

Biegler signaled to someone out of sight down the hall. "I haven't heard that one, but I wouldn't doubt they say that about me." He looked at Nell. "Would you step into the hall, miss?"

Nell felt the man's voice pulling her toward him. It was so calm and reasonable. He seemed nothing like a pit bull. More like a good, steady Labrador. Nell moved slowly toward him, her eyes imploring Vida to follow.

But Vida would not be led. Nell realized that her sister must have noted long before she did that Biegler wasn't holding a gun, and that even if he were carrying one, he could not use it for fear of setting off the bomb that the fume-filled room had become.

"You want to take me to jail, don't you, Mr. Biegler?" Vida said in a challenging voice.

"That depends. If you'll cooperate with us in trying to achieve a just resolution, you might be able to avoid punishment altogether."

Vida laughed harshly. "You mean if I squeal on Kyle Auster, you'll give me a get-out-of-jail-free card?"

Biegler sighed and backed deeper into the hall. "Something like that. It depends on exactly what your role in all this has been."

Nell saw something change in her sister's eyes. Then Vida murmured, "Run, baby girl. Run." Nell screamed, but Vida was already reaching into her pocket. She took out her cigarette lighter, a blue Bic, and held up her thumb. Strong arms seized Nell and dragged her toward the door. Someone charged up brandishing a gun, and then a muted roar sucked the air from Nell's lungs.

Laurel sat cross-legged on the floor behind the couch, watching Kyle Auster. Warren had forced his senior partner to sit on the hearth with his back against the marble fireplace. Warren himself was pacing the great room and periodically checking the progress of Merlin's Magic on the laptop. Thankfully, the children had not appeared. Laurel figured Warren's bizarre behavior upstairs had frightened them enough to keep them out of sight until someone else came for them. It hurt Laurel's heart to think of Beth terrified, but Grant would comfort her. He happily picked on his sister every day, but if anything truly hurt or upset her, he immediately went into a protective mode.

Laurel felt a strange kinship with Kyle. After all, they both wanted the same thing, short term. Escape. Beyond that, Auster was trying to keep both himself and Warren out of jail, which made sense to her. But Warren seemed to be in the grip of some sort of guilt reaction to whatever had been going on at the office. He was like a killer who wanted to be caught. Conversation had dropped to nothing, and Auster appeared resigned to being stuck where he was. Yet something told Laurel he was only acting. Twice she had seen him wipe tears from his cheeks. Warren must have seen this, too, but when he deigned to look at his partner, his face held only disgust. Laurel tried to stay ready for anything. Even a futile escape attempt by Auster might give her a chance to smash the Sony against the floor, or even to get the kids out of the house.

"May I say something, Warren?" Kyle asked in a shaky voice.

"If you must."

"All your life you've done the right thing. All your life you've been the golden boy. But this past year, you've done some things you don't feel good about. Things you probably never thought you'd do."

Laurel watched her husband, trying to judge the effect of these words.

"Your reasons are your own business," Kyle went on, "but right now, you're overcome with guilt. You think you're about to be exposed. Ruined. You're going to lose the respect of all those patients who think you're Albert Schweitzer. So what do you do? Try to pull the whole house down around you before that happens. You want to show the world that nobody's more disgusted with Warren Shields than Dr. Shields himself."

Auster laughed ruefully. "Partner, I *know* about self-disgust. And I know about confession. I can tell you from experience, it doesn't help the soul one bit. You'll feel better for about five seconds. Then you'll pay for the rest of your life. And if you keep doing what you're doing now, all those bad things you're dreading *will* come true. Patients won't ever look at you the same way again. You may even lose your right to practice medicine. Is that what you want?"

When Warren refused to acknowledge him, Kyle gestured at Laurel. "Look at your wife. You're browbeating her, trying to make her confess that she fooled around with somebody. Well, what if she did? Whose fault is that? You want to feel bad? Ask yourself that. Laurel's a good woman, a beautiful woman, and if she's looking somewhere else for love, then you haven't been taking care of business at home."

Warren's eyes ticked up from the computer, but Kyle pressed on.

"If she confessed right now and gave you what you think you want—all the dirty details—where would you be then? Fucked, that's where. Nine ways from Sunday. The two of you would have nowhere to go, because you're never going to get over it. I know you, man."

Warren's eyes smoldered. "I didn't know you'd specialized in psychiatry."

Kyle actually laughed. "I wouldn't waste my time. I already know more about human weakness than most of those cranks ever will. I went to school on myself."

Warren's gaze dropped back to the computer.

"I know you're listening to me," Kyle said stubbornly. "You're a control freak, Warren. Everybody knows it. And that's fine most of the time. Good for business. But now things are slipping out of control. That's how life is, okay? It's in the nature of things. Entropy, whatever. And a guy like me, when the water starts rising, I go with the flow. I let the current carry me, and I make the necessary adjustments to keep things in proper trim. You, on the other hand, are like a robot optimized to run within a certain set of parameters. When life breaks outside those parameters, you're lost. Your programming no longer suits the environment. You're like a submarine stranded in the middle of an interstate. And partner, there is a big-ass tractor-trailer headed straight for you. I'm trying to drag you out of the way, but you just won't let me. You're staying where you are because you don't know how to move."

"What's your point?" Warren said in a monotone.

"Just let me do what I need to do, and you'll have the rest of your life to find out who Laurel's been kissing behind the barn, if that's what you really want. But if you go to jail, she'll be screwing anybody she feels like anytime she wants to, because you're not going to be there to service her."

"I'll take that chance."

Auster was about to speak again when the telephone rang. Warren made no move to answer, so the machine in the kitchen picked up. Laurel's greeting played, and then a panicked woman's voice reverberated through the house.

"Please pick up, Dr. Shields! Please! This is Nell from the office. Everything's gone crazy! Everything blew up! Vida's hurt bad. She might die. Hello? Hello . . . ? Are you there?"

"Everybody into the kitchen!" Warren shouted, bounding for the answering machine. He looked back to make sure Laurel and Kyle were following, then stabbed a button on the machine, putting it into speakerphone mode.

"Nell, this is Dr. Shields."

"Thank God!" Nell sobbed, and then a car horn sounded in the kitchen.

"Where are you?" Warren asked.

"A pay phone. I'm scared to go to my apartment. I didn't know what to do."

"Calm down, Nell, and tell me exactly what happened."

Suddenly everything tumbled out of her in a frantic rush. "Vida tried to burn the patient records at the office, the computers, too. She lit everything off with me and Agent Biegler in the room with her. Everything just exploded! Gas, alcohol, they almost didn't get the fire out. The whole building could have gone up!"

Kyle had gone pale. He leaned over to Warren's ear and whispered, "Ask her if the records were destroyed."

Warren angrily shoved him away. "Where's Vida now, Nell?"

"The ICU at St. Raphael's. I haven't seen her since the explosion. I called the hospital, and a nurse told me they're going to fly her to the burn center in Greenville, if they can get her stable. What should I do, Dr. Shields?"

While Nell talked, Laurel had been studying Warren's pocket, the one that held his gun. The butt had sunk completely out of sight, but she wondered whether she might be able to get it out with a quick grab. Should she call Kyle's attention to it? Kyle was stronger, but then his hand was bigger. He might not be able to get it into the pocket before Warren flattened him. She considered grabbing a pot from a cabinet and trying to hit Warren over the head, but something stopped her. Maybe it was Nell's story, which was obviously affecting him deeply. Or maybe it was her memory of the attack with the can of beans, which hadn't worked out so well.

"You mentioned an Agent Biegler," Warren said. "He didn't try to arrest you?"

"When the fire blew up, something hit him. One of his men said I was arrested, but they didn't have handcuffs or anything. I don't really get it, because I was closer to the explosion. Biegler was trying to save me, but . . ." Nell sobbed once, then went on, "Something knocked him down, and then this other guy came charging in, but he was trying to take care of his boss. There was so much smoke . . . and blood. I tried to get Vi up, but she was knocked out, and . . . she's burned really bad, third-degree for sure. Oh, God . . ."

"Slow down, Nell. Take your time."

"When I saw that Vida couldn't move, I crawled into the hall for some air. Then I just kept crawling, and suddenly I was outside. When I realized I was by myself, I started running. The fire engines were coming then. I shouldn't have left Vi, but I was so scared, Dr. Shields—"

"It's all right. Anybody would have done the same. Where are you now?"

"Not far from the office. Should I turn myself in or what?"

Auster shook his head violently.

"Do you think you can get downtown?" Warren asked.

"I think I can get a ride, maybe."

"Okay. Go to my lawyer's office on Bank Street. Don Billings is his name. Tell him I sent you to him, and he can call me to verify. Tell him I said I'd pay all your bills."

Kyle was gaping now.

"What should I tell him?" Nell asked. "What should I say and not say?"

"Once you're with Billings, he's your attorney. Don't waste time trying to protect Kyle or me. You're the important one. You've got your whole life in front of you."

Kyle looked as if he were about to stroke out, but he was obviously afraid to speak on a line that might be tapped.

"I wouldn't lift a finger to help Dr. Auster," Nell said. "That cheating bastard screwed my sister over so bad . . . I *hate* him."

"I know what you mean," Warren said, looking back at his partner. "Don't worry. Kyle's going to get what he deserves before this is over."

"Don Billings?" Nell repeated, her voice shaky. "Bank Street?"

"That's right. Everything's going to be all right, Nell."

"Thank you so much, Dr. Shields. I knew you'd help me."

"Good-bye, Nell. Be careful." Warren hung up and confronted Auster, who was backing toward the foyer. "Did you tell Vida to burn our records?"

"Hell, no! You know Vida. She spearheaded every scam I ever tried up there. She told me this afternoon that the records had to disappear, but that's all. Man, she's the one who told me to come over here and get the bonds and ledgers. She even put these damn rags on me!"

"Let's talk about Vida and Nell for a minute."

"We don't have a minute!" Kyle cried, his face blotched red. "You heard Nell. They *arrested* her. You can bet your ass they have warrants out for you and me. Biegler's liable to pull up here any second, now that you answered that phone."

"If he does, so be it."

"*What?*"

"I don't care if I go to jail, so long as I go knowing the truth."

"The *truth*? About what?"

Warren turned on his heel and walked back down to the great room. Laurel knew he was going to check the Sony again. She said a silent prayer that the program hadn't cracked her password, then grabbed Kyle's stinking shirt and pulled him close.

"He changed the code for the safe room, but it doesn't matter. The bonds and ledgers are on the guest room bed. Go!"

Auster was already moving, but he looked over his shoulder and whispered, "What about you?"

"I've got to get my kids out."

As Laurel started for the stairs, she saw a blur in the corner of her left eye that might be Warren moving. She sprinted up to the landing, but paused when Warren screamed, "Put that box down, Kyle!"

"Can't do it, partner," Auster replied. "Let me pass."

Laurel peered over the rail of the landing. Kyle stood in the hall below, just within her sight, while Warren waited at the intersection of the hall and the foyer, blocking his exit. They were separated by less than ten feet, with Warren's pistol pointed at the box covering Auster's belly.

"Move aside, Warren," Kyle said with surprising force. "I'm not your problem."

"Put the bonds down," Warren repeated. "Right now."

Laurel wanted to continue up the stairs, but if one step creaked, Warren would hear her. She waited without breathing, terrified that Kyle would try to bluster his way past Warren to the door. After about five seconds, Kyle sighed, then bent and set the box on the floor. "At least Laurel got away," he said.

Stunned, Warren looked around in panic, then up the staircase. As Laurel's eyes met his, she sensed movement just beyond him.

Incredibly, Kyle now held a gun in his hand, a small nickel-plated automatic. Laurel stared in amazement as he aimed at Warren's chest, silently urging him to pull the trigger. Then she heard herself scream a warning: *"Warren, watch out!"*

Warren ducked left as Kyle fired, the sound like a solitary firecracker. A red flower bloomed high on Warren's shoulder, and then his gun boomed twice in reply.

Auster dropped like a sack.

Laurel stood frozen above this surreal tableau until a drumroll sounded overhead. Grant and Beth suddenly appeared above her, looking down from the second-floor rail.

*"Mom, what happened?"* Grant cried in alarm. *"Are you okay?"*

Beth's face was nearly bloodless, her eyes round and white. "I'm scared, Mama!" she whimpered. "Come get me!"

A groan of agony rose from below. Laurel looked down and saw Kyle lying facedown on the floor, a pool of blood soaking his lower back. He was trying to crawl, but only his upper body was moving. Warren was looking up at Laurel and the kids, his right hand gripping his left shoulder.

"Mama, come get me!" Beth wailed. "Mama, *pleee-ase*!"

Warren nodded permission. "Go! I'll take care of Kyle."

Laurel raced up the stairs and swept Beth into her arms without even slowing. "Come on," she hissed at Grant. "Move!"

"Where are we going?" Grant asked, running after her.

"Your room." They reached the upstairs hall.

"How come?"

"We have to get out of here!"

"How?"

"Your tree."

Grant's eyes widened. "But you told me never to climb on that anymore!"

"Today you get to."

She darted into Grant's room and crossed to his right-hand window. Outside, the roof sloped steeply down to a gnarled mass of oak branches already thick with spring leaves. There was a tree house in the oak, and from its platform a zipline ran forty meters into the backyard, where it terminated over a sand pit. A few weeks ago, Grant had learned that he could sneak out of his window, slide down the roof, and climb down to his tree house using the high branches of the oak. Laurel had forbidden this dangerous activity, but that was before her husband went nuts. The only question now was, could a six-year-old girl do what a nine-year-old boy could? Laurel was betting she could, with her mother's help. She knelt and looked Beth in the eyes.

"Grant's going first, okay? Then you and me."

"Mama, I can't," Beth said in a shaky voice. "It's way too high. Let's use the stairs."

"We can't, honey bun. Daddy might see us."

"What's wrong with Dad?" Grant asked. "Why is he acting psycho?"

"Daddy's sick, honey. He doesn't know what he's doing right now. We need to get away from him, just for a little while. Ready?"

Grant pumped his fist. "Spider-Man time!"

Laurel flipped a latch and raised the window. To her horror, their home security system chimed in response. Warren must have set the chime only moments ago, because it hadn't rung when Kyle opened the front door.

"Hurry!" she urged. *"Go!"*

Grant climbed quickly through the window and started down the slope of the roof, using both his hands and feet. Then Laurel crawled through, keeping one hand on Beth, who was crying in terror. "Come on, baby," she said, reaching back into the bedroom. "We're going to be fine." She was pulling Beth up to the sill when Warren's feet came pounding along the hall.

Laurel snatched Beth through the opening, banging the child's head on the window frame. Beth shrieked in pain, but Laurel didn't stop moving. She set her daughter firmly on her lap, meaning to skid down the steep, shingled slope on her behind. Then Warren snatched her hair and tried to drag her back through the window. Laurel screamed for him to let go, but he only pulled harder. A chunk of hair ripped out by the roots.

She'd lose every strand on her head to get Beth out of danger.

Beth squirmed around on Laurel's lap, probably to get better purchase on her mother's chest. Laurel had thrown back one hand to jerk Warren's hand free, but she needed that hand to hold Beth fast.

*"You're going to make her fall!"* Laurel screamed. *"Let go!"*

Warren's other hand caught Laurel just under the chin and began hauling her into the open window. She couldn't even draw breath. If she didn't stop fighting, she might black out and drop Beth. With tears of frustration in her eyes, she went limp.

As she waited for Warren to let go, she prayed that Grant had made his escape and not waited for his mother and sister.

"Grant!" Warren shouted. "Get your tail back up here, boy!"

The oak limbs shook as though a huge raccoon were moving in the tree below. Then Grant's feet hit the floor of the tree house with a bang.

*"I'm talking to you, Son! You do not want to make your father angry!"*

The hand loosened slightly at her throat.

"Pass her up to me!" Warren ordered. "Come on!"

Laurel did. As he lifted Beth through the window, Laurel saw a saucer-size bloodstain above his left collarbone.

"The bullet clipped my trapezius," Warren said, noticing her gaze. "It's nothing. As if you care."

She turned away, fighting a mad impulse to scramble down the roof to the safety of the oak tree.

Then a whir like the world's biggest fishing reel

sounded from below. Laurel looked to her right and saw Grant sailing away from the house like a commando in a POW rescue movie. He was kicking his feet to make the wheel mechanism speed along the zipline. She felt like cheering out loud.

Warren cursed in fury, and something dark moved behind her. Leaning back, she saw his gun come up and steady in his hand, as if to fire at Grant's receding form. She knocked the gun aside and scrabbled onto her knees, facing Warren in the window like an angry mother wildcat. She was spitting mad, her skin as hot and itchy as if electricity were crackling along it. "Point that gun at him again," she snarled, "and I'll *claw your eyeballs out.* I swear to *God* I will!"

Grant hit the sand clean and started sprinting without even a hitch in his rhythm. Compared to doing a 180 off a half-pipe, it was nothing. He looked over his shoulder as he ran and saw his father silhouetted in the window of his bedroom, staring silently after him while his mother waved from the roof to keep running. The sight scared him more than anything had in a long time.

He ran toward the creek first, because it was downhill, but then he cut left and started making for the Elfmans' house. As he did, Christy broke out of the trees below and raced to catch him, elated to have someone to run with. The corgi circled Grant as he ran, smiling as she always did. All he could think was that he needed to get to a telephone. He wasn't sure whom to call, and he had no idea what to tell Mrs. Elfman. *My dad's sick? My mom needs help?*

He swerved around some azaleas and kept pumping toward the Elfmans'. He could see Mrs. Elfman herself, standing in her backyard by the pool, wearing a big flowery dress. It looked like she'd already seen him. A second later, her yardman appeared beside her. Grant liked George a lot better than Mrs. Elfman. He was glad George was there. Grant figured he must look pretty scared, because a second later George started running toward him, and even Mrs. Elfman started walking fast in his direction. He *was* scared, too.

He wasn't sure what was wrong with his father, but he knew his mom was terrified. He'd never seen her face so white or her hands shaking, and he'd sure never seen her wallop his dad in the face. But what scared Grant most of all was what he'd seen in the TV room upstairs. It was hidden in his dad's pocket, but the outline was plain as day. Grant's throat had been tight ever since he realized what that outline meant, and when he heard the shots later, they'd come as no surprise.

"Whoa there, little man!" George called, dropping to his knees so that Grant would be eye to eye with him. "What you running from so fast?"

Grant was breathing so hard that he couldn't talk. By the time he found his voice, Mrs. Elfman was coming up. She took his hand and looked down at him with all the kindness in the world.

"What's wrong, Grant Shields? You have to tell us, if we're going to help you. Did some little boy blow his finger off? I heard firecrackers over there."

Grant shook his head, trying not to cry. "It's my dad," he panted. "My dad's sick!"

"Sick how?" asked George. "Did he grab his arm or his chest? Is he awake?"

Grant pointed at his own temple. "He's sick up here.

He doesn't know what he's doing. He's got a gun, and I think he shot somebody. My mom tried to get us out, but only I got away."

"Dear Lord in heaven!" Mrs. Elfman exclaimed. "You poor child. Run call the sheriff, George. Double quick. Tell him to bring every man he's got."

# CHAPTER
# 14

Danny McDavitt was sitting on the elevated deck at the Athens Point Airport, drinking a lukewarm Schaefer and listening to Marilyn Stone give him an informal legal assessment of his custody situation. No alcohol was sold on the premises, but a mechanic friend had come up with a cold six-pack for Danny. He and Marilyn had been talking for over an hour, but he was in no hurry to get home. The only other thing on his mind was what might be happening with Laurel, but he'd checked his cell phone a dozen times, and she'd sent no text messages.

"Bottom line?" said Marilyn. "Starlette can get physical custody of Michael, and she can probably limit you to minimum visitation. Every other weekend. It all depends on the judge. But she will *not* be able to institutionalize Michael if you're willing to take him on. No judge is going to warehouse a special-needs kid when there's a parent ready and willing to take on that responsibility."

Danny nodded. "Every other weekend's not good

enough. Michael needs one-on-one attention, all the time."

Marilyn was obviously sympathetic. "What about his teacher? Laurel Shields would make one hell of a witness for us, if she'd get up and tell the truth about Starlette."

Danny sipped his beer but said nothing. He was trying not to think about Laurel. After Marilyn landed the Cessna, he had broken down and sent Laurel a third text message, this one an almost panicked plea to alert him as soon as the encounter with Warren was over. But she still had not answered.

"What's the problem there?" Marilyn asked. "You don't think Laurel would do it?"

"She probably would. I'll have to talk to her about it."

"You do that. Every day counts, Danny."

He forced a smile. "I sure appreciate you taking this time."

"Oh, I expect a free lesson in return."

"I'll make it two."

"One's enough. How's Starlette acting now?"

"You don't want to know. Bitch city. Running up my credit cards like the Germans are about to roll into Paris."

"SOP for a woman who thinks her husband's about to dump her. You need to get out while you can. Take your chances."

Danny was about to reply when his legitimate cell phone rang. He checked the LCD and saw that the call was from the Sheriff's Department. "Excuse me, I need to take this."

Marilyn turned up her Schaefer and drank it off with an unladylike gurgle.

"Danny McDavitt," he said.

"Major McDavitt, this is Dispatch. I've been told that the sheriff needs the aerial unit to pick him up at Lake St. John. You know where that is?"

"I do." Lake St. John was a popular recreation spot forty miles up the river. "When are we talking about, Carol?"

"Now, sir."

"Now? What's going on?"

"Radio silence on this one, Danny. No specifics on cell phones either. You're the pilot on the board. Jim's in Las Vegas with his wife for his anniversary. How soon can you get to the airport?"

"I'm at the airport now."

"Good. I called Mr. Markle already. They should be getting the aerial unit ready now."

*The unit.* Danny almost laughed, but something in her voice stopped him. "This is a real emergency?"

"Yes, sir."

"What's the sheriff doing at Lake St. John?"

"Fishing. I'll give you his GPS coordinates once you're airborne."

Danny didn't want to spend his afternoon searching the river for some lost fisherman when Laurel might need him. But there were only two chopper pilots, and if Jim Redmond was out of town, then Danny had no way out of the duty. "Roger that," he said in a tone of surrender. "Call me back in ten minutes with the coordinates."

"What's the emergency?" asked Marilyn.

"Our illustrious sheriff wants a chopper ride back from Lake St. John. He's tired of fishing."

"Are you serious?"

"Nah," said Danny, getting to his feet. "It's probably somebody lost on the water. Unless one of the sheriff's campaign contributors sprained an ankle wakeboarding."

Marilyn laughed. "That sounds like the Billy Ray Ellis I remember from high school."

"You're not that old, I know."

She winked. "I was a ninth-grader when Billy Ray was a senior. He was the cat's meow back then. Big football star, all the girls after him. Of course, it was mostly white boys then. Different game."

"You'd better believe it."

"I think it's safe to say Billy was elected sheriff on his high school rep and his status in the Baptist church," Marilyn said in an arch tone.

"Politics. The same everywhere. He's okay, actually. I've known a lot worse in ranking uniforms."

The lawyer nodded thoughtfully. "We should do this more."

"I agree."

"If you'd hire me, we could."

Danny's smile faded. "I'm thinking about it."

By the time Danny reached the hangar, the mechanics had rolled out the Sheriff's Department helicopter and prepped her for flight. She was a Bell 206B, eight years old but still in good shape. White with blue and gold stripes, and a big gold star painted on the fuselage. The machines he'd flown in the air force were five times this size and infinitely more sophisticated, but the Bell handled well in the air, a kite compared to the massive predators he once flew. A Pave Low IV could carry twenty-four fully equipped commandos into battle; the Bell 206 had two seats up front and room for one passenger and a stretcher in back. Not much else.

"How goes it, Danny boy?" called Dick Burleigh, the silver-haired chief mechanic. "Ready to crank and bank?"

Burleigh had served as crew chief on a Huey with the First Air Cav in Vietnam. After surviving the Ia Drang and A Shau valleys, he'd moved to Baton Rouge and serviced news choppers for thirty years. At sixty-something, Burleigh decided to retire to Athens Point, where he started filling in at the airport for kicks. Pretty soon, he was running the maintenance department. For Danny he was a godsend.

"You tell me, Dick," he said. "How's she running?"

"Hot as a preacher's daughter."

Danny laughed and shook hands with Burleigh, then nodded to a blond kid in coveralls trailing behind him. "Let's forget about those beers, huh, guys?"

Burleigh smiled. "Long as you're okay to fly, Major."

Danny gave the old crew chief a salute. "My inviolable rule is, don't drink and fly. However, one night in the Caribbean, I had to go up and chase down a Bolivian drug boat with half a bottle of tequila in me. Long story, but we knocked down ninety keys of marching powder that night."

"You get to keep any of it?" asked the kid, his eyes twinkling.

Danny chuckled. "Nah. But there were reports of confiscated reefer weighing in a little light after some of those takedowns. MPs never got to the bottom of it, either." .

"You take her easy, Major," said Burleigh, his smile gone. "Wind's getting up, and you got thunderheads blowing in from the northwest."

"That's the way I'm headed, too."

"Maybe the sheriff ought to drive back to town. He could make it in the time it takes you to fly both ways."

*No,* Danny thought, *Billy Ray likes the chopper too much for that.* "I'm just an old rotorhead, Chief. I live to serve. Have a good one."

The mechanic winked and opened the Bell's door. Danny climbed into the right seat, fastened his harness, cinched it tight, and hit the starter. Then he put on his headset and ran the preflight checklist. He didn't miss having to put on his helmet, night-vision goggles, body armor, or any of the other gear required to fly the Pave Low. Compared to his military flying, this was like barnstorming in the 1920s.

When the main rotor system hit 360 rpm, Danny felt the chopper reach neutral buoyancy. He pulled up on the collective, which put the Bell into a low hover. After trimming the ship with his left foot pedal, he lightly touched the cyclic and tilted the rotor disk forward. A few moments later, the bird gained translational lift and launched herself into the sky.

At that moment, Danny's cell phone vibrated. He applied friction to the collective and let go long enough to grab the phone from his pocket, assuming that Laurel had finally texted him back. To his surprise, he found himself holding his legitimate phone instead. The Bell drifted a little as he flipped it open. The new message was from the Sheriff's Department dispatcher. There were only four words in the text box:

CODE BLACK/THIRD DEGREE.

Danny's ass puckered as he stared at the coded message.

Code Black meant a hostage situation.

Third Degree meant loss of life.

With visions of Columbine and Virginia Tech in his head, he twisted the throttle, pushed the chopper to 122 knots, and stormed toward the thunderheads rolling down from the northwest.

Kyle Auster was dead.

Laurel saw his body lying on the hall floor when she followed Warren down the stairs with Beth in her arms. She buried her daughter's face between her breasts, then looked over the rail. Kyle lay faceup with his eyes open, as still as a human body could be. His absurd shirt was hiked up to his nipples; Warren must have done that while working on him. How strange, she thought, to shoot a man and then immediately try to save him. Despite Warren's two shots, she saw only one wound, at the midline, above Auster's navel but below his heart. Dark blood covered his pale belly, matting the hair that so many gullible women had lain against in adultery.

"Did you call 911?" she asked from the landing.

Warren had already reached the ground floor. "No point."

"He died before you came upstairs?"

"No, but he was slipping away fast. I think the bullet hit his spine. He couldn't move his legs. It must have clipped his descending aorta as well, because he seemed to be bleeding out internally."

"What a shot you are," she said bitterly.

Warren was looking down at the body. "He shot first. You saw it."

"Such a waste. I can't . . . I guess I can't really believe it."

"Mommy, I can't breathe," Beth said.

Laurel turned her daughter's head but kept her facing away from the rail. Beth hadn't spoken since the events on the roof; she only sucked her thumb and lay glassy-eyed against Laurel's chest.

"Cover him up with something," Laurel said.

"You do it. Let me have Beth."

"You're not touching this child."

Warren looked up, his jaw set hard. "Don't think anything has changed. Kyle is dead because of a choice he made. Every choice has consequences. Yours included."

"Who the hell do you think you are? God? Get over yourself! You just shot a man. This insanity is *over.*"

"Come downstairs. Into the kitchen."

Laurel shielded Beth's eyes and walked down to the foyer, then followed Warren to the kitchen. Beth was a lot heavier than she'd been only a year ago. Laurel's back and shoulders were already aching. While Warren stared out the kitchen window, she took a glass down from the cabinet.

"What are you doing?" he asked, still looking out over the front lawn.

"Getting her some water. She's tired out. No, actually she's not. She's traumatized by what you did upstairs. Probably scarred permanently. What is *wrong* with you?"

"Give her a teaspoon of Benadryl."

"Is that your professional advice? Drug our daughter to sleep?"

Warren rolled his eyes. "This will be a lot less traumatic for her if she sleeps through it."

Laurel's stomach tightened. "What will?"

"Don't worry about it. She can sleep in the safe room."

Laurel felt as though she were having a conversation with a robot. "Warren, you just killed your business partner. Your office almost burned to the ground. Your employee tried to kill a federal agent. Don't you realize the police will be here any minute?"

"That's why she needs to be in the safe room."

Laurel whispered, "You're not putting our daughter into that room alone. She'd be terrified."

"She'd also be safe. Bullets can't penetrate an inch of steel plate."

A bolt of alarm shot through Laurel, despite her fatigue. "Do you seriously intend to hold us hostage inside a ring of armed men?"

At last Warren's face betrayed some emotion. "This is our house, Laurel. *My* house. *My* land. I expect the police to respect our rights and leave us alone to deal with our own family problems."

She closed her eyes, trying to blot out his face long enough to think, but it was impossible. The enormity of what had happened finally sank into her soul, and the floodgates opened. As she cried, she experienced an epiphany that revealed the road to freedom. The password to that road was a lie. But unlike the lies of omission she had been telling for the past year, she was going to have to sell this story. *At least Kyle won't have died for nothing,* she thought. In death, he was going to do her a service he could never have done in life.

She carried Beth to the built-in banquette in the corner of the kitchen. Beth tried to cling to her, but Laurel set her firmly on the seat and rubbed her forehead for half a minute. "Warren," she said, straightening up and putting her hands on her hips, "I can't let you put Beth at risk like this. I'm going to tell you what you want to know. But first I've got to know that you'll bring this insanity to an end. I don't care what you do to me, but you've got to let Beth leave the house."

Hearing resolve in her voice, he looked away from the window and focused on her. "Do you really think Beth is in danger from me? You're the one who put our children at risk. If you tell me the truth, the real truth, you might be surprised by how things turn out."

Laurel tried to read his meaning, but it was impossible. "Send Beth outside first. As a sign of good faith. Then I'll tell you."

He smiled sadly. "I can't do that. You haven't proved yourself worthy of trust. She's in no danger." He took a step toward Laurel. "Tell me."

She realized then that he wasn't holding the gun. Was it still in one of his pockets?

"I'm waiting," he said.

She pictured the awful scene upstairs, when he had told the kids she was having an affair. That was sufficient to bring more tears to her eyes. "It was Kyle, okay?" she said softly. "I saw him for almost a year."

Warren's eyes narrowed, and he moved closer. Close

enough to hit her. "Kyle. You *were* having an affair with Kyle?"

She nodded. "I didn't love him. But I wanted to hurt you. I knew that would hurt you more than anything else. If I cheapened myself like that."

Warren moved closer, close enough to kiss. "You made love with him?"

"No. I fucked him."

Warren flinched. She expected a blow any second.

"And you knew about the other women? About Vida? The nurses?"

Laurel nodded. "That was part of it, I think."

"Did Kyle love you?"

She was about to say no, but then she thought of Danny's letter. "He thought he did. Kyle was crazy. He'd never had anyone like me before. He said he would give up all the others if I would run away with him. But I didn't want that. I just wanted to make you realize what you were doing to me. How you were ignoring me."

Warren tilted his head to the right, like a scientist studying an animal in the midst of some curious act. "You're lying," he said at length.

"You don't know the truth when you hear it."

"If Kyle was the one who wrote that letter, you would have let him shoot me. But you didn't. You warned me."

"Of course I did! I didn't love Kyle! I love you. Besides, you're the father of my children."

Warren shook his head. "You're lying *now*. Kyle could have smashed your laptop while I ran to answer the kitchen phone, but he didn't. He didn't care about that Hotmail account at all."

"I could have done the same thing."

"No, I was watching you. And you did try, once. Kyle never did. He even screamed at you to tell me the password. He didn't care about your computer, because he knew it was no threat to him."

She searched her mind for some rational argument, but there was none.

"You're *still* trying to protect someone," Warren said, his voice low and dangerous. "Who is it?" He grabbed her by the shoulders and shook her violently. "Tell me who he is!"

"Daddy, stop it!" Beth screeched. "You're hurting Mama!"

"Mom's fine," Warren said, stopping his assault but not taking his eyes from Laurel's face. "If you were really having an affair with Kyle, you can answer one simple question for me."

Her stomach rolled over.

"Kyle had a unique feature below the waist. What was it?"

She lowered her voice. "I'm not going to discuss another man's genitals with you in front of our daughter."

"Let's go to the great room, then."

Laurel closed her eyes as though disgusted, but she was thinking desperately.

"You don't know," Warren whispered. "Because you've never seen Kyle's . . . package."

But she *had* seen it, once. A couple of years ago, at a Halloween party that lasted into the wee hours. A few drunken guests had peeled off their costumes and leaped into their hosts' heated pool. Naturally one of them was Kyle. He'd been standing behind a plastic cubicle that served as a changing room, out of Warren's line of sight but well within Laurel's. After stripping off his pants, he'd turned toward her long enough for her to take in his full nudity; then he'd burst into the open and dived into the steaming water. Laurel had a clear memory of the event, but no matter how hard she focused, she saw nothing but a normal, middle-aged penis of average size.

"Time's up," Warren said. "You lose."

"There's nothing different about him."

Warren's smile was triumphant. "Kyle had hypospadias. Do you know what that is?"

Laurel had heard the word, but she couldn't recall what condition it described.

"His urethra opens on the underside of his penis, rather than at the tip. It's fairly common. One in three hundred live births. And if you'd been sleeping with him, you would definitely know about it."

She looked away.

"You can go check his corpse, if you're curious. No? Then I repeat: tell me who you're trying to protect. If you don't—"

The kitchen phone rang loudly. Warren let go of her, glanced at the caller ID, then walked to the kitchen window. "And awaaay we go. It's started now."

Laurel stood on tiptoe. Over the hedges in front of the window, she saw a Sheriff's Department cruiser parked at the end of their driveway. One man inside.

Warren pressed the speakerphone button, then came back to the window. "This is Dr. Shields. Who's this?"

"This is Deputy Ray Breen, Doctor."

"Afternoon, Ray," Warren said in a cheerful voice. "What can I do for you?"

"Well, Doc, I just drove out to check on some things."

"Is that right? What things would those be?"

"Well, your wife and daughter for one. We heard y'all might be having some trouble out this way."

Laurel closed her eyes as Breen's deep drawl echoed through the house. This was why she hadn't called 911 in the beginning.

"No trouble," Warren said. "Nothing serious, anyway."

There was a long pause. Then Ray Breen said, "Well, I'm afraid your boy says different. He's over to the neighbors' house scared half out of his wits. He says maybe you shot somebody."

Warren laughed loudly. "No, no. Kyle Auster and I were cleaning a pistol, and it accidentally discharged. Put a hole in the floor, but other than that, no harm done."

This time the pause was longer. "I'm glad to hear it, Doc. But I'd feel a whole lot better if I could just say hey to everybody for a second. One at a time, if you please."

Warren's tense face gave the lie to his nonchalant voice. Maybe Deputy Breen wasn't so dumb after all. Warren took the phone off speaker, picked up the receiver, covered the mouthpiece with his palm, and whispered to Laurel, "Tell him you're fine. Everything's fine."

"I won't."

"If you don't—if you say something's wrong in here, or that I shot Kyle—you can bet your life they'll come busting in here with guns blazing. And I can't be responsible for what happens after that."

She wondered if this was true. So far, she'd seen only one car outside. But there had to be more. And the local cops she'd met seemed more likely to use guns than diplomacy to resolve a standoff. She nodded once, and Warren held the phone up to her face. "Deputy Breen?"

"Yes, ma'am. Can your husband hear me?"

At that moment, Warren pressed his ear to the receiver. "No."

"Are you all right today?"

"Yes."

"Are you in any danger?"

"Danger?"

"We heard there might have been some gunplay in the house."

"Just an accident. It's all right now."

"And your daughter? Is she all right?"

"Oh, yes."

"Could I talk to her?"

"Of course."

Warren knelt in front of Beth and said, "Say hello to the man, Beth. He's a nice man."

"Hel-lo," Beth said, reverting to her usual telephone ritual. "What's your name?"

"She's busy, Ray," Warren said, standing erect with the phone. He listened for a few seconds, then said, "Kyle's busy right now, too. . . . Uh-huh. . . . I understand that. Look, our practice is being audited by the IRS right now, and we're having a pretty tense day going over our books. Kyle is deep into them with the calculator right now, but as soon as he's done, I'll have him call you."

Laurel couldn't believe what she was hearing. In all

the time she had known Warren, she had hardly ever heard him lie. Now he was spinning out bullshit with the facility of Kyle Auster. As he continued to evade Breen's questions, she thought about what the deputy had said. Grant had obviously reached a neighbor's house, probably the Elfmans'. He would be terrified, but Bonnie Elfman would take good care of him.

"Listen, Ray," Warren said, his tone growing testy. "The thing is, I'm waiting for something in here. We're running a computer program, and we're waiting for a certain result. Once I have that, we'll all come out and visit with you guys for the rest of the evening, if you want. But this is business, Ray. It's important. You know what I mean? . . . Of course you do. All right. As soon as I have what I need in here, we're all coming out. . . . Kyle, too, absolutely. . . . Good talking to you, too."

Warren hung up, jerked the curtains over the kitchen window, and turned to Laurel with manic energy. "Get some sheets out of the laundry room to cover Kyle. I'll stay with Beth."

Laurel started to argue, but then she remembered that her clone phone was sitting on the shelf in the laundry room. Warren was letting her go alone because he knew she wouldn't leave Beth inside the house with him. "I'll be right back," she said, touching Beth's arm. She walked into the pantry, which led to the laundry room.

"The door to the garage is bolted," Warren called, in case she had a lapse of maternal judgment.

She reached up and slid her Razr off the detergent shelf. Her heart leaped when she saw 3 NEW MESSAGES on its LCD screen. Flipping open the phone, she bent over the laundry basket and made rummaging noises among some folded sheets. The first message read, *I'm not going anywhere. I'll b close by if u need me. I love u.* So much hope and relief suffused her heart that she felt giddy. The second message read, *Saw both cars home. What should I do?*

"What's the holdup?" Warren called.

Laurel picked up two folded sheets as she read the third message: *Text me the instant u r out of there! Crazy with worry!*

"Me, too," she whispered, sliding the phone into her back pocket.

She carried the sheets out to the kitchen and set them on the granite countertop. "What now?"

"I'm going to move Kyle out of the hall," Warren said softly. "You're coming with me."

"I think I'm going to give Beth that Benadryl after all," Laurel murmured. "If we're lucky, it'll cause short-term memory loss."

He frowned and picked up the sheets. "I need some food. We all do."

"I'll cook something," Laurel offered. "Breakfast would be easiest."

He nodded.

She looked at Beth lying on the banquette. "Would you like an egg with a hat on it?"

Beth actually sat up at this suggestion. "And grits and biscuits? And grape jelly!"

"Tell you what," Warren said to Laurel, "you do the work with the sheets. Leave Beth with me. I'm going to shut all the blinds, then start the food."

Laurel hesitated, then nodded in agreement. She took the sheets and went down the hall with Danny's messages running through her mind. She hadn't thought to check the time stamps, but he obviously hadn't followed her advice to leave town. Running simply wasn't in him. So where was he now? *He must have driven by the house at least once,* she thought. *Or else that was his plane I heard before. He knows I'm here with Warren. And that, combined with me not showing up in the clearing, started him worrying. But what can he do?* Danny sometimes flew the Sheriff's Department helicopter and so was fairly tight with the sheriff. If he'd heard the report of a shooting out here, Laurel was sure he would find a way to get himself into the loop. Once that happened, it would only be a matter of time before someone came to save her and Beth. Danny would have a tricky job trying to explain his concerns without betraying their affair, but she felt sure he could do it.

She looked down at Kyle's body. His eyes were still open, but the opaque irises held no life. The dead face already looked more like a wax figure of Kyle than the man himself. Pity rose in her, but she knew that her duty was to the living, not the dead. She thought of texting Danny that Kyle had been shot, but Warren might be watching from the end of the hall.

Unfolding one of the sheets, she laid it gently over Kyle's corpse, then with considerable effort rolled the body over. Then she stood and dragged it to the guest room door. With the sheet under him, Kyle slid fairly easily on the polished hardwood. Getting him over the threshold was harder, but she turned away from him, grabbed his ankles under her arms as though hitching a cart to a mule, and in three great heaves dragged him onto the carpet and clear of the door.

With the walls of the guest room around her, an almost irresistible compulsion to call Danny took hold of her. As she reached out to close the door, Warren appeared there with Beth in his arms.

"Good enough," he said, keeping Beth's head turned away. "We miss you."

She swallowed hard, then followed Warren back to the kitchen. *Danny knows I need help,* she told herself. *He knows everything he needs to know. I've got to keep the phone secret, no matter what. It might make the difference between life and death.*

"You take over," Warren said, pointing at the iron skillet heating on the stove. An egg carton and a can of Pillsbury biscuits lay beside it. "I'm going to check the computer."

*The computer.* As it had been from the beginning, her laptop remained the greatest danger to her. At any moment, the Merlin's Magic program could give Warren access to hundreds of messages from Danny: love letters, embedded digital photos, all the stuff she'd been insane ever to put on her hard drive. All the things someone in love can't live without. "No worries," she said brightly. "Beth and I have got it under control."

Warren seemed about to take Beth with him to the great room, but then he walked away alone. "All the doors are bolted," he reminded her. "And I took out the keys."

"Thanks for that information," Laurel replied in a tone that said, *Stop upsetting our daughter.*

"Don't open the blinds," he added. "And tap the skillet with a fork while I'm down there."

"Just go already!"

He vanished into the great room.

She clanked the skillet a couple of times, then lifted Beth onto the counter beside the Viking cooktop. Laurel felt almost drunk with adrenaline. A new plan had come to her, and she had no time for second thoughts. There was risk, yes, but she was almost certain that she and Beth would survive it. She cracked four eggs open and dumped them into the skillet with her right hand while holding Beth's hand with her left. "Daddy's not right in the head now, punkin," she whispered. "Can you tell that?"

Beth nodded with wide eyes and whispered, "Daddy lied to that policeman on the phone."

"Yes, he did. I need you to do one thing for me, darling. One easy thing, and then we can go outside where Grant and the nice policemen are. Will you do that for me?"

Beth nodded again.

"Do you remember where my laptop is? Down on the coffee table?"

"Uh-huh. Where Daddy is."

"After Daddy comes back up here, I want you to take your glass of water down to the great room like you're going to play. Then I want you to unplug the computer and dump your water into my keyboard."

Beth opened her mouth in shock. "*What?*"

"Pour it right into the keys, where the letters are. But be sure you unplug it first. And don't touch the computer with your hands afterward. That's important. Just dump the water into the keyboard from high above it. Far away. No touching."

Beth blinked several times, processing Laurel's request. "I can do that. But won't Daddy be mad?"

"He's going to be mad at me, not you. But that's what we have to do to make all this stop. Okay?"

Beth smiled. "Okay."

"Unplug the computer first. And don't touch it with your hands."

"I know. Electricity, right?"

Laurel smiled with satisfaction, then retrieved Beth's glass from the table by the banquette. She knew from experience that it would take a couple of seconds for the water to penetrate the Sony's keyboard, and unplugging the computer from the wall socket would step it down to battery power rather than the 110 volts coming from the mains. The danger of lethal voltage arcing back to Beth was almost nonexistent, but the probability of frying the computer itself was high. As Warren came back to the kitchen, Laurel said, "Any luck with your computer program?"

"It's coming along," he said without looking at her. "A seven-space password has seventy-eight billion possible combinations. Even more, really, depending on how many characters you choose from."

"How interesting."

He looked at her oddly. *Stay cool,* she told herself. *Don't get cocky. He's going to go ballistic in about two minutes—*

"Where are you going?" he asked Beth, who had been spinning in circles like a ballerina on Warren's side of the island, but now was walking toward the hall.

"Nowhere!" she said breathlessly. "I'm tired of sitting around."

"Well, we have to sit around awhile longer."

Laurel saw that Beth didn't have the water glass in

her hand, but it was nowhere in sight either. She had stashed it somewhere, like a good little conspirator. Probably on the floor.

Laurel needed Warren to move to her side of the island. She rotated the burner control beneath the eggs to HIGH, then turned toward the sink and began loudly washing the bowl she'd used to hold the broken egg-shells.

"Hey," Warren said. "Hey! You're burning them!"

"What?"

"You're burning the eggs!"

She spun from the sink and let her anger show. "Is your butt nailed to that stool?"

He got up and stalked around the island. Laurel went back to rinsing the bowl. She was turning off the water when a cracking sound came from the great room, followed by a screech.

"What the—?" Warren looked around anxiously. *"Elizabeth?"*

He scanned every corner of the kitchen and den, then ran for the great room. Laurel scrambled around the island and went after him.

"Where are you?" Warren shouted. "What are you doing?"

Laurel heard a primal scream of fury just before she reached the great room. The acrid stink of burned plastic filled her nostrils. Beth was cowering by the arm of the sofa, the empty water glass still in her hand, her eyes on her enraged father.

Warren stood over the silent Vaio, staring down with mute incomprehension on his face. When he looked down at Beth, she bolted toward Laurel, tossing the glass aside as she ran. She leaped into her mother's arms, and Laurel backed slowly toward the arch behind her.

"Elizabeth?" Warren snapped. "Did your mother tell you to do that?"

"No!" Beth shouted, stunning Laurel. *"I hate that computer! It's making you crazy!"*

Warren glared at his daughter like a sea captain staring down a mutinous member of his crew.

"Of course I told her to do it," Laurel said with a calm she did not feel. "It had to be done. I'm sure you can hire a lawyer to get those e-mails from the company, and that's probably what you should do. But this nightmare has to end. It *has* ended. I'm not playing this game anymore."

He opened his mouth but did not reply. Then he squeezed his hands into fists, which he pressed hard against his temples. Laurel was starting to believe that she had actually won when he closed the space between them in four quick bounds and backhanded her to the floor.

Beth screamed as they fell.

# CHAPTER

# 15

Deputy Carl Sims turned right off of Highway 24 and drove through the wrought-iron gate into Avalon, a subdivision he had only seen through the windows of his patrol cruiser. Carl had grown up in Sandy Bottom, an all-black neighborhood in the river lowlands of Lusahatcha County, well outside the city limits. The only whites who spent any time in Sandy Bottom were the well-checkers who operated the oil wells owned by the white businessmen in Athens Point. When Carl was a boy, pumping units had operated right in people's yards, but few of the residents ever saw a dime of the money that oil generated. Even if they managed to save enough to buy the land their houses stood on, they weren't going to get mineral rights with it. Not in Sandy Bottom.

Carl drove past several six-thousand-square-foot houses set deep in the trees, then turned onto Lyonesse Drive and stopped at a makeshift roadblock. Deputy Willie Jones had parked his cruiser so that it blocked most of Lyonesse, and a sawhorse with orange tape on it blocked the rest. Willie was twenty-six, four years older than Carl, but he always treated Carl as if they were the same age. He walked up to Carl's Jeep Cherokee and grinned broadly.

"What's up, my brother? You off duty, huh?"

"Was. Not anymore."

"This be some shit, don't it?" Willie said with nervous excitement. "Dr. Shields all barricaded in his house and shit? Don't make no sense to me."

Carl nodded soberly. Warren Shields had been treating both his mother and father for the past six years, and they spoke of him almost reverently. Or they had until Carl's mother had her stroke, which was what had brought Carl back to Athens Point rather than to Atlanta, where his girlfriend lived. Now only Carl's father could praise Dr. Shields in intelligible words. Dr. Shields had spent several hours with Carl and his father over the past year, advising them on how best to care for Eugenia Sims, and Carl had instinctively liked the man. Shields treated his father with the respect due an older man, and he treated Carl just as he would anybody else, no better or worse. Carl liked that. Shields reminded him of doctors he'd known in the service, truly color-blind and focused on their work.

"You don't think they'll tell you to shoot Dr. Shields, do you?" Willie asked, his smile suddenly gone. "I mean, not without trying to talk him out first?"

Carl shook his head. "Let's hope not."

Willie gave an exaggerated nod.

"Is the sheriff here?" Carl asked.

Willie shook his head. "He fishing over in Louisiana. They sent Major Danny up to get him in the helicopter."

*Bad luck,* Carl thought. "Who's in charge now?"

Willie curled his lips and shook his head. "You know who. They done called out the TRU, ain't they? Old Cowboy Ray hisself. Him and his little brother are up there unloading all their SWAT shit. Looks like the FBI at Waco or something."

The Tactical Response Unit was Athens Point's version of a SWAT team. It comprised fifteen officers recruited from both the municipal police and the Sheriff's Department. About half had military experience, most in the National Guard. Carl was one of the few who had served in Iraq; he was the team's designated sniper.

*"Hey, Willie!"* crackled Jones's radio. *"Any sign of Carl yet?"*

Willie rolled his eyes at the heavy redneck accent coming from his radio. "Deputy Sims just pulled up, sir."

*"Well, send him back here. We're setting up the position, and I want to get his input on interlocking angles of fire."*

"Jesus," said Carl.

"Uh-huh," Willie agreed.

"Has anybody even talked to Dr. Shields yet?"

Willie shrugged. Then his radio crackled again.

*"We've set up the command post in the Shieldses' front yard, under a stand of trees. Tell Carl to get his ass up here, ricky-tick."*

"You heard the man," said Willie.

Carl exhaled long and slow, trying to prepare himself for the blast of testosterone he would encounter a few hundred yards up the street.

"I hope the sheriff gets here soon," Willie said.

"You and me both, brother."

Carl took his foot off the brake and idled up Lyonesse. Nearly two months since the TRU was last called out. In that case, they'd received a report of a man barricaded in his downtown house with his family. What the TRU found when it arrived on the scene was quite different: a local engineer lying in his bathtub with a homemade bomb in his lap and his family safe outside. The TRU didn't have a trained hostage negotiator, so anybody might wind up talking to the subject, depending on circumstances. In the engineer's case, the sheriff had spent two hours talking to him through the bathroom window, shielded by the wall, a flak jacket, and a bulletproof helmet. Sheriff Ellis had less than two years on the job, and his last law-enforcement experience had been as an MP in Germany twenty years before. He was a God-fearing man who had a good rapport with people, but it hadn't been enough. The engineer blew himself up while the sheriff prayed for his immortal soul, repainting the bathroom with what had been his insides a millisecond before. Sheriff Ellis was wounded by ricocheting shrapnel that turned out to be a chunk of jawbone.

Carl had watched all this through his 10X Unertl scope, from a deer stand he'd mounted in a tree in a neighbor's yard. He'd wanted to destroy the bomb's works with a bullet, but since the device was clutched in the engineer's lap, he couldn't do it without killing the man. The hand holding the detonator was concealed behind the cast-iron side of the tub, so that option was out. The only other way to stop the bomb from exploding would have been to fire a round through the engineer's brain stem, short-circuiting his nervous system, but the rules for bombers were different in Mississippi than they'd been in Iraq—at least when the only people they threatened were themselves.

Carl put the incident out of his mind as he rolled up Lyonesse, because thinking about it only led him to the incident before that one—the one that had caused friction between him and the sheriff. He didn't need to cloud his mind with that right now.

Ahead, five cruisers sat parked on the street before a big Colonial set fifty meters back from the road. Mixed among them were civilian vehicles that belonged to the off-duty TRU men who'd been called up. Carl knew that his tactical commander was anxious, but he obeyed the speed limit and slowed for the speed bumps. He wanted to give the sheriff every opportunity to arrive before Ray Breen did something ill-advised.

Law enforcement in Athens Point was a curious thing. The police department had jurisdiction over the city, and by tradition the Sheriff's Department took the outlying county. But technically the sheriff had jurisdiction over the city as well. Before 1968, both departments had been 100 percent white, but gradually the police department came to more closely resemble the city itself, which was 55 percent black. The county as a whole had a similar percentage, but geographically blacks tended to congregate in the city, while the outlying county was mostly white. This had somehow resulted in an unbroken line of white sheriffs (Carl figured it was the shape of the voting districts). He would have preferred working for the black police chief, but the pay and benefits were better in the Sheriff's Department, so he'd opted to work in the county.

Most of his fellow TRU deputies were white country boys of a type Carl knew well. The majority were ten to fifteen years older than he, and some were over fifty. In a town with high unemployment, men didn't give up jobs with benefits unless they were pushed out—usually after an election. But despite the age and background of the men, there was an attitude of benign tolerance toward black officers in the unit. Prejudice still existed, but it was an amorphous thing, difficult to point at and impossible to prove, except in a few cases. Even the hard-core, Southern-rock NASCAR types accepted that civil rights reforms were here to stay, and they tried to make the best of it.

Beyond this, Carl was a special case. His military record as a sniper gave him an almost magical immunity to prejudice. In his experience, white country boys were fairly primitive in their social habits, creatures of dominance and submission, like the hunting dogs he'd raised as a boy. Physical prowess meant a lot, the ability to withstand pain meant more, but nothing ranked higher in their estimation than combat experience. If a man had shed blood in the mud and held his nerve under fire, then it didn't make a damn bit of difference what color he was—not to most of them, anyway. As a sniper with a near-legendary number of confirmed kills, Carl occupied rarefied air in the redneck firmament. The fact that he was black had put some of those good old boys in the curious position of almost fawning over a guy they might have tried to kick the shit out of if he'd wandered into their neighborhood at night.

Carl parked his Cherokee behind the rearmost cruiser and got his rain slicker out of the cargo compartment. He decided to leave his rifle case locked in the vehicle. The slower things moved, the more time there would be for hormones to stabilize and adrenaline to be flushed away.

He saw the mobile command post over the roofs of the cruisers. The camouflage-painted camper trailer had been towed under a small stand of trees and braced with cinder blocks. The steady rumble of a generator echoed over the flat ground, which meant lights in the trailer, if not air-conditioning. Carl reminded himself that he was only a deputy, not the ranking member of an autonomous sniper-scout unit, as he had been in Iraq. His job when he stepped into the trailer would be to take orders, not give them. And any advice he offered was likely to be rejected unless it reinforced what his superiors had already decided.

His biggest worry right now was the Breen brothers, one of whom was the commander of the Tactical Response Unit, subject only to Sheriff Ellis in a situation like this one. The Breen brothers looked to have been cut from the same piece of wood. They had farmer's tans, cracked skin, and slit eyes that betrayed so much meanness it made people take a step back, even when they were out of uniform. Both were lean and gaunt, the younger one, Trace, so much so that Carl wondered if he'd suffered some nutritional disease like rickets as a child. But maybe Trace just stayed so pissed off all the time that his anger had begun to consume him. Ray, the elder of the pair, was bulkier and had a more open face than his brother, despite his cowboy mustache. He'd served in the army during the lean years after Vietnam, as an MP, like Sheriff Ellis. He was also a Weekend Warrior like Ellis, but though Ray's unit had been called up for Bosnia, he hadn't seen action there either. He'd worked as a welder for a while, but got fired because he kept getting into fights. Only when he hired on with the Sheriff's Department had he found his calling; he wore the uniform like a suit of armor, and Carl could tell that the power of the job was what got Ray Breen out of bed every morning.

Ray reveled in the high-tech equipment of his Tactical Response Unit. Over the past few years, he had somehow scrounged together an arsenal that could adequately supply an urban SWAT unit. The TRU had automatic weapons, flash-bang grenades, shaped charges, advanced commo gear, and night-vision devices. In his off hours Ray read Tom Clancy, Dale Brown, and Larry Bond, or played *Rainbow Six: Splinter Cell* on his son's Xbox 360. If Carl chanced to meet Ray Breen in Wal-Mart or at a high school football game, the commander would squint and give a slight nod, as though to say, *We're part of an elite team. These civilians know we're always on the look-out for trouble.*

Ray had pulled Carl aside dozens of times to talk shop, asking detailed questions about the capabilities of various sniper rifles, scopes, and night-vision systems. But inevitably, after all the hardware questions had been answered, Breen would circle down to the question he'd really wanted to ask: *What's it like to blow some unsuspecting raghead's shit away from a thousand yards?* Carl always answered the same way: *I tried not to think about that side of it, sir. It was a job, and I focused on the mechanics of it.* Guys like Ray Breen never grasped the true nature of sniping. It was as much about concealment as it was about shooting. Carl had once spent two days constructing a hide in Baghdad, then another waiting motionless with his scout to take a single shot that a twelve-year-old kid could have made in his backyard in Sandy Bottom. But he didn't blame the TRU commander. The homeboys he'd played ball with at Athens Point High had asked the same question after they got a couple of beers in them. All human beings, Carl had learned, were fascinated with death. Only those who knew death intimately, as he did, understood its essential mystery.

Carl's eyes tracked a thin form slinking out of the CP trailer. Trace Breen. In the vernacular of Carl's father, Trace was a skunk. Lying was mother's milk to him. He had no military experience, and Carl assumed he'd ridden his brother's coattails onto the TRU, as nominal communications officer. From scuttlebutt around the department, Carl had gathered that Trace had worked a dozen different jobs before becoming a deputy, none of them productive. He'd been a roustabout at construction sites (where materials tended to disappear at night); he'd sold stereos out of the back of a van (most of those stolen, too); he'd worked as a hunting guide (poaching alligators at night); he'd also run dogfights, and pursued various other fly-by-night enterprises that went nowhere. Even now, Trace had some kind of cell phone scam going, selling disposable phones out of his car. Carl figured a truckload of the things must have been hijacked over in Texas or somewhere.

"Hey, Red Cloud!" Trace had caught sight of Carl. "Ray wants you in the CP like yesterday. You better double-time it, soldier."

Carl let the nickname roll off him. He didn't like anyone outside the Marine Corps using it. The local guys only got wind of *Red Cloud* after discovering an article about marine snipers in Baghdad on the CNN

Internet archives. Carl raised his left hand to acknowledge the remark, then headed for the command post.

Unlike the other white deputies, Trace Breen made no effort to conceal his dislike of African-Americans. If Carl passed him alone in a corridor, Trace would look pointedly at the ceiling or chuckle softly, as though amused at the idea of a black man in a deputy's uniform. If they met in public, Trace either pretended Carl didn't exist or snickered in the ear of whatever trashy blonde happened to be hanging off his arm. Lately, Carl had heard rumors that Trace might be dabbling in the drug business—specifically crystal meth—a trade he'd apparently worked at as a teenager. Carl had already decided that if he picked up concrete information about this activity, he would follow wherever it led. The sheriff might not want to bust his own deputies, but Carl figured if he made the arrest, Billy Ray Ellis would have no choice but to follow through.

Carl stopped before the trailer door and looked up at the Shields house. If what the dispatcher had told him was true, his mother's soft-spoken physician was barricaded behind the idyllic facade of that house, and he might already have killed someone. If Shields had done that, Carl might well be asked to take the man out, and soon. Before darkness fell, probably. He scanned the northern sky, hoping to see Danny McDavitt's chopper zooming out of the dark clouds gathering there, but he saw nothing.

The trailer door opened suddenly, and Carl stood face-to-face with Ray Breen. Breen wore a dark brown cowboy hat pulled low over his mustached face, but it was the flak jacket that startled Carl. Body armor was SOP for hostage situations, but still. Carl realized then that deep down he had not quite accepted that Dr. Shields had taken anyone hostage.

"Where's your weapon, Deputy?" Breen asked.

"In my Jeep."

Ray frowned. "It ain't gonna do us any good there, is it? Come on, Carl. We don't have a lot of daylight left."

"Eighty minutes," Carl said. "Less, if those clouds come over, which it looks like they will."

Breen gave a tight grin and slapped his shoulder. "I knew you were already thinking. Get your gear, son. This is big."

Carl didn't move. "Could I ask you something, sir?"

The grin vanished. Breen sensed resistance, and he didn't like it. "Go ahead."

"Has anyone talked to Dr. Shields yet?"

"Yeah, me. His wife and daughter are in there, and probably his partner, Dr. Auster. I spoke to the wife and kid, but I think Auster's dead."

"Why?"

"Shields wouldn't let me talk to him. We know there were shots fired, but the kid who got out isn't positive who fired them. He thought he saw a man lying on his back in the hall, but he was on the second-floor landing and didn't get a good look."

Carl wondered if this was the best intel they were going to get.

"We think they're in the main downstairs room now," Breen went on. "What they call the great room. I talked to the architect, and he's bringing a set of plans out here. There's big windows facing the backyard, but they're those fancy ones with the blinds built into them, between two panes of glass. They pretty much wipe out all visibility."

Carl nodded, surprised to find himself grateful for this obstacle.

"That ain't all," Breen said. "There was a fire at Dr. Shields's office about an hour ago. We don't have many details, but right now it's possible that Shields set that fire himself. A nurse at the hospital also told me there are some state or federal agents in the ER. There might be some kind of investigation going on that we don't know about. Something to do with Dr. Shields."

Carl said nothing. None of this made sense to him, but then he had few facts to work with. For the time being, he'd have to leave the situation in the less-than-masterful hands of Ray Breen and pray that the sheriff got here quick. Even that prospect made him feel only slightly better. The sheriff had been a petroleum land man for much of his life. The only thing that might stop Sheriff Ellis from doing the same thing Ray Breen would do was fear of a negative reaction from the voters in the next election. What gave Carl the most comfort was knowing that Danny McDavitt would be sitting beside the sheriff during any negotiations that might happen in the next few minutes.

"Get your rifle, Carl," Ray said. "The sheriff's still thirty minutes out. The wheels could come off this thing any second."

"Yes, sir," Carl said, starting back toward his Jeep.

He kept looking northward as he walked. More rain was coming; he would have known that with a blindfold on. Carl was a country boy, too.

He could smell rain ten miles away.

• • •

Danny crossed the Mississippi River just east of Lake Concordia and dropped out of the rain clouds at five hundred feet. This leg of the Mississippi was dotted with oxbow lakes, and Lake St. John lay just ahead. He flew around the eastern rim of the C-shaped lake, his eyes tracking the well-trimmed lots that bordered the eastern shore. As he neared the midpoint of the seven-mile horseshoe, he saw a cluster of brightly colored pavilion tents beside a large cypress lake house. A group of men had gathered in a muddy cotton field across the road, and they began waving him down when they caught sight of the helicopter.

Danny descended rapidly toward the group, then flared at the last moment and touched down softly in the newly planted field. A big man wearing a brown uniform and clutching a Stetson to his head ran beneath the spinning rotor blades and opened the door on the Bell's left side. Billy Ray Ellis was a big man, still muscular at fifty-three, with burly forearms covered in black hair. Despite his limited law enforcement experience, he was so popular in the county that he'd beaten the incumbent sheriff by twenty percentage points. Ellis heaved his bulk into the seat beside Danny, yanked the door shut, pulled on the second headset, and started talking as he fastened his harness.

"Get this baby back in the air, Danny. Push her hard as she'll go. We got a bad situation waiting for us."

Danny pulled pitch and applied power with the collective, then nudged the cyclic. The Bell tilted forward and bit into the sky. "What's happened? The message I got said Code Black. Is it a school shooting or something?"

Ellis shook his big head. "Do you know Dr. Shields? Warren Shields?"

Danny felt as though the bottom had fallen out of the chopper. "Yeah," he managed to choke out. "I taught him to fly last year."

"That's right, I forgot. Well, apparently, Dr. Shields has barricaded himself inside his residence, and he's holding his wife and daughter hostage."

Danny closed his eyes, fighting vertigo. After several moments of composing himself, he opened them again, picked out a landmark on the ground, and said, "How do you know that?"

"Shields's nine-year-old son managed to escape the house and get to a neighbor's place. Jumped off the roof or something. It's the daughter who's still in the house. The boy thinks his daddy shot somebody. We don't know who that was yet, but it could be Shields's partner, Kyle Auster."

"That's unbelievable," breathed Danny, trying to mask his panic.

"I agree. There was also some kind of fire at their medical office a little while ago. Details are sketchy, but some people were hurt bad. It may be that Shields set the fire. I don't know if the man's lost his mind or what. I always liked him myself."

"Who's on the scene now?"

"Ray Breen's assembling the TRU as they arrive."

*Shit.* "Good, good."

"Ray talked to the wife and little girl on the phone—"

Relief flooded through Danny like a narcotic.

"—but Shields wouldn't put Dr. Auster on. Sounds fishy, don't it?"

Danny nodded and pushed the engine to its limit. As soon as the sheriff got distracted, he would take out his clone phone and see whether Laurel had managed to send him any messages.

"Shields sure has a pretty wife," Ellis said thoughtfully. "You know her?"

"She teaches my son."

"Oh," said the sheriff, his voice suddenly grave. "That's right." Ellis was a deacon in the Baptist church, and he tended to assume the manner of a pastor when discussing anything he saw as a sad circumstance. An autistic son obviously qualified in his book. "Have you heard any rumors of marital problems?" he asked, changing the subject. "Anything like that?"

Danny stared stone-faced through the windshield. "Nothing. But then I never hear anything like that."

"Me either. But in my experience, when this kind of thing happens, there's marriage trouble at the bottom of it. Does Shields have a hot temper?"

"No. The opposite, in fact."

The departmental radio suddenly crackled to life in Danny's headset.

"Sheriff, this is Ray at the command post. I got a fella down here claiming to be a government agent, and he's causing me all kind of problems."

Ellis picked up the mike and keyed it angrily. "What kind of government agent? An FBI man or what?"

"One ID says he's a special investigator for the attorney general, and another says he's with the state Medicaid office. Name's Paul Biegler. Says he's down here investigatin' Dr. Shields and Dr. Auster for some sort of fraud."

The sheriff knit his heavy brows in puzzlement. "Is he standing right there, Ray?"

"No, sir. I got him waitin' outside the trailer. He claims he was in that fire over at Dr. Auster's office. Claims one of the employees tried to blow the place up. He's got bandages on his face, and he says he was wounded by shrapnel or something. He's got two other boys with him, and he's trying to take over the damn scene."

"*What?* Repeat that."

"I said, Biegler says he's got federal warrants for Dr. Shields and Dr. Auster, and that makes this a federal case. He says if we don't give him tactical command, he's going to call the FBI down from Jackson to take over."

Danny saw the sheriff's knuckles go white. "Bull*shit* he's going to take over our scene. You keep that son of a bitch on ice until I get there, you hear?"

"Yes, sir. A big ten-four on that."

"How far out are we, Danny?"

Danny scanned the river for landmarks, then checked his airspeed. "Twenty minutes, tops."

"Tell him I'm almost there now, Ray. And put a man on him. Let me know if he makes any calls to Jackson."

"You got it, Sheriff."

"Out."

Ellis turned to Danny. "What in the Sam Hill is going on? Sounds like our good doctors have got themselves into serious trouble. It wouldn't surprise me to learn that Kyle Auster was up to no good. But Dr. Shields? I just can't see that one."

"Me, either," Danny agreed. "He's a straight arrow."

"I got to think about this. You remember what happened with that engineer on Milburn Street? Blew hisself all over me without so much as a by-your-leave. And he was alone in the house. If Dr. Shields really has his wife and daughter in there, and if he's really shot his partner, I might have to send the TRU in there hard."

Danny closed his eyes in silent prayer. Most of Ellis's deputies had only moderate training, and their practical law enforcement experience was limited. Worse, the TRU was commanded by a deputy with juvenile delusions of heroism. The possibility that those men might make an assault into Laurel's house with grenades and automatic weapons nauseated him with fear. He could not allow that to happen.

When Sheriff Ellis settled back in his seat with his thoughts, Danny let go of the collective and pulled his cell phone out of his pants pocket. No new messages. Nevertheless, he flipped open the phone and began keying a message with his left hand. The first he sent read, *On my way there wi sheriff. u or Bth hurt? Auster alive? If yes, condition?* He started to put the phone away, then sent an immediate follow-up: *No one knows we have this link. Tell me all u safely can. How W armed? He intend imminent harm?* As Danny slid the phone beneath his left leg for easy access, Sheriff Ellis spoke again.

"Must be pretty important messages to slow us down for."

Danny gritted his teeth. "We're not going any slower. This is like taking your hand off the wheel in a car, but leaving your foot on the gas. I increased friction on the collective, so it stays in place."

Ellis's eyes were still on the cell phone.

"Problems with taking care of my boy," Danny lied. "My wife didn't come home to let the babysitter go on time."

"You can't just call her?"

"We don't talk so much these days."

Ellis grunted. "That's a shame. Marriage ain't easy, but you got to stick with it."

*Thanks a million, Dr. Phil.*

"You don't go to church, do you, Dan?"

*Oh, boy.* "Not much, Sheriff. Not for a while now. I'm not much for group worship. I get my quiet time in the woods. And in the air."

"I hear you, brother. But it's not the same, you know. You ought to come see us at First Baptist. I think you'd be surprised."

*Not if this is any indication.* "I may give it a try."

"At least talk to Reverend Cyrus about your marital problems."

Danny cleared his throat and spoke as diffidently as he could. "Sheriff, could I offer a little input on the hostage situation?"

"Absolutely. This is one of those situations where there's ten tragic things that could happen, and only one good thing."

"You're right. Sheriff, I would think long and hard before I considered sending Ray Breen and his boys into that house. Even the people who do that kind of thing for a living—I'm talking about Delta and the SEALs—they're hesitant to go into a situation with innocent friendlies in a confined space. I'm not saying anything against Ray, but if you turn insufficiently trained men loose in a house with automatic weapons,

God only knows who'll wind up dead. The wife, the little girl, some of our own guys maybe. I'd sure hate to see that, and I know you would, too."

Ellis was nodding as though in agreement. "You said a mouthful there. A standoff's a tricky thing. On the other hand, I've got a responsibility to that wife and little girl, not to mention this community. How would it look if we just stood by while Dr. Shields executed his wife, his daughter, and his partner? That wouldn't say much for my department, would it?"

Danny tried to hide his true feelings. Ellis was already as focused on how the drama would play out before the voters as he was on the safety of the people inside the house. "No, you're in a tough position, that's a fact. And I wouldn't presume to tell you what to do."

"But . . . ?" Ellis prompted.

"If it comes down to having to take Dr. Shields out, I'd have Carl Sims do the shooting."

"From long range, you mean."

"Yes, sir. I've seen that boy shoot, and he's as good as the snipers in the Secret Service. He could take out Shields with zero collateral damage, even if the doctor was holding his little girl in his arms."

"He could," said the sheriff. "But *will* he? That's what's on my mind."

Danny cringed inside. Six months ago, Sheriff Ellis had given Carl Sims authorization to shoot a young black man who had taken a hostage while robbing a local bank. In Ellis's mind, he had given a clear order to kill, effective as soon as Sims had a clean shot. But Carl interpreted the order differently and blasted the robber's gun hand into pulp instead. Danny heard that the sheriff had nearly had a stroke over this, and only the media praise he'd gotten afterward for his "restraint" had saved Carl Sims's job. Instead of getting a pink slip, Carl got a medal, one that probably didn't mean much after the hatful he'd received from the Marine Corps.

*It's all fucking politics,* Danny thought. *Even the life-or-death calls.*

He wanted to beg Ellis to at least consult with the FBI in Jackson, but he knew the sheriff would reflexively reject this idea. Why? Because the FBI could have a SWAT team at the Shields house in three hours, even if they had to come by road. If they used a chopper, they could be fully deployed in two. And unlike the Sheriff's Department, the Bureau had strict rules of engagement for hostage situations, written in the wake of Waco and Ruby Ridge. They would only assault the Shields house as a last resort, after all other means of resolution had been exhausted. Billy Ray Ellis wanted no such constraints on his decision-making. Short of a written order from the governor, he would not hand over tactical command of the scene to a federal agency, not in his county. Some men might see a federal assumption of authority as the ultimate out, an ideal way to cover their ass, but ex–football stars didn't think that way. Danny kept his mouth shut, figuring he could accomplish more from inside the tent than out of it.

"Are you pedal to the metal, Danny?" Ellis asked tersely.

"We're at the VNE now, sir."

"The what?"

Danny pointed at a small gauge in front of the sheriff. "Velocity never exceeded. She can't do another knot without burning up the engine."

"Okay, then. Just keep her at the redline."

As the sheriff glanced out at the ever-darkening clouds, Danny checked his phone for text messages.

There were none.


Carl Sims slowly worked his way back to the front of the Shields property, naturally moving from tree to tree, assessing the cover-and-concealment potential of each position. Snipers liked open spaces about as much as deer and rabbits did; they would do almost anything to avoid them. Twelve minutes after he'd started, he returned to the stand of trees that half hid the trailer serving as the TRU's tactical command post.

He needed to take a leak. The most sheltered spot was a narrow space between the trees and the rear of the trailer. He set his rifle butt-first on the ground and leaned it against a pine, then unzipped his fly and began to urinate against the next tree. He'd developed this habit as a boy and refined it in Iraq. Pissing against a tree or a wall could be almost silent, if you did it right; this practice had probably saved his life once in Baghdad. He was half-finished when he heard voices on the air. He quickly zeroed in on the source as a small, screened window in the back of the trailer. After zipping up, he moved toward the opening and peered through it from an off angle.

Ray and Trace Breen sat hunched over a Formica table, smoking cigarettes and talking in low voices. A pack of Camels and a .40 caliber pistol lay between them on a topographic map of the area. The smoke was so thick in the trailer that a steady draft of it was being forced through the window beside Carl's face. He had to struggle not to cough.

"Hell, I *wish* he'd pop off a round in there," said Ray. "Something. Shit, if he don't, we're liable to be here all night listening to the sheriff holler through a bullhorn."

Trace nodded and blew out a long stream of blue smoke. "Yep."

"I tell you what else worries me. Our sharpshooter."

Trace snickered at the word.

"You know what I'm talking about?" Ray said.

"Damn straight. That nigger might of killed a bunch of towelheads over in Iraq, but I don't think he's got the stomach for shootin' Americans."

Ray was nodding. "You saw what happened at the bank. Sheriff told him to take the perp out, and what did he do?"

"Blowed the motherfucker's hand off instead. What if he missed? A hand's a hell of a lot smaller than a head."

"Moves a lot more, too," Ray observed. "That coon can shoot, I'll give him that. But what he can't seem to do is follow orders. Which is strange in a marine."

"Awful strange."

Carl was tempted to shove the barrel of his Remington 700 through the window screen and scare the piss out of both Breen brothers, but he didn't. He had been quiet before, but now he stood with the sniper's stillness, a motionless state he equated with absolute zero, that condition of coldness in which not even electrons spin around their respective nuclei. Carl could remain in that state for many hours, and had, more times than he could remember. His respiration and heartbeat slowed until it seemed an age between each, an age during which he had almost infinite leisure to pull his trigger without being disturbed by the movement of breath or blood.

"You want to know something?" Trace said. "Something you don't know?"

"If you ain't told me yet, maybe I don't need to know. 'Cause Lord knows you can't keep a secret."

"I kept this one."

Ray chuckled and took a drag on his cigarette. "How long you kep' it?"

"Twenty years."

Ray coughed up smoke. "If this has anything to do with my wife, I'm gonna kill your ass. I'm telling you that right now."

Trace shook his head. "It's about that cocky sumbitch up in the house. The doctor."

"Shields?"

"Yep."

"What do you know about him?"

Trace's eyes smoldered with secret knowledge. "Plenty. Remember when he kilt that boy in his parents' house? Jimmy Birdlow?"

"Course I do. We were just talking about it outside."

Trace nodded. "Well, I was there."

Ray sat up at the table. "What?"

"Sure was. This was back when I was gettin' high a lot. And Jimmy was *always* gettin' high. He wanted some Dex to stay awake, and we didn't have no money. We just happened to be over in that neighborhood, and the Shieldses' house was the closest one that didn't have no lights on. Jimmy figured he'd just slip in and grab a TV, something he could trade for the pills. But the old man must have been awake, 'cause next thing I know, I'm staring in from the back patio at Jimmy and Mr. Shields screaming at each other. Jimmy was trying to explain, but the old man wouldn't give him a chance. He started yelling how he was going to call the police. And the next thing I know, Jimmy pulls out a gun."

Ray was staring at his younger brother with wide eyes. Carl blinked slowly, then leaned forward so as not to miss a word.

"Jimmy wouldna shot him," Trace asserted. "He just didn't want the man to call the law."

"Why didn't he just run, then?" Ray asked.

"He tried to, but Shields's daddy tripped him up. Then he got between Jimmy and the door. Then the mama come in there, too, wearing her damn housecoat."

"When did Shields show up?"

"Hell, I didn't even know he *was* there till he shot Jimmy in the back. Sumbitch didn't give Jimmy no warning or nothing."

Ray leaned back in his chair and silently regarded his brother.

"Bastard," Trace muttered. "Blew Jimmy's heart out the front of his chest."

Ray shook his head. "You said Jimmy was holding a gun on his daddy."

"He wouldna shot him!"

"You think Shields knew that? Jimmy broke in their goddamn house! I'd of shot him, too. You're lucky he didn't shoot *your* ass through the window."

Trace shook his head bitterly. "I tell you one thing, if I had a gun that night, I'd of killed that motherfucker dead."

"Boy, if a bird had your brains, he'd fly backwards. I can't believe you didn't wind up in Parchman before your twenty-first birthday."

"I ain't stupid. And I'll tell you something else. I hope that sumbitch tries something up in that fancy house. I *hope* the sheriff sends us in there. 'Cause I will blow his shit away, no lie. For what he done to Jimmy."

"Jesus, Trace. You need to calm down."

"You said the same exact thing a minute ago!"

Ray sucked thoughtfully on his cigarette.

"I don't like him," Trace insisted. "People act like he's a damn saint or something. You ever see him out at the baseball field? Sumbitch thinks the rules don't apply to him. Or his kid, neither."

"I forgot," said Ray. "Shields's team beat your boy's like a drum last spring, didn't they?"

"Cheated us, is what they done."

Ray stubbed out his cigarette and stood as best he could in the low-ceilinged trailer. "Nobody's called on the radio. Let's get out there and see if we can't make something happen before Billy Ray gets here."

"Damn straight. What about that government man? Beagle."

"Fuck him. Billy Ray ain't gonna give him the time of day."

Trace pushed himself up off the table, leaving his cigarette burning in the ashtray. "Damn straight."

Like a lizard clinging to the window screen, Carl watched the two deputies leave the trailer. He wasn't sure what, if anything, to do about what he'd heard. Sheriff Ellis wasn't going to change the makeup of the Tactical Response Unit in the middle of a crisis. And

Trace Breen's presence at a shooting twenty years ago couldn't be corroborated by anyone; therefore, his motive for revenge could not be proved. As for the racist remarks about Carl, that was just the reality that underlay the veneer of courtesy he encountered every day. The president of the United States couldn't change that, much less the sheriff of Lusahatcha County. But Ray Breen was right about one thing: marine sniper Carl Sims did not intend to kill another living soul unless it was to save a life in clear and present danger.

He shouldered his Remington and walked soundlessly around the trailer to join his fellow deputies.

# CHAPTER

# 16

Danny just beat the storm clouds to Athens Point. He flew low over the city, angling along the hills, then cutting eastward once he'd passed the old sawmill. His nerves were jangling, but at least he knew Laurel was alive.

Five minutes ago, Trace Breen had tried to patch Dr. Shields through to Sheriff Ellis on the radio. The connection had been poor, but Danny had heard Laurel's voice when the sheriff asked Shields for confirmation that she was all right. Laurel told Ellis that Beth was asleep, but she fell silent when he asked her about Dr. Auster. After Shields took back the phone, Ellis had informed him that he was flying next to the doctor's old flight instructor. Shields asked Danny how he was doing, and Danny said fine. The whole conversation had the feel of a family phone call, like talking to relatives on vacation in a foreign country. The connection died soon after that, and when Trace called Shields back, the doctor didn't answer.

"I want you to stay close to me when we land," Ellis said as they dropped toward the earth. "I'm thinking this chopper might make a good diversion if we have to go in hard."

Danny nodded, trying to swallow with a mouth devoid of saliva.

"That's the neighborhood, isn't it?" Ellis said, pointing down to some patches of open grass in the forest below.

"That's it. Shields's land is in a bend of Larrieu's Creek."

Danny picked out the serpentine creek and followed it eastward. Soon he saw the slate blue roof of the Shields house, nestled in a curve of trees that grew along the waterway.

"Damn," said Ellis. "There's at least fifty meters of open ground on all sides of that place."

"Except that back corner." Danny pointed through the windshield. A broken line of trees marched up from the creek's ravine to the southwest corner of the house.

"That must be where the son got out," Ellis said.

They could see the cruisers gathered in front of the house, and a roadblock at the entrance of Lyonesse Drive. Someone had even put up a red flag as a wind indicator, Danny noticed, on a pole standing in the clear space behind the department's camper trailer.

"There's the command post," said Ellis. "Set her down, Danny."

"Twenty seconds."

The sheriff unhooked his harness as Danny pulled back on the cyclic and flared in. Then Ellis opened the door and jumped to the ground like MacArthur going ashore in the Philippines. "Remember, stay close!" he called over his shoulder.

Danny checked his phone for new messages. Finding none, he climbed out and secured the main rotor to the tail boom with the tie-down kit. There was liable to be some real wind before he flew out of this place again.

When he was satisfied, he walked over to the command post, where a small knot of men had gathered around the sheriff. Three of them wore dark business suits, and one seemed to be getting in the sheriff's face pretty good.

The aggressive stranger's hair was cropped short, and it had receded on both sides of his scalp, leaving a sharp V of aggression in the middle of his forehead. He looked about forty-five, but the flesh of his face was tight, with no sagging around the jaws. The kind of guy who woke up at 5 a.m. every day to run four miles. As soon as Danny was close enough to hear, he realized that the man in the suit was the agent Ray Breen had been complaining about: Paul Biegler.

"States' rights versus federal authority," the sheriff was saying. "Somehow, it always seems to come down to that with you people. I guess you want to refight the Civil War right here, Agent Biegler."

"Yankee sumbitch," someone muttered.

"I was born in Arkansas," Biegler snapped, cutting his eyes at Trace Breen.

"Well, I don't have time to debate constitutional issues with you," Ellis said. "I've got a crisis to resolve."

"How?" asked Biegler. "You don't have any intelligence."

Ellis drew himself to his full height. "You people may think we're all dumb down here, but we—"

"Information!" Biegler snapped. "You don't have

any *information* about your subject. Intel, Sheriff. Ring a bell?"

For a moment Ellis was speechless, so Biegler charged on. "I've spoken to Kyle Auster's office manager at the hospital. She's in critical condition. Third-degree burns over forty percent of her body. She told me that she and Auster were behind the fraud. They've been having an affair for years. Shields went along with some of it for the past few months, but that's all."

"If Shields is the good guy in all this," said the sheriff, "then why did he shoot Auster?"

"Maybe Auster provoked him."

"Or maybe this office manager's really been screwing Dr. Shields," suggested Ellis, "and she's trying to do whatever she can to protect him."

Biegler shook his head. "Vida Roberts has worked in medicine for twenty years, Sheriff. She knew she wasn't going to make it when she talked to me. That's a deathbed confession. Admissible in court."

Ellis's face was getting redder by the second. "So, what are you saying? We should just pack up and go home? Let these two fine fellows work things out on their own?"

"Of course not! I'm saying that if Auster's still alive, you've got two different subjects in there. Two different psychologies. And you don't know who's really controlling things."

"I think Auster's dead," Sheriff Ellis said with conviction. "I just talked to Dr. Shields. I heard his voice when he said Auster couldn't come to the phone."

"You'd better be sure."

Ellis gave the agent a patronizing smile. "Well, I sure thank you for your brilliant insights."

"Sheriff, listen—"

"Now, I'd appreciate it if you'd carry your ass about four hundred yards that way." Ellis gestured back toward the highway with a sweep of his big forearm. "Down past my perimeter. I don't want to see you back up here unless you've got something that will give me a tactical advantage in this standoff. Are we clear?"

Biegler's eyes went flat as a shark's, and he spoke in a low voice. "I can federalize this scene, Sheriff. I *will* bring the FBI down here from Jackson."

"This thing's gonna be over with before you get anybody down here."

Biegler sighed. "If you think that, you don't know much about hostage situations."

"I reckon we'll see, won't we?"

"Ellis, if you fuck this up, you'll answer to the attorney general. And I'm not talking about the one in Mississippi."

"Go suck an egg."

Sheriff Ellis walked away from the trailer and signaled Danny to join him.

Biegler stared after them for a few moments, then turned and marched off toward the roadblock.

Trace Breen barked a laugh. "That sumbitch is shakin' like a dog shittin' a peach pit."

"You sure told his ass," Ray agreed.

Ellis rounded on his deputies, his dark eyes blazing. "You TRU boys have been spending a boatload of my budget on training and equipment. Well, you got till exactly dark to prove you're worth it. Understood?"

The smiles vanished. "Yessir," Ray snapped out. "Let's get to it, boys."

Danny had to stretch out his legs to stay up with Ellis

as the sheriff strode down the border of the Shieldses'
front yard.

"Where are we headed?" Danny asked.

"Neighbors' house. Frank Elfman's. They got Dr.
Shields's boy over there. I think we ought to hear him
out ourselves before we shoot anybody, don't you?"

Danny felt the coiled spring in his chest loosen just
a little. "Absolutely."

Laurel lay on her side on the great room sofa, her
arms and legs once again bound tightly with duct tape.
Warren had taped her ankles first, so she had risked
slipping the Razr from her pocket and sliding it beneath her before he taped her wrists. The forty seconds
it had taken him to do that were the tensest she'd experienced since the ordeal began.

Beth lay sound asleep on the red leather sofa in the
study, thanks to a sedative dose of Benadryl calculated
by her father. Warren himself was sitting at his study
desk. His large, flat-panel computer monitor hid his
face from Laurel, and she was thankful, because it allowed her ready access to her cell phone. The Roche-
Bobois sofa was a modern piece, with spare lines and
minimal padding on the arms. There wasn't much of
a crease in which to hide the Razr, but she had stuffed
the phone as deeply as she could into the crack between the arm and the seat, leaving only a thin line of
exposed metal.

Danny had sent two messages since she'd checked
the phone in the laundry room, the first telling her he
was on the way with the sheriff, the second asking
several questions about the situation inside the house.
She'd sent back a message that read: *KA dead by W.*

*Self-defense. Me & B all right 4 now. Tied up tho. More 2 come. Be patient.*

Danny's question as to whether Warren intended harm was harder to answer. Warren had hit her twice after Beth shorted out the laptop, and hard. But he hadn't shot her. What he had done was download another copy of Merlin's Magic into his study computer, so that he could try to break into her Hotmail account online. She wasn't too worried about that, since she didn't save e-mail messages online. There might be one or two of Danny's last e-mails in her online mailbox, but she didn't think so. Even if there were, the password-cracking program had to start again from scratch.

She was more worried about the safe room.

After taping Laurel up, Warren had carried his father's old deer rifle and some plastic trash bags into the safe room. His shotgun was presently leaning against his desk in the study. He'd been quite open about what he was doing, announcing that the trash bags could serve as temporary toilets. There was already enough food and water in the safe room to last for days, if not weeks, and the gun was self-explanatory. But he had not tried to move Laurel or Beth in there. She had a feeling that Warren saw the safe room as his last resort, a final redoubt in the event of a police assault, rather than a place to commit some terrible crime. His primary goal still seemed to be the discovery of her lover's identity, through cracking the Hotmail account.

She wanted to tell Danny about the guns and the safe room. But if she did, what would happen? Would she trigger an immediate rescue attempt? Were there people outside capable of bringing off a rescue without loss of life? She thought about the hostage rescues she'd read about or seen on the news. In most cases, it seemed, at least some hostages died before the hostage taker was killed.

*Before the hostage taker was killed . . .*

She craned her neck and looked at the top of Warren's head, just visible over his monitor. Rather than hatred, she felt pity for him. She had the sense of looking at a mental patient, a man who had been perfectly normal one day and woke up schizophrenic the next. Warren's mind had locked itself into the track of marital infidelity, and he could not disengage it. Did he deserve to die for that? Could she send out words that might doom him in the next few minutes?

Danny's assertion that no one outside knew of their phone link gave her pause. Was he simply trying to keep their love affair secret? Or did he not trust the sheriff completely? For that matter, was the sheriff even in charge out there? Nell Roberts had mentioned federal agents on the phone. What if the FBI was outside? Would Danny trust them? She needed to know more before deciding what further message to send out.

"Warren?" she called. "Would you come over here, please?"

"Why?"

"I need to ask you something."

More than a minute passed before his chair squeaked and he rose to walk into the great room. *Time means nothing to him,* she thought. *He's receding from the world.* The house phone had rung a half dozen times, yet he hadn't answered since he'd let her talk to Sheriff Ellis. She forced away the memory of Danny's voice during those few precious seconds; she couldn't focus when she let that sound loose in her head.

As Warren came toward her, she recalled how boyish and wild he'd looked this morning, after staying up all night searching for something Nell Roberts had warned him about. The irony was exquisitely tragic: Nell had tried to save Warren from Kyle and Vida, and by so doing had led Warren to Danny's letter, which might ultimately cause his death. Warren stopped three feet from her and sat on the ottoman he'd used earlier. He looked as though he'd aged fifteen years since this morning.

"I want to ask you something," Laurel said softly. "We've been married for twelve years, and in all that time you never raised a hand to me. You've been calm, rational, even kind most of the time. And now, in the span of a few hours, you've become a totally different person. Can you help me understand that?"

"You never betrayed me before."

"I don't think that's it. I really don't. If I'd told you a week ago that you were going to beat me and tie me up, you wouldn't have believed it. Not even because of adultery or anything else. And in front of our six-year-old child? You couldn't even have *imagined* that."

He blinked but said nothing.

"I'm worried about your mental health, Warren. I'm serious."

The faintest of smiles touched the corners of his mouth. "Your worries no longer worry me."

This set her back. "And our children's worries?"

"They'll know someday who really cared about them."

"What does that mean?" Laurel struggled against her bonds in frustration. "You're talking like a Delphic oracle. You keep telling me I've broken a trust. All right, what if I have? From what Kyle said, you've done the same thing with your patients. Or with yourself. Maybe both. I don't know, because you won't tell me. But he was talking about prison, Warren. Whatever you did must have been pretty bad. I don't understand it, but then I don't have to. Because I can forgive you, whatever you've done. I know you're a good man, deep down. So why can't you forgive me?"

"It's different. Completely different."

"How? Stealing is a lesser sin than adultery?"

"You don't know what you're talking about. You don't know what I've done, or why."

"I want to!"

"And I want to know what you've done. Are you going to tell me?"

She bit her bottom lip. She had certainly thought about confessing. If she admitted her affair with Danny, Warren would believe her, she knew. After the initial shock had passed anyway. Because every word she spoke would ring with the conviction of truth. The question was how Warren would react once he'd accepted that truth. If her lover had in fact been Kyle, or someone else of that caliber, Warren would probably scream and yell in disgust, then kick her out of the house and divorce her. But Danny McDavitt was a different thing altogether. For Warren, the essential nature of masculine honor was sacrifice, and he respected Danny more than almost any man he'd ever met. He admired Danny's war record, of course; that was a given. But he also saw Danny as a dedicated family man. When he and Danny coached the girls in soccer last year, little Michael had come along for most practices, and all of the games. Many times Laurel had caught Warren staring as Danny patiently tried to engage his son in activities with the other kids. And what she'd seen etched into her husband's face at those times was a combination of pity and admiration. Once, Warren had actually climbed into the car after practice and said, "Danny McDavitt's a better man than I am. If Grant had been born like that, it might have killed me." This happened months before Laurel and Danny started seeing each other, but Laurel sometimes wondered if Warren's admiration for Danny had formed some perverse part of her attraction to him.

*No confession,* she decided. *If Warren were to find out now that I'm in love with Danny—and that Danny loves me—he'd self-destruct.* A colder woman, she thought, might reveal the truth to try to drive her husband to suicide, but Laurel couldn't consider it. First because she didn't want her children to lose their father. Second because Warren might decide to make his wife and children precede him into death. A lot of fathers had done so in the past. All you had to do was watch the news to know that. And last, of course, there was the selfish consideration. Danny might be in love with her, but he was unwilling to give up custody of Michael to marry her. Even if Warren died tonight, it would bring her no closer to a future with Danny.

"We both need to talk about the bad things we've done," she said. "But not right now. Right now we need to find a way out of this trap we've made for ourselves. We need to make sure our children are safe."

Warren actually looked as if he was considering it. "What about Kyle?"

"What about him? He tried to kill you. You acted in self-defense. I'll testify to that."

Warren looked toward the study. "I just want you to know one thing. Everything I've done this past year was for the children. And for you. Even the bad things."

"Warren, how can that be? Please help me understand!"

"I can't. You know how I am. Some things I just can't talk about."

The phone rang again, but he ignored it.

"Don't you think you should answer? They're probably getting pretty antsy out there."

He nodded. "They are. I can see them on my computer."

Laurel was thunderstruck. She had entirely forgotten about the security cameras they'd installed when the house was built. She'd never used them, but Warren had the cameras connected to his computer via wireless connection, and he was obviously monitoring them now. No wonder he was so calm! Sitting there while the phone rang endlessly! He'd know the assault was coming in plenty of time to retreat to the safe room. She needed to text Danny about the cameras right away.

"I don't think they know I can see them," Warren said. "Or they'd be concealing themselves better."

"The cameras are pretty hard to see," Laurel observed, remembering how well the architect had hidden them in the molding outside.

"You insisted on that, remember?"

*Yeah, great.* "So, you're not going to answer the phone anymore?"

"Ray Breen's an idiot. Sheriff Ellis isn't much better."

"You need to talk to somebody. So they don't come charging in here and hurt Beth."

Warren nodded slowly. Then, after a few moments, he said, "Danny."

Laurel's heart thudded. "What?"

"I wouldn't mind talking to Danny. He was in the chopper with Ellis, remember?"

"Yes."

"Danny's a family man, all the way. And his wife is a little . . . difficult. The major would understand what I'm going through."

Laurel wanted to smash Warren's face. Here in the heart of hell, she was being compared to Starlette McDavitt, one of the women she despised most in the world.

"Ask for Danny, then," she said. *You son of a bitch.*

Like a man suddenly remembering he'd left something on the stove, Warren got up and walked back to his computer. Laurel rolled to face the sofa back, then slid her Razr from its niche and began working the keypad with her thumb.

Bonnie Elfman had led Danny and Sheriff Ellis to a TV room at the back of her house, where they found Grant Shields sitting on a wicker sofa with Deputy Sandra Souther, pretending to watch TV. Ellis had questioned the boy gently enough, and he got a recap of what Ray Breen had already relayed to him: a nine-year-old's perspective on a violent family argument and possible murder. Now the sheriff was trying to tease out details.

"How many shots did you hear, son?" he asked. "One? Or maybe two?"

Grant closed his eyes like a psychic trying to guess what card someone was holding. "Three, I think."

Ellis glanced at Danny. "How many guns does your dad own?"

The boy's eyes opened. "Um . . . three."

"What kind are they?"

"He's got one of every kind. A shotgun and a deer gun and a pistol."

The sheriff smiled. "You're a smart boy, aren't you?"

"I don't know."

"What about you? Do you have a .22 or anything?"

"No, sir. Dad says I'm not old enough. I am, though."

"I believe you are."

As Ellis slid his chair closer to the boy Danny's cell phone vibrated against his thigh. He took it out and read the new text message with an accelerating pulse. *W mentaly unstable. Handgun & shotgun close. Rifle n safe room. Stocked for days. Intent uncertain, but W not n hurry. Trancelike. Bth asleep & close 2 him. PS B careful! He can c u! secuty. cams!* Danny replied, *Understood. Take care. I love you,* knowing as he did that the contents of these secret messages were almost certain to be read by the sheriff one day.

"Grant?" said Ellis. "Have you ever seen your daddy as upset as he got today?"

The boy's eyes started to glisten. "No, sir."

"Close even?"

Grant shook his head. "He was like a different person or something."

Ellis nodded, then glanced up at Danny. "You want to ask anything?"

Danny squatted in front of the boy that he had once believed would become his stepson. Grant had his father's face and sandy blond hair, but his eyes were Laurel's. "Is there anything else you want to tell us, Grant? Anything at all?"

Grant shook his head, but then without warning two rivers of tears washed down his cheeks. "Please don't let them hurt my daddy, Mr. Danny. He didn't mean any harm. He's sick, that's all. He's not thinking right! That's what my mama told me."

Danny took hold of the boy's hands and squeezed. "Don't you worry, son. We're going to make sure everybody gets out of there safe and sound."

Grant wiped his face and nodded. "Okay."

Danny started to get up, then added, "Your mom's a strong lady. She's going to do whatever she has to do to get back to you."

Grant looked unsure. "I don't know. She acts that way, but sometimes I see her crying when she doesn't know I'm looking."

Danny nodded as though this were part of his everyday experience. "All grown-ups cry sometimes. I've seen some of the toughest soldiers in the world cry. That doesn't mean anything bad."

"Do you cry, Mr. Danny?"

He felt his throat tighten. "Sometimes I do, Grant. You just wait here and try to think about something else. You'll be back with your mom before you know it."

"And my dad," Grant said firmly.

Danny nodded again.

"We'd better get moving," Sheriff Ellis said brusquely. "We've got that ops meeting to get to."

Danny squeezed Grant's hand once more, then stood.

"Sandra?" said Ellis. "Why don't you find this boy a soda pop or something?"

"He said he didn't want anything."

"All boys want a soda pop."

Danny forced himself to walk out of the room, thinking that on a night like this, Grant might be luckier to be like Michael, just for a while.

"Slow down, Missy! There's a bunch of cars up there."

Nell Roberts was barely holding herself together. She'd felt some relief after talking to Dr. Shields, but it hadn't lasted long. She'd called her second cousin Missy Darden to pick her up and run her downtown to Dr. Shields's lawyer's office, but the office had turned out to be closed. Nell got the lawyer's home number from information, but when she called it, she got an answering machine. After convincing Missy to drive her out to the man's house, she'd worked up her nerve to knock on the door, but no one answered. Throughout this odyssey Missy had questioned Nell endlessly, but Nell remained evasive, unsure how her cousin would react to the news of Vida's injuries.

"There's some kind of roadblock up there," Missy said, pointing to Dr. Shields's street. "You want me to stop here or what?"

"No, keep going. But slow."

"What the heck is going on, Nell? Why are they guarding Dr. Shields's street?"

"I don't know."

"It's something to do with that lawyer, isn't it?"

Nell scanned the lawns and grassy lots beyond the lines of cars parked along Cornwall, Avalon's main street. Knots of people were gathered along the curb, many of whom she recognized. Most wouldn't know her anywhere but in the window of Dr. Shields's office, but some would. A white deputy standing in the road ahead was turning cars back toward the highway. A young black deputy stood at the roadblock, talking to a couple of men in polo shirts. She was pretty sure he'd been to the office for his departmental physical.

"What do I do?" Missy asked, easing her Mustang forward. "Come on."

"I'm going to get out. You go on back to work."

"No way. It's too late for that anyway."

Nell had her hand on the door handle when she saw Agent Paul Biegler less than fifty feet away. He was standing behind a black sedan, talking to his two assistants. He had a pressure bandage on his right cheek.

"*Uh-oh,*" Nell said, sliding low in her seat. "Get out of here!"

"Why? What's wrong?"

"Just back up and park somewhere!"

"Okay, okay, calm down."

Nell shut her eyes and tried not to freak out. She'd known something bad was happening out here. Dr. Shields had pretended different on the phone, but she knew his voice too well to buy that. He was trying to protect her, rather than himself. God only knew what kind of trouble Dr. Auster had caused out here.

"Missy, I need your help. Will you come with me?"

Her cousin shrugged. "Why not? Maybe I'll finally find out what all the fuss is about."

# CHAPTER

# 17

Five men and four cowboy hats were jammed into the mobile command post around Danny: Sheriff Ellis; TRU Commander Ray Breen; Detective Rusty Burnette; Carl Sims (wearing a black baseball cap); and Trace Breen, who was supposedly there to facilitate communications. Each passing minute had made it clearer that the tiny trailer had been designed to accommodate only half their number with comfort.

On the positive side, the architect's plans for the Shields house had finally arrived and now lay spread across a Formica dinette table half the size of the blueprints themselves. One page showed the landscape contractor's plan, and on this Carl had marked the surveillance and sniping positions now occupied by TRU officers. Sheriff Ellis stood like a bent tree over the table, and Ray Breen leaned against the door to keep out unwanted visitors.

During the time it had taken to gather everyone in the trailer, Danny had formed a pretty clear picture of how each man felt about the situation. The Breen brothers believed Kyle Auster was dead and were ready to assault the house with flash-bang grenades immediately. Detective Burnette favored delaying the assault until they had more information about where everyone was inside the house. Only Carl Sims kept close counsel.

"All right," Sheriff Ellis said, bringing the meeting to order. "Two things. What we know, and what we don't."

"Three hostages in the house," said Ray Breen. "One probably dead already. The subject is armed and dangerous, which his own son told us. And we're losing light fast, quicker because of this storm coming up."

"Thank you, Ray," said the sheriff. "What don't we know?"

"We don't know if Dr. Auster's alive or dead," drawled Detective Burnette. "We don't know what part of the house they're in, which it's a damn big house, by the way. We also don't know exactly how the subject's armed, though he's well-armed for sure. And most of all, we don't know why he's done any of this. He claims he's gonna come out when he gets done with this computer program he talked about. Told Ray he'd come out quiet and peaceful." Burnette glanced over his shoulder at the door. "Right, Ray?"

"That's what he *said*. Don't make no sense to me, though. What's a guy doing messing with a computer when he's already shot somebody and his own boy's running from him?"

"We don't know," Burnette said doggedly. "That's my point. Considering what I heard that government fellow yelling about, I'm thinking our two doctors might be up there destroying evidence while we sit out here jawin'."

"You've got a point there," Ellis said. "I hadn't thought about that."

Danny watched the faces, his gut aching with guilt. He could answer several of the most important unknowns, but he had no intention of doing so. Not yet. If he revealed his secret link to Laurel, the consequences were impossible to predict, but he doubted that many of them would be positive.

Ellis looked at Carl. "What's the shooting situation?"

"Not good. I don't know where they are yet, obviously. I'm thinking they might be in that great room. Three reasons. The blinds are shut, there's a phone in there, and the blueprints show a hardwired Internet connection in that room. But the blinds and curtains are drawn all over the house, and he's got cordless phones and Wi-Fi in there."

Danny couldn't believe he'd forgotten to ask Laurel what room they were in. At this point he wasn't about to wait. He took out his cell phone and keyed in the message. Trace Breen watched with suspicion but didn't challenge him.

"You all heard Agent Biegler," said Sheriff Ellis. "We need to end this thing before we get the FBI crawling up our backsides."

"Amen," said Ray.

"How are we going to pinpoint them in the house?" Burnette asked.

"Directional mikes should tell us which room they're in," said Ray. "Exact position's going to be tougher. If the supervisors would've coughed up for the FLIR unit we been begging for, we'd be sitting pretty."

"FLIR couldn't see through those blinds," Danny

interjected. He had extensive experience with the miraculous technology known as forward-looking infrared radar—he'd had a state-of-the-art unit on his Pave Low—but while FLIR could detect humans in absolute darkness (and sometimes through glass and water) it couldn't "see" through an opaque solid.

"What about our little private-eye video camera?" Ellis asked, referring to a tiny camera on the end of a flexible tube, often slipped by detectives beneath doors to film couples in flagrante delicto.

"On the blink," Ray groused. "That's what you get when you buy cheap. The mikes'll be enough. All we need is to know which room he's in. We'll come in from six different points at once, and so fast he won't know what's hit him."

Danny made a soft cluck of disapproval with his tongue.

"What is it, Major?" asked the sheriff. "You have a better idea?"

"When I first moved back to town, I saw a story about a rich guy who'd lost a grandkid in a fire. If I remember right, he was going to donate a couple of thermal imaging cameras to the fire department, to let firemen see through smoke. I don't know how good they are, but—"

"I don't think they've been delivered yet," Ray said. "And the ones they have now are real low quality."

"Call Chief Hornby and make sure, Trace," ordered the sheriff.

The younger Breen hurried outside with a cell phone to his ear.

Danny tried desperately to think of another way to

locate Shields within the house; he didn't want to reveal his link with Laurel simply to answer the question of position.

Ray Breen said, "We could slip up to the windows and have a look. You can probably see around the edges of those blinds."

"They looked pretty flush through my scope," Carl told him.

"Shields would see you coming," said Danny.

Ray looked skeptical. "How you figure that?"

"Through his cameras."

"Cameras!" cried a chorus of voices.

Danny tried to look nonchalant. "Sure. I assumed you'd seen them. They're hidden by ornamental woodwork, but you can see the lenses if you look close."

Ray pushed up to the blueprints and started riffling through them. "Well, I'll be damned. There they are."

"Shields has probably been watching us ever since we got here," Burnette said.

"No probably about it," said Carl. "I'll bet he's got those cameras networked to his computer. With a laptop and a rifle, he could move from window to window and pick us off without breaking a sweat."

"He could have shot us before now," reasoned Burnette. "But he hasn't shot anybody."

"We haven't moved in yet," said Sheriff Ellis, studying Danny. "You've got sharp eyes, don't you, Major?"

"I pay attention."

"What else have you noticed?"

"Nobody's saying anything about the safe room."

"The what?"

"That house has a safe room in it. A panic room,

whatever you want to call it. A steel box with a re-inforced door, stocked with food and water."

"I *know* that ain't on the blueprints," Ray said in a suspicious tone.

"Maybe they added it later," Burnette suggested.

"How do you know about that room, Danny?" asked the sheriff.

*Because I made love to Shields's wife in it once.* "Dr. Shields told me about it when I was teaching him to fly. I think they did add it near the end of construction."

"That goddamn architect," Ray grumbled. "Useless."

Sheriff Ellis was rubbing his chin, his eyes seemingly fixed on some distant tragedy. "If Shields drags his family into a room like that, we're screwed, blued, and tattooed. He could execute 'em one by one and we couldn't do nothing but stand outside and listen."

The trailer door banged into Detective Burnette's back, and Trace Breen squeezed inside, panting with excitement. "Chief Hornby says they got those new thermal cameras last week. Two of 'em. They're still in the boxes, but Jerry Johnson's been reading the manuals, and—"

"Can they see through glass?" Ellis cut in. "Or window blinds?"

"The chief thinks they can. He said the two of 'em together cost more than a used fire engine."

Sheriff Ellis pumped his fist like a weary gambler catching a break at last. "Get them over here, Trace. Jerry Johnson with them. Tell the chief if they're not in a car and on the way in two minutes, I'm sending Danny in the chopper."

Trace nodded and went back outside.

"Okay," said the sheriff. "Let's say we've pinpointed Shields and his family in the great room, and negotiations fail. How do we proceed?"

"Blow out the windows and go in with flash-bangs," said Ray. "Dr. Shields will be bleeding from the ears and blind as a bat. He won't be able to pull a trigger even if he wants to. Then—"

"I'm not so sure about that," Carl said quietly. "I know the tests say people can't pull a trigger after a flash-bang goes off, but I know guys who've done it."

"Shit," Ray scoffed. "Marines, maybe. Not some civilian doctor."

"I'm just telling you it can be done. Don't assume that he can't do it."

"That's why we're gonna take him down in that first second. Double-tap him and it's all over."

Danny closed his eyes. The prospect of Ray Breen and his men firing automatic weapons in a room with Laurel and her daughter in it was unthinkable, especially in the chaos that would follow the detonation of grenades designed to shock terrorists senseless. But this was standard operating procedure once negotiations had failed. It wouldn't be enough to oppose Ray Breen's plan based solely on fear of collateral damage; he'd have to come up with a better one himself.

"The house is pretty exposed," Detective Burnette observed. "How are we gonna get close when he's got those security cameras?"

"Spray paint," Ray answered with a grin. "There's a line of trees running up to the back corner of the house, where the kid got out. I'll take two guys up that way with some black spray paint. No more cameras."

"What if you spook him?" asked Burnette. "He might panic and start shooting."

"We've got to kill those cameras, Rusty. What if we cut the electricity to the whole house?"

Danny sensed an opening. "Shields told you he was waiting for his computer to tell him something. If he's fixated on that and we cut the power, we might really push him over the edge."

Sheriff Ellis nodded in agreement.

"A laptop would have battery power for a while," Burnette pointed out.

"We don't know he's using a laptop," Danny said. He looked over at Carl. "Do those blinds go all the way to the top of the great room windows?"

Carl shook his head. "Not quite. There's some open glass right at the top—a little arched pane—but that's like fifteen feet up, and no trees tall enough to get the right shooting angle."

"Could you use the chopper as a shooting platform? I could get you a perfect angle on those high windows."

The sniper's dark face seemed to darken even more with skepticism. "Helos are too unstable for precision shooting. Plus, that's double-paned glass. I wouldn't want to guarantee my shot from a moving platform."

"Understood," said Danny. "But I've seen it done. I had a Delta sniper shoot prone from the belly of my ship. He didn't like doing it, but he hit his targets."

Carl looked around at the faces of the other men. "I'll give it a try. But add in the deflection of the glass, and that's a tricky shot. If my target's alone, okay. But if there's a hostage close, she could get hurt."

Ray was watching them incredulously. "What do you two experts think Dr. Shields is gonna be doing while Carl's hanging up there trying to shoot him? He's gonna blow your asses out of the sky, that's what! He could shoot down that helicopter with a deer rifle."

This was true, Danny knew. "I don't think he'll be expecting a shot from the chopper. If I turn on the searchlight, he'll think we're trying to get a look at him."

"And if Carl misses the first shot?"

"Then you guys would bust in like you want to."

Sheriff Ellis was the kind of man who talked to help himself think. "If Carl saw Shields holding a gun in his hands, especially in a threatening manner, we could definitely justify taking him out."

"What if we go in and we don't see a weapon?" asked Ray.

"Fire to disable?" said Ellis. "Don't you train for that?"

Ray shook his head. "Double-tap. Two to the body, one to the head, makes you good and dead."

"Jesus. What happened to surgical strikes?"

"That's just not practical in close-quarters combat," said Carl. "Things happen too fast, once you go in. There may be a weapon you can't see. Body armor you can't see. Once things go that far, you have to shoot to kill."

Ellis nodded. "I'm glad to hear that from you, Carl. Ray seems a tad eager today."

Danny noted with some relief that the closer they got to the moment of truth, the less cavalier the sheriff was about ordering an assault.

A soft but persistent buzz drew several pairs of eyes

to Danny. With hot blood flowing into his cheeks, he held up a hand in apology. Then he took out his cell phone and, after making sure no one else could read the screen, read the newest text message: *Me lying on sofa n grt room. W n study atdesk. Bth lying on study sofa.* Here was the very information that the TRU was using every available resource to try to discover. The best thermal imagers in the world couldn't give this kind of detail. Danny considered telling the sheriff that he'd simply tried to text Laurel Shields (whose cell number he might reasonably have, since she was Michael's teacher) and had gotten lucky. But sooner or later they would discover that the cell phone Laurel was using was not registered to her, but to a friend of Danny's. *No,* he decided. *I've got to keep this ace up my sleeve until the last possible moment—*

"I thought we wasn't supposed to be talking to nobody on the outside," Trace said from behind Danny. "Who's *he* talking to?"

Sheriff Ellis said, "Major McDavitt has a family emergency. So how 'bout you shut up and focus on your job?"

Trace ducked his narrow head. "Yessir."

Thinking of Laurel's message, Danny moved closer to the blueprints and said, "I was actually in this house a couple of times, back when I coached soccer with Dr. Shields."

"Really?" said the sheriff.

"Yep. And if I remember right, Shields has a computer sitting on the desk in his study, which is right off the great room." He pointed. "Right there. If Shields was telling the truth about working at his computer, he might be sitting at that desk to do it. And if I'm not mistaken, the study windows are just like the ones in the great room."

Carl nodded. "They are."

Danny looked at the sheriff and let his voice take on its pilot's authority. "I think I see a surer way to end this thing. It was your idea to start with, Sheriff."

Ellis stood a little straighter.

"If the thermal imagers pinpoint Shields in that study—or in the great room—I should take the chopper up as a diversion, just like you suggested on the way here."

The sheriff nodded to confirm that this had, in fact, been his idea.

"We put Carl on the ground with his rifle scoped on those windows and the thermal imager beside him. When I turn on my searchlight, Shields will come to those windows like a moth to a candle. When he does, Ray can blow the windows out with plastique—*all* the back windows. Shields will be silhouetted like a duck in a shooting gallery. And that's when Carl takes his shot."

The sheriff's eyes narrowed. "Carl only?"

"There's your surgical strike. One shot, one kill. No collateral damage."

Ray Breen was winding up to argue, but Ellis silenced him with an upraised hand. The sheriff's eyes bored into those of his sniper. "Will you make that shot, Carl?"

Carl looked back steadily. "No problem, sir. There's a pecan tree forty-three meters from the back windows. I ranged it with my laser. I can set up behind that. The doctor won't even know I'm there."

"I didn't ask if you *could* make the shot," Ellis growled. "I asked if you would."

The sniper's face tightened as he realized exactly what was being questioned. "Understood, sir. I'll make the shot."

"No wounding, nothing like that."

Carl nodded once, his jaw set firm.

Sheriff Ellis didn't look convinced, but he finally turned away and gazed at the semicircle of faces pressed close around him. "All right, listen up. I like Major McDavitt's thinking on this. But my first plan is to *talk* Dr. Shields out of there."

Ray Breen snorted, but he tried to make it sound involuntary.

"I know Shields has stopped answering the phone, but that doesn't mean he won't answer the next time we call. If he won't answer, I'll go to the bullhorn. *But*—at the rate we're losing light, our options are going to shrink mighty quick."

"Storm's coming up fast," Burnette noted.

"And maybe the FBI, too," Ray intoned.

Ellis grimaced. "Ray, set up your directional mikes."

"They're being set up now."

"Good. The second those thermal imagers get here, I want 'em up and running. I want to know where every person in that house is and hear every word they're saying. Once I've got that intel, I'll make my tactical decision." Ellis dug into his pocket for something—chewing tobacco, Danny figured—but came up empty. "Anybody else got anything to say?"

Nobody did. Except Danny, who throughout the meeting had been haunted by an image so vivid that it might be a premonition: Ray Breen charging into the great room with an MP5 submachine gun on full auto—and one solitary slug finding its way into Laurel's heart—

"I'd like to say something," Danny said quietly. "What I'm about to tell you is only what I've heard Delta Force and SEAL commanders tell their men before an assault. Don't ask me what assaults, because I can't tell you."

The room went silent as a prayer vigil, just as he'd intended. He looked Ray Breen in the eyes. "This is no training exercise. And it's damn sure no movie set. If you men assault that house, you're as much a threat to the hostages—and to each other—as you are to Dr. Shields. You have no way of knowing how Mrs. Shields or her daughter will react to your intrusion. The little girl might bolt for her father the instant those windows go down. You've got to know what you're going to do in that event *before* you go in."

"What *would* you do, Ray?" asked the sheriff.

"Depends if he's holding his gun on the little girl, I guess."

"That's no time for guessing," Danny said.

"You think he'd hold a gun on his own daughter?" asked Burnette.

"Who the fuck knows?" Ray snapped. "He's the nutjob taking people hostage."

Sheriff Ellis looked down at the blueprints, his eyes clouded with doubt. "If Dr. Shields is holding his little girl when the windows go down, Carl is the only man authorized to shoot."

Half of Danny's fear left him in a single sigh.

"Jesus!" cried Ray. "A million things could screw

up Carl's shot. We need to be able to do whatever's required to get the job done."

"A sniper ain't no better than we are up close," Trace argued.

Carl looked at the younger Breen with barely disguised contempt. "You want to put a thousand dollars behind that mouth?"

"Any day, boy."

"You'd have to borrow it to pay me."

"Shut up!" bellowed the sheriff. "My order stands. All this is hypothetical right now anyway. Everything could change in five minutes. Danny? Anything else?"

"Only this. I never knew a real hero who wanted to be one. We've got one objective: the safety of those people inside. Keep your minds on that, and maybe we'll end this night without killing anybody."

"Which is exactly what we want," Ellis concluded.

A soft beeping sounded in the trailer.

"Shit fire!" Trace exclaimed, his eyes on the comm rack. "That's him!"

"Who?" asked the sheriff.

"*Him.* Dr. Shields! His house, anyway."

"Answer it!" snapped Ellis.

Trace picked up the phone and, after trying to swallow his bobbing Adam's apple, said, "Hello? Deputy Breen speaking."

Everyone watched his rodent's face bunch in concentration. "No, that's my brother. Is that who you want to talk to? . . . Okay. Wait a minute, please."

Sheriff Ellis stepped forward, expecting to be handed the phone, but Trace put his hand over the mouthpiece and shook his head.

"He's asking for Danny, Sheriff."

Ellis looked nonplussed. "Danny?"

"Um, 'Major McDavitt' is what he said. Ain't that Danny?"

The sheriff turned and looked back at Danny.

Danny shrugged, unable to guess what Shields wanted with him. Unless he'd somehow forced Laurel to confess their involvement, that is—

"Major, do you want to talk to Dr. Shields?" Sheriff Ellis asked stiffly.

"We'd better think it through before I try that." Danny looked at Trace. "Tell him you're going to find me, and I'll call him back."

Trace was about to do this when Ellis said, "Ask if he'll talk to me instead."

Trace followed his orders, then hung up, looking embarrassed. "He said Danny or nobody, Sheriff. Then he hung up."

Ellis rubbed his strong chin. "Okay . . . everybody get into position. Stay on the secure radio net, but keep the chatter down."

The trailer emptied fast. Soon only Trace Breen remained with Danny and the sheriff.

"Where are you supposed to be?" Ellis asked Trace.

"Right here. This is my post."

"Well, clear out for a minute."

Trace looked happy to oblige.

After he'd gone, Ellis gave Danny a penetrating look. "What do you make of this development?"

"I don't know what to make of it."

"Are you and Shields pretty tight?"

"Not at all. We coached ball together, like I said. And I taught him to fly. But he's not the kind of guy who makes friends easy. There's always a distance there."

Ellis nodded. "That's my feeling, too. So what does he want with you? I don't get it."

Danny shrugged again. "Do you want me to talk to him?"

"Somebody needs to. Or the next thing that's gonna happen is him getting shot."

"I'd hate to see that happen. But I'd hate to see an assault even more."

"You've made your point." Ellis spat in the little sink against the wall, then grabbed a pot of coffee off the counter. After sniffing it, he poured some into a Styrofoam cup. "Take a short break, Danny. I need to think for a minute. There's something we're not seeing here."

"Seems like it," Danny said, wondering if Ellis was smarter than he was given credit for being.

"I need to pray about this, is what I need to do."

"I'll leave you alone, then."

"Don't stray far. I may call you any second."

Danny nodded. "I'll be right outside."


Grant Shields was sitting on the sofa in the Elfmans' TV room, trying and failing to focus on the first *Harry Potter* movie, which Mrs. Elfman claimed her grand-kids loved best of all of them. Grant had seen all the *Harry* movies so many times that he could recite the lines with the characters. The bad thing was that Harry was always thinking about his dead parents. The lady deputy sitting beside Grant didn't seem to notice, but he could feel himself clenching his fists and bouncing his feet up and down. He had no idea what was happening at home. All he knew was that something very bad could happen, and soon. The way his dad had been acting worried him, but not nearly so much as all the cops and guns he'd seen outside.

"How's our little man doing?" Mrs. Elfman asked, poking her head into the room for the fifteenth time.

"He's doing fine," said Deputy Souther.

Mrs. Elfman walked in and set a big orange bowl beside Grant. It was filled with tortilla chips and bright green paste.

"Guacamole!" she announced. "I know you love it, because your mom told me so."

Grant nodded and mumbled thanks, but he didn't want any guacamole. He did like it, most of the time, but only his mom's. Mrs. Elfman's tasted funny. Too much lemon, or something.

"You call me if you need anything else, young man," she said.

Grant nodded and kept his eyes on the TV, so Mrs. Elfman wouldn't see how worried he was.

After she left the room, the lady deputy said, "She's kind of pushy, huh?"

Surprised, Grant nodded and stole a glance at his babysitter. Her first name was Sandra. She was younger than his mom, but not by much. She seemed nice, too, and not fake nice. As he looked back at the movie, he felt her warm hand cover his.

"I know you're scared," she said. "But it's going to be all right. They're going to get everybody out of there safe. Your mom, and your sister, and your dad, too."

Grant's eyes burned, then filled with tears. Deputy Sandra sounded like she believed what she said, but he wasn't sure. Not at all. And right then he decided that he couldn't just sit there while whatever happened, happened. He had to see it for himself. There might even be something he could do to help. Since he'd turned nine, his mom had been relying on him more and more for physical things. He was almost as strong as she was, and he could already outrun her.

"I need to go to the bathroom," he said, holding his belly as if he had a stomachache.

"I'll ask Mrs. Elfman where it is," Sandra said, starting to get up.

"That's okay, I already know." Grant got up and walked out of the room, his mind already racing through the Elfmans' backyard and down to the creek, where no policeman would be able to see him.

Sandra stood and followed him to the hall door, where she could watch him go into the bathroom. She smiled the way his mom did when he was sick, and Grant sensed that she might be able to read his mind a little, the way his mom could sometimes.

That was okay.

Mrs. Elfman's bathroom had a window.


Deputy Willie Jones was tired of manning the road-block. Gawkers just kept coming, more and more every few minutes. They came on foot and in cars, the neighbors on foot, the townspeople in cars. Willie didn't know how the rumor spread so fast. Probably cell phones. Turning back the cars was no trouble, but the foot traffic was another matter. Fifty people were standing along Cornwall Street, most in little groups of five or six. Some had tried to walk up Lyonesse, but Willie had nipped that in the bud. They had some nerve, though.

Several men had tried to question him, but he'd kept as quiet as one of those guards outside Buckingham

Palace. The things they said, though. Half the people out here believed that Dr. Shields had already murdered his whole family, and some thought he'd taken his neighbors hostage. From what Willie had gathered, though, not much had happened since he'd arrived.

He'd been keeping a close eye on Agent Biegler, as Ray Breen had instructed. Biegler and the two men with him had spent most of their time huddled around the trunk of a black Ford Crown Victoria parked a little way up from the roadblock. Then a couple of minutes ago they'd climbed into the Ford and driven off toward town, which suited Willie fine.

He was thinking of calling Ray Breen and asking to be relieved when a young white woman with dark hair walked quickly up to the roadblock. Another white woman about her age was trying and failing to keep up with her. Willie started to hold up his hands, but something in her eyes stopped him. She looked like the witnesses he'd spoken to after bad highway accidents, pale and shaken, with eyes like a wounded deer's.

"Can I help you, miss?"

The woman looked nervously over her shoulder. "I hope so. I need to see the sheriff."

"The sheriff's kind of busy right now."

"I know, but I think he'll want to talk to me."

"Why's that?"

"I was at the fire today. At Dr. Shields's office."

This got Willie's attention. "Are you a patient of his or something?"

"No. I work for Dr. Shields. I met you when you came for your physical. It was my sister who almost got killed in that explosion. I've been trying to talk to you for a while, but that Agent Biegler's been watching the roadblock. He just drove off, so I came right up. Can we hurry? If he sees me, he'll arrest me for sure."

Willie thought about calling Ray for an okay, but then he realized he could kill two birds with one stone. "Hey, Louis!" he shouted, waving to one of the deputies who were turning back the rubbernecks in cars. "Get over here and man the barricade!"

As soon as Louis started toward him, Willie took the woman by the arm and led her to his cruiser.

Danny found Carl Sims sitting on a camp stool beneath a pavilion tent someone had set up outside the command trailer. The sniper was putting a light coat of oil on the long, gray barrel of his rifle, a Remington 700 with a custom stock. The air out here felt twenty degrees cooler than the musty air in the trailer.

"Rain's almost here," Carl said. "Got to maintain your equipment."

"Amen," Danny agreed, glancing at the chopper sitting in the open space beyond the trailer. He thanked his stars yet again for Dick Burleigh's Vietnam experience.

As Carl wiped down the gun, his dark, corded arms rippled. He looked like a teenager preparing for a deer hunt in the dawn light. Danny had seen hundreds of boys like him over the years, seemingly too young for the jobs they were asked to do, but maybe the only ones resilient enough to do them and survive.

"You been in the shit, ain't you, Major?" said Carl. "Overseas, I mean."

"I've been in a few places I wouldn't want to go back to."

Carl smiled, his teeth bright in the false dusk. "I know what you mean."

Danny reached into an Igloo on the ground and pulled out a can of Dr Pepper. "Something on your mind, Carl?"

Sims held the rifle at a right angle to his body and looked down the length of the barrel, checking something Danny couldn't even begin to guess at.

"That guy at the bank," Carl said. "The one whose hand I shot?"

*The one the sheriff's hung up on.* "Yeah."

"I recognized him from grade school. Soon as I saw him in my scope."

"I thought it might be something like that."

Carl lowered the rifle and began working at it again. "Wasn't just that, though." He looked around to make sure they were alone, then spoke in a softer voice. "I killed a lot of people in Iraq, Major. More than the twenty-seven they credited me with."

Danny waited for whatever was coming.

"I knew why I was killing those people, you know? Most of 'em, anyhow. But this stuff here . . . I don't know. In a few minutes, I'm going to have my mama's doctor in my crosshairs. And it just don't feel right."

"I know."

Carl looked confused. "But inside the trailer . . . you were talking like you want me to shoot the man."

Danny sighed heavily. "I'm not in command here, Carl. If it were up to me, the FBI would be running this scene, and you and me would be waiting for word somewhere dry. But that's not going to happen. Not with these boys."

The sniper nodded dejectedly. "I heard that."

"There's exactly two professional soldiers here tonight," Danny said with quiet conviction, "and they're both under this tent. If the sheriff reaches the point of ordering an explosive entry, you are the best hope that Mrs. Shields and her daughter have of surviving this night. You alone. Do you understand?"

Carl stopped wiping the gun. "You're saying I should knock down the doctor before Ray and them screw things up."

Danny moved closer to the sniper, then squatted so that their eyes were level. "You want my opinion? If we're within two minutes of an assault, and you have a clean shot . . . take it."

Carl's eyes widened. "Without waiting for authorization?"

"Sheriff Ellis thinks you're slow on the trigger, right?"

The sniper nodded resentfully.

"Prove him wrong."

The trailer door popped open behind them. Danny looked around and saw Sheriff Ellis walking toward them.

"Danny," Ellis said, "I think you need to talk to Dr. Shields. We're losing our light. If we have to go in, I don't want to wait till dark to do it."

Danny took a swig of Dr Pepper and held it in his mouth till it burned. If he was going to talk to Warren Shields, he needed to be awake and alert.

"Sheriff!" someone called. "Sheriff Ellis! I got somebody you need to talk to!"

Danny swallowed and turned. Willie Jones was hurrying up with a pretty, young woman beside him. As they drew closer, Danny saw terror in the woman's face.

"Who's this?" asked the sheriff.

"Nell Roberts," Willie said. "She works for Dr. Shields. She was at the fire today. She's been trying to avoid that Biegler dude. He tried to arrest her earlier today."

Ellis motioned Nell under the pavilion tent. "What are you doing out here, miss?"

"I didn't know where else to go! I'm worried about Dr. Shields."

"Worried about Dr. Shields?" Sheriff Ellis gave Danny a look that said, *What did I tell you?* "Are you and Dr. Shields personally involved, miss?"

Nell's cheeks reddened. "No! He wouldn't do anything like that. And I wouldn't either. He's not like Dr. Auster."

"What do you mean by that?"

"That's what I came out here to tell you. Dr. Auster is a liar—a liar and a crook. He's gotten Dr. Shields in trouble, but it's not Dr. Shields's fault. Dr. Shields is a good man. Ask anybody. I don't know what's going on out here, but I can promise you Kyle Auster is behind it."

Sheriff Ellis took a long breath, then slowly expelled it. "So, if I told you that Dr. Shields is holding his family hostage in his house, and he maybe killed Dr. Auster, what would you say?"

Nell shook her head as though this were an impossibility. "I'd say Dr. Auster asked for it somehow. He probably tried to kill Dr. Shields."

Danny recalled Laurel's text message: *KA dead by W. Self-defense.* Nell Roberts apparently knew her bosses well.

The sheriff turned to Danny. "What are we going

to do with this young lady? I don't want Biegler to get
ahold of her."

"Why don't you put Willie with her, and keep her
close to the trailer? If I'm going to talk to Shields, I may
want to ask her some questions. Psychological stuff."

Ellis nodded. "You heard the Major, Willie. You're
Miss Roberts's babysitter from now on. Stay right outside the trailer."

"Yes, sir," Willie said with a grin.

"You ready, Danny?" Ellis asked. "This may be our
only chance to end this thing without casualties."

"Ready."

"Oh, shit," said Carl. "Sheriff?"

Danny and Ellis turned together. Flanked by two
subordinates, Paul Biegler was marching toward the
pavilion, and he was marching like a man in charge. He
brought the rain with him. Before he reached the edge
of the tent, a staccato rattle of heavy drops sounded on
the nylon overhead.

"I don't need this," said Ellis.

"Bad omen for sure," Carl muttered, a note of su-
perstition in his voice.

Biegler stopped outside the pavilion and stood in
the rain like a visiting captain awaiting permission to
come aboard a ship.

Sheriff Ellis offered the opposite of hospitality. "I
thought I told you not to come back here unless you
had information that would improve our tactical situation."

Biegler nodded. "That's exactly why I'm here. Mind
if we get out of the rain?"

As Ellis took a slow step back, Danny sensed a sub-
tle shift in the balance of power at the scene. From the

moment Biegler and his men stepped under the protection of the tent, everything changed.

"What have you got?" the sheriff asked. "We don't have much time for talk."

"Warren Shields is dying," Biegler said.

Ellis's mouth went slack. "Say what?"

"He's got an inoperable brain tumor."

"Lord have mercy," Carl breathed.

"How do you know that?" Ellis asked. He turned to Nell Roberts. "Did you know that?"

Nell shook her head, clearly in shock. "I knew something was wrong, though. He's been acting different for a while now. Oh my God . . . oh, no."

Biegler's voice gained authority as he spoke. "Shields was diagnosed eleven months ago at the office of a neurologist at the Stanford Medical School. One month later, he applied for a life insurance policy in the amount of two million dollars. He was approved."

"How?" asked Danny.

"The neurologist at Stanford recorded Shields's office visit and tests as something else. The two of them went to medical school together. Roommates."

"Jesus," said Danny, realizing that he and Laurel had begun their affair at about the same time her husband was diagnosed.

"How did you find this out?" Ellis asked.

Biegler drew himself to his full height. "Unlike some people, I cultivate contacts outside my own agency. I've had everybody I know running Dr. Shields through national computer databases. When the neurologist's name came up, I called him. It didn't take much pressure to get the truth out of him."

"How could Dr. Shields keep something like that secret?" asked Carl.

"He's essentially treating himself," Biegler explained. "With steroids mostly. Every three weeks or so he flies out to Stanford, under cover of going to a bicycle race."

Ellis shook his head in disbelief. "Are you saying his wife doesn't even know?"

"Nobody knows. Nobody but Shields and his neurologist. The guy said Shields has only one mission in life now: providing for his wife and kids before he dies. Nothing else matters to him."

In the silence that followed this remark, Nell Roberts began to sob, but the sound was mostly covered by the rain.

"Well, hell," said Sheriff Ellis. "That's a shocker, and no mistake. But I'm not sure how it changes anything."

Biegler's eyes went wide in wonder. "Are you kidding? It changes *everything*."

The trailer door banged open again, and this time Trace Breen jumped out, shielding his eyes with his hand. "It's him again, Sheriff! Dr. Shields. He's still asking for Major McDavitt!"

Biegler gave Danny a long look. "Why is he asking for you?"

"Let's go find out," said the sheriff.

# CHAPTER

# 18

Danny sat at the Formica-topped table in the command trailer, waiting to speak to Warren Shields. The odors of sweat and mildew had mingled into an unpleasant soup in the cramped space. To Danny's surprise, Sheriff Ellis had allowed Paul Biegler to follow them into the trailer; he stood two steps behind Danny, his posture tense. Trace Breen was present to work the comm gear, and his brother stood by the door with Carl Sims at his shoulder. Danny figured Ellis would kick Carl out when he saw him, but the sheriff's attention was on weightier matters.

"Put those on," said Trace, pointing at a headset on the table.

Danny picked up the headset, which was connected to a small gray box that read HELLO DIRECT on the top. Wires ran from this to a rack of audio gear against the trailer wall. A portable DAT recorder and three small speakers sat atop the rack.

"If those speakers are going to be on," Danny said, "turn them way down. I want Shields to think it's just him and me on the phone."

Sheriff Ellis nodded to Trace, who made an adjustment in the rack.

Danny tried to remember all he knew about Warren Shields. Danny had thought he was under stress from the effort of hiding his cell phone link to Laurel. But hearing that Shields was suffering from terminal cancer had blasted his perception of the past year to smithereens. Every assessment he had ever made of his and Laurel's relationship had been missing a critical factor. Moreover, it seemed impossible that Laurel would not notice an illness that serious. Had she known about the cancer and kept it from him? If so, she wasn't the person he'd thought she was. *What have I done to that poor man?* he thought. *What have I done to that family?* When Danny first began falling in love with Laurel, he had struggled hard against his feelings. Laurel had done the same, or so it had seemed. Even after they lost that battle, guilt had shadowed their relationship for a while. But eventually it faded, in the growing certainty that they were meant to be together for the rest of their lives. Now that old guilt had broken up through the dark soil at the bottom of Danny's heart, where he'd buried it, like some poisoned flower after a heavy rain—

"Danny?" prompted Sheriff Ellis. "You still with us?"

"I need a pen and paper. To make notes."

"I don't think we got any here," Trace said.

"In a command post?"

"Here," said a deep, even voice.

Bodies moved behind Danny, and then Carl handed him a small notebook he'd been holding, along with a waterproof pencil. "Logbook," Carl explained. "All snipers carry them."

"Thanks, Sergeant," Danny said, using Sims's former military rank instead of *deputy*.

Carl melted into the back wall again.

Danny picked up the headset, thinking that if Warren knew he was Laurel's lover, this would be the shortest hostage negotiation in history. He made eye contact with the sheriff and Agent Biegler in turn. "Anybody has any suggestions, tell me now. When I start talking, I'm going to face the wall so I'm not distracted. I'm not a trained negotiator. I'll be flying by the seat of my pants. You don't want me doing this, I'm happy to step aside. But once I start, please stay out of it. No second-guessing on the fly."

Sheriff Ellis nodded, but Biegler stepped forward and looked down at Danny. "Don't mention his illness, if you can help it. For some reason, this man trusts you. You want to keep him on an even keel and get him out of there peacefully. Stay away from anything that aggravates the emotional component."

"What am I supposed to talk about? The weather?"

"You won't know that until Shields starts talking. But keep him cool. And don't offer him anything without getting something in return. No food, no medicine, absolutely no reduction in criminal charges. Only I can grant that, through the attorney general. Anything Shields requests gives us leverage, and we have to gain a concession for it."

Danny had a feeling that Biegler had flown up to Quantico for a weekend course in hostage negotiation. "I don't think he's concerned with criminal charges, Agent Biegler. And I don't think we have anything he wants." *Unless he wants me.* "But I'll keep your advice in mind."

"I need to know if Auster is dead or alive," Biegler added.

*He's dead as a hammer,* Danny thought. "Understood."

"Just get the little girl out of there," Sheriff Ellis said. "We don't want her in the line of fire if we have to assault the house."

"I think I've got the gist," Danny said. "Let's get to it."

"Dialing now," said Trace.

Danny put on the headset and waited. After three rings, he heard a click. Then Warren Shields, sounding not at all like himself, said, "Dr. Shields."

"Warren?" Danny said, feeling more than a little awkward. "This is Danny McDavitt."

"Finally," Shields said, with obvious relief. "It's good to hear your voice, Major."

"Yours, too." Danny wasn't sure how to begin, so he just went with his gut. "Doc, we've got a lot of confusion out here today. You want to tell me what's going on?"

Shields sighed heavily. "Laurel betrayed me, Danny. She's been having an affair with somebody. Worse than that . . . she's in love with him."

*He doesn't know it's me,* Danny realized. Elation almost lifted him out of his chair. "That doesn't sound like your wife to me. How do you know?"

"I found a letter from the guy."

*God. He must have found a handwritten letter. If he'd gotten into her e-mail account, he'd know everything.* Danny had always signed his handwritten letters "Me," just in case someone saw them. "That's what all this is about?" he asked. "An affair?"

"Afraid so. Pretty pathetic, huh?"

"Not really. That's a big blow, finding out a person isn't who you thought they were. That the world isn't the way you thought it was."

"You got it, Major. That's exactly it. You're living your life under certain assumptions, and then you find out they're all wrong. You thought you were walking on firm ground, but you're really walking through a swamp of shit."

Danny wrote *Depressed/Wronged man* in Carl's logbook. He'd known plenty of guys who got Dear John letters while serving overseas. A few had shown their letters to Danny in the hope that he could read something between the lines that they couldn't. He'd never found a way to lessen the pain for any of them.

"You must be pretty angry," Danny said. "I know I would be. The thing is, though, I don't get what you're trying to do in there. You're talking about a man-and-wife kind of problem. But you've got a lot of trouble stirred up out here. A lot of firepower. Can you help me out on your thinking?"

"It's simple, really," Shields said, as if it really might be.

"Is it?"

"Absolutely. I just need to know who the guy is."

Danny's gut clenched. "The guy she's having an affair with?"

"Yep. That's it in a nutshell."

"And Laurel won't tell you?"

"Nope. She's protecting the guy. I mean, the asshole dumped her—it's right there in the letter—but she's still protecting him. Do you believe that?"

Danny had forgotten to turn toward the wall. He did so now and tried to block out all the eyes staring at the back of his head. "Maybe she figures it could only make things worse, since it's over. You know?"

"How could things be worse than they are now?"

Danny realized that both their voices had the cavernous sound created by cheap speakerphones. He wondered if Laurel was hearing his voice as he spoke. "Maybe she figures that if you have a face to put to your negative thoughts, it's going to hurt a lot worse. Which could be true, you know?"

"No way. It's *not* having a face that's so bad. If I knew who the guy was, I'd probably laugh. I'd probably think he's a total loser."

*Maybe he is,* Danny thought wretchedly.

"I thought for a while that it was Kyle. My partner. But it wasn't."

As Danny wrote *PAST TENSE* in the logbook, he realized that someone had turned up the speakers in the trailer.

"I hear an echo," Warren said suspiciously. "Who else is listening to this?"

Danny gestured angrily for Trace to turn down the speakers. "Nobody. They've got me on some kind of headset. Sheriff Ellis wanted to eavesdrop, but I told him I wouldn't talk to you unless it was just the two of us."

"Good man. Good old Danny."

Someone grabbed the pencil out of his hand and wrote *AUSTER?!* in Carl's logbook. It was Biegler. Danny snatched the pencil back and waved him away. He knew Auster was dead, but he had to play out the charade to protect his link with Laurel.

"About your partner," he said. "I should tell you that you've got a lot of people worried about him out here."

Warren laughed softly. "That's kind of hard to believe."

"I wouldn't kid you, Doc. The folks out here would feel a whole lot better if Dr. Auster would come to the phone and say a few words. Just a quick hello would be enough."

"I *told* Ray Breen," Shields said with obvious irritation. "Kyle's busy going over our tax documents. There's a Medicaid investigator in town trying to put us in jail."

"Is that right?" Danny glanced back at Biegler.

"I'm surprised he's not out there with Ellis."

"I haven't seen him. Just a whole bunch of deputies and cops."

"City cops outside the city limits?"

"They're part of the local SWAT team. You've caused quite a commotion out here, my friend."

"I guess it would. Look, Major, can you tell me anything about Vida Roberts? We heard she was hurt in a fire at our office."

Danny wrote, *Concerned about future/at least for others. Used "we."* People scrambled to read what he'd written. "She's in the ICU, that's all I know. I can check on her if you like."

"Please."

"One more thing," Danny said. "Your daughter."

"Beth?"

"Right. How would you feel about sending her out here to me? Just while you and Laurel get this thing worked out?"

"Beth's fine, Danny. She's in no danger. I hope nobody out there thinks I'd hurt my own child."

"No, no. Not under normal circumstances, that is. But Grant was pretty rattled when he came out of there earlier."

"Grant didn't understand what I was trying to tell him. He doesn't like having to grow up. He'd love to stay a kid forever. But no one can do that, can they, Danny?"

"That's a fact."

"I knew you'd understand."

Danny grimaced, then plunged ahead. "Well, I do and I don't, Warren."

"What's that?" Shields asked, his voice cracking with what sounded like fatigue.

"I said I don't really understand what you're doing. I've only known you a couple of years, but one thing I do know is that you're a man of honor."

Shields didn't reply for a while. Then he said, "Thank you, Major. That means a lot coming from you."

"I'm glad. But, Warren, the things you've done today . . . scaring your kids, putting their lives at risk, holding your wife prisoner . . . those are not honorable things."

Danny felt someone yank his shoulder. He turned and saw Biegler shaking his head and mouthing, *Stop!* Danny put out a hand and shoved him backward. Biegler looked ready to attack him, but Sheriff Ellis wrapped a bearlike forearm around the government agent's chest and held him back.

Danny kept waiting for Shields to reply, but the doctor said nothing.

"I can see how you might *feel* justified," Danny went on. "In an angry state of mind, I mean. But you can't justify those things, Warren. Not in my eyes. Some of the fathers we coached against might do this kind of thing, but not you. You're too good for this. And you know that things as important as your marriage need to be considered in a calm state of mind. You've got to put a cold eye on them, as my old commanding officer used to say. Then you can see what's really there. What's really happened."

There was a long, staticky silence. Just as Danny thought the connection might have been lost, he heard Warren say, "I'm feeling pretty alone in here, Major. Like I've lost my bearings. You know?"

Danny felt the first glimmer of hope. "That's why I'm here, buddy. I'm going to help bring you back down to earth."

Warren laughed strangely. "I'm not sure there's any way back from where I am now. I'm not even sure how I got here. It's like there's another directional vector besides north, south, east, and west. And I'm stuck on it. Does that sound crazy?"

"Not to a man who's been there himself. Sometimes life gets out of whack like that. I almost flew into the Arabian Sea one time, because my head was all turned around from personal stuff."

"That's hard to believe."

"Believe it." Danny hadn't smoked a cigarette in twenty years, but he wanted one now. "How long has it been since you slept, Doc?"

"A while now."

"How many hours?"

"Ahh . . . close to forty."

Danny scrawled *40hr deficit* in the logbook. No wonder the guy was on the ragged edge. "Forty hours without sleep. Would you go out to the airport and fly in the state you're in now?"

"Of course not."

"Good. Because I sure wouldn't fly with you. So, here's my question. If you wouldn't fly in this state, why would you make decisions that could cost you everything you have?"

This time the silence stretched for more than a minute. Then Shields said, "I've already lost everything, Danny. And now my wife's gone, too. That's all I was clinging to . . . doing right by her and the kids. I feel like I've been in a raging river, clinging to a branch on the bank. But now that branch has been yanked away. There's nothing to hold on to anymore, and nothing at the end of the river but black water. A bottomless hole. Ah, forget it. You don't know what the hell I'm talking about."

Danny started to say he did, but then he remembered Biegler's warning. "Hold on, Doc, I'm having trouble hearing you. Let me call you right back."

He smothered the headset mike in his fist and motioned for Trace to break the connection, which, to Danny's relief, he did almost instantly.

"Why the hell did you do that?" Biegler asked.

Danny turned to Sheriff Ellis. "I need to talk to him about the health issue."

"His cancer?"

"He's already there himself. You heard him."

"That's an unacceptable risk," said Biegler. "You might send him into an emotional tailspin."

Danny felt the same exasperation he'd felt when serving under incompetent officers. "You think the guy doesn't know he has a brain tumor?"

"I'm saying what's the point of reminding him? If he's not focused on it, let's not go there."

"He's there *now*. Look, I know this guy. He's a physician and a realist. He'd rather hear the truth than a load of bullshit. That's why he asked for me in the first place."

Biegler looked at the sheriff.

"I'm with Major McDavitt on this one," Ellis said. "Dr. Shields is upset because he can't get a straight answer from his wife. Let's don't make things worse by lying to him ourselves. Let's talk straight to the man."

Danny nodded thankfully and picked up the headset.

"You guys had better be right," Biegler said.

Danny closed the mike in his fist again. "Biegler, you remind me of every REMF I ever met in a combat zone. You want a guaranteed result with zero risk, and your ass covered if the shit hits the fan. But that's not how it works in the real world. So please shut the fuck up and let me work here."

Biegler reddened and started to reply, but Trace Breen preempted him with "What's a REMF?"

"Rear echelon motherfucker," answered his brother.

Trace grinned. "Damn straight."

Ellis glared at his comm officer, then motioned for him to call Dr. Shields back.

Laurel lay motionless on the great room sofa, listening to Christy scratch at the pet door Warren had installed during the winter. Now that it was spring, the young corgi spent her days running the creek bed, only returning in the evenings for food. Surprised to find

her little door latched, the hungry dog scratched relentlessly at it, wondering why she was being shut out of
her family abode.

Warren seemed not to hear Christy. He had put
Danny on the speakerphone so that he could keep
working at his computer (which probably meant monitoring the Merlin's Magic program in its digital war
against her Hotmail account). It was surreal listening
to Danny's voice floating out of the study. She felt that
if she could only saw the duct tape from her legs and
wrists, she could run right out the back door and into
Danny's arms. But of course she couldn't. First she'd
have to pick up Beth—who still lay supine in Benadryl-
induced sleep—and then trust Warren not to shoot
as she fled, something she wasn't nearly so confident
about as she'd once been. The pessimism he had revealed to Danny had stunned her. Yes, the situation
was bad, but Warren was talking like a man resigned
to death, not to jail or legal fines.

The phone rang again, and Warren pressed the
speaker button. "Danny? Can you hear me now?"

"Five by five, Doc."

"Five by five," Warren repeated, with longing in
his voice. "I wish we were flying over the river right
now."

"Let's go, buddy. I've got the chopper waiting outside. You always said you wanted to try it."

Warren laughed softly. "They'd never let us go
now."

"Oh, I don't know. I've got some pull with the
sheriff."

"Don't bullshit me, Danny. I saw them spray-paint
my cameras."

Laurel's stomach tightened. Had they spray-painted the cameras in preparation for an attack?

"I won't lie to you," Danny said. "You know that. I think it's time we get down to cases. What do you say?"

"I'm listening."

"The thing is, these boys out here have got a manual for situations like this. That's what they go by, and they don't make exceptions. They're trying to be professional, that's all. You can understand that."

"Sure."

"So we don't have time for small talk. I want you to know something, Warren. I know you had a tough blow about a year ago. Tougher than this thing with your wife."

Laurel raised her head from the couch.

"What are you talking about?" Warren asked warily.

"I'm talking about your cancer."

Laurel's face grew hot, and her heart beat hard against her sternum. Cancer? What was Danny talking about?

"I understand why you kept that secret," Danny continued. "God knows a man's health is his own business. But I think maybe this particular illness is affecting your judgment a little."

Warren's reply was almost a whisper, but Laurel could just make out his words. "I don't know what you're talking about."

"Come on. You asked me not to bullshit you. Do me the same courtesy, okay?"

There was a long silence, and then Warren said, "Who found out about it?"

Laurel heaved herself up into a sitting position. Warren's face was concealed behind his monitor, but she stayed erect, hoping to get a glimpse of his eyes. The last fragments of disbelief were falling away. The evil sleeping in the shadows of her failing marriage had suddenly slithered into the light. She felt as if she'd been walking past a decaying house every day, averting her gaze though she knew something dark and hungry lay within.

"Does it matter who found out?" Danny asked.

"Listen, I may be sick, but my judgment is fine. The thing's in my brain stem, not my cerebral cortex. Not yet, anyway."

*Brain stem?* Laurel thought. *Cerebral cortex? He has a brain tumor?* In a dizzying rush of memories, she saw the womanish fat around Warren's usually trim hips, the strange hump at the back of his neck . . . *Steroids—*

"You're the medical expert," Danny said. "But look at what you're doing here. These aren't the actions of the Warren Shields I coached soccer with. Or the steady, thoughtful physician I taught to fly."

"Are you sure? Every man can be pushed too far, you know? Every man has a breaking point. Eventually you have to push back."

"Are you talking about Laurel again?"

"Of course."

"I don't think she's your main problem, Warren. I think this other thing is magnifying that into more than it is."

Laurel's memory had revved into overdrive. All the bike races Warren had traveled to and returned from without trophies, his failure to call home and check in, unusual shortness with the children, surprising moments of maudlin sentimentality—

"I'll tell you about this 'other thing,' as you call it," Warren said. "I think about it a lot, Danny. I think about all my patients who've died. Older people, most of them. But not all. Looking back, I try to remember if the young ones were marked somehow. Whether they might have done something to bring their fates down on themselves. But they didn't, Danny. One day God or Fate just said, 'I will not let you be happy. I will not give you children. I will not let you breathe another day. I will take away your ability to move.'"

"Warren—"

"No, listen. This is important. I've tried to believe, all my life. To have faith that there was justice in life, some larger plan or meaning. But I can't do it anymore. I've watched some of the best people I ever met get crippled or taken before they reached thirty, forty, whatever. Babies, too. I've watched babies die of leukemia. I've watched infants die from infections, bleeding from their eyes and ears. Terrible birth defects . . . I look for a reason, a pattern, anything that might justify all that. But nothing does. *Nothing does.* Until I got sick myself, I played the same game of denial that all doctors do. But, Danny, my cancer ripped the scales from my eyes. I go to these funerals and listen to smug preachers telling grieving people that God has a plan. Well, that's a lie. All my life I've followed the rules. I've toed the line, given to the less fortunate, followed the Commandments . . . and it hasn't mattered one bit. And don't tell me about Job, okay? If you tell me God is testing me by killing me . . . that's like saying we had to destroy a village in order to save it. It's a cruel joke that we play on ourselves. And don't tell me it's all made right in the afterlife, because you know what? The agony of one infant dying senselessly mocks all the golden trumpets of heaven. I don't want to sit at the right hand of a God who can torture children, or even one who sits by and allows them to be tortured. Free will, my ass. I made no choice to die at thirty-seven. This one's on God's account, Major. We look for meaning where there is none, because we're too afraid to accept randomness. Well, I've accepted it. Embraced it, even. And once you do that, the world just doesn't look the same anymore."

Laurel felt herself coming unmoored from reality. She had never heard Warren speak more than three sentences about God outside of church. To hear him launch into a tirade on the absurdity of faith disoriented her. But it was what lay behind his words that had driven her into shock, an unalterable fact that would change her future almost as profoundly as Warren's—terminal brain cancer.

"I hear you, buddy," Danny said at length. "I've heard that same opinion expressed vividly in war zones. But the thing is, even if you're right, it doesn't mean the choices you make don't have consequences. In fact, if that's how you see the world, you have to be even more careful about what you do. Because no divine power is going to balance the scales in the end. You know? You have to do it yourself. Or do what you can, anyway."

Laurel could see the edge of Warren's face behind his monitor. He was nodding. "That's exactly what I'm doing now, Danny. Balancing the scales."

"How do you figure that?"

"You think I'm going to leave my kids to be raised by *her*? Raising children is a sacred charge. I can't trust her to do that any longer."

Fear and shame began eating through Laurel's shock.

"Well, what other option do you have?" Danny asked.

"That's what I'm thinking about."

"Well, why don't you tell me what you're thinking?"

Another long silence. "I don't think you'd understand. You still look at things the old way."

Laurel had never heard a voice so bereft of hope. Warren's whole life for the past year had been an exhausting round-the-clock performance carried out for her and the children. An imitation of health.

"I might surprise you there, buddy," Danny said. "You want to talk about randomness? I've seen a lot of men on the south side of twenty die for no reason at all. Shot or mortared out of a clear blue sky, sometimes by their own side. I've heard them screaming in the back of my chopper with no hope of getting to a field hospital in time. And they don't scream to God, Doc. They don't scream to Daddy, either. They scream to Mama. Because they know Mama loved them more than anyone else ever could. More than even God, if there is one. You hear me, Warren? I don't care how much you love Grant and Beth—when the shit hits the fan, it's Mama they'll cry for. And the shit *has* hit the fan, okay? Daddy's going to die. And the last thing you want to do is leave those kids at the mercy of somebody besides their mother. I don't care how angry you are, brother. I don't care what she did to you. And *they don't either.* I know you don't like hearing this. This is tough love, buddy. This is the stuff that makes a battle-field seem like a safe place."

"I hear you," Warren said quietly. "I do. But it just doesn't register. I can't explain it to you."

"Well, try. Nobody's going anywhere just yet."

Laurel saw Warren sag back in his chair, but she still couldn't see his eyes. She wondered if Danny was lying, if armed policemen were preparing to burst into the house. She tried to stay ready for it. Her first move would be toward Beth, though she doubted she could reach her with taped ankles.

"I had a dog when I was a kid," Warren said. "Did I ever tell you that?"

"I don't believe you did."

Laurel faintly remembered Warren telling her he'd owned a dog as a boy, but he hadn't gone into detail. In fact, he'd only revealed this on the day he agreed to buy Christy for the kids. He'd never spoken of it before or since.

"He was just a mutt," Warren said. "I found him out in the woods. A neighborhood kid was pouring drain cleaner on him. I took him home and washed him off, named him Sam. We went everywhere to-gether. He was my . . . my best friend, I was going to say. My dad didn't like Sam, but he put up with him. Anyway, a couple of years later, we got a bad rain. The neighborhood drainage ditch ran right behind our house. An open ditch, you know? About five feet deep. In a bad rain, it became a torrent. Five feet of water rushing through there like a locomotive. Just past our house, it turned into a massive whirlpool, because all that water was being forced into a twelve-inch pipe that ran underground to the creek.

"That particular day the wind blew a yellow ball Sam always chased into that water, and he went after it. He got the ball, but by that time the current had him. He couldn't get back to the bank. I went to jump in after him, but my dad ran off the patio and grabbed me, held me back. I would have drowned, but I didn't care. When you're eight, you don't worry about stuff like that."

Laurel was scarcely breathing.

"Sam fought for maybe a minute after he got to the whirlpool, and then it sucked him down. I was crying and praying he could hold his breath till he shot out the other end of the pipe, but it was a couple of hundred yards, at least. Maybe three hundred. I found him just before dark, down in the creek. Drowned. I've thought about him a lot, banging through that long black pipe, trying to fight, struggling to breathe . . . but the pipe was just too long. He never had a chance. That's how I feel now, Danny. A year ago, the current pulled me into the ditch. I've fought like hell to stay afloat, but I'm just about out of gas. And when I found that letter this morning, it just . . . I finally got sucked into the pipe. I can't breathe . . . I can't see. And I sure as hell can't get back to where I started. All I can do is wait to shoot out the other end of the pipe." Warren's chair creaked as he leaned backward. "And you know how that story ends."

Laurel tasted salt in her mouth. Her face was covered with tears. How could she have been married to a man for twelve years and not heard that story? How could she be the kind of wife that a man would not want to confide his worst nightmare to?

"You're in a bad place," Danny said. "I can hear

that. All I'm going to say to you is this. You need to look at this marriage situation as if you weren't sick. If you weren't sick, and there was another man in your wife's life, what would you do? You'd be angry, sure. But in the end, I think you'd have to let her go and be the best father you could be. Show her what a bad mistake she'd made by leaving you. But you show a woman that by being what you already are—a man of honor, not a pissed-off redneck who can't keep his shit in one sock."

Laurel wondered if Danny had gone too far.

"I think it just comes down to this," Warren said. "Other people's problems look simple, but when it's your own problem, it's complicated. I'm glad you talked to me, Danny. But in the end, I'm the one who has to decide how to end this thing."

The finality in his voice summoned a new kind of fear from Laurel's soul.

"Don't go yet," Danny said quickly, his voice betraying stress for the first time. "You said a while ago that you were waiting for something. Something on your computer. Are you still waiting?"

"I am. Laurel caused me some problems there, but I've got another computer working on it."

"What is it you're waiting for?"

"The name, Danny."

"The name?"

"The guy who was screwing my wife. Still is, for all I know."

Laurel wondered if Danny was alone, or if other men were watching him right now.

"She's got that on a computer in there? The guy's name?"

"I'm pretty sure she does. Don't worry about it. I'll let you guys know once I have it."

"How long is that likely to take?"

"No way to know. It's a probability thing. Could be ten minutes, could take ten hours."

Danny cleared his throat. "I don't think we have that kind of time, Warren. Not anything like."

"Why not? The sheriff getting antsy out there?"

"I told you about the manual. Remember? These guys have a list of steps out here. They cross one off, then go to the next one."

Warren thought about this. "I see. Well . . . I wouldn't advise anybody to trespass in this house. The yard's all right. But a man's home is his castle. Even the law says that. And as far as I can tell, nobody's got cause to come into this house uninvited. Uniformed or not. I wouldn't take kindly to that, Major. Not at all."

"I hear you, Doc. I'll relay that to the sheriff."

"You do that. Maybe we'll talk again."

Warren's hand reached out from behind the computer and switched off the speakerphone. In the silence that followed, Christy's scratching paws became the dominant sound in the house. It made Laurel think of Warren's drowning dog.

"Shouldn't you let Christy in?" she called. "I know she's starving by now."

Warren didn't answer for a while. Then he said, "Are you hoping they'll shoot me when I bend down to unlock the pet door?"

Laurel closed her eyes and wondered how two human beings who had shared a bed for so long could grow so far apart.

# CHAPTER
# 19

Danny ripped off the headset and shoved his chair away from the table.

"What was all that stuff about God?" Ray Breen asked from the door. "Did you hear that shit? Sounds like he's gone atheist or something."

Sheriff Ellis shook his head. "Dr. Shields is questioning his faith, that's all. Death is the most difficult test of the spirit, Ray. I've seen many a devout man question God in the face of cancer. Especially when it hits children. No, the truth is, I feel for the man."

"Well, I'm happy to hear it," Biegler said sarcastically. "But none of that brings us any closer to a resolution. I suppose you noted that we heard nothing whatsoever from Kyle Auster?"

Ellis nodded. "I think Dr. Auster's dead. Danny?"

"Dead."

"Well," said Ray. "What are we waiting for then? Shields ain't gonna let his little girl out of there. And he sure as hell ain't gonna let his wife out. I don't think we got any choice but to go in and get them."

"We need to know what's going on inside that house," said the sheriff.

"Randy's got the directional mikes on the windows," Trace said, "but he's getting a lot of noise. No clear voices. He texted me while Major Danny was talking. He thinks Shields is in the study. The wife and kid aren't saying anything. Nothing audible, no how. The thermal-image gadgets got here, but they ain't set up yet."

"Audio's enough for what we need," Ray said. "Let's get a location on Shields and go."

Sheriff Ellis still looked reluctant to give the order.

"What else are we gonna do?" Ray said impatiently. "The man's in hell already. You heard him."

"The man's scared to death," Carl said softly. "That's what I heard."

Everyone turned and looked at the sniper.

"We need to focus on Mrs. Shields and her daughter," said Danny, trying to plumb his own motives even as he spoke. "God knows Dr. Shields is in a bad place, but he poses a serious threat to his family. An imminent threat, if you ask me. There's no telling what he'll do if that computer finally tells him who his wife's been seeing."

"He'll kill her," said Ray. "You tell a guy that crazy who's been doing his wife, he's gonna off 'em both. Or the one he can get to, anyway. No question about it."

"Damn straight," Trace said from the comm rack. "I would."

"Maybe," said Sheriff Ellis. "I want the signal from those directional mikes routed in here."

"I got it now," said Trace.

"Well, turn it on!" Ellis snapped. "The worms are eating us up in here, I swear."

Agent Biegler said, "We need to be ready to go at a second's notice, Sheriff. Is the rest of your team in position?"

"*We?*" said the sheriff. "What's this *we* stuff? You ain't got a dog in this hunt, Biegler."

"I'm part of this operation, whether you like it or not."

"My men are in position," Ray said. "The charges are already set on the windows. Sonny Weldon's on the switch."

"Good," said Ellis.

"What's the chance of flying glass hurting the hostages?" Danny asked.

Ray shrugged. "There's a thin bead of explosive around each of those big panes. We're going to cut the glass, basically. It should drop pretty much straight down. With really bad luck, somebody could get hit by small shards, but I don't think so."

*Shards moving at 12,500 feet per second,* Danny thought, making a mental note to text Laurel to stay far from the windows prior to the assault. And to lie on top of Beth, if possible. With this thought came the realization that the men in the room were not watching Sheriff Ellis expectantly, but him. Even Ellis seemed to be waiting for Danny to give some last-minute guidance. Danny figured they must have bought into the plan he'd outlined earlier, whether they'd voiced their agreement or not.

"Let's put one thermal imager in front of the house and one in back," Danny said. "Make sure the one in back is at Carl's position. The operator will serve as his spotter. Carl's used to working that way. Make sure the fireman who's read the manual is operating the unit

by Carl. He'll have some idea what he's looking at."
Danny peered between sweat-soaked uniforms to the
sniper's face. "Sound okay to you, Carl?"

"Best we can do, probably. I had a thermal rifle
scope in the Corps when I needed it, but this ought to
be good enough for general target acquisition."

"Let's pray it is. After Carl has a positive lock on
Shields—and I mean *positive*—I'll take the chopper up,
hover over the backyard, and hit the searchlight. That'll
bring Shields to the windows." Danny looked at Ray.
"Then you blow them out, and Carl takes his shot."

Danny looked at the sheriff, worried that he'd
usurped the man's authority, but Ellis only nodded in
agreement. In this kind of situation, the natural hierar-
chy asserted itself.

Trace Breen held up his hand for silence. "Listen! I
got a mike signal ready. It's noisy, but just be patient.
Your ears'll sort out the words after a minute or so."

"Wait a second," said Ray. "I think it's time our
shooter got into position."

"Deputy Sims," said the sheriff, "get to your sniping position."

Danny was surprised that Ellis had let Carl stay
so long. But when he thought about it some more, he
understood. Carl Sims was Death. In the command
trailer, death was contained. But once they put Carl
behind that tree in the backyard—with clearance to
shoot—Warren Shields was a dead man. This certainty
roiled Danny's gut in a way few things ever had, and
only one thing weighed against the essential wrongness
of it. Shields's cancer.

*He's dead anyway,* Danny told himself.

Carl hesitated at the door, looking back to Danny

for a final, unspoken authorization. Danny closed his eyes, then gave the slightest of nods, knowing that his gesture carried the weight of a Roman emperor's thumb in the arena.

While Carl slipped silently out to his position, Laurel struggled like a mangy dog to scratch beneath the duct tape binding her ankles. Her soul might be in free fall, but her body could still drive her mad. Red welts had risen where the tape chafed her skin, and she had already scratched two of them bloody. As soon as she got momentary relief, her mind went back to Warren.

In the past ten minutes, she had seen deeper into her husband's heart than she had during her entire marriage. The despair he'd revealed to Danny had shattered her so completely that hope seemed only a quaint dream dimly recalled from childhood. Guilt suffused every cell of her being, and yet to dwell on it now was pointless. She had to act.

"Warren?" she said. "Could I speak with you for a minute?"

"What about?" came the disembodied voice from behind the computer monitor. "My tumor?"

"Not only that."

"Talk."

"Would you please come over here?"

"I can hear you fine from here."

This was going to be much harder without eye contact. "I think you know what I'm going to ask you. Why didn't you tell me about your diagnosis when you first got it?"

"There was no point."

"No point?"

"It would only have made things worse."

"Why do you think that?"

He sighed and leaned back in his chair. "I've seen it again and again in my practice. People get cancer, and everything in their lives changes. Sometimes it's not so bad . . . a thyroid cancer, testicular, some lymphomas, things that are caught early and dealt with. But if you get one of the big ones, the deadly ones, people never look at you the same way again. It's almost a tribal reaction, or an evolutionary one. People avoid you. You're tainted by death. Even if the surgeons swear they got it all, people think, 'Any day now, it could come back. He's a goner.' "

"I don't think that's necessarily true anymore."

His face moved out from behind the monitor. The frankness in it chilled her. "You have a lot of experience with cancer patients?"

"I realize you see more than I—"

"Laurel, I might as well have pancreatic cancer, okay? The worst thing is, people start treating you like you're dead long before you die. If you're a salesman, you make customers uncomfortable. Your boss smiles to your face, but he's already looking for somebody to replace you. People say they support you, but it's bullshit. Remember that actor who played *Spenser: For Hire* on TV? Robert Urich? He got synovial sarcoma about ten years ago. He went public and told the world he was going to beat it. What did the network do? Canceled his series. He lived five more years. If you're a doctor, it's worse. You scare the hell out of patients. Nobody wants to be reminded of his mortality. They look at a guy like me, midthirties, perfect physical shape . . . dying of cancer? Patients don't want to see that. They don't want to believe it can happen. I don't blame them. I didn't want to believe it either. But I did, finally. And I didn't intend to be treated like a dead man for my last few months of life. I'll be dead soon enough."

She tried to imagine herself in his situation, knowing he would soon lose everything, even his children. But Warren was right; there was simply no way she could. "I can understand you keeping it from your patients. Even from Kyle. But why didn't you tell me at least? Just me? You know I would have kept it secret. I could have helped you with everything. Getting to the treatments . . . anything you needed."

His head disappeared again. "I thought about it. But what could you do besides feel sorry for me and worry about the future? I wasn't going to endure the former, and I intended to spend every minute I had left on earth making sure you never had to do the latter. You see? What's the point?"

Laurel felt like knotting a piece of cord and whipping herself until she bled.

Warren got up and came around the desk. He stopped in the squared-off arch between the great room and the study. She rarely saw him unshaven, and the dark growth of beard gave him a desperate aura. He looked like a distant cousin of himself, someone she had met once long ago and then forgotten.

"Marriages go through hell when one partner is dying," he said. "People leave each other during illnesses like this. They get divorced. They have sexual problems, and not in the way you'd think. Sometimes the sick partner wants sex, but the other person just can't stomach it. They can't be intimate with this deathlike figure that used to be the person they lusted after. We all have strong feelings of repulsion against death and illness. I didn't want you thinking about any of that until you absolutely had to." He squeezed his fingers into fists. "And I meant to keep that day from coming, too."

"How?"

His gaze was unblinking. "Think about it."

She felt lost. She hadn't yet learned the rules of logic for the world where death was both inexorable and imminent. "I don't know."

"You asked me why I got the gun."

Her stomach turned over. "Oh, God. Warren, you wouldn't."

"You think I want my son's last memory of his father to be a hairless skeleton shitting himself in the bed? A shell of a man who can't talk or remember anything or even feed himself? No, thank you."

"Don't talk like that. Please."

"Why not? You want to pretend it wouldn't end that way?"

"I can't believe you've been dealing with this alone."

"Everybody deals with this alone. Sometimes there are just people around, that's all. Nobody can really help you."

"I think you're wrong," she insisted, hoping her faith wasn't absurdly naive. "You have to be willing to *let* someone help you."

An expression of boyish shyness came over his features. "Well . . . I'm not that way."

"I know. But maybe it's time to change. Just a little."

"I can't. I have to deal with this myself."

"Is that what you're doing now? Look at me, Warren. This is *crazy.*"

"No, it's not. I simply didn't foresee your betrayal. I should have, I see that now. But I was preoccupied. Isn't it funny? I've been spending my last months on earth trying to provide for someone who stopped loving me a long time ago."

"That's not true."

His eyes found hers again, and they were devoid of all illusion. "Isn't it?"

"I've always loved you, Warren! I just wanted you to really let me in, to let me love you, and you couldn't. I don't think it's your fault. It's just . . . I think your father wanted to make you tough, and he did such a good job that you *can't* be soft, you can't be vulnerable at all. And when you armor yourself like that, there's no way love can get in."

"Or out. Right?"

She nodded sadly.

"And now?"

She hung her head, searching for words to explain what she felt. "I don't know. Now we need to pull together to try to beat this thing somehow."

He laughed as though amazed. "You can't quit, can you? You can't stop pretending that the world is different than it is."

"Where there's life, there's hope. Corny maybe, but I believe that. And you're a fighter, God knows."

He drew his hand across his throat like a knife. "No one beats this, Laurel. It would take a miracle. And there are people on earth a lot more deserving of miracles than I am. What end would it serve, anyway? You're in love with someone else."

She stared back, unable to lie anymore. "I don't know. I feel like the whole world has been pulled inside out. I didn't know how things really were."

"So now that you know I'm dying, you love me again?"

What could she say to that?

Warren cocked his head as though listening to some faint sound beyond her hearing. "It's too late. I understand that now. For a while, some options remain open, but then they close. If you don't act while a door is open, it can shut forever. That's how life is. If you have a dream when you're young, you'd better act on it then, or the chance will be gone. You'll never run a world-record sprint at thirty-five. You don't become a rock star or a pro baseball player at forty-five."

"We're not talking about childhood dreams!" she cried, suddenly angry. "We're talking about a marriage! Two beautiful children!"

"That's right. We're talking about family. Trust, remember?"

Even as she watched him with hope in her heart, his face hardened into a mask of merciless judgment.

"You can't step back into that sacred circle after you've left it to fornicate with another man." He raised his arm and pointed at her like some Puritan judge. "You carried his seed into this house. The house that I built to protect you and our children. You carried that man into this house *inside your body*. And you *reveled* in it! *Didn't you?*"

"No."

Warren stepped closer to the sofa, his hand delving into his pocket. "Don't *lie*. We're through with lies. Admit what you did."

"I didn't do that."

"You made him wear a condom?"

"I didn't cheat on you!"

"Liar!" Another step closer. "You make me sick!"

She glanced past him at Beth's sleeping form, searching for the strength to keep lying. It could only be a mercy now. "I never betrayed you, Warren. I've had a hundred chances, but I never did."

He raised his hand high as if to strike her. "*LIAR! WHORE!*"

She shut her eyes and waited for the blow.

"Get up!"

"I can't. My feet are taped together."

"Get up, damn you! Get your—"

"Mama? What's the matter?"

Beth's tiny voice stopped Warren's roar the way a toddler running into the street stops a truck. She was standing in the arch between the study and the great room, her little arms folded protectively across her chest. Wild-eyed, Warren whirled and glared down at her, and she began to whimper. Laurel tried to get up, but he reached back and shoved her down again. Then he screamed like a man going mad.

"He's going to kill her," said Danny, quickly checking the instruments on the helicopter's panel. "We can't wait any longer."

"Christ!" Sheriff Ellis cried from the left-hand seat. "Take us up!"

"I can't yet!" Danny waited in near panic, urging the rotors to full rotational speed. The light was gone now, thanks to the storm clouds. For all practical purposes, night had fallen.

"Black Seven, this is Black Leader," said Ellis, calling Ray Breen. "We're going airborne in a matter of
seconds. As soon as we're in a hover over the backyard,
Major McDavitt will hit the spotlight, and I'll give the
command to go. The command will be 'Go,' repeated
three times. A no-go order will be 'Abort,' but don't
expect to hear that. Acknowledge."

"Black Seven, ten-four."

"Black Diamond, are you in position?"

"In position," Carl Sims replied. "I'm aiming at the
target indicated as most likely by the thermal imager."

"Are you ready and willing to fire?"

"Yes, sir. I'll acquire the target as the windows go
down, and fire on your command."

*No hesitation in that voice,* Danny thought. Death
was hovering over the Shields house.

"You're cleared to fire on Dr. Shields as of this moment," the sheriff said. "As soon as the windows go
down, take the soonest available shot."

"Understood," said Carl.

"It better be. Everyone else acknowledge by turns
that you're in position."

The radio started clicking. "Black One, copy that.
In position."

"Two, in position."

"Three, in position."

"Black Four, in position."

On it went, up to fifteen. The Bell's rotors were
churning now, pulling the craft away from the earth.
Danny pulled pitch with the collective and put her into
a hover, then pushed the cyclic and applied power. The
chopper rose into the darkness over Avalon.

Danny swung away from the house, knowing that

the noise of the engines would already have drawn Warren's attention. *Do a pedal turn, hover over the backyard, and hit the searchlight. Shields will think the sheriff is trying to see into the great room through those arched windows above the blinds. He'll probably open one of the blinds a little and peer out, trying to get a fix on the chopper. . . .*

*Two seconds later he'll die.*

With that thought came a hint of new awareness, but Danny didn't have time to dwell on it. He was making his turn, then crossing over the house to the backyard at seventy feet. He imagined he could see Carl Sims scoping the glowing windows, waiting for the brightly colored blob on an LCD beside him to become a living man. In that moment Warren Shields would cease being Carl's parents' doctor and instead become a warm target consisting of center mass with a head and four limbs attached. Carl's bullet would arrive like a freight train compressed into a quarter-inch-wide spear of copper-jacketed lead—

"Go lower!" shouted Sheriff Ellis. "Hit the spotlight!"

Danny switched on the thirty-million-candlepower searchlight mounted beneath the chopper's nose and aimed it at the second story of the Shields house, keeping it away from the lower windows to be sure it didn't interfere with the thermal imagers. He nudged the cyclic until they were hovering over the center of the backyard, just forty feet off the ground. He'd already sent a text message warning Laurel to keep away from the windows; he only prayed she'd been able to read it in time.

"Black Team," said Sheriff Ellis, "prepare to go on my order."

Danny could see the strain Ellis was under in the set of his jaw and the flexed muscles of his big forearms. He reminded Danny of a first-time skydiver preparing to jump—

*"Black Leader, this is Black Diamond!"* cried Carl. *"We've got a problem, repeat, a problem at my position."*

"This is Black Leader, what's happening?"

"I've got a kid on the roof of the house!"

Ellis glanced at Danny, his eyes unbelieving. "You've got *what*? Say again!"

"A kid on the roof. A child—on the back roof of the house, south side."

Danny peered down at the roof, wondering whether Laurel could have gotten Beth up there while Warren was talking to him. He saw no child, though, no movement of any kind.

"Is it the little girl?" Sheriff Ellis asked.

"Negative," said Carl. "Male child, maybe ten years old. He's trying to get *into* the house! Through a dormer window."

"It's Grant!" said Danny, sighting the little shape at last. He aimed the searchlight just to the right of the dormer. "See him? There he goes."

An agile figure vanished into the house with simian speed, then pulled the window shut after him.

"Damn it!" bellowed the sheriff. "Where the hell is Sandra Souther?"

"Doesn't matter," said Danny, holding his hover. "What do we do now?"

Ray Breen's voice crackled from the radio. "Let's

hit Shields before the kid can get downstairs. Right now!"

Sheriff Ellis's lips parted, but no words emerged. Danny wasn't sure what the best course was, but he knew one thing: you didn't learn how to handle this kind of situation on a football field. Ellis was far out of his league.

"What's happening on the thermal camera?" Ellis asked.

"We lost the kid, but my target is steady," Carl answered. "Target may even be a little closer to the study window. Can't tell for sure."

"Let's do it!" barked Ray. "This is our chance!"

Ellis's head bowed in the ghostly glow of the cockpit lights. *He's praying,* Danny realized. *Oh, Jesus—*

"Hold it!" shouted Carl. "Target's moving laterally now. Toward the kitchen."

Ellis's head snapped up, and he squinted uncertainly at the house.

"Abort," Danny said softly.

As though Danny were speaking through his mouth, Sheriff Ellis cried, "Abort! Abort! This is Black Leader. Abort!"

"Come on, Billy Ray!" pleaded Ray.

"Abort," Ellis repeated, his voice firm. "Everybody stay in position. Trace, can you route the directional mike signal to the chopper?"

"I think so."

"I've lost my target," said Carl. "He's off the thermal. I think he's in the kitchen."

"This is Black Six, with the thermal cam in front of the house," said a new voice. "I have a faint reading in the kitchen area."

"That's Shields," said Ellis.

Ray Breen's pumped-up voice distorted the headset speakers. "Forget Carl! Let's do it the old-fashioned way!"

Danny felt a rush of panic, but Ellis only shook his head and said, "Stand down, Ray. Land by the command post, Major."

"Are you *sure*?" Ray pressed.

"Goddamn it!" Ellis yelled. "I gave you an order! Do not, repeat *not*, blow those windows. Acknowledge!"

Two clicks sounded in the headsets. Ray Breen couldn't bring himself to speak, so angry was he over the aborted assault.

Danny swung the Bell around the house toward the stand of trees that sheltered the trailer. As he flared for the landing, he saw the sheriff's hands shaking in his lap. Sensing that he was being watched, Ellis quickly rubbed his palms together as though for warmth. Danny hadn't judged the man a coward for his nerves. He knew that the minute he took his own hands off the controls, they would be shaking, too.

# CHAPTER

# 20

Danny crashed through the door of the command trailer on Sheriff Ellis's heels. Trace Breen's head whipped up from his comm gear, a dip of Skoal bulging his bottom lip. Ellis walked to within a foot of him and demanded to know what was happening in the house. Trace shrugged like a crackhead being asked for directions.

"Do you hear the boy?" Ellis asked. "Grant Shields?"

Trace shook his head.

"Any violence?" Danny asked.

"I don't know. The last thing I heard after Dr. Shields screamed so crazy was the little girl crying and asking for chocolate milk."

"*Chocolate milk?*" Ellis echoed.

"Uh-huh. They're in the kitchen now. The mikes don't pick up much there, 'cause it's deeper in the house."

"Chocolate milk," the sheriff repeated, grabbing some paper towels to wipe the sweat and rain from his face. "Christ. What about the thermal camera?"

Trace keyed a walkie-talkie. "Black Six, this is base. What do you see on the thermal?"

"I saw three figures turn into two. I think maybe the mother picked up the girl. They're real faint now. Deeper in."

"Any sign of a fourth figure?" Ellis asked.

"You see anybody else?"

"I picked up a reading after Carl lost the boy on the back side, just a little green glow, but it's in and out. Fades almost as soon as I see it."

"Where at?" Trace asked, before Danny could prompt him.

"Kind of central, I guess, almost like it's between floors. Stairs, maybe?"

Danny looked at Sheriff Ellis. "The boy might not have let his parents know he's inside. He might be looking for a way to help his mother. I'll bet that's why he went back."

"This is a Chinese fire drill," Ellis said. "They're in there drinking chocolate milk, and two minutes ago we were about to blow the man's head off." He tossed the crumpled paper towels onto the blueprints on the table. "Should we just pack up and get the hell out of here? Let these folks solve their own problems?"

Danny was about to say *Maybe,* when Paul Biegler stepped through the door and said, "You should flush your badge down the toilet if that's your plan. You didn't have any idea what this job was about when you stood for election, did you?"

Ellis sniffed and regarded the Medicaid investigator with unconcealed disdain. "I thought it was about catching criminals and protecting the community. Not getting between husbands and wives in domestic disputes."

"Warren Shields *is* a criminal," Biegler asserted. "He may not be in Kyle Auster's class, but he has committed multiple felonies. Would it ease your conscience if he'd hit an old lady over the head and grabbed her purse instead of committing fraud?"

"Get out of my command post," Ellis said mildly. "Before I knock you out of it."

Biegler stepped fearlessly up to the sheriff. "You should have blown the windows and taken him out while you had the chance. Now you've got three hostages instead of two."

Ellis stared back silently, but Danny saw a vein bulging in his neck.

"What do you say, Major?" Biegler asked Danny, his voice edged with mockery. "I say it's time to get the FBI in here. Past time. Old Billy Ray here just proved he hasn't got the sand for this job—"

The sheriff hit Biegler so fast that Danny didn't see his fist cross the space between them, and so hard that the government agent dropped where he stood and lay motionless on the floor.

"I warned him," Ellis said. "Get him out of here, Trace."

Trace Breen jumped up from the radio and dragged Biegler out of the trailer by his heels, gulping in awe all the way.

"Lock the door when you come back," Ellis ordered.

After Trace had locked the door, the sheriff said, "Ray'll be coming in any second, soon as he calms down. Tell your brother to guard the door and keep

Biegler out. I don't want to see that son of a bitch again tonight."

"Biegler or Ray?" Trace asked.

"Biegler!"

Trace nodded and went back to his radio.

Sheriff Ellis led Danny to a corner and spoke softly. "I hate to admit it, but I'm about out of ideas. Do we just wait, or what?"

Danny shook his head. Grant Shields's sudden reappearance had given him a chance he had thought lost moments ago. "Sometimes the best thing is to do nothing, but this isn't one of those times. If things aren't getting better, they're getting worse. You know?"

Ellis nodded. "Agreed."

"I've got one idea, and I want you to seriously consider it."

"I'm listening."

"I want to go into the house. Physically go in and talk to Shields face-to-face."

Ellis stared back in disbelief. "Unarmed, you mean?"

"If I go in with a gun, he's liable to shoot me."

As Ellis's eyes searched his, Danny realized that the sheriff wasn't the middling-dumb country boy that people like Marilyn Stone thought he was.

"I get the feeling I'm missing something," Ellis said. "First off, Shields asks to talk to you—not me, not his lawyer, not his pastor—you. Then he talks to you like you *are* his pastor. And now you want to walk unarmed into a house where a disturbed man who's probably already murdered one person is holding his family at gunpoint. Have I got that right?"

Danny had tried not to think too much about the

risks of his plan, but Ellis wasn't going to let him off that easy. He hadn't known himself how he felt until a split second before Ray Breen was going to blow the windows—before the 7.62 millimeter bullet in Carl's rifle would have blasted Warren Shields's laboring heart into mush. After Carl sighted the boy on the roof and Sheriff Ellis turned to Danny for guidance, Danny could easily have said "Go," rather than "Abort." If he had, Shields would be dead now, and Laurel would be a widow. A single woman, free to spend her life with whomever she chose. Danny wanted Laurel more than he'd wanted any woman in his life. But when the power had been given him to possess her—twice now, he realized—he'd been unable to take her. The first time because he wouldn't give up his son to have her; this time because he couldn't live the rest of his life with a decent man's blood on his hands. But something deeper than this had stopped him, something he still couldn't quite pin down. He was trying to unravel the feeling when five sharp bangs rattled the trailer door.

"Open up, damn it!" roared a muted voice. "It's me, Ray!"

Trace got up, but the sheriff waved him back to his seat.

"Talk to me, Danny," Ellis urged. "Time's short."

Danny raised his hand to his mouth as though he were about to throw up. The dark epiphany that had begun as he hovered over the backyard had finally revealed itself to him. "Shields wants us to kill him."

Ellis's eyes went wide. "What? You mean . . . like suicide by cop?"

"Exactly."

"Because of the cancer?"

"I don't know. Yes and no. Deep down, he's a John Wayne type. No matter how bad Shields may want to kill himself, he sees suicide as a coward's way out. I don't think dying of cancer scares him. The pain of it, I mean. It's the *indignity*. He's too proud for that."

Ellis's eyes seemed focused on something beyond Danny. "I can relate to that. My daddy died of lung cancer, and I watched every minute of it. That's no way to go."

Ray Breen's next bovine bellow shook the aluminum skin of the trailer. "I'm soaking wet, goddamn it! Let me in!"

*"In a minute!"* Ellis roared back. Then his jaw muscles clenched, and he stroked his incipient jowls. "Tell me why I should let you go in that house. What hope have you got?"

"Shields trusts me. I might be able to get close enough to get the gun away from him."

Ellis snorted. "If that's your plan, forget it. That's begging to get killed. Ask any cop."

Danny almost felt emboldened to confide in the sheriff about Laurel. The man had a grasp of the complexities of life; but how far would a Baptist deacon bend the rules?

"What is it?" Ellis asked. "It's come-to-Jesus time, Danny."

Danny almost spoke up, but in the end he decided that revealing the truth meant giving up the only edge he had in the situation—and might result in his being barred from the scene. "I can't put it into words," he said lamely. "But Shields respects me. If I can look him in the eye, man-to-man, I might be able to make him see reason."

"And if you can't?"

"Maybe I can get his wife and kids out."

"You're willing to die for that chance? An outside chance?"

"He won't kill me."

"Why not?"

Danny thought about it. "He doesn't believe he has the right."

Ellis clucked his tongue three times, then turned to Trace Breen, who was watching them warily. "Have you heard anything?"

"Just mumbles and static. They're too far from the windows. You want to try moving the mikes around?"

"Try anything that might work." Ellis turned back to Danny with sudden purpose. "I can't let you do it. Dr. Shields may not be responsible for his actions. I don't just mean he's distraught. That brain tumor may have unhinged the man. He could kill you, no matter what you believe."

Danny shrugged. "I've been in tough spots before."

"That was different. That was for your country."

"This is just as important."

"Not in my view." Ellis looked at his watch, then gave Danny a long, slow look. "Not unless you know something I don't."

"No, sir. You know what I know."

"Then forget it. You stay with me. Trace, let your brother in."

Trace got up and went to the door.

"And tell me the second you hear anything on the mikes."

"You want me to tell Carl to move around front? In case he can get a shot there?"

"Leave Carl where he is."

Ray almost knocked his brother down as he stormed into the trailer, water cascading off the brim of his Stetson. His eyes burned with outrage.

Before he could vent his anger, Ellis said, "Ray, get your best men up to the front door and the pantry door in the garage. We're gonna go in the old-fashioned way, soon as you place your people. I want those hostages out of there."

Breen stared back, the light of satisfaction growing in his eyes. "And Shields?"

"If he poses any threat whatever to your men or to his family, take him out."

Danny's pulse began to hammer in his throat. He raised his hand to his neck as if to somehow slow the racing blood.

Ray looked from the sheriff to him. "Y'all still planning to use the chopper as a diversion?"

"I can't think of a better one," said Ellis. "Move out, Ray."

Breen went out, leaving a trail of muddy boot prints behind him.

"I want to monitor the directional mikes from the chopper," Ellis said. "I want 'em loud and clear, Trace. Make it happen."

"You got it, Sheriff."

"And keep a thermal cam on the kitchen windows." Ellis walked to the door without even looking at Danny. "Let's go, Major. We'll listen from the ground, but I want the rotors spinning."

Ellis disappeared through the door. As Danny

moved to follow him, Trace grinned with such malice that Danny stopped. "What is it, Deputy?"

The feral eyes glinted in the dim light. "That fucker's dead now."

"Shields?"

"Yep."

"That pleases you?"

"Damn straight."

"Why?"

Trace picked up a red paper Coca-Cola cup and spat a brown stream of tobacco juice into it. "Chickens coming home to roost. That's why."

"What do you mean by that?"

The yellowish skin above Trace's chin worked around the plug of snuff in his bottom lip. "What do you care?"

"Sounds like you've got a personal problem with Dr. Shields."

"What if I do? From what I seen tonight, I don't think I'm the only one."

The deputy's eyes flashed with glee. Danny almost crossed the little room and grabbed his scrawny neck, but that would only bring questions he'd have to lie to answer. Instead, he wrapped a Sheriff's Department poncho around his shoulders and walked out into the rain.

Carl Sims had been staring so hard at the readout of the thermal-imaging camera that his eyeballs felt paralyzed. Even for a sniper accustomed to searching terrain through a rifle scope, this was torture. The LCD monitor displayed a full spectrum of colors as it read the heat differentials in front of its supersensitive sensor system. The coolest areas appeared blue; warmer objects looked green; while the hottest targets transitioned from yellow to orange and finally to bright red. The human beings moving behind the window blinds were faint, amorphous blobs of constantly changing color and intensity, amoebas that pulsed, merged, separated, and then vanished altogether, only to reappear in some other place. The rain didn't help matters (the camera had already gone on the blink a couple of times; clearly it did not like moisture), but the air-conditioning inside the house did. With the air cooled to below seventy degrees, the thermal camera could detect just enough contrast to reveal the human beings moving within that air—even with the window blinds interposed between the sensor and its targets.

Carl had never been in such a bad shooting situation. He'd thought he had seen it all in Iraq, but he was wrong. He had shot through high winds, blasting sand, rain, automotive glass, and even through the water of a swimming pool; he knew exactly how a bullet would behave in each of those situations. He'd shot during the day and he'd shot at night. He'd shot prone, sitting, standing, and from a moving vehicle. He'd killed nine men from distances greater than a thousand yards. But never had he sat a stone's throw from a well-lighted house with his vision totally obscured by window blinds, trying to locate his target on a camera before he could even put his eye to his rifle scope. In Iraq, if he needed thermal-imaging capability, he'd simply switched to a thermal-imaging rifle scope, which gave him the equivalent of X-ray vision, zeroed in to put a bullet wherever he wanted it. But this . . . this was a sniper's nightmare.

He didn't want the pulsing blobs to return to his side of the house. If they did, according to the sheriff's new orders, Carl would have to give the order to blow the windows himself, which meant that he would be guessing which blob was Dr. Shields. After the windows dropped, it would take at least a full second to acquire his target in the Unertl scope and pull the trigger. That was if he was *right* about which blob was Dr. Shields. If he was wrong, it might take two or three seconds to acquire. The shooting was nothing in this case; target acquisition was everything.

This situation was tailor-made for a commando assault, not a sniper shot. Delta, the SEALs, Force Recon, the FBI's Hostage Rescue Team—any of those units would have had the Shields family out of there hours ago, and without a single casualty. But none of those units was here tonight. Tonight it was Ray Breen's Weekend Warriors. Carl had trained with the guys out there in the black body armor, and though they might look like commandos, they weren't. Most had the reaction times of an average bowling team, not the Olympic-caliber reflexes of a Delta Force operator. Yet any minute—once Major McDavitt's helicopter lifted into the air again—they were going to crash into that house with guns blazing. The major's earlier words played relentlessly in Carl's head: *There's exactly two professional soldiers here tonight, and they're both under this tent. If the sheriff reaches the point of ordering an explosive entry, you are the best hope that Mrs. Shields and her daughter have of surviving this night. You alone.* Carl closed his eyes and prayed the major could find a way to persuade Dr. Shields to surrender peacefully. Failing that he supposed, he should pray that the red blobs would return to his side of the house. Any other outcome was likely to mean disaster.

Laurel stood on the sink side of the kitchen island, exactly opposite Warren and Beth, as Warren had instructed her to do when he cut the duct tape from her wrists and legs. Beth sat on a barstool with both hands wrapped around a mug of Borden chocolate milk that Warren had heated in the microwave. No one had said much since Beth calmed down, a feat accomplished by prodigious lying on Laurel's part, more fluff about Mommy and Daddy playing a grown-ups' game.

Warren's discussions with Danny seemed to have drained him, or perhaps sleep deprivation was finally taking its toll. Laurel couldn't remember going forty hours without sleep herself, except perhaps during final exams in college, and probably not even then. Warren had done it often as an intern, but that had been years ago. His nerves were stripped bare; the slightest sound made him jump, and he spoke in quick, snappish phrases. She had decided to focus on Beth and to avoid provoking him at any cost.

Earlier, when Danny's helicopter had cranked up and hovered over the backyard, Laurel had felt sure that rescue was imminent. Yet this belief had not brought her joy. Even before she'd received Danny's text message warning her to stay away from the windows, she'd become certain that the price of freedom would be Warren's life. As Warren strode toward one of the great room windows to check out the hovering helicopter, Laurel had steeled herself for the sight of her husband's head being blown apart like JFK's in the Zapruder film, her own personal Technicolor nightmare, one that would haunt her till the day she died. In the end, though, nothing had happened. It was as though they had edged up to the brink of disaster, then pulled back.

Beth slid off her stool and walked over to the table where she'd eaten breakfast thirteen hours before. To Laurel, the memory of that meal was like a glimpse of some other universe, one far removed from the absurd one that contained them now. Warren tracked Beth with his eyes as though about to stop her, but he didn't. Laurel watched her daughter pick up one of Grant's miniature skateboards—Tech Decks, they were called—and start rolling the two-inch-long board across the glass table. With Beth diverted, Laurel looked across the island at Warren and stared until he had no choice but to make eye contact.

"I'm sorry for everything I've done," she said. "And for everything I haven't done. I want to make things better. Tell me what I can do."

He stared back at her like a man who has forgotten how to speak. His bloodshot eyes roamed her face, perhaps searching for some clue to what had brought them to this pass. As he worked his jaw and swallowed with obvious effort, she realized that he was severely dehydrated. He hadn't used the bathroom for hours, nor had he drunk anything. The left corner of his mouth was red; she thought she saw the budding vesicles of a fever blister, which he only got when he was under extreme stress.

"Let me get you some water," she offered. "And some ibuprofen, maybe?"

He didn't respond at first. Then he rubbed his mouth and said, "Ice water."

As she turned toward the sink, Beth cried, "Christy! Dad, it's Christy!"

The corgi had disappeared earlier, probably terrified by the thunder of Danny's helicopter, but now she was back, scratching at the doggy door like a starving beggar.

"Can I let her in, Daddy?"

"Not now, honey."

"Please?" Beth pleaded. "Please, please, please, *please.*"

As Laurel filled a tumbler with water from the tap, Warren surprised her by saying, "All right. She probably needs food."

Laurel heard Beth unlatch the pet door, then Christy's claws scratching the planks of the hardwood floor.

"She's got something in her mouth," Beth said. "It's a bag, Daddy. I wonder what's in it."

"Don't touch that!" Warren snapped. "It's dirty."

Laurel turned from the sink as though moving underwater, certain even before she saw it that Christy had retrieved the Walgreens bag from behind the hedge. Survival instinct drove her toward the dog, but it was already too late to bury this evidence.

"I'll throw that away!" she said, but by then Warren was taking the bag from Christy's mouth.

As he opened the bag, an urge to bolt from the house almost overcame Laurel, but she forced herself to stay put. Warren looked into the bag, and his eyes narrowed in puzzlement. "Christy must have knocked over the tall container," he said. "I didn't know she could do that."

Laurel felt like a cartoon character staring helplessly upward as a thousand-pound weight hurtled down from a cliff top. She was every bit as stupid as the Coyote—

"Wash your hands, Beth," Warren said. Then he walked to the trash compactor, opened it with his foot, and tossed the Walgreens bag inside. "Use the pantry sink."

"Aww, they're clean." Beth stroked Christy's orange back as the dog ate noisily from her dish.

"Go!"

Beth jumped up and vanished into the pantry.

Laurel stood motionless before the island, recalling an afternoon in college when a bolt of lightning had blasted apart a tree just forty feet away from her on a golf course. The very air had seemed to ignite around her, and she'd stood in the ozone-tinged aftermath like an air-raid survivor, too dazed even to be thankful for her life.

"My water?" Warren said.

She looked down at the tumbler in her hand. "Oh." She handed him the glass, her hand shaking.

"I guess I'll get my own ice," he said, going to the freezer.

"I'm sorry."

As he shoved the glass into the automatic ice dispenser, Laurel realized that the dog, rather than almost delivering her destruction, might have delivered her salvation instead. Her plan would be risky, but she saw no safe way out of this trap.

"Warren? I have something to tell you."

He took a thoughtful sip from his glass. "What is it?"

"I wanted to tell you this morning, but you were so upset about the audit—or that's what I thought, anyway—that I decided to wait. But now that I know about"—she lowered her voice—"your illness . . . you need to know this. It just might change how you feel about everything."

He set his glass on the table and folded his arms across his chest. "What are you talking about?"

Laurel suddenly sensed that she was making a mistake. But what other gambit did she have? "I'm pregnant," she said simply. "I just found out this morning."

He blinked once, slowly, like a lizard in the sun. Other than that, he gave no sign of having heard her.

"Did you hear what I said?"

"We've only had sex twice in the last month."

She prayed that Danny wasn't hearing this. "It only takes once, you know. It only took once with Grant."

Warren looked down at her belly, but of course she wasn't showing. If anything, she looked thinner than she had a month ago.

"More lies," he said.

She somehow managed a confident smile. "Open the trash compactor. Look inside that bag Christy brought in."

He stared at her awhile longer. Then he opened the compactor and fished out the Walgreens bag. Out came the tampon carton.

"Keep going," she said.

He looked into the empty bag, then opened the tampon box. He stared for several seconds, then drew out the e.p.t box, and his expression changed from irritation to a kind of wonder. Pulling the used test strip out of its little baggie, he studied it for a while, then looked up at her with suspicion.

"When did you take this test?"

"I told you, this morning."

"Why did you hide it?"

"Because you hadn't even come to bed the night before, and you were obviously upset. I decided to wait until you'd resolved the audit."

Warren stared at her like a parent listening to a lying toddler. "If you're pregnant, the baby's not mine."

He seemed so utterly convinced of this fact that Laurel's smile faded. "Why not?"

"Because I can't father a child anymore."

There was a roaring in her ears like the birth of an avalanche. "You . . . why not?"

"Because of the drugs I'm taking. Massive doses of steroids, plus some experimental compounds Kenneth Doan prescribed for me. He got me into a Genentech trial. I'd be surprised if I have even one viable sperm left."

"You must have!" she said quickly. "There's no other explanation."

"Of course there is."

"All clean!" Beth announced, bounding into the kitchen with her wet hands held high. She patted Christy on the back, earning a warning growl, then climbed onto a chair and started rolling a Tech Deck across the table.

"Let's continue this later," Laurel said, wringing her hands. "Please."

Warren's eyes looked even more reptilian than they had before. "Beth, honey?"

"What?" She twirled the little skateboard in a circle.

"Mommy's got a surprise for us."

Beth looked up from the board, her eyes on Laurel. "What is it, Mommy?"

"You're going to get a new brother or sister soon," Warren said.

Beth's mouth and eyes opened wide. "A baby sister?"

"Maybe," Warren said. "We don't know yet."

"I want a baby sister! No more *boys*!"

Warren set the Walgreens bag gently on the counter. "Do you have any more surprises, Mom?"

"It's your baby," she whispered. "There's no other option but virgin birth, and I'm no virgin."

"That's for sure."

"Where's Grant?" Beth asked. "I want to tell Grant we're getting a baby sister!"

"Grant's spending the night with Gram," Warren said, his eyes never leaving Laurel's face. Gram was Laurel's mother; she lived thirty-five miles up the river in Vidalia, Louisiana.

"I want to stay with Gram, too! No fair!"

"Hush, Elizabeth," Warren said. "We'll see about that later."

"Does Gram know about my baby sister?"

"Quiet!"

Beth's head snapped down, and she went back to twirling the skateboard.

Warren stepped close enough to Laurel to kiss her. "If this baby was mine, you would have told me as soon as you heard I was sick. After I got off the phone with Danny."

"Who's sick?" Beth asked. "Is Daddy sick?"

"Quiet, baby," Warren said in a silky voice.

"Please don't do this," Laurel implored.

"You were trying to give me hope before. You would have told me about it then, if it was true."

She answered with quiet urgency, trying not to communicate her growing panic to Beth. "I wasn't sure if it would make things better or worse. I was afraid you'd feel you were missing that much more."

"A man lives to pass on his genes. You know that." He lifted his hand and tenderly brushed a strand of hair from her eyes. She shuddered. "There's only one reason you would have kept this secret from me."

"You're wrong."

He picked up the Walgreens bag and slapped her with it.

Beth screamed.

*"Dad, stop it!"* shouted a voice from the hallway.

Everyone froze as Grant stepped from the hallway into the kitchen. "Stop yelling at Mom! She hasn't done anything!"

Warren looked his son from head to toe, and Laurel saw pride in his eyes. "There's my son," he said. "It's written all over him."

It was true. Grant had Warren's muscular body and regular facial features; but it was her eyes that looked out of his face.

Warren took three steps toward Grant and held out his right hand. "I knew you'd come back, Son. You had the wrong idea before."

Grant drew back, but then Warren raised his hand, and Grant slapped it in some kind of high-five ritual. "There's guys outside with guns," Grant said. "Lots of them, and some of them are mean. We have to get ready."

"Yes, we do," Warren said calmly. "We're all here

now, just as it should be. I want you kids to go into the safe room."

Laurel shivered at the name.

"Are you and Mom coming?" Grant asked.

"In a minute, yes."

"I'll wait until you go, then."

"Mind me, Son."

Grant looked back at his father with a combination of disappointment and defiance. "I'm not a little kid anymore, Dad. I want to help. I can do stuff now. Grown-up stuff!"

Warren looked appraisingly at his son, then knelt and beckoned him closer. When Grant came forward, Warren spoke softly into his ear. Grant nodded several times, then hurried past Laurel into the pantry.

"Where's he going?" Laurel asked.

Warren smiled. "Don't worry about it."

# CHAPTER

# 21

Danny was so stunned by the revelation of Laurel's pregnancy that he could hardly think. He and Sheriff Ellis sat shoulder to shoulder in the helicopter, headsets on, with the rotors already whirling at full rotational speed.

"I don't think we can wait until Carl gets a clear shot," the sheriff said, his worried face illuminated by the cockpit lights. "I know you want to, but I can't risk Shields barricading his family in that panic room. He could cut their throats and laugh at us while he was doing it."

"He hasn't done that yet," Danny pointed out.

"No, but he's coming apart in there. I didn't like the sound of his voice. I've got that Jim Jones, Kool-Aid feeling."

Danny wanted to argue, but his mind kept jumping back to the fact that Laurel had lied to him about sleeping with her husband. This morning she'd told him flat out that she hadn't. But she *had*.

"Shields doesn't believe her about that pregnancy either," Ellis added. "I think that pushed him over the edge." He elbowed Danny. "You think Shields is the father of that baby?"

*Jim Jones,* Danny thought, twenty seconds behind the conversation. *Kool-Aid.* "I don't know. Might be the guy who wrote the letter."

"Shields is a doctor, so he must know what he's talking about. He says he couldn't have got her pregnant. Aw . . . in five minutes it won't matter anyway."

Danny closed his eyes, trying to work his way to the heart of what had really been going on in his life.

"Fuck this," Ellis said, abandoning his deacon's rectitude. "Take us up, Danny!"

Danny pulled pitch and the Bell leaped into the night sky. In seconds he was looking down at the glowing yellow windows of the Shields home in miniature, an aerial shot of the perfect suburban home. A Steven Spielberg movie.

"This is Black Leader," Ellis said. "TRU will carry out explosive entry on my command. Acknowledge by turns."

Danny gripped the controls with too much force, trying in vain to bleed off his anxiety.

"Black One, in position."

"Two, in position."

Ellis pointed down toward the front yard. "I want you to flare out there and hit your light, pull him to a window. He might come alone, and I'll blow the doors then."

Danny shook his head as though to clear it. "You can't send Ray in there, Sheriff. You've got to let Carl take the shot."

"There's no more time! And Carl's still on the back side of the house."

"Move him!"

"It's too late! We're going in. Shields has left us no choice."

"Six, in position."

Danny descended to 150 feet and flew left turns as he waited for the acknowledgments to come in. From this altitude, the beating of the rotor blades would sound to someone in the house like a giant robot pounding on the roof. *Maybe that baby is Warren's,* he thought. But the sheriff was right; Shields was a doctor and he'd sounded certain about his inability to father a child. Danny flashed back to the morning's school conference, when Laurel had started to tell him something, then pulled back at the last moment, when the next parent showed up at the door—

"This is Black Six," crackled the headset. "I've got movement on the front thermal cam. It's real faint, but it looks like a large figure moving from the pantry toward the central hall. The foyer area."

"What's he doing?"

"I don't know. It's just a green blob, Sheriff. Like a ghost."

"Keep me posted. Carl, stay ready. If Shields moves back into the great room, we may blow those back windows yet."

"Understood. I'm glassing the windows, and my spotter's on his thermal. I'm ready to fire."

Danny looked down at the house, praying for the X-ray vision promised in the comic books of his youth. Where was Laurel? What was Warren doing? Would he really execute her? *Yes,* answered a voice in his head. *Not to kill her, but to murder the child she's carry-*

*ing. It's his only chance at revenge against an invisible enemy. He'll shoot her in the stomach. . . .*

Danny thought about the cell phone in his pocket. He should already have used it to try to find out what was happening inside. But with Warren moving around the house, what good were texted answers? Every passing second could change the reality in there. *Maybe it's time to call her,* he thought. But would that give the TRU the edge they needed, or get Laurel killed before they could even blow the doors?

For once in his life, Danny had no idea what to do.

Grant sat huddled in the pantry with the lights off, just as his father had told him to do. He had one job: pull the big breaker switch if he heard shooting. He knew all about the breaker switch, because his dad had told him about it when they lost power during Hurricane Katrina. It wasn't hard or anything. He'd seen twenty different cartoon characters pull the same kind of switch to make the lights go out.

Grant was confused about what was happening with his parents, but he was glad to have a job to do, and he didn't want to disappoint his father again. No matter how crazy it might seem that his dad was acting, Grant knew there was a reason for it, because his dad always did the right thing. His mom had told him that. Plenty of times. And now wasn't the time to start doubting it. He was only a kid, after all.

As he stared up at the big switch lever, his back pressed into a corner, someone slid open the pantry window. Grant jumped because he was startled, but after that he stayed absolutely still. He'd been hunting enough times to know what to do when you didn't want to be seen. No movement. No sound. Not even a breath.

It didn't surprise him that the alarm system didn't chime. The same silence had greeted him when he sneaked back through the window upstairs. He figured the cops had turned off the system somehow.

A dark head came through the window, and with it the smell of cigarettes. Then the head vanished, and a leg with a boot on the end of it came through. Four fingers curled under the window frame. Then the head returned, followed by shoulders and the rest of a body. Grant tensed, preparing to spring to his feet and tear out of the pantry, but his father's instructions held him back. He could not abandon his post.

He heard a grunt, followed by creaks and stretchy sounds like those his grandmother's knees made when she got up from her easy chair. The intruder stood tall in the darkness. He was wearing a uniform, Grant realized, just like the one Deputy Sandra had been wearing. Grant thanked God there was a shelf above his head, or the guy would probably have seen him already.

When the man took a step forward, Grant's eyes bulged. This man had coached the baseball team Grant played against in the city championship last year. His son was a pitcher on the team, a boy who cussed all the time and tried to pick fights after he lost. The referees had threatened to throw the coach out of the game for yelling cuss words.

*Trace . . .* that's what the kids called him. *Coach Trace.* Like the Natchez Trace.

Grant watched Coach Trace move quietly to the pantry door, then open it slowly. When light from the kitchen fell across him, Grant saw a gun in his hand. Then Coach Trace vanished.

A fist closed around Grant's heart.

He gritted his teeth and tried to figure out what to do. His dad had told him to stay put, that he wouldn't be safe roaming around the house. He'd also said that switching off the lights was an important job. A *critical* job. And Grant was supposed to wait until he heard shooting to do it. Coach Trace clearly meant to shoot somebody—maybe even his dad—but was that when Grant was supposed to switch off the lights? He didn't think so. Because that would be too late. He pulled off his shoes, walked barefoot to the door, and followed Coach Trace into the kitchen.

Danny was hovering a hundred feet over the front yard when a panicked voice filled their headsets.

"Sheriff, this is Gene on the front thermal! I think somebody may have gone into the house!"

"*What?*"

"I had a figure in the shrubs near the pantry window. I thought it was Dave, but then it suddenly faded to half intensity. Now it's gone. I think maybe the guy went into the house."

"Damn it!" Ellis cursed. "This is Black Leader, have any of you entered the house?"

No one replied.

"Acknowledge proper position by turns!" Ellis demanded. "Come on, damn it!"

"Black One, in position."

"Two, in position."

"Three, in position."

The transmissions came in like a military roll call, all

the way to fifteen without pause. Sheriff Ellis breathed a sigh of relief after the last. "Must have been a mistake. For a minute I thought we had a rogue on our hands."

"Let's get this show on the road," Ray Breen said.

Ellis motioned for Danny to start descending.

Laurel stood motionless in the foyer, recalling her attempted escape from the safe room, when Warren had threatened to kill both her and himself. *That was the turning point,* she thought. *My last chance to get out.* But it had been no chance at all, really. Because Warren would have carried through with his threat. She was certain of it now. *It would have saved the children,* she thought with a stab of guilt. *But who could have made that choice?* Surely she'd had reason to hope for some other outcome at that point.

She stared at the door that concealed the entrance to the safe room, recalling stories she'd read about gas station clerks ordered by robbers to go into a restroom and lie on the floor. *I won't go in,* she told herself. *I'll fight here rather than die passively in there. Maybe Grant will help me.*

She turned toward the front door. Police waited on the other side of it, but Warren had bolted all the doors and hidden the keys. She stepped backward and looked down the hall toward the kitchen, which was dark now. Warren was escorting Beth up the hallway. The scene looked completely normal, father and daughter walking toward the stairs to go up and read a bedtime story—except for the pistol hanging from Daddy's hand.

*Something's different,* she thought, her pulse quickening.

She looked at her husband's face, haggard and swollen, only the eyes vital, alive with a zealot's conviction. *He's going to kill us,* she realized. *This is the end.*

Panic of unimaginable power surged through her, infusing her with the strength to try anything. Her hands quivered with energy, as though they knew that any moment they might be employed to choke the life out of a stronger enemy.

*My cell phone,* she thought suddenly. *Should I call Danny and tell them to come in shooting? Warren won't let me do that. But I could just open the line—*

Something moved behind Warren, blanking Laurel's mind of everything but what was in front of her. *Was it only a shadow? No . . . it had substance—*

*There!* A darker outline in the darkness of the kitchen—

She forced her eyes to focus on Warren's, trying to protect the newcomer. In the dark blur behind her husband, the shadow floated swiftly up the hallway, thin and fluid and somehow more dangerous than Warren's gun. She felt an instant of guilt for not warning Warren, but then Grant's voice shattered the silence—

*"Coach Trace! Coach Trace!"*

The shadow whirled toward the piercing scream, and Warren spun also. His gun went up as he turned, and Laurel saw then that the shadow had made a fatal mistake, one that Grant must have known it would. By spinning toward the sound, the stranger had turned his back on Warren, and by the time he tried to correct his error, Warren had already fired. *Grown-up stuff indeed . . .*

Warren's bullet struck the shadow somewhere vital, because she heard the heavy thud of dead weight drop-

ping onto wood, a sack of feed hitting a barn floor.
Then Grant charged out of the dark and snatched a
pistol from the fallen man's hand.

"You got him, Dad! You got him!"

Grant leaped into his father's arms and hugged him
tight.

*"What the fuck was that?"* Sheriff Ellis shouted into
his headset mike.

"Gunshot," said Danny, terrified that Warren had
just executed Laurel. "Sounded like a pistol, but what
was that the boy screamed?"

"We gotta go *now*!" Ray Breen yelled. "Give the
order, Sheriff!"

"Negative!" Ellis shouted. "Somebody yelled *Trace*.
Trace, was that you? What are we hearing down there?
Did anybody fire?"

The communications officer didn't respond.

Danny tilted the chopper to get a better view of the
house. Rain still peppered the windshield, making it
hard to see clearly.

"Trace!" Ellis yelled. "Get me Dr. Shields on my
radio!"

"We can't wait!" Ray shouted. "We gotta go!"

"Shut up, Ray! Keep this channel clear!"

The radio hummed and crackled, and then a woman's voice filled Danny's headset. "Sheriff, we've got a
problem."

"Who's this?"

"Sandra Souther. I'm in the command trailer."

"Where's Trace?"

"Um . . . I think he's in the house."

Ellis blanched. *"What?"*

"Dr. Shields just called the phone in here. Nobody was answering, so I came in and picked up. Dr. Shields said Trace just tried to shoot him in the back, and he had to kill him."

Sheriff Ellis looked at Danny with dawning horror.

"You'd better put a rope around Ray Breen," Danny said. "Fast."

"Ray, this is Billy Ray," the sheriff said in a voice Danny had never heard from him before. "I know you heard that, brother. You're to stand down and let me handle this, copy? Get a grip on yourself for sixty seconds and let me handle it."

"Fuck that," Ray muttered. "I lead the TRU. We're going in."

"*Ray!*" Ellis balled his right hand into a fist and spoke harshly. "If you enter that house without authorization, you're out of a job."

"*I don't give a shit! Black Team, prepare to go on my command. Five seconds—*"

"I'll arrest you for murder, Ray. As God is my witness, you'll go to death row in Parchman. And you've put too many men there to want to see it from the inside."

Danny listened in dread for Breen's go order, but it didn't come.

"Sandra, this is Sheriff Ellis. Can you hook me up to Dr. Shields?"

"Maybe. Hang on."

"Why in God's name would Trace do that?" Ellis murmured, seemingly lost.

"He had a personal grudge against Shields," Danny said. "I don't know what it was. I just found out myself. I should have told you." Danny touched the sheriff's arm. "You can't let Ray into that house. Now or later, you can't do it."

"He's the TRU leader," Ellis said. "Those boys down there trained under him, and I'm not changing horses in midstream."

Danny looked hopelessly down at the house glowing in the dark.

"He'll kill Shields, no matter what you tell him."

"Shields put us all here. That's the bottom line. If it ends ugly, it's on his head. Trace Breen didn't start this nightmare. Warren Shields did it all by himself."

*No, I helped,* Danny thought. *With a little hands-on assistance from the man's wife—*

"I've got Dr. Shields for you, Sheriff," Sandra said. "Go ahead."

"Dr. Shields, this is Sheriff Ellis. Can you hear me?"

"It's faint, but I hear you."

"Did you just shoot one of my deputies?"

"Yes, sir. Trace Breen snuck in here and tried to shoot me in the back. If my son hadn't warned me, I'd be dead now."

*"You're a goddamn liar!"* screamed Ray.

"Keep this channel clear!" Ellis ordered. "Doctor, no matter how justified you may feel, you just shot a duly appointed officer of the law. You have only one option. You must surrender. I'm giving you three minutes to walk out of your house with your hands held high in the air. You must walk out alone, unarmed, without any member of your family. Do you understand?"

Shields didn't reply.

"Dr. Shields? Did you hear me?"

"Yes."

"The clock starts now. I beg you to come out peacefully."

Shields said nothing else.

"Hang up, Sandra," Ellis said.

"He already broke the connection."

Ellis looked at his watch. "Whoever's on those thermal cams, tell me if it looks like they're going into the panic room."

"The kids may be in there already," said a voice. "But I think the adults are in the kitchen."

Ray Breen said, "I never seen no chickenshit like this in my life, Billy Ray. The son of a bitch killed one of our people, and you—"

*"Shut up and listen!"* Ellis hollered like a quarterback silencing his linemen in a fourth-quarter huddle. "We're not waiting three minutes! We're going in *one* minute. Copy?"

Danny wasn't sure he had heard right until Ray Breen said, "I got you now. We're ready."

"Black Six," Ellis said, "if Shields gets within thirty feet of that panic room, we're going in. Keep me posted."

*Christ,* Danny thought. *Shields could be in there thinking about giving up, and he'll still be thinking about it when Ray Breen blows his head off.* Sheriff Ellis's strategy was sound; giving an unbalanced man a real deadline could easily push him into executing his hostages. But Danny couldn't shake the feeling that they hadn't done all they could to talk Shields out of the house. Or was that simply his guilt talking? Was there any hope that Shields would surrender? The doctor believed he'd just defended himself against an intruder trying to murder him. He was deep into a siege mentality. He was also terminally ill. Did it even matter to Warren when or where he died?

"Take us up another hundred feet," Sheriff Ellis ordered.

Danny started ascending. *Where's Laurel now?* he wondered. *What will she do when they blow the doors? Drop to the floor or stand there like a doe in the headlights while bullets spray through the house? Is there any chance she'll try to protect her husband?* Danny didn't think so, but even the slightest prospect of this terrified him, because he was certain that Ray meant to kill Shields no matter what.

"Thirty-five seconds," Ellis said, his eyes on his wristwatch. "Stay ready, Ray. Everybody key off your watches. Thirty seconds . . ."

A silver sheet of rain hit the windshield, and Danny fell through a black hole, straight into Afghanistan. Forty-two marines were trapped on a mountaintop in the worst storm the company's Tajik adviser could remember. Taliban guerrillas commanded by mujahideen who'd fought the Russians twenty years earlier were scaling the rock walls like ants to finish off the Americans. It was only a sideshow to the battle raging at Tora Bora, but to the marines marooned on the mountain, it was the end of the world. An army Black Hawk had already been shot down as it hovered to fire a Hellfire missile into a cave mouth. An Air Force A-10 had held off the guerrillas for a while, but now even the Warthog had been grounded. When night fell, there would be no stopping the Taliban. They were already too close to the marines for artillery to knock them off the mountain, and the Spectre gunships in the theater were committed to Tora Bora. At any moment, Danny expected the marines to call in artillery on their own position, as Joe Adams had famously done on Hill 385 in Korea. Anything was better than being captured by Afghan tribesmen.

Then a Delta Force officer volunteered to drop onto the mountain and set up a protective perimeter, if a helicopter pilot would try to airlift the trapped marines to safety. To do so would mean almost certain death. Danny didn't want to die. He had no illusions about war. He was forty-three years old, and he hadn't reached that age by volunteering for suicide missions. Yet he'd felt a voice rising up his throat, trying to volunteer him. Why? Was he trying to live up to the legacy of his father, the red-faced crop duster who'd fought in the Big One? He certainly had no faith in his immortality under fire. But at bottom, he realized, it was simpler than all that. If someone didn't take a bird up there, those marines would die. Forty-two husbands, fathers, and sons. Fate had placed their lives in Danny's hands. Of the two other pilots there that day, one had a son he'd never seen, and the other always had his eye on the main chance, which meant flying milk runs for rock stars, not dying in Afghanistan. So without thinking very much, Danny had raised his hand and said, "I'll go." The most meaningful reward he ever got in the military was the look in the Delta operator's eyes after he volunteered. The look said, *You are a crazy fuck, and you're probably going to die, but, brother, you are One of Us.*

Danny landed on the mountaintop three times before they got him. He wrung performance out of that chopper that the engineers who'd designed it would never have believed. His Pave Low took more AK rounds than by any physical law it should have survived, and the blasting sand and water stripped off half the paint and all the decals by the end of the second run. But eventually the ship gave up the ghost. It took an RPG round to kill it. Danny's door-gunner screamed a warning, and Danny jinked at the last second, but the hissing rocket clipped his tail rotor and the controls went gooey on him. He didn't even remember the crash, only an absolute certainty that the end had come, and that it had come in a chopper, as he had always known it would. He thought of his father as he fell, with his beloved Pave Low windmilling in the air like Pete Townshend's guitar arm. There was a bright flash in his head, then the face of a girl he'd loved in high school, and then . . . nothing.

Only later did he learn that his crew were killed on impact. Danny was ejected, seat and all, through a hole the mountain ripped in the cockpit during the ship's final spin. A piece of shrapnel tore through his left leg, and some Afghans fired a burst of AK rounds at him, connecting once in the same leg. And then a miracle occurred. Inspired by Danny's desperate barnstorming, the pilot of one of the AC-130 gunships over Tora Bora threw away his regulation book, diverted to the besieged mountain, and rained hell and death down on the Afghans for ninety minutes straight. The Delta Force operators tied Danny to a stretcher they found in the wreckage of his chopper and carried him down the mountain, fighting a rearguard action all the way. The last six marines came with them. A hundred meters from the bottom, elements of the First Marine

Division rushed up like a camouflaged tide and swept them back down to safety.

They gave Danny and his dead crew a Mackay Trophy for that action, but the ceremony was hollow for him. He never again saw any of the marines he'd saved that day. He did receive a couple of letters, one from a wife in Kansas, thanking him for saving her husband. The jarhead had added a postscript himself at the bottom: *Semper fi, buddy. You're always welcome here.* They put in a snapshot of their kid, too, a freckled girl standing in short rows of corn. Danny had only read the letter once, but he kept it in his top dresser drawer, to remind him that sometimes you just had to say "Fuck it" and do the right thing, no matter what it cost. If you did, you never knew what someone else might do to help you. Or what good might come of it.

"Ten seconds!" Sheriff Ellis cried, his voice pitched high from the stress. "Take us down, Danny!"

Danny loved Laurel; he hadn't the slightest doubt about that. And he hated his wife, for using his son as a hostage. He had an obligation to Michael that nothing could remove, but didn't he also have an obligation to Laurel? What if she was carrying his child? God forgive him, a *healthy* child who could speak and listen? Laurel had given him everything she had to offer and asked nothing in return. She'd simply trusted that he'd do the right thing by her. And that he had not done—

"Five seconds," said Sheriff Ellis. "This is Black Leader, we're going to hover low and hit the spotlight. Everybody—"

Danny twisted back the throttle and slammed down the collective, and the helicopter dropped like King Kong off the Empire State Building.

*"Shiiiiiiitttt!"* Ellis screamed, his face bone white with terror. *"What's happening?"*

"We lost the engine!" Danny shouted, intentionally throwing the ship out of trim. "Brace yourself!"

Anything less than a crash might have left Ellis capable of issuing orders on the way down, so Danny had pulled an emergency autorotation, virtually killing the engine and causing a controlled crash in which only the energy stored in the still-whirling rotor blades could spare them from death. Red emergency lights lit up the instrument panel, and the *whoop-whoop* of the low rpm warning filled the cabin. He waited until the last possible instant to flare, then yanked up on the collective, certain that the primal terror scrambling the sheriff's brain would prevent him from giving the go order. The Bell bounced hard on the front lawn, its rotor tips spinning bare inches from the brick front of the house.

*"What just happened?"* Ray Breen shouted. *"Are you guys okay?"*

"Holy Christ!" yelled Ellis, clutching his chest in terror.

Danny unhooked his harness and scrambled out of the chopper onto wet grass. When the sheriff saw this, he assumed the ship was about to explode and tried to do the same, but Danny leaned back inside and yelled, "Give me ten minutes! Ten minutes alone with him! Stay on those mikes!"

Comprehension dawned in Ellis's eyes, followed by a blaze of anger, but Danny broke away and sprinted around the chopper to the front door of the house. He slammed into it with all his weight and started banging on it like a fugitive at a church door.

*"Open up! It's Danny! Warren, it's me! It's Danny!"*

Over his shoulder he saw two alien figures in black body armor break cover and charge him. They'd closed to within twenty feet when the door fell away and someone yanked him inside.

# CHAPTER

# 22

Warren slammed the door and stared at Danny with wild eyes. "What the hell are you doing?"

"Trying to save you!" Danny replied, panting from his exertions.

He saw the gun in Warren's hand, then Laurel over his shoulder, watching with terror in her eyes. Through her fear Danny saw the glow of gratitude. Warren looked nothing like the man Danny had taught to fly. High on his left shoulder, his shirt was stiff with clotted blood. He had the face of some soldiers Danny had seen, those who had been asked to do too much, or to witness too much, and had somehow found themselves still walking the earth after all their friends were dead.

"Where's your kids?" Danny asked, trying to orient himself from memory. The kitchen and den were a few yards behind Laurel; the hall to Danny's right led to a guest room, then to a back door to Warren's study. Behind Warren was the great room, which opened onto the study and the master suite.

"Beth's in the safe room," Laurel answered, after

her husband refused to. "I don't know where Grant is."

"We need to get Grant in the safe room, too."

"Grant's fine where he is," said Warren.

"No, he's not. That three-minute deadline was bullshit. They were coming to get you when I set down on your front walk."

Warren processed this in silence.

"I want to talk to you, but we need to get everybody into the hall first."

"Why?" Shields asked.

"They have thermal imaging devices out there. They can see through the window blinds. But the hall walls will shield us."

Warren slowly shook his head.

"It's twenty feet!" Danny shouted, pointing to his right.

Shields seemed to reconsider. "You go first."

Danny had hoped the doctor would lead the way, giving him a chance to grab Laurel and try for the front door. But if he'd tried that and failed, whatever trust he now enjoyed would be lost. He backed slowly down the hall, his eyes on Warren's gun. His left heel slipped on something, then caught. He looked down and saw a dark, tacky stain on the floor. Blood. He'd seen whole slicks of it in the belly of his chopper. He figured the stuff on his shoe belonged to Kyle Auster.

Shields wasn't following him, he noted, and Laurel was still stuck behind her husband in the foyer. "Warren, if you stay where you are, they'll blow down that door and toss in a flash-bang grenade. The C-4's already in place."

Warren blinked twice, then came toward Danny,

motioning for Laurel to follow him. He stopped after the hall walls closed around him. Danny held out his hand and beckoned Laurel forward. He could tell she wanted to run into his arms, but she moved slowly, as though Warren might decide to shoot her at any moment.

"You two stay on opposite sides of me," Warren said nervously.

Laurel obeyed like a convict worried about a brutal guard.

Warren kept his gun hand on Danny's side, as though he expected Danny to make a play for the weapon.

"I violated orders to come in here," Danny said, trying to keep his voice under control. "So I hope you'll listen to me. There's a boy out there who shot twenty-seven people in Iraq. And that's just what they recorded officially. He's got a bullet chambered with your name on it."

Warren's face didn't change at all.

"That's welcome news to you, isn't?" Danny said. "That's what I realized when I was hovering over your house. That's how you want to die."

The doctor's right cheek twitched.

"Warren?" Laurel said softly. "Is he right?"

"I'm right," Danny said, not taking his eyes from Warren's face. "But you're not going to get that surgical sniper's bullet. You're going to get Ray Breen and his weekend commandos blasting in here with grenades and submachine guns. And if anybody gets in the way, like Grant or Beth or Laurel, well, that's just too bad. Do you hear me, Warren?"

"Yes."

"Is that how a good father checks out?"

The cheek was twitching steadily now.

"You know it's not," Danny pressed. "How a man dies is his own business, but he's got no right to take anyone else with him."

"Grant and Beth can leave," Warren said. "But not *her*." He jabbed his pistol toward Laurel. "She stays till the end."

*The end of what?* Danny thought. *The end of you, or of all of us?*

Behind Warren, Laurel put a shaking hand over her eyes. For an instant Danny wondered if she might smack her husband's head or make a grab for the gun, but she was past that point now. She was barely functioning.

"Let's get those kids out of here," Danny said.

*"McDavitt's a goddamn traitor!"* Ray Breen shouted over the radio. *"He's telling Shields everything we got out here! Can't you hear that mike signal? I can't take any more of this shit!"*

Sheriff Ellis said, "Danny's about to walk out of there with those kids, Ray. Keep this channel clear. I'm giving Danny the time he asked for."

Carl Sims lay on the wet grass behind his pecan tree and listened to the menagerie of voices on the radio net that linked the members of the Tactical Response Unit. Ray Breen was going to need a straitjacket or a horse sedative if he got any madder. Even if he didn't, he was exactly the wrong person to send into a hostage situation. Carl had figured the sheriff would pull Ray off the TRU after his brother was shot; it just seemed like common sense. But this wasn't the Marine Corps, and Carl wasn't in command.

He didn't know why Major McDavitt had risked his life to charge into the house alone, but Carl was glad he had. Anything was better than sending Ray and his cowboys in there with grenades. Carl made sure the extra poncho he'd brought was keeping the rain off his rifle, then went back to studying the LCD on the thermal camera. He suspected that the major might have gone in to move Dr. Shields back into his line of fire. If so, Carl didn't plan on disappointing him. Any doubt about shooting the doctor had vanished. It was simple arithmetic now.

One death was better than five.

"The kids, Doc," Danny said again. "Where's Grant?"

Warren was staring at Danny with a strange new intensity. "What are you really doing here?"

A shiver of fear raced along Danny's shoulders. Warren's hollow eyes seemed suddenly to hold the very knowledge that Danny would have given anything to keep from him. Had he somehow sensed the truth? Had physical proximity triggered some primitive sensory apparatus that could detect sexual chemistry between people?

"Do you always have to be the hero?" Warren asked.

"I'm no hero. I just care what happens to this family. I don't want to see your pictures on the front of tomorrow's *Citizen* over a story about a terrible tragedy. And I don't want to listen to every asshole in town saying, 'It just goes to show, doesn't it? You never can tell.'"

Warren's mouth smiled but his eyes remained disconnected from the movement.

"So let's get those kids out of here, huh?"

The dead smile vanished.

"The baby I'm carrying is yours, Warren," Laurel said, averting her eyes from Danny. "I know it. That's the one ray of hope in all the darkness you've been living with this past year."

Danny searched her face, but he saw no sign that she was lying. Maybe Shields *had* fathered the child.

"I told you," Warren said, "it can't be mine."

"You said it was unlikely. Not impossible."

Shields looked at the floor, then at his gun. Laurel was playing a dangerous game.

"Is it possible?" she asked softly. "Just possible?"

"Maybe," he whispered. "But if it is . . . I don't even know if you could keep it. My cells are so screwed up now from the chemicals and hormones, the risk of birth defects would be so high—"

"I don't *care*," Laurel averred, so firmly that Danny believed her. "If you're dying, then we have to risk it. You're going to live to see this baby born!"

Danny didn't know whether she was speaking from the heart, but her eyes flashed with conviction, and her words rang with truth.

Warren's face was glistening. *Maybe he's finally breaking down,* Danny thought. Maybe the hope of something positive before his death was enough to lift Shields out of the hell he had lived in so long. Danny prayed that Sheriff Ellis was hearing this conversation—and holding Ray Breen on a tight leash.

Warren wiped his eyes, then looked back at his wife. "I want you to get a blood test. Will you do that?"

She nodded, but Danny saw that the idea had scared her.

"A DNA test?" Danny asked, thinking that this

alone was proof that Shields saw them both alive in the future.

"No, that takes too long. Mark Randall can come in here and draw some blood, and they can have it typed at the hospital lab in thirty minutes."

Danny felt dizzy. "You mean *now*?"

"Why not? Randall lives practically around the corner, on Sagramore Street."

"Warren . . . we don't have that kind of time."

"Why not?"

"Because the guys outside are about to blow this house apart. You want them to sit around while you perform some kind of in-house paternity test?"

"I don't see why that's asking too much. It could resolve everything."

"How far along is she?" Danny asked. "How could they even get a needle to the fetus without, I don't know, ultrasound or something?"

Laurel spoke with a feminine power that made both men turn. "If you truly loved me, it wouldn't matter whose child I'm carrying."

Warren gaped at her.

Danny wondered why the hell she'd said that. Did she have a death wish? Asking a man to accept another man's child from the woman he was married to . . . that was definitely outside the envelope. Wasn't it?

"You don't know what love is," Warren said. "I see that now."

"On the contrary," Laurel replied. "It's you who has no idea what love is."

Danny was trying to think of a way to get her off this tack when a disembodied voice said, *"Merlin has broken the password! It's MAGIC!"*

Danny nearly jumped out of his skin, thinking someone else from the TRU had slipped into the house. When no gunfire erupted, he figured Grant was playing a video game on one of the home computers. But when he saw Laurel's face, he knew he was wrong. She was terrified.

A triumphant blast of trumpets echoed through the house. Then the voice repeated, *"Merlin has broken the password! It's MAGIC!"*

Warren's face was shining as though all his fatigue had suddenly melted away. "Everybody into the study!" he cried.

Waving his pistol, he herded Danny toward the back door to his study. Danny had little choice but to walk ahead. As he did, some of Warren's words during their earlier negotiation came back to him:

*"I've got another computer working on it."*

*"What is it you're waiting for?"*

*"The name, Danny."*

*"What name?"*

*"The guy who was screwing my wife. Or still is, for all I know."*

Danny stopped in the study door, his heart banging in his chest. *My name is about to pop up on his computer screen. . . .* "Warren, if we go in here, one or all of us is going to die. They'll see us on the thermal cam, and they'll fire this time."

"At least I'll die knowing the truth." Warren pushed past him with Laurel in tow. She brushed against Danny as Warren yanked her down the single step, and the scent of her pierced him to the core.

"You won't live to read the screen!" Danny yelled.

"You're free to go, Major. But not Laurel. Everything that's happened today was leading to this moment."

Danny couldn't abandon her. He stepped down into the study, but he made sure that the men outside knew where he was. "If you're set on committing suicide, all right. But I'm not giving up on you. Maybe they won't fire if I'm in here with you."

Seeing that Danny meant to stay, Warren gestured for him to stand on the far side of the desk, opposite the Aeron chair that faced the computer screen. Then Warren stood Laurel to the right of his chair—between himself and the study windows—and sat before his computer. His wife was now a human shield, one that had probably merged their two figures into one on the thermal camera outside. Shields's ultimate goal might be suicide, but he meant to live long enough to discover who'd been screwing his wife.

*"Merlin has broken the password!"* the computer announced yet again. *"It's MAGIC!"*

Warren laughed like a gleeful twelve-year-old playing a video game. As he began clicking his mouse, Danny flicked his eyes back and forth, working out the geometry of the room. He had to get Carl a shot, fast. If Warren pulled Danny's name out of Laurel's Hotmail account, he was a dead man. Shields had already shot a deputy and his medical partner. How hard would it be to shoot the guy who'd impregnated his wife?

Warren had set his pistol in his lap so that he'd have both hands free to work the computer. Laurel stood two feet to his right, with the desk separating her from Danny. Her eyes locked onto his, willing him to do something, anything, to stop her husband from opening her e-mail messages.

*What's Warren looking at now?* he wondered. *A list of old e-mail from me?* Danny never signed his name to casual e-mails—notes about where and when to meet, like that. But the longer ones—those describing his feelings for Laurel—he'd always signed. And being a woman, Laurel had probably chosen to save exactly those for posterity.

"What do you see?" Danny asked, trying to stall.

Shields shook his head in wonder. "I'm reading a message telling my wife to meet her lover at the usual place. Strange, isn't it?"

*That one won't be signed,* Danny thought. *But the next one might.*

"And I'm waiting to find out who the father of my wife's child is. This is a real red-letter day, wouldn't you say?" Warren clicked the mouse again, probably moving to the next e-mail.

Laurel's face twitched with fear.

*Five more seconds could kill us both,* Danny realized. *Screw the risk, Carl has to shoot—* "Warren, you've got to stop this! You've given Laurel the third degree all day long. They could blow you away right now! Right where you sit. You make an easy target because you're sitting—"

Warren's hand flicked out like a striking snake and grabbed Laurel's right wrist. A split second later he was on his feet, jerking her hand out of her pants pocket.

*It's her phone,* Danny realized. *He's seen her phone!*

Danny started around the desk, but Warren's gun snapped up, its black eye staring a hole in Danny's chest.

• • •

"Third degree?" echoed Sheriff Ellis, sitting in the command trailer with Sandra Souther. "*Third degree.* Jesus, Danny's telling us to shoot. He's telling us to kill Shields." Ellis grabbed a walkie-talkie off the table. "This is Black Leader, we're going to blow the windows on Carl's order. Repeat, Black Diamond has tactical command. Carl, the second you have a shot, take it."

"Understood. I'm looking at the thermal image, but there's no separation. Either the wife or Major McDavitt is in the line of fire."

"Danny said Shields is sitting down. If you can't see him on the thermal, blow the windows and take your chances."

"Will do. Be cool, everybody . . . I'll say when. Scoping now . . ."

"Damn it, Billy Ray," cursed Ray Breen. "Let my men take this bastard out. This is exactly what we train for."

"Negative," said the sheriff. "Carl has the call. Acknowledge, Ray."

Ray clicked his radio twice.

Warren held his wife's Motorola Razr high like a trophy. The silver flip-phone had obviously been open while in her pocket, and Danny was sickeningly sure that this Razr was her clone phone, the one she used exclusively to talk to him.

Warren lowered the phone and looked hungrily at its screen. "You've had your hand in your pocket all day. Even when you were taped up. That was one too many times."

Laurel was wavering on her feet. Danny wished she would faint and give Carl a clear shot.

"Let's see who you're trying to call," Warren said, working at the tiny keys. "Or were you texting somebody?"

As Laurel's eyes found Danny's, Warren's thumb stopped working at the keypad. He looked up at his wife, and a shudder went through him. Then he stuck the barrel of his gun into Laurel's belly. "I knew that wasn't my baby."

"Warren?" Danny said softly. "Buddy?"

Shields laughed strangely, then tossed the cell phone to Danny.

Danny caught it and looked down at the screen, which displayed a message beneath SENT MESSAGES. On it were five words written in the pseudo-shorthand of cell phone messaging:

        U haf 2 kil hm!

"You have to kill him," Danny said as though reading the message aloud, but he was speaking to Carl Sims.

"I guess there's only one thing left to learn," Warren said. "Who fathered the bastard in her belly." Keeping his pistol pressed firmly against Laurel's stomach, he reached down with his left hand, moved his computer mouse, and clicked a button.

"Warren, don't," Laurel begged in a voice close to breaking. "Don't look."

But he did. He stared at the screen like a man witnessing his own death. "No. Goddamn it . . . it can't be."

Danny expected the gun to swing toward him, but instead Warren clicked frantically at the mouse. "It's not here! Doesn't he fucking sign anything?" He swept the monitor off the desk with a crash.

"It's over, Warren," Danny said with relief. "You can't find out what you want to know. Not tonight. Put down the gun, man."

Shields stared at Danny as though reality had finally sunk in. After hours of insanity, he was no closer to learning the truth than he had been at the beginning. A glimmer of real hope sparked in Danny's heart—

Then his cell phone began to chirp.

Warren's eyes dropped to Danny's pants.

As Danny cursed himself for forgetting to silence his phone, Warren seized Laurel's neck in the crook of his elbow and dragged her around the desk with his gun jammed into her stomach. When he reached the point where Danny stood between him and the windows, he threw Laurel to the floor.

"Put up your hands!" he said, aiming at Danny's chest. "I don't want to kill you, Major, but I need to know what the sheriff's telling you."

Danny put up his hands.

Warren patted Danny's pockets with his left hand. When he found the cell phone in the back pocket, he shoved his pistol hard beneath Danny's sternum and fished out the phone with his other hand. Then he backed away, taking care to keep Danny between him and the windows, and flipped open the phone.

Warren didn't yet understand what had happened with the phones, but he would in seconds. Danny prepared to dive onto Laurel, which would clear Carl's line of fire and shield her from Warren's revenge.

"Danny?" Warren said softly. "Look at me."

Danny knew he should dive, but now that it had

come to this, he found himself unable to do it. He had betrayed this man. And he couldn't consign him to the grave without accepting responsibility for what he'd done.

Warren's gaze cut through him like the eye of God, to the darkest reaches of his soul. Danny sensed no judgment in the gaze, though, only grief. A profound sadness that a man Shields had believed to be noble had turned out to be merely, even terribly, human.

"It was you?" he asked. "All along? It was you?"

Danny nodded once.

Warren flinched as though Danny had shoved a needle into his heart. "Why? Can you tell me that?"

Danny saw no point in speaking anything but the truth. "I love her."

Shields seemed to take this explanation with equanimity. He looked down at Laurel, who watched him fearfully from the floor. It struck Danny then that there were four of them in the room: the woman; two men; and the unborn child, who might belong to either man. Perhaps the same realization struck Shields. Whatever emotion came to him, he could not endure it. He screamed something unintelligible, then swung the pistol at Danny's head. Danny leaped out of its path, lost his balance, and rolled onto the floor. He'd planned to cover Laurel with his body, but she was too far away now. He clapped his hands over his ears and tucked into a fetal position, facing away from the windows.

"*You coward!*" Shields screamed. "*You're supposed to be a hero! Look at him, Laurel . . . there's your fucking hero!*"

Danny closed his eyes and prayed for death to take the right man.

• • •

Carl stared at the thermal imager like a snake watching a transfixed bird. Every atom of his instinct told him that the only red blob still standing represented Warren Shields. A moment ago it had been twice its current size—

"Blow the windows," he said into his headset.

He put his right eye to the Unertl scope, closed it against the coming flash, and squeezed two pounds of pressure out of the rifle's three-pound trigger.

The dim rectangles of the study windows flashed white in his left eye, and bright yellow light spilled across the lawn. Carl glassed the study with robotic efficiency, searching for Dr. Shields—

*There.* The doctor stood alone, aiming a pistol at something below the windowsill. You couldn't ask for more justification to fire. As Carl applied the last pound of pressure, Laurel Shields lurched into his sight picture and seized her husband's gun hand. Carl longed to revoke his shot, but his motor cortex had already sent the signal to his trigger finger. Shields and his wife both flew backward—

*Dear sweet Jesus, no, please no—*

Searing flashes lit up the interior of the Shields house, then detonations like impacting mortar rounds rolled across the lawn.

Carl jumped to his feet and started running.

Even with his hands over his ears, Danny heard the shattering concussions of the grenades. When he felt confident there would be no more, he scrambled over to Laurel, who lay motionless on her back, her eyes closed.

"Laurel! Can you hear me? Are you hit?"

She didn't respond. Blood was seeping through her top. She'd been hit in at least four places, the wounds widely dispersed. How was that possible? He'd heard only one rifle shot after the windows went down.

*Glass,* he thought. *Shards of window glass.*

A man screamed to Danny's left. Danny turned and saw Warren on his back, gasping for air and waving his pistol as though having a seizure. His shirt, too, was peppered with blood.

Danny got to his feet and stamped on Warren's wrist, pinning his gun to the floor. He was about to reach down for the weapon when someone screamed, *"Get on the floor! Get down!"*

Danny turned and saw what appeared to be a creature from outer space. Clad from head to foot in black ballistic nylon and Kevlar body armor, it had enormous insectlike goggles covering its eyes—

*Ray Breen.*

"Get out of the way!" Breen shouted, brandishing a submachine gun. "Or I'll drop you where you stand!"

Danny held up both hands. "He can't fire! I'm standing on his arm! I'm going to take his weapon!"

*"Get out of the way, Major!"*

Keeping his left hand aloft, Danny bent and tugged the gun from Shields's unresisting hand, then tossed it away, into the great room.

Two more figures in black appeared behind Breen, but the TRU commander didn't lower his weapon. Instead, he moved to his right, angling for a clear shot at Shields. Not knowing what else to do, Danny dropped to his knees and shielded the doctor with his own body.

"Somebody stop him!" he shouted, realizing as he did that Ray Breen was the senior officer in the room. "Get Sheriff Ellis!"

*"Get off that bastard!"* Ray yelled. *"This thing ain't gonna end but one way!"*

Breen's gun was an MP5, Danny saw, capable of firing eight hundred rounds per minute on automatic. If he pulled that trigger, both Danny and Shields would die.

"Go ahead," Warren rasped from beneath Danny. "Shoot."

Breen moved closer, trying to fire around Danny—

"Put the gun down, Ray."

Danny turned and saw the long gray barrel of Carl Sims's Remington 700 jutting through a shattered study window. Carl held the rifle almost casually, at waist level, but no one in the room doubted that a bullet fired from it would strike its intended target.

*"He killed my brother!"* Ray shouted in a voice beyond reason.

"I don't want to shoot you," Carl said softly. "But I will."

Breen studied the sniper's face, then turned back to Shields and aimed his MP5 past Danny, right at the doctor's head. Carl didn't raise his rifle an inch, but when he spoke, something was in his voice that had not been there before. *Disdain,* Danny thought.

"You're always asking me how many men I killed over in Iraq. The truth is, I don't know. But I know this: I've killed better men than *you.*"

The gun in Ray Breen's hand quivered under the stress of the war raging inside him. After several seconds that held eternity within them, he lowered the weapon to his side. As Danny crawled toward Laurel, Ray lunged forward and drove his boot into Shields's rib cage with a crack.

Then every light in the house went out.

# CHAPTER

# 23

Two seconds after the room went black, something knocked Danny's legs from under him. His tailbone cracked against the floor, but he forgot the pain when a cold pistol barrel invaded the soft flesh between his jawbone and windpipe. He tried to jerk his head back, but a strong hand grabbed his hair and shoved the gun deeper into his neck.

"*Get up,*" hissed a voice in his ear. "*On your feet, or I'll pull the trigger.*"

Danny obeyed.

Shouts of anger and confusion reverberated through the darkness, but the whispering gunman dragged Danny across the room with total assurance. Danny stumbled on something, but his captor held him erect. *Night-vision goggles?* he wondered. His shoulder brushed a doorjamb as tactical lights arced through the room, and then he passed into cooler air.

"*Move to the right.*" A knee drove into his back. "*Hurry!*"

Danny saw light ahead. He thought of crying out,

but the gunman read his mind. *"Make a sound, I'll blow your brains all over the hall."*

It was Warren, Danny realized. Of course it was. Who else could it be? But where were they going? Why didn't Shields just pull the trigger and be done with it?

"Toward the light!" Warren urged, running him up the hall now.

"Where are we going?"

"You've got a date with destiny, you lying piece of shit."

Grant knew he'd waited too long to pull the circuit breaker. But how could his dad expect him to wait in the pantry while everything was happening somewhere else? He'd waited as long as he could stand it, and then—just after he'd sneaked out to find his father—the whole back of the house had blown up. By the time he got back to the pantry, men were yelling and screaming all over the house. But Grant still did what his dad had told him to do and sent blue sparks flying from beneath his hands.

Now he was running through the dark, making for his father's study. In the great room he collided with something hard—something that shouldn't have been there. Two strong hands seized his upper arms, and a face like something out of a video game appeared before him, a black-goggled grasshopper's face lit by the beam of a spotlight shining through the great room windows.

"Get that kid out of here!" someone shouted.

Grant was hauled off his feet, carried out through the garage, and set down in the driveway. It was still raining. The shouts of panicked grown-ups ricocheted through the night. The masked figure looked down at him for a moment, then raced back inside the house. Desperate to learn what had happened to his parents, Grant ran around to the front yard, the last place he'd heard Mr. Danny's chopper.

The big helicopter straddled the front sidewalk like a futuristic bird that had somehow landed in the present by mistake. Its rotors were still spinning. Grant moved toward it but kept close to the shrubbery so that no other deputies would see him.

As he neared the chopper, he froze. His father and Mr. Danny were crossing the open space between the front door and the helicopter.

"Dad!" Grant shouted. "Mr. Danny! Wait for me! Wait up!"

When he reached the two men, Grant realized that his father hadn't heard him. He grabbed his dad's arm, then jerked back as an almost unrecognizable face whipped around and glared at him.

"*Grant?*" exclaimed his father, as though he'd never expected to see his son again.

"Get out of here, Grant!" said Mr. Danny. "Run!"

"No way! I want to come with you guys!"

"You can't," said his father. "You have to stay here, Son."

"I'm coming," Grant insisted. "I'm not staying here by myself."

His father looked down at him with an expression Grant had never seen on his face before. It made Grant want to cry. Then his father yanked open the chopper door and said, "Get in the back, Son. Hurry. Harness yourself in."

Grant scrambled into the helicopter, a machine that

hummed and shook as if it were more alive than he was. Mr. Danny and his father climbed into the front seats, and then Mr. Danny did something and the whining overhead got louder. Grant could feel the rotor blades trying to pull the ship off the ground. His father turned around to say something, but then the front door of the house opened and two of the black-suited men ran out. Both were waving guns, but Grant knew they wouldn't run beneath the spinning blades. One of the men leveled his gun and aimed at the front of the helicopter. In the next instant Mr. Danny shouted something and the ship leaped into the air. As Grant tumbled out of his seat, he saw treetops sweep past the window, and then the moon, shining high and white through a break in the clouds. He only wished his mom were there to see it.

Danny had flown in crazy conditions before, but never with a gun jammed into his gut. The pistol wasn't the same one Shields had aimed at Laurel; this one was a nickel-plated automatic. *Trace Breen's gun?* he wondered. *Or maybe Kyle Auster's, if he had one.* Shields kept the pistol where his son couldn't see it, but the range was still point-blank. Close enough for the burning powder to set Danny's shirt on fire as the bullet ripped through his abdomen from side to side.

The chopper hurtled eastward at fifteen hundred feet, the house already far behind. Danny wondered what kind of response Sheriff Ellis was mounting to this new development. He'd started calling over the radio only seconds after they lifted off, but Shields had shut off everything but the interphone circuit.

"Where are we going?" Danny asked, as casually as he could. "Havana?"

"Upriver," Warren said tersely. "Thirty miles. Vidalia, Louisiana. Take us up to two thousand feet."

Danny turned north and started ascending. Vidalia was a town of five thousand mostly working-class people who lived on the floodplain across the river from the great bluff at Natchez. "Why Vidalia?"

Warren tilted his head backward. "We're dropping Grant off at Laurel's mother's house."

"I see. So this trip's just for you and me?"

Warren didn't answer.

Danny had a lot of experience flying at night, but almost always with the aid of night-vision goggles, and in a much more powerful chopper. Flying the Bell 206 through mountains of storm clouds was a completely different thing. He wasn't afraid, but he was concentrating hard enough that the gun against his side kept surprising him. Blue-white flashes of lightning illuminated the towering cloudscape, and he could hear Grant's cries of awe despite the fact that the boy wasn't wearing a headset.

Danny couldn't see much on the near-lightless land below, but the rivers and lakes he used as landmarks gleamed like black mirrors as the chopper raced over them. The Buffalo River, Lake Mary, the Homochitto River, and then the Mississippi, curving east toward Natchez.

"Did I hear you say we're going to Gram's?" Grant yelled, moving forward and setting his chin on the tight seam between Danny's and Warren's shoulders.

Warren concealed the gun beneath his bloody shirt-tail and slid the headset off of his right ear. "That's right, Son."

"Where's Mom?"

"Home."

Danny kept his face expressionless.

"Is she okay?"

"She's fine. Those men weren't there for her. You'll see her soon. Get back into a seat and fasten your harness."

"What about you? Your shoulder's bleeding bad."

"I'm fine," Warren said, touching his shirt, which was now matted against his wounded shoulder.

"Wow!" Grant cried. They had crossed over the bluff at Natchez, and the land fell precipitously away. Two hundred feet below the old city, the lights on a long string of barges winked up at them. "Cool," the boy said. "They have two bridges here."

"Get into a harness, Son!"

"Okay, okay." Grant's head vanished.

"You don't know Laurel's okay," Danny said softly. "You didn't even check."

Warren grimaced. "Shut up."

"What?" asked Grant. "What are y'all saying up there?"

"Nothing, Son. Look for landmarks down there. Can you see the riverboat casinos?"

While Grant searched the broad black river, Warren said, "Laurel's mother lives just off Carter Street, the main drag. Right behind the levee. Maybe you know that already."

"No."

Danny started descending after he passed over the two great bridges spanning the river. There was only one brightly lit road in Vidalia, the highway leading westward across Louisiana. The section that ran through the town was called Carter Street. Danny found it easily, and soon he made out the grassy hump of the levee, running at right angles to the highway.

"That's it," said Warren, pointing down at a small house with an older Lincoln Continental parked on the street in front of it.

"Where do you want me to land?"

"Street's fine. There's no traffic."

The neighbors began opening their doors and windows as the chopper dipped under two hundred feet. By the time it landed in the middle of their street, a crowd had gathered in the rain, thinking they were witnessing either a crash or an invasion.

"I see Gram!" Grant shouted. "She's standing on the porch!"

"Jump out and run to her, Son."

Grant's head reappeared above the junction of shoulders. "What about you?"

Warren seemed unable to find his voice. Danny leaned forward and saw tears in the doctor's eyes. "Major Danny and I have to help the police do something," Shields croaked. "But Mom will be here soon."

"Are you sure? What's wrong, Dad?"

Warren covered his eyes with his left hand, but his right still gripped the gun. Danny wondered if Shields would really shoot him in front of the boy. On balance, Danny figured he would.

"I've just got a headache," Shields said. "I stayed awake too long. You need to go, Son. You take care of your mother, all right?"

Grant stared at his father in confusion. "Till you get back, you mean?"

"That's right. Go on, now. We're late already."

Grant turned to Danny, his eyes dark with foreboding. "Mr. Danny . . . ?"

"Do what your father told you. It'll be all right."

"Go!" Warren snapped.

Grant seemed on the verge of tears. Danny's heart went out to the boy, but then Grant fell back on his loyalty to the man he trusted above all others. He nodded to his father and said, "Don't worry. I'll take care of Mom." Then he climbed out of the chopper and ran toward a small, gray-haired woman standing on the porch of the little house with the Lincoln out front.

"I'm sorry," Warren said almost inaudibly.

"You owe that boy every second you have on this earth," Danny said. "I know you hate my guts, but you need to stop this suicide trip and get your family back together."

People in the crowd were venturing toward the helicopter. Shields stabbed the gun into Danny's side. "Get us airborne."

"Where are we going?"

"Heaven. How does that sound?"

"I don't believe in it. And neither do you."

Shields's eyes shone with something like madness. "Valhalla, then. Isn't that where heroes go when they die?"

"Only if they die in battle."

An ironic chuckle. "Well, then. That's where we're going."

Danny didn't know if it was better to die on the ground or in the air. But one thing he did know: in the air, he had a chance to live, because he would have control of the aircraft. A passenger bent on both homicide and suicide complicated matters, but that was better than the bullet he would get for refusing to take off.

He pulled up on the collective, touched the cyclic, and lifted the Bell over the streetlights, swinging gracefully back toward the bridges. There was no real advantage in flying over Natchez, but something was pulling him to the Mississippi side of the river.

"Why don't we call the sheriff and check on Laurel?" Danny suggested.

Warren lifted the shiny pistol and pressed its barrel against Danny's left temple. "Why don't you shut up and fly."

"Tell me where."

"Just keep us over the river."

"How high?"

"Two thousand feet's fine."

Danny spiraled upward in a slow climb, wondering how long the gun would stay at his head. It didn't leave him much maneuvering room. He'd already begun forming the rudiments of a plan. If he could roll the chopper and pull enough g's, he might be able to open Shields's harness and dump him out before the doctor shot him. But he couldn't do that with a gun to his head.

"Are you afraid to die, Major?"

Shields had asked the question in a philosophical tone. Danny shrugged. "To tell you the truth, I should have died long before now."

"You didn't answer my question."

"I don't want to die."

The gun barrel entered the shell of Danny's left ear. "But are you *afraid* to die?"

Danny thought about it. He felt a lot of things at

this moment, but the least of his emotions was fear.
"I'll tell you what I think. It isn't dying that's hard. It's
living."

Shields's jaws flexed angrily. "What are you trying
to say? Are you saying I'm a coward?"

"No. I'm saying life ain't a bowl of fucking cherries.
I'm saying you owe that little boy whatever time you
can give him, no matter what shape you're in. I think
he's tough enough to watch you die. It might not be
pretty, but he'll get over it. A hell of a lot easier than
he'll get over this shit."

Shields's jaw was working so hard it looked as if he
were trying to grind his teeth away. "You've got all the
answers, don't you? Or so my wife seems to think."

"I don't have any answers!" Danny snapped, tired
of Shields's paranoia. "I'm just trying to get by, same
as the next man. All I'm saying is, it's living that takes
courage. In my experience, the hero who charges the
machine-gun nest is sometimes the guy who didn't
have anything to go home to. To me, the real hero is
the guy who goes home to face whatever life hands
him, no matter how tough it might be."

"That's easy for you to say. You're a lucky son of a
bitch. And life handed you my wife."

Danny put the Bell into a hover above the river. Far
below, through sheets of rain, twinkling headlights
moved steadily between Louisiana and Mississippi.
"I've caught the short end a few times. You've been
dealt a tough hand, I'll grant you. But I've seen guys
get a lot worse, with no time to set things right or even
say good-bye to the people they loved. In muddy holes,
on piles of sand, burned alive in a fucking Humvee.
It's like you said back at the house. It doesn't make

any sense. You want an answer, Warren? You've got two kids who love you. Two healthy kids who need everything you can give them, and who'll give you everything they have in return. That means more than you know. Take it from me."

Shields lowered the gun back to Danny's waist. "I killed a cop tonight," he said in a guilt-ridden voice.

"Well, I'd say he asked for it. He was a mean bastard who would have caught it one way or another down the road."

"They'd still jail me for it. Or execute me." Shields began to laugh strangely. "If only I could live all the years it would take them to execute me after sentencing me to death! I'd take that deal, all right."

Danny wondered if he had any chance of getting back to the ground alive. As they hovered in the dark, he noticed that several cars had stopped along the northern span of the bridge. Then he saw red lights flashing at the Mississippi end.

"Whose baby is Laurel carrying?" Warren asked with sudden intensity.

Danny turned to him. In the cramped cockpit, their faces were as close as lovers'. "I don't know."

"Christ! Can't anybody just tell me the truth?"

"I truly don't know. But it doesn't matter anyway."

Shields closed his eyes. "Do you really think she's dead?"

For the first time, Danny sensed an opportunity to save himself. But despite Shields's closed eyes, the gun still pressed into his left hip. If they had been flying without the doors—as Danny sometimes did—or if Shields had neglected to fasten his harness, a high-G maneuver might have set the stage for Danny to dump his hijacker out of the chopper. But that was useless speculation.

Danny looked back at the flashing red lights. They were static now, at the center of the bridge. "I don't know. All I do know is, Laurel was right. If you really love her, it doesn't matter who the father is."

Shields's eyes popped open. "How can you say that?"

Danny shrugged. "Age, maybe? You'll get there eventually."

"No. I won't."

It was so easy to forget the man was dying. Danny wondered if Shields forgot it himself sometimes. For the first second or two after he woke up in the mornings, maybe. Danny had a paraplegic friend who'd experienced that. He said there was nothing worse than the crushing weight of remembering that he was paralyzed and couldn't get out of bed. "I think love means giving up something," Danny said. "Maybe the thing that means the most to you. Pride, maybe? That's what she was talking about. That's what they want us to do, you know? Only then do they truly believe you love them."

Some of the anger had drained out of Shields's eyes. "You really love her, don't you?"

Danny didn't answer. He'd already confessed once, and he saw no reason to do it again when repetition might buy him a bullet.

Shields raised the gun to Danny's temple again. "Say it, Major."

"I love her," Danny admitted, suddenly aware that all his world-weary talk about death was bullshit. He'd found a woman he wanted to spend every day of his life with, and he had two kids of his own who needed him desperately—maybe even three. The thought that those children might come in harm's way without their father there to protect them—that scared the hell out of him. It also gave him the resolve he needed to kill Warren Shields if he could.

"You want to kill me, don't you?" Shields said.

Danny shook his head, but his heart wasn't in it.

Warren leaned against the left-side door on his side and lazily aimed the gun at Danny's belly. "I *wanted* to love her," he said, looking puzzled. "I just . . . I guess I knew her too well."

*You didn't know her at all.*

Warren raised the gun until its muzzle touched Danny's cheek. "If you lived through this night, what would you do?"

"Best I could."

"Would you take care of them?"

"Them?"

"Laurel. My kids."

Sensing a route to life, Danny nodded.

A quarter mile behind and below the doctor, more red lights spun and flashed on the bridge.

"It's not fair," Shields muttered.

"It never is," Danny said, amazed that the man could have practiced medicine for years and not learned this lesson. Until his own diagnosis, Shields had actually believed himself immune to the vagaries of fate. Danny knew a lot of pilots like that. "The house always wins, Doc. It's just a question of when. The way I see it, you're alive now. Today. Let tomorrow take care of itself. Your family needs you. Let's take this machine back to Athens Point and find out about your wife."

"They've sent up another chopper!" Shields said, pointing with his arm across Danny's chest.

Danny turned, scanning the night sky for lights. There was only one other chopper in the county, a JetRanger that belonged to a private businessman. Danny didn't think they could find a pilot to fly it in this weather, but this was an extraordinary emergency. As he searched the sky, the Bell rose unexpectedly—maybe an updraft off the bluff, he thought. Then he turned to ask Shields what the hell he was talking about and saw that he was alone in the helicopter.

Danny hung suspended in the darkness above the river, as alone and alive as he'd ever been. Shields was probably still alive, too, tumbling down through space. The nickel-plated pistol lay on the empty seat, unnecessary now.

*He's hit by now,* Danny thought, looking at the altimeter. They were high enough that Shields would have reached terminal velocity prior to impact. Danny had heard grisly stories from a Vietnam-era CIA pilot, comparative descriptions of what happened when a prisoner was thrown from a chopper and landed in water as opposed to smacking dirt or concrete, or was ripped to shreds in treetops, strung through the canopy like red and pink ribbons. Shields was dead, no doubt about it.

Danny pushed down the collective and dropped toward the river, searching for the body. The two bridges threw off ambient light, but not enough to help him sight Shields. He didn't really want to see the corpse, but Laurel was certain to ask, not to mention the sheriff. In that moment Danny realized that he believed

Laurel was still alive, in spite of her wounds and un-consciousness.

He started to switch on the searchlight, but then he noticed people lining the rail of the bridge above him. There was no way anybody had seen Shields leap from the chopper, but if Danny started searching the water with a light, it wouldn't be hard to figure out what had happened. God, how Laurel would suffer if that story got out. Her kids, too. Grant Shields would go through life dreading questions about his father. *What happened to your real dad? Uh, he died. How? Killed himself. Wow, dude, I'm sorry.* Danny didn't want the boy to suffer through that conversation again and again. And with a little luck . . . he might not have to.

Danny executed a quick pedal turn, then swept up-river, jinking from side to side like a pilot under du-ress, but steadily cheating toward the Louisiana bank. The inside of a river bend is the shallow side, since it doesn't bear the full pressure of the current trying to cut its way into the land. Danny headed into a patch of darkness along the inner shore, not far from a seafood restaurant, a place where he knew there was a sandbar. When he saw the pale line where the water met the sand, he picked up the shiny automatic and fired two shots through the windshield.

Then he rolled back the throttle, shut off the fuel, and pulled his second autorotation of the night.

He wouldn't have done it if the chopper wasn't in-sured—Lusahatcha County couldn't afford to replace an aircraft—but it was. Had there been no chance of witnesses, he might have done things differently—jetti-soned the doors, for one thing, SOP for ditching—but with towns on both sides of the river and the levee close, someone might well witness the "crash." And the aircraft might be recovered. He needed all the witness statements and physical evidence to bear out a scenario in which two men had fought until the end. That would be the story for the sheriff, anyway. Laurel's children could be told something more palatable, at least until they were old enough to understand.

As the Bell fell toward the shallows, Danny took his feet off the pedals and let the ship spin beneath her rotors, as she might if her pilot had been ripped away from the controls. After four or five rotations, he felt like puking, but he steadied the craft just in time to flare before impact. As the dark water rushed up to meet him, he made sure he was less than twenty feet from shore, then dropped the Bell into the river.

Helicopters always roll when they fall into water. The rule is to not fight the roll but assist it, but Danny never got the chance. When the first rotor hit the water, the ship was slammed onto its side as though by the hand of God. River water poured through the smashed Plexiglas, and the Bell began to sink. Danny knew he should have taken a big breath before impact, but he hadn't thought of it. Now he fought to escape his harness with barely enough air to keep his brain alight. The massive power of the Mississippi carried the chopper downstream like a piece of driftwood. A millisecond before fear became panic, Danny's training asserted itself, the belt disengaged, and he swam through the hole where the door should have been, praying he was still close enough to the bank to swim to safety after he surfaced.

He broke through to the air and into what seemed a ring of flaming islands. Pools of JP-4 floating on the water. By the light of the burning fuel he saw the sand-bar. Kicking hard, he fought his way toward the grainy shingle, then crawled high enough on the sand to be safe if anything exploded.

"Be alive," he said to Laurel. "Just be alive."

Fifteen minutes later, Danny was led to the backseat of Sheriff Ellis's cruiser and given a blanket and a hot cup of coffee. He stank of kerosene. He was lucky that he hadn't caught fire during his swim to shore. A dozen cruisers were parked on the crushed-oystershell lot of the seafood restaurant, some from Lusahatcha County, some from Adams County, and others from Concordia Parish. A crowd of officers stared at the burning wreckage floating downriver. Before long, Ellis heaved his bearlike form into the front seat. He cranked his bulk around, laid his forearm on the seat, and studied Danny, his eyes unreadable.

"They told me Laurel's in surgery," Danny said.

Ellis cleared his throat. "Mrs. Shields grabbed her husband's arm at the instant Carl fired. To save your life, apparently. Carl's bullet hit Dr. Shields's gun. Mrs. Shields was struck by shards of glass and fragments of the gun, but also by some fragments of Carl's bullet."

Danny steeled himself for the worst. "How bad?"

"She just got into surgery. They stabilized her in the ER."

"You're not telling me anything."

"They don't know yet, damn it. They don't know what all got hit, because the wound tracks have to be probed."

"Any head wounds?"

"No."

*Thank God.* "What about her stomach?"

"The verdict's still out on the baby, according to the ER doc. You rest and get your head clear. You've got a lot of questions to answer."

Danny looked downriver at the burning fuel, fading now as it slid southward toward Athens Point. The lights on the bluff across the water seemed to look down in reproach, but he didn't care.

"You should have told me about Mrs. Shields," Ellis said. "You and her, I mean."

"What would you have done if I had?"

"Probably sent you home."

"Exactly."

Ellis grunted. "Well, look what's happened this way."

"Shields's kids are alive. Laurel's alive, at least for now. It could have ended a lot worse."

"Trace Breen is dead."

"Whose fault you figure that is?"

A long and weary sigh seemed to shrink the sheriff.

"Don't say that around Ray. Not if you want to live another day."

Danny took a sip of coffee, savoring the heat as it migrated down to his chest. "Ray has no business leading the Tactical Response Unit. He hasn't got the temperament for it."

"I agree with you there."

"I want to go to the hospital, Sheriff."

Ellis grunted again, disagreeably this time. "I'm not sure that's a good idea. You don't want the rumors starting any faster than they have to."

"I don't care about rumors."

"She might."

"St. Raphael's, Billy Ray. Come on. Back to Athens Point. Haul ass. I've chauffeured you enough times to earn a ride."

Ellis took a deep breath, then blew out more air than Danny could hold in both lungs. "Don't spill that coffee."

He closed his door, started the cruiser, and swung it up over the levee. Soon they were on Louisiana 15, headed north through empty black cotton fields with Ellis's lights flashing red against the rain, the kind of night run Huey Long had favored in his heyday. This was the fastest route back to Athens Point, since Highway 61, on the Mississippi side, ran southward through Woodville, thirty miles east of the city. As the cruiser roared along the deserted highway at ninety-five miles per hour, Danny went over the sequence of events prior to the assault, when Warren had caught Laurel sending her final text message: *U haf 2 kil hm!* Danny didn't understand why she'd risked so much to send that message, for it had seemed only to state the obvious.

"Tell me about those last few seconds in the chopper," Sheriff Ellis said, breaking Danny's reverie. "They told me you said you were fighting with Shields, lost control, and crashed in the water by the sandbar."

"That's right."

"And he was ejected through the windshield?"

"The door," Danny amended. If Shields had gone out through a shattered windshield, his body would show severe lacerations. "His door was knocked off or open. I don't know which."

"I heard you said he went through the windshield."

Danny shook his head. "Door. But he wasn't wearing his harness, so he hit the instrument panel first. He's probably broken up pretty bad. I was too busy to see much."

Ellis drove without speaking for a while. Then he said, "Did you see him drown?"

"No. I was trying to save myself."

"Uh-huh."

"What is it?" Danny asked angrily. "Spit it out."

"Well, Jimmy Doucet's an Adams County deputy. He was parked on the bridge, and he says he saw somebody fall from the chopper before you dropped down low."

"That's bullshit," Danny said mildly. "He couldn't see anything from up there. It was pitch-dark and raining."

"Jimmy's got good eyes. He says he saw something big fall past your lights."

"A buzzard, maybe. I was a quarter mile north of that bridge, and two thousand feet above it."

"That's what I told him." Ellis looked back over the seat with an inscrutable expression. Not anger, and not outright suspicion either. It was almost a sly look. "Come on, Danny. You took him out, didn't you?"

"What?"

"Shields got cute with you up there, and you killed him."

"How the hell would I kill him? He had the gun."

"Maybe you took it away from him."

"You'll find the body. Halfway to New Orleans maybe, but you'll find it. And you won't find any bullet holes, except in his shoulder. Auster shot him."

"If the gar and the gators don't eat him first," Ellis

said. "Maybe you pitched him out, then. You could fly a chopper sideways through a keyhole if you wanted to."

Danny felt himself going pale. "I told you what happened. I've got nothing to add."

Ellis smiled. "Course you did. Better for everybody this way, anyhow. The helicopter's insured, so what the hell. I'll have a brand-new one sitting on the pad in two weeks. And I still want you to fly it. We just have to get past whatever bullshit inquiry Ray Breen will try to bring on your head."

Danny sighed. "I think my flying days are over."

Ellis looked back again, his disappointment plain. "How come?"

Danny just shook his head.

The sheriff faced forward, the downward angle of his big head radiating disappointment.

Up ahead, the lights of the Athens Point Bridge shone out of the darkness. The cantilevered span had been built during the Stennis era, when Mississippi had expected to get a bigger share of the space program than it ultimately did. Danny still remembered the ferry that the bridge had replaced, and how he'd stand on the thrumming deck with his father while the green hills receded behind them and the Louisiana lowlands slid closer. Some people believed the bridge had kept Athens Point alive during the lean 1980s, when the oil business crashed. Now there was talk of a big new bridge at St. Francisville, just thirty miles down the river. As Danny wondered how that might affect his hometown, he suddenly understood why Laurel had sent that last text message. She wasn't instructing him to kill her husband. She was giving him *permission*.

She'd realized that after the revelation of Warren's cancer, Danny might be too mired in guilt to act without mercy. And she'd been right. He had remained on his feet to confess his guilt when he should have been diving to cover her with his body. That mistake might yet cost Laurel her life.

Sheriff Ellis barely slowed down as he crossed the Athens Point Bridge. A minute later, they turned into the parking lot of St. Raphael's Hospital. As Ellis parked under the admissions bay, Danny leaned forward and squeezed his shoulder. "You did all right, Sheriff. I'll see you around."

He got out and walked toward the double doors, the pressure of Ellis's gaze on his back. Then a voice caught up with him.

"I hope she's all right, Danny."

Danny held up his right hand but kept walking.

"I've got to ask," Ellis called. "Is that kid yours or what?"

"It doesn't matter," Danny murmured. "That's the thing."

He walked into the hospital, ready for anything.

# EPILOGUE

*Three Weeks Later*

Danny stood sweating outside the city courthouse in the only suit he owned. May had arrived, and it was already eighty degrees before noon. He was waiting for Marilyn Stone, his lawyer, whose office was around the corner. They were due for a meeting at the office of Starlette's lawyer.

Starlette herself had left town soon after the rumors about Danny and Laurel began filtering out of the Sheriff's Department. She'd taken the children and flown back to Nashville, threatening to file for divorce and take everything Danny had—his money and the kids. Danny had been in a daze since the night of the stand-off, so he hadn't argued too much. He'd simply called Marilyn Stone and asked her advice. She'd promised to do all in her power to ensure that Danny didn't lose custody of Michael, and also to get him reasonable access to his daughter. Starlette ultimately chose to file for divorce in Mississippi rather than in Tennessee, where they'd married, because Mississippi was still a "fault" state, and you could pay a heavy price for adultery.

"Danny!" called a female voice. "Over here!"

He looked down Bank Street, which housed many local attorneys' offices. Marilyn stood on the sidewalk in the bright sunshine, looking nothing like the plain Jane who showed up at the airport twice a week for flying lessons. She wore a navy suit and lipstick, and she appeared to have curled her hair. Danny waved and walked slowly forward. He dreaded having to sit across a table from the woman who was willing to institutionalize their son to get revenge on her soon-to-be-ex-husband.

"Guess what?" Marilyn said, her eyes twinkling.

"What?"

"Starlette caved."

He stopped. "What do you mean?"

"I mean she's willing to give you custody of Michael."

Danny blinked in the sun, trying to process this unbelievable statement. "What do you mean? When did this happen?"

"She didn't even get on the plane in Nashville this morning."

"What?"

Marilyn nodded. "I just found out myself."

"But . . . why?"

"I'd like to say it was my great lawyering, but the truth is much simpler. Three weeks as Michael's sole caregiver was all it took. When Starlette's lawyer told her she couldn't institutionalize Michael if you were willing to take him, she cracked."

The sudden release of weeks of tension nauseated Danny.

"This won't be free," Marilyn cautioned. "Nobody's that lucky."

"What do you mean?"

"You'll have to pay a price to get Michael. A big price."

Danny shrugged. "Whatever."

"Starlette wants your interest in your last oil well. Your entire interest."

Danny rocked on his feet. He didn't even want to calculate what twelve feet of pay sand was worth at $60-a-barrel oil. Whatever financial security he had, that was it. "Okay," he said. "Done."

Marilyn put a hand on his shoulder and squeezed. "I already said yes for you."

He laughed ruefully. "I guess you know me."

"A potential client once told me that he'd heard divorce was expensive. I said it was—very expensive. When he asked why, I quoted another client back to him: 'Because it's worth it.'"

Danny was still trying to anchor himself in time and space. "When do I get Michael?"

"Starlette's loading him on a Continental flight in about an hour. You can pick him up at the Baton Rouge airport at six-fifty-three p.m."

Danny decided right then to rent a plane; the distance was short, but Michael loved to fly with his dad. "I don't know what to say. You've changed my life, Marilyn. And you've saved my son's life."

"Come with me," she said, smiling strangely. "I have one more thing to do for you."

She took his hand and led him into her office, past the male receptionist, then up a flight of stairs to a door at the end of a narrow hall. "This is my VIP dining room. I had some food brought in, because I figured we'd be hungry after our meeting."

She opened the door.

Laurel was standing behind a table laden with boxes from the Indian restaurant a couple of blocks away. She was wearing a bright blue skirt and a white linen top, and she looked like nothing so much as the lovely teacher who had welcomed Michael with a smile two years ago. Danny had only seen her in black since Warren's death, and then only from a distance. The change almost took his breath away. He looked back to thank Marilyn, but all he saw was a closing door.

"I heard," Laurel said. "About Michael."

Danny nodded. "I can't really believe it."

"You see? The worst didn't happen."

"No."

Laurel's face was still pale, and she had lost seven or eight pounds she could ill afford. Danny saw darkness under the makeup beneath her eyes.

"Are the kids in school?" he asked.

"Only a few more days."

"Have you made any plans for the summer?"

She looked away. "I was thinking of getting out of town for a while. I can't take all this gossip. Grant and Beth have had a really hard time at school."

"You probably should," Danny said, trying to mask his disappointment.

"I guess you're going to be busy with the divorce?"

"I don't know. With Michael more than that, I imagine."

Laurel nodded, then gestured at the bags on the table. "Are you hungry?"

"I couldn't hold anything down."

She smiled as if at a fond memory. "Me either."

"I miss you, Laurel. Bad. I've been worried about you."

Her smile cracked, and she put up her hand to cover her eyes. He started to go to her, but she waved him back. "It's been hard," she said. "I have a lot of guilt about what happened."

"I don't feel too good about it myself."

She dropped her hand, revealing bloodshot eyes. "I don't know where to go, Danny. Do I get in the car and drive to the beach? Take the kids to Disney World? There's this huge hole in our lives now, and I don't know how to fill it."

He cleared his throat. "I have an idea."

"What?"

"Go down to the travel agency and buy three plane tickets for Disney World. Forget the Internet. Tell everybody you know that you're leaving town. Pack up the SUV where all the neighbors can see you. When it gets dark, load up the kids and drive out to Deerfield Road. We'll close the gate and shut out the world. There's fifty acres for everybody to get to know each other in. I can move out to the cabin by the pond, and you guys can take the house. We'll fish, cook out, let your dog chase the four-wheeler, whatever. If the kids get bored, I'll rent a plane and fly us anywhere they want to go. Even Disney World. Nobody will know where you are or what you're doing. And you can have all the time you need to get over things."

He thought he saw hope in her eyes, but he wasn't sure.

"Do you think . . . ," she said, faltering. "Would it be all right, considering the kids? Or would it just be selfish?"

He walked around the table but stopped a foot away from her. "There's something I haven't told you. I didn't think you were ready to hear it."

She drew back, obviously afraid of learning yet another nightmarish fact about her husband's death. "Do I need to know this?"

"You do. Before Warren died, he asked me if I would take care of you and the kids."

She looked back at him in disbelief. "Don't lie to make it easier for me."

"I swear by all that's holy. He asked me to take care of you. He was a good man in the end. He wasn't thinking of himself."

Fresh tears flowed from Laurel's eyes. Then she collapsed against his chest and began to sob. He stroked her hair and held her gently, letting her cry it out.

"What do you think?" he asked at length. "About that fake vacation?"

She nodded into his chest.

"When?" he asked.

"Tomorrow." She pulled back and looked up at him with guarded hope. "Will you take care of us?" Before he could answer, she took his hand and placed it on her abdomen. "All of us?"

Danny felt the heat of her body through the linen. Memories of all the days he had thought he would die young flooded through him, bringing an awareness of years granted that seemed a pure grace, given those he had seen stolen from men much younger than he. "I will," he said. "Till there's no life left in me."

She closed her eyes and leaned on his shoulder. "That better be a long time from now."

He squeezed her tight, knowing only one thing with certainty: that every moment was a gift.

# ACKNOWLEDGMENTS

Special thanks to CW4 John P. Goodrich, USA. Ret., for his assistance in understanding what it means to fly a helicopter in peacetime and in war.

My heartfelt thanks also to Tom Johnson, a Vietnam helicopter pilot and wonderful writer whose book, *To the Limit*, I recommend to everyone with the highest possible praise.

Thanks also to Jane Hargrove, Chuck Mayfield, Jerry Iles, M.D., Betty Iles, Geoff Iles, David Gaude, Doug Wike, and Curtis Moroney.

As usual, I take responsibility for any and all mistakes in the book.

I would also like to stress that the actions and attitudes of the deputies in this novel are not representative of the deputies or police officers I have known in Mississippi. The simple fact is that in a thriller someone has to be the bad guy. In real life, the law enforcement officers I have known have been dedicated and sometimes heroic individuals who serve the public for very little compensation. Without their constant labor, few of us would get any sleep at night.

I urge everyone to make an effort to see how they might be able to help their local departments to acquire such technology as FLIR, which is mentioned in this novel. The greatest beneficiaries will be you and your children.

# THE DEVIL'S PUNCHBOWL

## GREG ILES

## Coming in January 2009 from Scribner

Midnight in the garden of the dead.

I wonder whether any previous mayor has taken a meeting in the city cemetery? Given that Natchez has existed since 1716, and knowing her history, I would not be surprised to find it so.

But why am I here?

If a patrolling cop should stop and ask, I will answer that I've come to meet a friend. But there will be no police here. At dusk they chain all four entrances shut to keep out the vandals who've cost the city hundreds of thousands of dollars in damage, much of it to irreplaceable statuary and wrought iron. The friend I'm waiting for knows that; it's one reason he picked this place. But I haven't come here out of friendship.

I've come out of guilt.

And fear.

The man I'm waiting for is forty-six years old, yet in my mind he will always be nine. That's when our friendship peaked, during the Apollo moon landing. But you don't often make friends like those you make as a boy, so the debt is a long one. The pricking at my conscience is the kind you feel when someone slips away and you don't do enough to maintain the tie, the guilt more acute because over the years Tim Jessup managed to get himself into quite a bit of trouble, and after the first eight or nine times, I wasn't there to get him out of it.

My fear has little to do with Jessup. Tim is merely a messenger who may bear tidings that confirm the rumors men have been murmuring over golf greens at the country club, passing beside high school gridirons, and whispering through the hunting camps like a rising breeze before a fall storm. When Jessup asked to meet me, I resisted. He couldn't have chosen a worse time to discover a conscience, for me or for the city. Yet in the end, I agreed to hear him out. For if the rumors are true—if a uniquely disturbing evil has entered into my town—it is I who opened the door for it. I ran for mayor in a Jeffersonian fit of duty to save my hometown. In my righteousness I was arrogant enough to believe that I could deal with the devil and somehow keep our collective virtue intact. But that, I fear, was wishful thinking.

My watch reads 12:21 a.m., yet there's no sign of Jessup among the faintly luminous stones standing shoulder high about me on Jewish Hill. Thirty-five minutes ago a lone pair of headlights drifted up the lane that stretches along the great bluff bounding Mississippi on the west. They trundled past me, the rumble of the engine behind them bouncing off the shotgun shacks across from the cemetery, then vanished around the bend, headed toward the Devil's Punchbowl, a vast defile in the deep woods of the county, still choked with kudzu despite the falling mercury of October. Two hundred feet below the bluff road, the Mississippi River gleams like a cold, black mirror, not the reddish-brown tide of mud that during the day flows straight from the pages of Twain. A curved sliver of moon hangs over the flat Louisiana delta, and pinpoint stars glitter high above me. I'm cold, I'm tired, and I have a babysitter watching my sleeping daughter at home. Annie is fourteen now, but I never leave her alone at night.

Having waited past the appointed hour, I'm tempted to leave. My car is parked on the narrow shoulder by the wall at the foot of Jewish Hill. If I were to slide down the steep hill and push through the shrubbery behind the wall, I could be homeward bound in thirty seconds. But my fear keeps me where I am. I first thought Jessup insisted on this unlikely trysting place and time to make our meeting convenient for him; he works on one of the riverboat casinos at the foot of the bluff, and midnight marks the end of his shift. But he claimed that the cemetery's isolation was a necessity for me—swore, in fact, that I could trust neither my own police department nor any official of the city government. He also warned me not to call his cell phone or his home for any reason. Part of me considers these precautions ridiculous, but a warier part knows that Jessup's employers routinely use surveillance equipment employed by the CIA. I used similar technology myself not so long ago.

I was a lawyer in another life. A prosecutor. I started out wanting to be Atticus Finch and ended up sending twelve people to death row. Looking back, I'm not even sure how that happened. But one day, I woke up and realized that I had not been divinely ordained to punish the guilty. So I resigned my position with the Houston district attorney's office and went home to my joyous wife and daughter. Uncertain what to do with my newfound surplus of time (and facing an acute shortage of funds), I began writing about my courtroom experiences, and like a few other lawyers slipstreaming in the wake of John Grisham, found myself selling enough books to place my name on the bestseller lists. We bought a bigger house and moved Annie to an elite prep school. An unfamiliar sense of self-satisfaction began to creep into my life, a feeling that I was one of the chosen, destined for success in whatever field I chose. I had an enviable career, a wonderful family, a few good friends, lots of faithful readers. I was young enough and self-righteous enough to believe that I deserved all this, and foolish enough to think it would last. Change came like the tractor-trailer that nearly ran me down when I was hitchhiking through Germany in college. As I stared down into the silent Rhine valley, a roaring steel giant crested the ridge behind me and blasted by like an artillery shell, spinning me to the pavement and sucking the air from my lungs. One second everything was static, familiar, in place; then reality shattered into fragments that flew far past the edge of the known universe. Lawyers grow familiar with the traumas that do irreparable damage—accidents, divorces, violent crimes—but my small-scale apocalypse was the death of my wife. I loved her. And four months after my father diagnosed her with cancer, she was dead.

The shock of losing Sarah almost broke me, and it shattered my seven-year-old daughter. For days we floated untethered in an airless, unwatered vacuum too empty even for tears. In desperation I fled the city, taking Annie back to the small Mississippi town where I'd been raised, where I had buried Sarah, back to the loving arms of my parents. There—*here*—even before I could begin working my way back to earth, I found myself drawn into a thirty-year-old murder case, one that ultimately saved my life and ended four others. By the time it was through, I felt more grounded than I had in years, and back in the soul-nourishing footsteps of Atticus Finch. That was seven years ago. Seven years ago we stood a simple stone less than a hundred yards from this spot. On it are chiseled the words: *SARAH ELIZABETH CAGE. Daughter. Wife. Mother. She is loved.* I'm thinking of walking down the hill to visit her when an urgent whisper breaks the silence.

"*Penn? Penn, are you here?*"

I whirl from the river, keeping a tall gravestone between me and the voice. A wiry figure is advancing along the rim of Jewish Hill from the interior of the graveyard. From my vantage point, I can see all four entrances to the cemetery, but I've seen no headlights, heard no engine. Yet here Tim Jessup is, materializing from the stones like one of the ghosts so many people believe haunt this ancient hill. He calls my name again, but I don't answer. I haven't spoken more than twenty words to Tim in years, not face-to-face. I want to study him without him sensing the objectivity in my gaze. He was a junkie once, and he still moves like one, with a herky-jerky progress in which his head perpetually jiggers around as though he's watching for police while his thin legs carry him forward in the hope of finding his next fix. Jessup claims to be clean now, thanks largely to his new wife, Julia, who was a year behind us in high school. Julia Stanton married the high school quarterback at nineteen and took ten years of punishment before forfeiting that particular game. When I heard she was marrying Tim Jessup, I figured she wanted a perfect record of losses. But the word around town is that Julia has worked wonders with Tim. She got him a job and has kept him at it for three years, dealing blackjack on the *Magnolia Queen.*

"*Penn? It's me, man. Come out!*"

Jessup is closer now, and the gauntness of his face is un-mistakable. Though he and I are the same age—born exactly one month apart—he looks ten years older. His skin has the leathery texture of a man who's worked too many years under the Mississippi sun. Passing him on the street under that sun, I've seen more disturbing signs. His salt and pepper mustache is streaked yellow between his nostrils and his mouth from decades of cigarette smoke, and his skin and eyes have the jaundiced cast of a man whose liver hasn't many years left in it. Jessup passes my position and walks to the edge of Jewish Hill, where a strained wire bench awaits lovers, mourners, and all the rest who come here. He peers out over the river, then looks down toward the road, where my car hugs the cemetery wall.

Now he knows I'm here.

Still I do not call out. There's something besides guilt and fear working in me. It's almost revulsion. What bound Jessup and me tightly as boys was that we were both doctors' sons. We each understood the special weight of that particular burden, the way preachers' sons know that emotional geography. Having a physician as a father brings benefits and burdens, but for eldest sons it brings a seemingly universal expectation that someday you will follow in your father's footsteps. In the end both Tim and I failed to fulfill that expectation, but in very different ways. Watching him now, turning haplessly in the moonlight in search of me, it's hard to imagine that we started our lives in almost the same place. Maybe that's the root of my urge to remain separate from him. For though Tim Jessup made a lifetime of bad decisions—in full knowledge of the risks—the one that set them all in train could have been, and in fact was, made by many of us. Only luck carried the rest of us through. With a sigh of resignation, I step from behind the gravestone and call toward the river.

"Tim? Hey, Tim. It's me, Penn."

Jessup whips his head around like a frightened deer, and his right hand darts toward his pocket. For an instant I fear he's going to pull a pistol. Then he recognizes me, waves me toward him, and starts walking in my direction. As he closes the distance, memory overrides the present, reminding me how unlucky this man has been. When he was a freshman at Ole Miss, Jessup agreed to entertain two seniors from St. Stephen's Prep, our alma mater, during a football weekend. Like a lot of other students, he made several high-speed trips to the county line to procure cold beer, which was not available in Oxford, Mississippi (and still isn't). During his third beer run, Tim managed to drive his Trans Am eighty-eight feet off the highway and into a hundred-year-old oak standing at the edge of a cotton field. Jessup and one of the high-school boys were wearing their seat belts; the third boy was not. The impact hurled him from the backseat through the front windshield and into the branches of a pecan tree, where with any luck he died instantly. Because of the alcohol found at the scene, both sets of parents sued Jessup's father, and Tim served a year in jail for manslaughter. Pleading the case down from vehicular homicide probably cost Dr. Jessup all the goodwill he'd built up in twenty years of practicing medicine, not to mention the cash that must have changed hands under the table. But despite the light sentence, things were never really the same for Tim after that. As his life slipped further and further off track, people blamed drugs, weakness of character, even his father, but in my gut I always knew it was the wreck that had ruined him.

"Penn," he calls softly, "I thought you'd chickened out." Jessup flattens both hands against his pants pockets, then scratches his arms above the elbows and glances back toward the road. Only after he's sure the road is empty does he turn and give me the glint of his eyes. "*Shit*, man. You shoulda *said* something."

I smile and hold out my hand, marveling that at forty-six, Jessup still sounds like a strung-out hippie. "You're the one who's late, aren't you?"

He nods steadily, like a man who will do anything to keep from being still. *How does this guy deal blackjack all night?*

"I couldn't rush off the boat," he says. "I think they're watching me. I think they suspect something."

I want to ask who he's talking about, but I assume he'll get to that. Looking at him now, in all his jittery anxiety, I realize just how badly I hope that I have come on a fool's errand, that all the rumors I've been hearing are the lurid speculation of bored townspeople. "I didn't see your car. Where'd you come from?"

A cagey smile splits the weathered face. "I got ways, man. You got to be careful dealing with this class of people.

Predators, I kid you not. They sense a threat, they react—BAM!" Tim claps his hands together. "No thought. Pure instinct. Like sharks in the water."

I start to ask him about the rumors, but he cuts me off before I can speak.

"In fact," he says, glancing back toward town, "we ought to get behind cover now." He gestures toward the three-foot-high masonry walls enclosing the plots of the Jewish families who emigrated to Natchez in the early nineteenth century. "Just like high school, man. Remember smoking grass behind these walls? Sitting down so the cops couldn't see the glow of the roach?"

I never got high with Tim during high school, not up here, anyway. But I see no reason to break whatever flow keeps him calm and talking. The sooner he tells me what he came to say, the sooner I can get out of here.

He vaults the wall with deceptive agility, and I climb after him. With a last anxious look up Cemetery Road, he sits on the cold ground and leans back against the mossy bricks in one corner. I sit against the adjacent wall, with my running shoes almost touching his weathered Sperrys. Only now do I realize that he must have changed clothes after work. The dealer's uniform he usually wears on duty has been replaced by black jeans and a T-shirt.

"Couldn't come out here dressed for work," he explains, as though reading my mind. What he read, though, was my appraising glance, and I realize that all the drugs he has taken throughout the years have not ruined what always was a sharp mind. I decide to dispense with small talk.

"You said some pretty scary stuff on the phone, Tim. Scary enough to bring me out here at midnight."

He nods, digging in his pocket for something that turns out to be a bent cigarette. "Can't risk lighting it," he says, putting it between his lips, "but it's good to know I got it for the ride home." He grins affectingly. "So, what had you heard before I called?"

I don't want to repeat anything Tim hasn't already heard or seen himself. "A few vague rumors. Celebrities flying in to gamble, in and out fast. Pro athletes, rappers, like that."

Tim is nodding again. "You hear about the dogfighting?"

My hope that the rumors are false sinks. "I've heard talk there was some of that going on. But it was hard to credit, given what happened to Michael Vick. I mean, I can see some rednecks down in the bottoms doing it, or out in the parishes across the river, but not high rollers and celebrities."

Tim sucks in his bottom lip and gives me a bad-little-boy smile. "What else have you heard?"

"I don't want to speculate about things I don't know to be true."

Jessup curls his lip in distaste. "You know you sound like a politician."

I suppose that's what I've become, but I feel like an attorney, sifting the truth from an unreliable client's story. "Why don't you tell me what you know? The real facts. Then we'll see how that matches with what I've heard."

He shrugs and takes the unlit cigarette out of his mouth, then studies it as though considering putting a match to it despite his fear. "Whores," he says. "You heard that?"

*Jesus.* "There's always prostitution going on. Especially around casinos."

"*Young* whores."

"How young?"

"Too young. And not all willing."

The flesh on my upper arms crawls. I had not heard that. "Is this rumor or fact?"

"I've seen it, brother." Tim winces like a man with an ulcer. "Bad."

"Is that the worst of it?"

"Depends on your sensibilities, I guess. There's the dope."

"I've heard that too. Forever."

"Not like this. They bring this stuff up from Mexico special."

"Special for what?"

"That's what I'm trying to tell you. All these rumors you've been hearing are tied together. This is a centralized operation, designed to pull the highest rollers down south. The whales from Vegas, especially.

"Whales?"

"Big players. The rap stars and pro athletes you already know about. Throw in the Arab playboys, Asian trust-fund babies . . . it's a circus, man. And they *love* that dogfighting. Blood sport." He shakes his head.

"Is it working? To pull them in?"

"Better than they ever dreamed. We had a jet fly in from Macao two weeks ago. This Chinese billionaire brought his own dog in to fight."

"Through the Natchez airport?"

"Hell, no. There's other strips around here that can take a light jet."

"Not many." I want to stand and pace, but Tim's paranoia is working its way into me: If I rise above the wall, I could be silhouetted in the moonlight. "Tim, you're scaring me."

"If you're scared now, you'd better tighten up the old bunghole. Because if dope and girls was all it was, I wouldn't be here. They'd kill me if they knew I was talking to you, man."

Now we've reached the heart of the matter. Tim either has facts for me, or he doesn't. "Who would?"

Jessup plunges his right hand into his pocket and brings out a Bic lighter. "No names. Yet." He flicks the lighter into flame and touches it to the end of the cigarette. He draws air through the cigarette like someone sucking on a three-foot bong, holds in the smoke for an alarming amount of time, then speaks as he exhales. "I've got a kid now, you know? A son."

I want to press Jessup, but I've dealt with enough criminals who turned state's evidence to know when to back off. "I know. I saw him with Julia in the Winn-Dixie a couple of weeks ago. He's a great-looking kid."

Tim's smile lights up his face. "Just like his mom, man. She's still a beauty, isn't she?"

"She is," I concur, speaking the truth. "So . . . what moved you to risk all that? What trumps dogfighting and underage prostitution?"

Tim takes another quick hit from the cigarette, then begins speaking letters aloud like we're back in a grade-school spelling bee. "F-R-A-U-D, Your Honor."

"Come again?"

"They're screwing the city, Penn. At least I'm pretty sure they are. On the receipts, I mean. They're shorting you on the taxes. Big-time."

Something has gone cold in me. Natchez had two casinos

operating when I ran for mayor, and a third had won approval from the state gaming commission. I'd always been against gambling in Natchez, not for any moral reason, but because the casino boats primarily drain money from the local poor and transfer it to Las Vegas and Atlantic City. But the pressure was on to draw major industries back to Natchez, and I couldn't afford to be choosy. What finally convinced me to allow the *Magnolia Queen* into town was the record-setting tax deal I negotiated with its parent company. From the day that boat went into operation, it has been paying—or was supposed to have been paying—the highest city tax rate of any casino in Mississippi. We put innumerable safeguards in place to prevent fraud, so I find it almost impossible to believe Tim's claim. And yet . . . I've sometimes wondered if the company acceded too easily to my demands. Did they know all along that they would never fully honor their commitments? "How could they do that, Tim?"

He expels a long stream of smoke. "Computers, brah."

"Keep talking."

"The casinos pay the city a percentage of their gross in taxes, right?"

"Every month."

"There's no way to steal money from discrete parts of the gaming operation, because everything's so tightly regulated by the state commission, and by the company's own security apparatus. Every square inch of the boat is videotaped around the clock, and wired for sound. State-of-the-art stuff. Military grade. The cameras are robotically controlled, and from Vegas, not Natchez. I saw Pete Elliot fingering his brother's wife in the corner of the restaurant one night."

"Jesus. I don't need to know that crap."

"I'm just saying—"

"I get it. Just get to the point."

"My point is, the only way for the company to rip off the city is to distort the gross. That way the city doesn't ask questions. You guys see a big enough number, and your cut of that number, you don't look any deeper. Right?"

He is right, to an extent. "The gaming commission looks deeper, though. How much money are we talking about?"

Jessup squints at his cigarette as though pondering an advanced calculus problem. "I don't know. Not that much, in terms of the monthly gross of a casino boat. But that's like saying a thousand years isn't much time in geological terms. We're talking serious money for an ordinary human being."

I realize that I am slowly wringing my hands. "Point taken. But where's the upside in doing this? For the casino company, I mean. They're practically minting money down there. Why risk killing the golden goose to steal a couple of extra million a year? Or even a month?"

Jessup nods. "Now you're thinking. Doesn't make sense, does it?"

"Not to me."

"Well, let's discount the fact that successful people—and companies—commit illogical crimes every day for greed alone. Let's just *assume* that there's a logical motive. What would it be?"

I'm no stranger to bizarre criminal motives, but in this case my prosecutorial experience offers no solution. "I can't see one. Not if I'm the casino company."

Jessup's eyes flicker in the moonlight. *"Exactly."*

I wait for an explanation, but Tim just sucks on the cigarette until it's dead, then lights another. The flame flares orange against the white marble gravestones of our walled haven. "What are you telling me, Tim?"

"I think it's one guy."

"One guy? Not possible. The casino companies never give an individual that kind of power."

"One guy with friends, I meant. A handpicked team."

"I don't buy it. The casinos do everything in their power to avoid exactly that situation."

"You're right. Everything *in their power*. And they're good at it. But they're not God. They make certain assumptions about people and situations, Penn, and that makes them vulnerable."

"Are you speculating here, or do you know something?"

The bad-boy smile again. "A little of both."

"Clearly you have a suspect. Who is it?"

"I told you, no names yet. But this guy has been with the company awhile. Long enough to put something like this together. And if anybody could do it, it's him."

"And you're saying he's also behind the other stuff? The dogfighting and the girls?"

"And worse. Absolutely. He's single-handedly pumped up the monthly gross like you wouldn't believe—well, I guess you would, since you've seen the numbers—but the point is, Vegas loves this dude."

A picture of Tim's suspect is forming in my mind.

"And while they're patting him on the back," Jessup continues, "he's robbing them blind."

*And my city*, I think. "If that's true, then *your man* is begging for a bullet in the head."

"No doubt about it."

"So, about the ugly side-action that brings in the big players. Where does all this happen? Surely not on the *Magnolia Queen*?"

"Hell, no. It's almost never the same place. They've used a couple of hunting camps more than once. One of them is on an island in the river. No law at all out there. Or what there is, the local bigshots own. Other times they've set up out on somebody's farm, but always close to the river. You'd think the high rollers would want swanky surroundings, but they eat up the rustic Southern vibe. Especially when those teenage girls start talking like honey and molasses; the suckers think they're Rhett Butler in the unrated version of *Gone With the Wind*."

As badly as I wanted to believe this is all a Jessup fantasy, it has the ring of truth. I know men who would like nothing better than to spend a weekend doing what Tim is describing. "Back to the mastermind behind all this," I say, wondering if the well-spoken but reticent suspect I'm imagining could also be a psychopath. "Does he have a death wish?"

"I'm not sure yet. I can't figure him out, and I've been studying him awhile. The guy is cold, Penn. On the outside he's like a mechanic."

"You mean a cardsharp?"

"Right. He started as a dealer himself, years ago. He's detached, clinical . . . a human computer with the dexterity of a magician. But there's more to this guy than that. Or maybe less. There's something missing in there. When the dogs are tearing each other to pieces, or some girl is screaming in the back of a trailer, he's definitely taking it in, not tuning it out . . ."

"So he's into that stuff himself?"

"Sometimes I think he's just counting the money in his head. Getting off on running this whole show. But other times I think he's like a high-wire walker who half wants to fall. Like he wants to see how far he can push the world before the world pushes back."

"I've known a couple of guys like that. I sent them to death row."

Tim stubs his cigarette out against the mossy bricks behind him, his face cold sober. "I think maybe that's why I'm here. Penn, you are the *only* guy I trust in this town. And it will take some no-shit intestinal fortitude to take this guy on. He's bought influence everywhere. And I mean *every-where*."

I settle back against the cool brick wall. "You picked a hell of a week to come forward." This is balloon-race weekend. We've got nearly a hundred hot-air balloons coming to town this year, and eight thousand tourists. "I've got the CEO of a major company coming in for the royal treatment, which I have to give him, hoping he'll locate his new recycling plant here."

Tim nods. "I read about it in the newspaper. Sorry."

I shrug, picturing an industry executive with a fantasy of a nice little Southern town in his head. "This particular CEO wants Mayberry, R.F.D., not a den of dogfighting and white slavery."

Jessup chuckles in the dark. "Has the guy ever cracked a history book? They were gambling, selling slaves, raping Indian women, and cutting each other's throats in this town before Paul Revere sold his first silver candlestick."

"That's not the pitch I'll be making this weekend," I mutter in frustration. "Anyway, there's not much doubt about what we have to do with your story."

Jessup is fishing for another cigarette. "What's that?"

"Take it to the state gaming commission."

He goes still. "You're joking, right?"

"No. What did you think we would do?"

"Not *that*. Not yet. It's too soon!" He forces his voice quieter. "Look, you want to arrest Mr. X for promoting dog-fighting? On my word? That bastard could get fifty people to swear he was on the *Queen* any day or night we name."

"I want him for that, yeah. And the prostitution. And the

fraud. But it seems the fraud's the best way in, isn't it? Unless you don't have any documentary evidence."

Jessup licks his lips like a nervous poker player. "I'm not saying I've got nothing. But I don't have much. Not on him. I could hurt some of our friends from the old days, but what's the point in that?"

"Tim . . . what did you come here for exactly?"

"I wanted you to know what's going on. In case, you know . . . something happens to me."

A sense of foreboding has taken hold deep in my chest. "Wait a second. What do you think you're going to do?"

He does not reply, but there is a dogged look on his face that I don't like at all. "Tim, you're not on some kind of hero trip? That's the way you get dead."

"I know that. I'm not an idiot. Despite what some people may think."

"Hey." I reach out and tap his shoulder. "Nobody who makes a twenty-seven on his ACT is an idiot. But you could be lacking some common sense. At least in the risk-assessment area."

His eyes seem to film and his gaze grows distant. "Oh, I've assessed the risk. You want to know what this guy's capable of? Every week, he sends out four pickup trucks with cages in the back, a hundred miles in every direction. His men come back with those cages full of *house pets*—cocker spaniels, poodles, Dalmatians—and every one of those dogs gets torn to shreds before the week is out. The trainers throw 'em into a hole with starving pit bulls to teach the fighting dogs how to kill."

A shiver of revulsion goes through me. As I try to absorb what Tim has told me, I recall that a woman who lives three houses down from me lost her nine-year-old whippet last month. She let the dog out to do its business, and it never came back.

"I got two dogs of my own," Tim says. "Golden retrievers. I keep them locked in the house now. They're both stir-crazy, but Julia knows never to let them out."

"Tim, I know this is bad," I say gently, "which is exactly why you and I can't take them on alone. We need your information, but then we have to let professionals handle it."

"Professionals?" He almost spits the word. "Didn't you

hear what I said on the phone? You can't trust *anybody* around here."

"My own police department?"

Jessup shakes his head as though incredulous at my ignorance. "They're not *yours*. Those cops were on the job before you got into office, and they'll be there when you're gone. Same for the sheriff and his boys. To them, you're just passing through. A political tourist."

His casual damnation of local law enforcement disturbs me. "I trust a lot of those men, Tim."

"For a smart guy, you can be pretty damn naïve sometimes. I'm not telling you all the cops are crooks. I'm telling you they're human. They're looking out for themselves and their families, and they like to have a little fun on the side, same as the next guy. How many guys do you know who wouldn't look the other way in exchange for a snapshot with a star NFL running back? I've been to a couple of these barn burners, okay? I know who I've seen."

Like the full import of a terminal diagnosis, the ramifications of what Jessup is telling me are slowly sinking in. "This is our town," he says slowly. "That still means something to me. They're screwing our hometown and laughing about it. Carpetbagger motherfuckers."

Despite my argument, I can't deny that I feel what he's feeling. "I understand your anger, Tim. But this isn't worth your life. It's not even worth a beating. This isn't the same town we grew up in. When you go to a restaurant, how many people in it do you know?"

He smiles wistfully. "Yeah. Time was, I was on a first-name basis with everybody I ran into in this town."

"No more."

"No." He points his forefinger at me. "But you came back. And you've stayed. You must think this place is worth saving, or you'd be living on an island somewhere, spending all that money you've made. Instead you're the mayor in a town where you couldn't pay most people to take the job."

He's right, though about every other day I think running for mayor was the worst mistake of my life. "I do think Natchez is worth saving, okay? But everybody has a different idea about what constitutes saving a town. One thing I know for sure: nobody would say it's worth your life to save us some gambling revenue."

Tim's eyes glisten. "It's not just that. God knows, I've made some bad choices in my life. I've disappointed a lot of people—my dad most of all. But what's going on now is really hurting people. Those young girls . . . innocent animals that just want to live, the same as any other creature. And I'm in a position to do something about it. What kind of man would I be if I just turned away and let it go on?"

"You didn't turn away! You came to me. And I'm going to inform the appropriate authorities. You've fulfilled your responsibility. Hell, you've done more than a lot of men would in your situation."

Jessup shakes his head with almost childlike deliberation. "You're not going to inform anybody of anything, Penn. It's too soon. You're a good enough lawyer to know that. Wait for me. God put me in this position for a reason . . ."

"Don't bring God into it."

"I'm not asking you to believe like I do. I'm just asking you to be ready to take what I bring you and do the right thing."

I feel obligated to dissuade him further, but part of me knows that in cases like this, often the only way to convict the people at the top is to have a witness on the inside, directly observing the criminal activity. Tim Jessup could be that man.

"What *are* you going to bring me?"

"The goods."

"Evidence?"

"That's right."

"Of what? Dogfighting and whores? Or the big-money stuff?"

"Whatever I can get. Just tell me you're with me. Tell me I can trust you."

"You can trust me, Tim. Just be careful, okay?"

He looks me full in the face, his eyes almost serene. "I will. Especially now that there's two of us in this."

I reach out and squeeze his arm. "You've come a long way against long odds, brother. Don't you go getting hurt now."

"Don't blame yourself if I do. The way I see it, I've got no choice." Jessup smiles suddenly. "Hey, you still dating that lady who runs the bookstore?"

"Laura? Yes, why?"

"No reason. I like her, by the way. But what happened to that newspaper girl? The publisher?"

The change of subject throws me. "Caitlin couldn't resign herself to living in Natchez. She likes life a little faster than it runs here."

Tim raises one eyebrow. "The water may not run fast here, but it's deep. I thought you might want to know that I've seen Laura's son down on the *Queen* a few times the past couple of weeks. He looked high to me."

This news hits me almost as hard as Tim's earlier revelations. I've spent a lot of time and too much political capital getting my girlfriend's nineteen-year-old son out of trouble with the law. If he has broken his promise to stay clean, the future holds some serious unpleasantness.

Jessup is watching me closely. "Was I right to tell you?"

"Are you sure he was high?"

Tim doesn't reply. He's holding up his hand for us to be silent. As he comes to his knees, I realize what has disturbed him: the sound of a car coming up Cemetery Road. We listen to the rising pitch of the engine, waiting for it to crest and fall. But it doesn't. There's a grinding sound of brakes, then silence.

"It stopped," Tim hisses. "It's right below us."

"Take it easy," I tell him, but I'm surprised by my thumping heart. "It's probably just a patrol car, checking out my Volvo."

Tim has his feet under him now. He crab-walks over two graves and lifts his eyes above the rim of the far wall. "Remember what I told you. Even if it is a cop, that doesn't mean we're okay."

"Can you see anything?"

"No! We're too deep in."

"Jesus, calm down. I'm the freaking mayor, all right? We're fine. Let me go take a look."

"*Stay here.*"

I scramble to my feet, then scissor my legs over the wall. Before I've covered twenty feet I hear the tinny sound of a police radio. This brings me immediate relief, but when I hurry back to tell Tim, I find the walled plot empty save for the dead. My old friend has vanished as silently as he appeared.

Given a choice between waiting for the cop to leave or walking down to face him, I choose the latter. For one thing, the cop might not leave. He might call a tow truck instead. For another, I *am* the mayor, and it's none of his business what I'm doing up here in the middle of the night. I could be having a dark night of the soul, visiting my wife's grave.

Instead of sliding down the face of Jewish Hill, I walk around to the steps, then cross the cemetery wall thirty yards up the road from the cop, so that I won't startle him by appearing suddenly from the graveyard. He's standing at the cemetery wall, shining a flashlight twenty feet up the hill. As the beam passes over the wire bench, my heels crunch on some gravel beside the road.

The cop whips his light toward me. "Hold it!" he shouts. *"Stop right there!"*

I raise both hands and call, "It's Mayor Cage, Officer. Everything's fine. I just had a little car trouble."

Despite all my reassurances to Tim Jessup, my heart only races faster. The cop shines his light right in my eyes. Surely he must have called in my license plate by now. He knows he's facing the mayor of the city. Just to be sure, I call out again.

"I'm Penn Cage, Officer! The mayor. Please put that light down."

Not only does the cop keep his light in my face, but he also starts walking toward me. Incredibly, as my eyes adjust to the glare, I see him reach down with his right hand and draw his sidearm from the holster at his hip.

*"Hey!"* I shout. "Did you hear me? It's Mayor Cage!"

"I heard you, all right."

He closes the distance between us without slowing, and before I can speak again, he hammers the flashlight into my solar plexus. As I drop gasping to the concrete, it strikes me that Tim Jessup knows a lot more about my city than I do.

The flashlight whistles as it drops toward my head.